1

NO HIGHER GROUND

By

Roman Godzich

Newer World Press

A Division of Hellecat Publishing

New York

Disclaimer

This is a work of fiction. Names, characters, businesses, places, events and incidents are either the products of the author's imagination or used in a fictitious manner. Any resemblance to actual persons, living or dead, or actual events is purely coincidental.

Credits
Edited and Copyedited by Charie D. La Marr
Cover design by Melarts
Book design and production by Newer World Publications
Formatting by Travis La Marr
Troubleshooting by Travis La Marr
Author photograph by Peter A. Rosenberg

Publisher's Cataloging-in-Publication data

No Higher Ground/Roman Godzich
ISBN- 13- 978-1979258722
ISBN- 10-1979258724

1.Science Fiction 2. Thriller 3. Moon 4. Aliens

Publishing Date October, 2017

First Edition

Newer World Publications
An Imprint of Hellecat Publishing
New York

Praise for No Higher Ground

"Imaginative science fiction based in hard science and realistically envisioned future geopolitics, NO HIGHER GROUND is a thriller with a wildly inventive reality. Surprising alliances and betrayals are set against stakes which reveal the war games we humans play are a mere footnote in the battles fought across the universe. An exciting debut."

- Nina Sadowsky, author of JUST FALL and THE BURIAL SOCIETY

"Roman Godzich is an enormously clever fellow, with a wit that is precise, original and unexpected. It is often the case that witty people are unable to make the transition to fully immersing prose. But Godzich is one of the rare and happy exceptions. He is able to handle serious matters with all the deftness that he handles daft ones. He has a poignant sense of balance and a profound depth of insight. His characters feel real and they are sculpted rather than sketched. A writer of considerable talent, one absolutely worth checking out..."

– Rhys Hughes, author of THE NOSTALGIA THAT NEVER WAS, THE HONEYMOON GORILLAS and over 40 other books.

For Dzika, Matthieu, Oos and Julian

*The best time to plant a tree is twenty
years ago. The second best time is now.*
– Chinese Proverb

Chapter One

Death kept falling from above but Sam could not stop grinning.

After disconnecting himself from the control system for the Narwhal Undersea Explorer, Sam Czerny checked to make sure the robotic control had stabilized itself. He kept grinning through the full ten minutes it took to remove the navigation suit that allowed him to control the explorer. It maintained a position one hundred and fifty meters above the Gakkel Ridge deep in the eastern Arctic Ocean. Then, he took a last look at the smoking underwater volcano on the display. The fuzzy yellow bacterial colony he had saved was fine.

He blew into his cupped hands. Despite being in California, Sam still felt as cold as if he had been diving with the robot in frosty Arctic waters, but he didn't care. After almost an entire day working the display, he was excited about what he found and what it meant for his research. Stepping out of the connection chamber, he squinted in the bright command room.

Anders Kroon was the engineer on duty and he looked up at Sam with a scowl. "Well, you look like shit. How long have you been in there? Let's see." He scanned his display. "Holy crap! Seventeen hours? Are you trying to break a record or something?"

Sam grinned. "Anders, that was awesome! My first trip to the third volcano and already I've turned up more carpets of microscopic life of a type we've never seen before. I can't wait to show the vids. There's more alien-like life in the Arctic than anywhere else on this planet! This was the most thrilling dive I've ever done." Sam stretched his arms over his head. Despite his fatigue he was buzzing with excitement.

"Well you look like thrilled shit, then. Oh, and while you were in there, people have been trying to reach you. Some of them seemed urgent but none of them seemed dire enough to interrupt you per the instructions you left."

Sam raised his eyebrows showing blue eyes that were bloodshot from staring at the display for so long. "Really? Who's trying to reach me?"

Anders swiped his hand in front of the display. "An interesting group. Someone named Trish Stern from DC. Looks like she's with Starshield-Shackleton. A Major Zhang Wei from Dongfeng City in China. A fellow by the name of Pierre Pacquelier in Florida and your better half, Helen. Each sounded urgent but none of them achieved the DIRE protocol that you defined."

Sam had not wanted any interruptions during the deep dive and left instructions stating anyone who didn't try to reach him at least four times in an hour was not serious enough to disturb him. They could wait. He only had an eight-hour session with the diving robot scheduled, but the researcher following him called and said he couldn't make it. So, Sam had swapped a future dive time for an uninterrupted long session. It had been well worth it.

"Let me get to my office and I'll start by calling Helen."

"Smart man." Anders smiled. "Always call the wife and the boss first. I guess it's easier if they're both the same person. When's your next shift?"

"I'll have to check. Next week, I think."

"Okay, I should be on next week, too. Can you send me a copy of your report?"

"An engineer wants to read a xenobiologist's report? Really?"

"I might read it. But I'll certainly add it to my list of things I've helped with. You can never have too many brownie points in academia, you know?"

"Yeah, you're right." Sam laughed. "I should pay more attention to that myself. I'll send you a copy. And Anders?"

"Yeah?"

"Thanks for all your work. You make the hard part easy so I can concentrate on the fun part. I do appreciate that."

"It's why I make the big bucks, man."

Sam left the command room and walked down the hallway to the beverage station where he got himself a hot chocolate booster. With the first few sips he could feel the caffeine and taurine raise his energy level. It made him feel better than he had a right to feel after so many hours of concentration during a long remote-controlled session and the pressure of a deep-sea dive. Such a dive was hard on the body.

Sam found his office and plopped into the chair behind his desk. He cleared off a few empty cups and brushed a bit of dust from the desktop before logging in and initiating the call to Helen.

"Ah! I see you're still alive." Helen was in her home office. Sam recognized the six-foot rendering of the great wave of Kanagawa on the wall behind her bright red hair. She was wearing a bottle-green blouse that matched her eyes and flashing the smile that always made him happy. "Did you find any alien polar bears yet?" This was her standard question to him ever since he first started studying the unusual life forms at the bottom of the eastern Arctic Ocean.

"Still no polar bears. But I did find what I think are at least nine new bacterial colonies. One of them is along a vent that's spewing a mix of arsenic and sulfur thick enough to kill just about anything on the surface. Some of these will have us rethinking what type of life forms we may find on the Jovian Moons when we get around to exploring them."

"Honey, I'm glad to see you're having a good time, but I need to put on my boss's hat for a minute. Your presentation is still not available for the funding meeting and the deadline is tomorrow morning. It makes me look bad when the other participants have sent theirs in and my own dear husband is late."

Sam brushed his hand through his wavy black hair. "I'm not late. You just said the deadline is tomorrow morning. I have the rest of the day to finish it."

"So, give me a preview. What's the gist of it? Can you send me an outline?"

"Er, not really." Sam grinned. "I want to include some of what I found today to make it as fresh as possible."

Helen folded her arms across her chest. "Samuel Czerny, you know I can tell when you're making things up as you go along. This is why I've been trying to reach you. I know that if I'm not on your back, you'll be off on some other fascinating bit of research and never complete the presentation on time. And much as I love that boyish grin of yours, it's not going to get you off the hook."

Sam looked down at his keyboard like a guilty child.

Helen continued. "Don't you give me that sad puppy look either.

3

You know I fall for it every time. But this is too important. If we don't get the funding, your projects are the ones that get cut first. Remember, studying alien life forms when none have been found is hard to justify. The people who give us the funds tend to be an unimaginative bunch. Lose the few supporters we have and we'll have to find another line of work for you. I can't defend your work if you won't."

Sam could see how upset she was. "You can't tell me Rothlesberger's Zombie Preparedness studies are more important or useful."

"Rothlesberger delivers well-told stories about how a zombie threat could spread. And he does it with charm and scares the living crap out of the financiers. That gets them to bring out the checkbooks and shower him with money. You need to work harder at getting them to understand astrobiology is worth studying. Maybe even put a little fear into them. Warn them that we need some sort of protocol for when we encounter little green men or little green viruses. And if we don't have one, we may lose precious time needed to defend life on our planet."

Leaning forward, he shook his head. "Helen, we've gone through that scenario a dozen times. Fear mongering may get us funding but it sets a bad direction for real research. Pretty soon it turns into funding defense projects rather than pure science. Astrobiology is still a young enough field and it shouldn't have that type of thinking corrupt it."

"Sam, that's exactly my point. If you're not making the effort to get funding for your research as pure science, nobody else will. Do you think it would be better to have them go and fund Ledbetter's work?"

Sam straightened up in his seat. "Ledbetter? That hack! He's still out there saying we should be looking for robotic explorers from other planets! How likely is that? Even if they do exist, the odds of finding them are so tiny that it would be like net fishing for trout in the Sahara."

He paused and then grinned widely. "You did it again didn't you? You got me to take your side and then cornered me into agreeing I have to finish this presentation tonight. I never should have married the boss."

"I wasn't your boss when we got married, Sam, and I have to say I have no regrets."

Helen's smile made his face light up as well. Every day he remembered why he'd fallen in love with her. She always knew how to get him to do the right thing—the thing that was best for him. Sam knew without

Helen looking over his shoulder, he would be doing some type of menial research he hated.

"Okay, Helen. I'll spend the rest of the day putting together a fantastic presentation that will have them begging to shower us with money. Promise."

"When you put your mind to it, you can convince anyone of anything. Remember; you got me to marry you. That was no mean feat. By the way, there have been a few other people trying to reach you. First of all, Trish Stern from Starshield- Shackleton. They're one of the companies that have been steady as far as funding us goes. You should see what she wants. Might be important. And a Major Zhang in China. I looked him up and he's a bigwig involved with the base they're building in the Fermi Crater. And some guy with a heavy French accent by the name of Pacquelier. He said he knows you and sounded all hyped up about something. Who is he?"

Sam started to say he wasn't sure. Then he remembered Pierre Pacquelier, a larger than life French scientist. They had been on a panel together at a science fiction convention a few years earlier. Some kind of a rocket propulsion specialist. They hit it off and had a few too many drinks after the panel. Pierre was a funny guy. His English was not just accented but also laced with literal French idioms that sometimes made him hard to understand.

"Okay, I guess I should call Stern from Starshield first since she has funding influence. The rest can wait until I have my presentation wrapped up and on your computer."

"Good idea. I'll be waiting for it. Later!" she said.

He gave her a virtual good-bye kiss and disconnected the link, only to have it immediately light up with another call. The display showed the call was coming from Starshield offices in DC. Sam brushed his hand through his hair and wished he'd taken the time to freshen up a bit. Putting a big money-raising smile on his face, he answered the call.

The display turned bright blue and a message indicating a secure encryption was in place. Sam found that surprising, as standard encryption made all calls secure many years earlier. He wondered if Starshield-Shackleton was doing more than space mining.

A few moments later the display resolved itself into a mustachioed face with black eyes squinting beneath a tussle of black hair. Sam always thought Pierre Pacquelier looked like Salvador Dali with the ends of his mustache cut off.

"Sam? This is you?" A thick French accent came from Pierre's image. He broke into a smile. "It is good to see you again, my friend."

He liked Pacquelier. "Pierre! How are you? I heard you've been trying to reach me. When was the last time we saw each other, the Sci-fi convention about a year and a half ago?"

"Yes, my friend. We were on some panel together, but I don't remember what it was. I do remember drinking and talking afterward. Anyway, I am calling to apologize and to receive your thanks."

"Huh?" Sam grunted. Pierre's habit of translating French word for word into English often confused him. "I don't understand what you mean."

"Of course, you do not because I have not told you. But when I tell you, you will have to forget, or at least pretend it is a surprise when they contact you."

"What's a surprise?"

"Okay, I am sorry. I am putting the cart before the oxen," He paused for effect. "Let me begin again."

"Yes, go on . . ."

"An alien artifact. Something made by aliens. Do you see what this means?"

Sam sighed. "Pierre, I've heard this a dozen times before. People think they've found an object that didn't come from Earth and it always turns out to be some natural or man-made thing."

Pierre smiled and shook his head. "I do not think this is one of those cases. For one thing, the artifact is much too big and regular to be a natural object. It is as large as a big building Sam, and it appears to be very, very old."

Sam frowned. "How old?'

Pierre took a breath. "First estimates date it to be about sixty-five to seventy million years old."

"Pierre, what on earth are you saying? Where is this thing?"

"Not on Earth, Sam. We found it in the Fermi Crater on the far side of the Moon."

Pierre suddenly looked to his left and then back at the screen. "O la! I must go now. See you soon."

The screen went blank as the call ended.

Chapter Two

University of California
San Diego

Lacing his fingers and placing his hands behind his head, Sam leaned back in his chair thinking about the call with Pierre. He knew Pierre tended to be enthusiastic about projects in general. He was the kind of guy who would take off at a gallop without ever looking at a map or plugging an address into a GPS. But to claim an alien artifact was on the far side of the Moon was pretty outrageous, even for Pierre.

More information was needed before Sam could even consider such a possibility. He woke his display and began asking questions. As he worked, he began to create a data map of answers. His focus was on projects on the far side of the Moon. In a matter of minutes, he had a document containing all the details available on current and past Moon missions. In addition, he had a list of white papers outlining future possibilities for lunar exploitation.

It added up to over four hundred and fifty screens of data. There was no way he could get through all of it at that moment. Helen was waiting for his presentation. She had given him five hours to come up with something. However, the summary of the data he had gathered was only thirty-seven pages. Reading that wouldn't take much time at all, and would leave him plenty of time to finish the report for Helen. The problem was that it was likely the summary would leave him with more questions than answers. But those questions would have to wait. He couldn't let Helen down. The future of his project depended on it.

Twenty minutes later a new call interrupted him. This one also said it was from Starshield-Shackleton in DC and showed the same encryption message. Sam welcomed the break in his work. There were many questions he wanted to ask Pierre—beginning with exactly who discovered the artifact. But instead of Pierre, the face of a woman with long blonde hair looked back at him out of wolf gray eyes.

Startled, he said, "Hi? I'm Sam Czerny, can I help you?"

"Mr. Czerny, my name is Patricia Stern, but please call me Trish. Everyone does. Mr. Czerny, as you know I'm with Starshield-Shackleton. I'm sure you know we're the organization responsible for funding your research at Gakkel Ridge."

Sam relaxed. He figured this had to do with his presentation. Maybe this person wouldn't be able to make the event and wanted an inside scoop. "Yes, yes, I can tell you I'm very grateful. We've made some interesting discoveries and the rest promises to be even more . . ."

Trish Stern interrupted him. "I'm not calling to discuss that particular project. I'm calling you about another project. If you recall the terms of the funding agreement, we can call on your expertise in regards to any project we may want you to work on."

"What?" Sam scrunched his eyebrows in confusion. Everything seemed to be taking him by surprise this day. "I'm not sure I follow." Something about her demeanor told him Ms. Stern was all business despite having asked him to call her Trish.

"Mr. Czerny, our contract states we have the liberty to pull you off of your current research project and put you on another one we deem more important and that would benefit from your special skill set. We can also exercise a clause stating you can't share any of what you learn without our authorization. We are now exercising that option, Mr. Czerny. I'm sending a copy of the agreement for your reference." She stared into the camera, studying his response,

A document arrival icon appeared in the lower right corner of his display. He opened it across half of the display and found she had highlighted the clauses in question.

After reading through it twice to be sure he understood, he realized she was right. The document also made it clear should he refuse, he would lose what funding he had and he would have to refund last year's funding within thirty days. There was no way that was possible. He was just getting by with the money he had left, there was no money left to reimburse her. Without her financial support, his project was proverbially dead in the water. Even if he could find someone else to continue the funding on such short notice, they would never agree to refund previous funds. It was obvious Starshield-Shackleton had him, and he knew it.

"Okay, Ms. Stern, I've read it and it appears you're right. I have no options and we both know that. There's no built-in escape pod. So, I guess you have my full attention. Tell me about this project, especially about the time-line. I have some urgent business I'll need to wrap up before I can shift into something else. I'll need about a week."

"Please, it's Trish," she said, giving him a gentle smile. "I'm afraid we can't give you that much time. Major Zhang Wei should be contacting you shortly. You are to meet him at the Dongfeng Space City tomorrow morning."

"Dongfeng? In China?" Sam was confused. How did China get involved in all of this?

"Inner Mongolia actually. It's in the Gobi dessert. The General is there now. He would be on the call with us but he's currently making the arrangements to get you there on time."

"Wait a second," Sam protested. "I need to settle some things before I can go. My wife is expecting a very important presentation from me by end of day today . . ."

Stern interrupted him again. "I believe that's been handled by the Major himself. I'm sure your wife will be fine with the arrangements. Starshield-Shackleton knows how to be very generous. I'll personally see that your presentation is put on hold until this current assignment is over." Her whole face smiled for the first time,

"Mr. Czerny, I want you to feel confident. This may all seem a little mysterious, but you'll be completely informed soon enough. Trust me, we don't go about something like this lightly. If we didn't see the real value in your participation, we wouldn't be talking to you right now. I'm certain by the time you've been able to be brought up to speed on this project, you'll even thank me that we called on you."

"Well, okay then, Trish, Apparently, I have some time right now since I won't be writing a report. Why don't you bring me up to speed?"

Sam didn't like her smile. He couldn't help feeling like he was a canary looking at a cat.

"Mr. Czerny," she began, "I'm afraid I'm not in the position to do that at this time. Major Zhang is far better prepared to provide you with the information you will need on a need-to-know basis."

"Please call me Sam," he said, thinking perhaps she might see him a little more as a person and a little less as just a resource. "And what I'll need to know is all of it."

She paused. "Sam, if all is going as per the major's plan, someone should be there soon to pick you up and get you on your way to Dongfeng City. I'm adding my contact info to this call. You can reach me anytime day or night. You may have a little trouble reaching me while traveling, but you'll be assigned a pair of handlers who should be able to help you. I look forward to seeing you soon. Goodbye."

Before Sam could respond, the display showed the connection had ended. He wondered what the project could be and whether it might have anything to do with Pierre's mysterious message. A sudden knock at his office door made him jump from his seat.

Opening the door, he found two Chinese gentlemen both dressed in black.

"Mr. Czerny?" asked the one on the left. He continued without waiting for an answer. "I am Zhi Chan and my associate here is Mr. Hong Wong." They bowed in unison. "Major Zhang Wei has asked us to escort you to the airport as soon as possible."

"Airport, huh? I'm afraid I don't have my passport with me. I'm going to have to stop at home to get it. It's only about ten minutes away, and it won't take me long to find it."

Mr. Hong Wong smiled and pulled an envelope from his inside jacket pocket and handed it to Sam. "You'll find your passport among the documents in there. We took the liberty of stopping at your home and gathering some things you'll need during your trip."

"Well, I need to stop by my home anyway and speak to my wife."

"We've handled that as well. She has spoken with Ms. Stern. We wish to make this trip a quick one. Now if you'll follow us to our vehicle, we need to take you to the airport with all haste, Mr. Czerny."

Sam thought for a second and then decided he might as well go along. If this had to do with what Pierre told him about, it would be foolish of him to miss out on the opportunity. Even if it did feel as if he had too little control and the people had their details sewn up a little too tightly. "Okay, I'm up for the ride. Lead on, McDuff!"

Zhi Chan gave him a perplexed look as he stepped forward and led the way. Sam noticed that Hong Wong fell in behind.

They walked out to the parking lot where a polished black limousine was waiting for them. Chan opened the door and they got in. The driver was behind a smoked glass partition and took off as soon as they were in the car.

It was the first time Sam had ever been in a car with an actual driver controlling it. Much like horses and then horseless carriages, self-driving cars had gone through a cycle where only the very rich could have them. Then they became ubiquitous and available to everyone. And now, like horses, cars with drivers were the toys of only the very wealthy. Sam took out his phone and began to dial Helen. He had no connection. That was odd since he usually had no problem connecting on the drive home and never had a problem near the office.

He held up the phone and cocked his head at his two escorts.

Chan spoke up. "Sorry, sir. The car is insulated against any type of radio-magnetic frequencies. Starshield uses these cars for different reasons and they value their privacy. It does make it inconvenient sometimes. Again, my apologies."

Chan continued. "We'll be arriving at the airport in a moment. We've reserved a special plane for you. We have access to all the special planes we need. After all, Starshield builds them."

At the airport, Sam noticed the limousine drove past the terminal and straight to the back end of one of the hangers. When they got out of the car, he saw one of the most unusual looking planes he'd ever seen. It sported swept-back wings and four engines sitting on a tail end surrounded by a half loop rudder almost as tall as the plane was long. The plane had only four passenger windows on the side facing him.

"What is that thing?" he asked Chan.

"That's the Starshield Shan Shee 4. It's a prototype of sorts, although this one has logged over a million miles. It's the fastest passenger plane Starshield has. You'll be meeting with Major Zhang in about four hours."

Chapter Three

S am followed the two escorts aboard the plane, ducking his head to get through the small portal as he looked around the inside of the plane.

The interior had only six passenger seats. Each one had an odd set of netted belts attached. What struck Sam as most odd was that Pierre Pacquelier was sitting in one of the seats.

Pierre rose and shook Sam's hand. "So good to see you in the analog, my friend. I was hoping you would make this flight." Pierre had one of those contagious grins and Sam smiled back.

When Sam got his hand back from Pierre, he scratched his head. "I thought you were in Washington when we spoke just a little while ago."

Pierre's smile disappeared and his eyes shifted left and right. "Ah, uh, yes, that was some time ago wasn't it?" He stared straight into Sam's eyes. Sam remembered Pierre told him to act surprised.

"So, what are you doing on this project? Come to think of it, just what is this project anyway?"

Pierre nodded his head. "Ah, I see they have not yet informed you. Well, do not feel different from us, my friend. We do not know much either. But I do know we are in a very special airplane right now. That alone must mean something."

"It does have an odd structure. It looks like it must be very fast given the sweep of the wings."

Pierre laughed. "I am betting it is faster than anything you have traveled in until now. We will be at our destination in under three hours."

"You've got to be joking," Sam replied. "How can anything get us to Mongolia in that time?"

"I am not joking. Not at all. This thing flies straight up into the stratosphere and then dives almost straight down at better than Mach 10. The flight is more like rocket than an airplane, I think."

Pierre looked behind his seat then said, "But I am being so impolite. My mother would be so ashamed of me. Permit me to introduce the other passengers on our trip."

Pierre stepped away and Sam saw two people sitting behind Pierre. The four seats faced each other. A tall balding man in his forties stood at attention and bowed. Sam expected him to click his heels.

"Boris Ivanovich Yelenko," Pierre introduced. "Boris is an amazing engineer and one of the geniuses behind the Lagrange Two Station."

Lagrange Two, Sam remembered, was a space platform floating some tens of thousands of miles from the far side of the Moon. Built as a starting point for deep space and Mars exploration, Sam remembered reading it was supplied with material mined and transformed on the Moon.

Yelenko's handshake was cold and formal. Sam got the impression he was looking at a high-ranking member of the military.

"It is an honor to meet anyone with such grand vision," Sam said. "Even more so when the vision is becoming reality."

Yelenko nodded. "Thank you. It is far from being a reality yet, but I am hopeful."

Pierre interrupted, pointing to a woman, no more than five feet tall with a rounded face and pitch-black eyes that hinted at an Asian ancestry. "This amazing woman is the one and only Doctor Amanda Won. Amanda's the brains behind the brains of the robots working on the Moon."

"It is nice to meet you," she said in a deep contralto voice that Sam found at odds with her small roundish frame. She held out her hand to shake his.

Pierre added, "And this is my friend Sam Czerny. Sam is the world's most notable xenobiologist."

Amanda Won and Boris Yelenko looked at Pierre curiously.

"What is a xenobiologist doing on this trip?" Amanda asked.

Before Sam could reply, the captain announced they needed to take their seats. Personal displays rose from their armrests as they sat.

The displays showed a short, animated movie that explained the craft would be taking off soon. Once it was over the ocean, it would be rising at an angle of eighty-two degrees until it reached low Earth orbit. This would involve about an hour at just under two G's of acceleration. They would then spend twenty-four minutes in level flight before beginning a rapid descent. The level flight and rapid descent would include more than an hour of micro-gravity. Then it explained how to use the unusual seatbelts.

Sam always wondered what it would feel like to be weightless. He found the prospect exciting.

The captain's voice came back on as the plane began to taxi down the runway. "This is Captain Jacob Morgan. We will shortly begin take off. Please make certain your seatbelts are fastened properly. At this time, I would also like you to drink the contents of the little bottle found in your left-hand armrest pocket. This contains a mood enhancer we have found helps handle the increased G's during our ascent."

Sam noticed everyone was removing their little bottles. He took his out as well. The label stated it contained three ounces of 'proprietary blend' as well as some vitamins and a little aspirin. Along with the others, he drank the fruit flavored drink. It didn't taste too bad.

By the time they reached the start of the runway, he was feeling sleepier than he expected. He figured all the time with the robot earlier in the day combined with the mood enhancer was having more of an effect than expected.

When the others began to nod off, Sam was too tired to notice. Suddenly, he felt so exhausted he didn't even remember he'd wanted to call Helen before they took off—just to make sure she was okay with his impromptu trip.

Chapter Four

Someone tapped Sam's forehead, making him open his eyes. He reached out his hand to prevent whomever it was from tapping him again and felt he'd pushed something away. Opening his eyes, he saw the little bottle he drank slowly spinning away from him. *I must be dreaming*, he thought as he watched it tumble end over end until it bumped into the wall. It bounced back and spun in the opposite direction.

Sam looked at his fellow passengers and saw they were all asleep. He noticed Yelenko and Pierre were holding out their arms like B movie zombies. Amanda, whose arms were tucked into the netting, had her mid length black hair floating about her head like a cloud. It looked pretty.

Realization brought him wide-awake. Given the lack of gravity, they were either at the apogee of their flight or somewhere in descent. A horrible thought occurred to him. What if the captain or whoever was in the cockpit was also sound asleep? The idea filled him with dread. Then he thought he was just being irrational. After all, there must be fail-safe precautions to prevent incidents like that from happening. But somewhere in the back of his mind, he remembered reading of disaster survivors saying they assumed someone was in control when it turned out nobody was. Could that be happening now?

Thinking it was better to not take any chances, he shouted out, "Anybody there? Come on, you aren't all going to go to sleep and leave me alone, are you? I mean, this is no joke. I don't have the first idea of how to fly one of these. Somebody is going to stay awake and fly this thing, right? Right? Someone, answer me!"

There was no answer. Maybe they all were indeed asleep. That thought was terrifying to him. Even if they were flying on autopilot, someone had to be awake in case something went wrong. Didn't they? Sam intended to find out.

"Okay, I guess I have to go and see myself, because you're freaking me out right now." He unlatched his seatbelt to go see if he could get a response by knocking on the cockpit door. Maybe the pilot had his headphones on and didn't hear Sam calling him.

He found getting to the cockpit door was not as easy as he thought. He pushed himself up from his armrests and felt his whole body continue to move up until he smacked his head against the cabin ceiling. This sent his body pivoting backward with his head moving toward the cabin floor and his feet toward the ceiling. The back of his head hit his seat cushion rather than any hard surface. At the same time as his toes struck the ceiling. The simultaneous strike stopped his pivoting and made his body turn to his right along its axis.

Sam calmed a bit and reminded himself he was a good swimmer. Moving through air this way was a lot like the way he used the controls to move his undersea robots.

Taking a deep breath, he reached out with his right hand and attempted to stop the rotation of his body along its axis. After a few taps that kept turning him in the opposite direction, he stabilized himself enough though he was drifting to his left. He tucked his knees into his belly and slowly straightened them until his toes brushed the back of Pierre's seat. This served to propel him at about one foot every three seconds towards the cockpit door. As he moved, Sam worked on a plan to stop himself. He noticed the cockpit's door handle was larger than one would normally see on a plane, so he decided that would be his target.

As he got close, he reached his hand out with every bit of strength he had and grabbed the handle. The rebound of his momentum pulled him backward. He resisted the urge to pull the other way, tightening his grip on the handle and every muscle in his body. He just held on until he came to a relative stop. Holding on with his left hand, he pressed his knees against the door and tried to turn the handle. It moved about ten degrees to the left. A second try rewarded his efforts as the door swung back and smacked his back against the wall. The door swung back and closed, then slowly opened again. This time it stayed open just enough for him to hold on to the side and stretch his left leg back. As the door opened wider, he held most of his body still and held on tightly as he peered around into the cockpit.

The problem was there was no cockpit.

All he saw was a bank of computer blades where he expected a pilot to be sitting. Sam realized the craft was either remote controlled or completely run by computer. He was inside a robot ship!

The lights in the cabin all turned blue and blinked three times before returning to normal. Sam felt a surge of anxiety wondering if this happened because he opened the cockpit door. Was the computer responding to the cockpit being breeched? He closed his eyes and listened for some kind of alarm or a shutting down of the programming.

Then he heard the same voice he'd heard before takeoff and breathed a sigh of relief.

"This is Captain Jacob Morgan again. We're about to begin the part of our descent where we will soon flatten out our flight. You will feel the return of gravity as we do that. Please make sure you are seated and that your seatbelt is attached. If any items are floating next to you, please make sure you catch them and stow them securely to prevent injury to yourself or any other passengers. You will find a net with a telescoping handle tucked in the pocket below your feet. I hope you enjoy the game of catch the objects. Gravity should be returning in about five minutes. I would also like to inform you that our destination has changed. We are no longer going to the Juiquan Facility in Dongfeng. We are now headed to the Wenchang Launch Center at Hainan Island."

Sam turned his head and looked out of the window. The sky was black. Darker than he had ever seen it. A bright blue curve of Earth filled about two thirds of the view. That felt odd to him and his gut clenched as he realized just how high they were. He wondered why the destination had changed. Looking at the other seats, he saw the other passengers were still asleep except for Boris Yelenko.

"You are flying while flying?" Yelenko asked, his slight Russian accent sounding intellectual to Sam's ear.

Sam wasn't sure if Boris was trying to be funny, but he kept a straight face when asking his question. "I didn't intend to. Did you know there's no pilot aboard this plane?"

"No, I did not, but I am not very much surprised. Most of what pilots do is follow a set of instructions. Even during weather events, they follow the protocol designed for those situations. With the diagnostic capabilities of machines today, I do not see why they cannot do as good a job or better, most of the time."

"What about unexpected occurrences?"

"What if a human pilot is not trained for them either? Do you think they would perform better? In fact, if you factor in their human emotions, which would have to be controlled in an emergency situation, they might even be less efficient than a computer under such conditions. Artificial Intelligence can store more memories and manage more 'what-if' scenarios. In other words, it would be easier to train a computer and have it retain everything it has been taught. Human memory is fallible."

"Well, I would think people would be more creative and flexible and would rely on their experience to adjust to the situation," Sam replied.

"Again, when you think about it, experience is just a data-set and an ability to retain it and sort through it. In a specialized set of tasks like flying, I think a machine will be just as likely to do well. Perhaps even better when it comes to being able to make the proper decision or set of decisions. I am not at all worried if that is what you are asking." Yelenko did look calm as he said this.

Yelenko noticed the bottle that tapped Sam in the head and woke him earlier. He reached under his calves and pulled out what looked like the type of fishing net children played with at the seashore. Expanding the rod, he snagged the bottle and brought it back toward himself. Sam saw him smile for the first time. "It is much like catching butterflies in the arboretum of Yekaterinburg when I was a child," Yelenko said.

The lights blinked and Captain Morgan, wherever he was, announced they had two minutes until they would feel gravity return.

"It might be a good idea for you to make your way back to your seat, or must I catch you like a butterfly as well?" Boris said.

Sam responded by flexing his legs and bouncing from the wall next to the cockpit door and shooting himself toward his seat. He pushed off a little too hard and had to stretch out his arms to keep from slamming into his seat headfirst. He managed to catch himself and turn in the right direction so he would be floating directly above his seat. Feeling the strain on his arms, he was grateful he had been doing regular workouts at the university gym.

"Just stay there," Boris advised. "As the gravity settles in, you should fall into your seat gently."

Just as Yelenko had predicted, Sam felt himself slowly lowering into this chair. He had to adjust himself to fit, but it was easy to do.

"The invisible Captain Morgan said we changed destination. I'm not sure why or what this Wenchang Base will be," Sam said.

Yelenko answered. "It's the southern most of the Chinese space cities. It's on an island that even has a sort of amusement park attached to it. It also has a military base. From there they've been launching a lot of the equipment for the base feeding the Lagrange platform."

"The Moon Base feeding the Lagrange platform? Tell me about that."

Yelenko smiled. "A lot of the station is being built on the Moon and then shipped to the site. The Moon offers much in the way of raw materials. The Fermi Crater Base has mining, smelting and manufacturing facilities as well as a rail gun launching system. It sends both raw rocks and completed parts to the Lagrange Station about fifty thousand kilometers from the Moon."

Several tones began ringing. They were not unpleasant but loud. Sam also felt his seat vibrate and he realized this was to wake any passengers who were still asleep.

Captain Morgan's ever calm and happy voice told them they would be landing in approximately twenty minutes.

"What? Do not tell me I missed the zero gravity!" Pierre's voice rang out. "Ah! That is just like me to sleep through the exciting part. Was anyone awake? Did anyone feel it at all?"

Boris spoke up. "Sam decided to go for a float, I awoke to seem him bobbing about the cabin like a feather on the breeze."

Pierre turned to look at Sam with surprise and a little respect. "Really? Sam, my friend, you never stop to stun me."

Chapter Five

T he craft landed and the passengers deplaned. It surprised Sam to see how bright it was outside but then he realized that it was just mid-afternoon local time. It was a good thing they had all gotten a little sleep since there was a good deal of day left for them. He figured they had enough hours left to begin whatever their work was immediately.

As they marched across the runway, a man in gray coveralls greeted them. He wore the same Starshield-Shackleton logo across his left shoulder that Sam noticed on the outside of the plane. It was a quarter moon bisected by a streamlined rocket ship. Sam thought it looked rather old fashioned.

The man had jet-black hair in a bowl cut, shining black almond eyes and a soft childlike look on his face. But Sam noticed his stance was one that projected confidence and ease.

"Can I get everyone together, please? My name is Dr. Tommy Park, and I am the local head of security for Starshield-Shackleton. Welcome to the Wenchang Base. We have been waiting for you. Please follow me to the conference room where we are holding the mission briefing."

As Sam, followed he heard Amanda mutter, "Mission?" to Pierre.

"I know. Isn't it all very exciting?" Pierre replied.

They went into a nearby building that looked like a warehouse from the outside. Once inside, they discovered a colorful environment not unlike a modern corporate office. They took a waiting elevator and Sam noticed it brought them down eleven stories before stopping. From there, Park led them into what looked like a pilot's ready room on an aircraft carrier.

The seats were all facing one end of the room where a large display screen sat behind a podium. A door at the side of the room opened and two people entered the room. Sam recognized one of them as Trish Stern. Next to her was a Chinese national with close-cropped gray hair and wrinkles at the edge of his eyes and corners of his mouth. Wrinkles that said that he was more often annoyed than smiling. Sam was sure he was Chinese because he wore a military uniform with the upright isosceles triangle and the letters CNSA and a Chinese ideogram—the logo of the Chinese National Space Administration.

Trish Stern stepped to the podium and addressed the audience. "Good afternoon. My name, for those who have not yet met me, is Trish Stern and I'm the project liaison for mission L2-41. I'm pleased to see we have everyone here. Before we go into the actual mission briefing, please let me say I'm proud of all of you. And I want to both thank you and wish you all the greatest good fortune during your trip."

Sam, who was sitting between Boris and Pierre whispered, "Trip?"

Boris turned and looked at him, shaking his head and Pierre looked like a child ready to fly from his seat in excitement.

Trish Stern pretended to ignore any audience reaction. "Now I have the great pleasure to introduce the mission commander. A man who has been working with the lunar mining and Lagrange Station projects for more than seven years. This is Major Zhang Wei." She stepped back and applauded as the major walked up to the podium and the small audience followed her example.

The major did not pause to acknowledge the applause. Instead, he tapped the control screen on the podium and lit up the display behind him. As he spoke, an animation of the Lagrange Station showed the various steps in the construction process. "As you know, we are entering the most important phase in the building of the Lagrange Two Station. We are about to attach new docking points and reactivate the old IIS pods we sent to the Lagrange Two more than forty-five years ago. Much of the technology aboard the pods is antiquated and obsolete at this point, but we can use the pods as human habitat while we build out the rest of the station."

Sam looked to his left and saw that Pierre looked like firecracker at the end of its fuse. He sat at the edge of his chair and looked ready to leap up and yell in celebration.

The major continued. "Currently, autonomous devices are running the operation. We have over twenty-eight different types of these devices at the Fermi Crater Base. They range from those dedicated to mining and manufacturing, to those used to carry materials to our launch site.

"Lee Jin-Dal," the major said, tilting his head toward a member of the audience sitting at the front of the room, "will be going to the actual Lagrange Point along with Boris Yelenko as the operational staff at the station. This is the first operation where we are sending lunar-made material to the station itself."

Trish Stern applauded, as did Pierre, who looked as if he would applaud anyone and anything to be able to release some of his excitement.

"The rest of us will focus on the Fermi Base. Liftoff is at 3:45 tomorrow morning. For those of you who have recently arrived, make sure your timing device synchronizes with base time. We have moved the launch site to this base due to the availability of a ready launch vehicle. We are taking advantage of the fact that the Moon is in perigee with the Earth in two days. In the packets handed to you when you stepped in, you should find a tablet. This will include an agenda for your training over the next four or five hours and a debriefing and preparation for lift off tomorrow."

Everyone in the room quickly opened their packets.

The major interrupted them. "Before you start, make sure you familiarize yourself with this part of the base. We have consolidated your activities on floors seven, eight and nine of this building. On floor six, you will also find free offices for those of you who prefer to work on your own. I will be holding a final briefing in this room at 1:45 AM. I expect to see you all there. Some of you have tight schedules, I suggest you review them now and get to it. Dismissed."

Sam thought the major looked at the audience as if he was expecting them to salute. Instead, some got up and shuffled out into the hallway while the others began to read their tablets right in their seats. After setting his password and making sure he was on base time, Sam looked at this agenda. He only had two meetings scheduled. One with a mission preparation specialist concerning what he would need to know for the trip to the Moon.

That was when it struck Sam. He was actually going to go to the Moon.

Over the last twenty-five years several thousand people had gone to the Moon and back. It wasn't exactly the heroic notion it had been in the early days of space exploration. He remembered his grandfather telling him how he'd watched Neil Armstrong's first steps on the surface of the Moon, staying up late at night when he was only a little boy. Those early astronauts were real heroes. Still, Sam could think of only two or three people he had met who could claim they'd set foot on the Moon. This was going to be quite a feather in his cap and would add to the prestige of his presentations as well as his resume. Helen would like that. It would be good for their projects and make getting grants easier.

Helen!

He'd completely forgotten he hadn't spoken to his wife at all since he promised her he'd complete the presentation. Even if she'd been briefed by Wong Hong, Trish Stern or whomever; he needed to call her and make certain she was okay with this. And besides, telling her he was going to the Moon was a damn good excuse for not having finished his presentation. Picking up his things and heading to the elevator, he hoped he could find a quiet office on the sixth floor for the private call.

When he got to the sixth floor, he opened a few doors before he realized the convention here was that a closed door meant an occupied office. He finally found an open door, closed it and settled in.

Powering up his comm device, he placed the call to his wife. After nothing happened, he checked to see if he had a connection. The device showed the same lack of bandwidth it had in the limousine. This building was just as shielded as the car had been. He wasn't going to be able to talk to Helen.

He took his tablet from his package and turned it on—quickly reviewing the document he had to read when he noticed the device had a camera. He opened the list of applications and saw the device had a connectivity app. The app indicated the device was getting bandwidth. It should have been obvious, he thought, they needed to have bandwidth in the building for these devices to work. It was only his comm device that could not connect, though he wasn't sure why.

He accessed the app and entered Helen's contact coordinates. In a few seconds he saw her face. He couldn't make out the background around her but it didn't look like she was at home.

"Sam!" he could see the surprise on her face. "I was wondering if I'd hear from you. Ms. Stern had said it was not probable, but I know how you are. If anybody would find a way, you would. She also told me you're on some type of top-secret project for them. It's so nice to see your face."

Once again, Sam thought about how much Helen's face always

made him smile, "It's been a bit of a whirlwind. I'm sorry about missing the presentation. This thing caught me completely off guard."

"Don't worry about that. Everything is fine here. The funds they sent us are more than I could have raised in three years of presentations and meetings. I don't know what you're up to, but I can tell you it's paying off." She scrunched up the space between her eyebrows. "At least tell me it isn't dangerous."

Sam smiled to reassure her. "Not dangerous at all. Right now, I'm on an island off of the coast of China and, get this, tomorrow I'm heading to the Moon! Fermi Base on the far side. I'm still not sure what I'll be doing there but I have suspicions. If it's what I think it is, it could be the biggest scientific discovery in hundreds of years." Sam realized he was beginning to sound like Pierre when he noticed Helen looking at him curiously.

"Can you still see me?" she asked. "It looks like the connection failed. I heard you say you were on an island and then you froze up." She waved at the screen.

"I can hear you fine. Can you hear me now?"

Helen just stared at the screen with her smile fading. "Well, I don't seem to be able to see or hear you, but in case you can still see and hear me, have a great time and come back to me in one piece. I love you, Sam." She blew him a kiss before the connection severed.

Sam was disappointed, but at least he let her know he was okay. And her smile and kiss would sustain him for a while. He wondered why the connection cut off so suddenly. Were they monitoring his activity here? There was more secrecy about this whole mission than he was used to. Maybe this was just how the military functioned. He never felt at ease with military people precisely because they never seemed to trust anyone. Still, he was only talking to his wife. He knew better than to tell her any classified information. They didn't have to completely disconnect the call; they could have just censored it if he said more than they wanted him to.

Maybe he would be able to connect with her from the Moon. That would be fun. Something to tell their grandkids.

He decided to start paying attention to the mass of data he needed to go through before his first meeting.

Chapter Six

Trish Stern was sitting at a desk reviewing the conversation Sam had with his wife a few minutes earlier. She had gotten a security alert informing her someone was connecting with an outside person and decided to monitor it. The fail-safe mechanism using a set of algorithms prevented Sam from letting his wife know where he was and where he was going as expected.

She couldn't blame him for calling his wife. While they had told him where he was going, they had not explained the need for secrecy. They'd swooped in and picked him up minutes after her phone call. He didn't have a moment to talk to his wife. And while that was what their goal was, it hardly seemed fair to take a man away from his wife like that.

"Damn you, Jeremy Ledbetter," she thought, not for the first time. To have their first choice of xenobiologists go out and get himself killed while paragliding was bad luck and bad timing. Sam Czerny wasn't quite as good as Ledbetter, but given the short window of opportunity, he would have to do.

The door to her office swung open and slammed against the wall. Major Zhang Wei stomped in and smacked his hand on her desk. "Did you see how close we came to a security breach? We need to do something about this man Czerny. I move we cancel him from the trip now. We have a valid reason with this security breach!"

Trish stood calmly and closed the door to her office. Then she turned to the major. "We've gone through this before. The people whose interests we represent and who are funding this adventure think otherwise. It has always been their insistence that a xenobiologist be on the team. They believe once we locate the artifact, the company would be remiss if we didn't bring in someone to study it. Someone who's not an obvious employee

25

of the company. I've managed to bring someone in who's not only quite reputable but who's beholden to us for donations we've made to his projects. This isn't a time for us to rock the boat. You and I have far too much at stake." She slapped her hand on her desk in the same spot he had. "And don't pound on my desk!"

Major Zhang returned to his usually stone-faced stare, betraying no emotions as he looked at her. "Do not presume that because we came to an agreement and you won, you have all decision-making authority. Don't forget the government committee has named me as the military leader of this project. As such, the decisions, even life or death ones, are mine."

Trish paused and stared at the man. She knew the major could be dangerous if he felt he was in a subordinate position, especially to a woman. He was such a holdover in some ways. Something of a misogynist when it came to women in decision-making positions. She had dealt with men like this her entire career and learned how to handle them.

"Major, I defer to you when it comes to running the project. But remember, there is a lot more at stake here than just a mining base on the Moon or a platform for deep space exploration. Your government has paid my company a lot of money for what we're doing. My own substantial interests are tied to the success of this mission. I'd hate to see you replaced because my company felt it needed to find someone in the Chinese military who behaved in a way that ensured success for all parties. We have options written into our contract stating we have the right to replace you if we find it necessary. Your government agreed to that."

Trish gave him a wide smile, showing him her teeth and letting him know she would bite him if she felt it was necessary.

The major, to his credit, neither cowed down to her nor stood up to her. "Then I leave the problem of Sam Czerny and security to you," he said quietly. "He needs to be put on a tight leash immediately. If not, I'll not be the one found negligent. He is your responsibility now. Take care of him. Immediately."

Without waiting for a response, he turned and exited, closing the door behind him but not quite slamming it.

Trish sat at her desk and used her tablet to look up Czerny's schedule. She saw she could move one of her meetings up sooner and then join Czerny in his operations briefing. That way, she could keep a closer eye on him.

Tapping into her tablet, she scheduled herself into the briefing. After all, she should have done that anyway from the beginning. She should have known it would be necessary when they had to bring in a new person so late in the process.

Damn that Ledbetter and his childish, irresponsible games! she thought. Bringing someone in to the loop at this late date would be no easy task, but she had no choice. Her company insisted a xenobiologist be on the team, and Sam was the only one qualified for the job. She had to make it work.

The briefing would be a good time to put a leash on Czerny. She hurried to get her work done so she could make the briefing.

Chapter Seven

Wenchang Military Base
Hainan Province

Amanda Won was fourteen minutes early for her mission briefing. She was always early for every meeting. Her mother always said being late was the height of rudeness. Every time she prepared herself for any meeting or event, she could hear her mother's voice with its thick South Korean accent. "You can always get back anything you lose except time. When you are late you are stealing time from other people. A terrible thing to do."

Heeding her mother's advice, she always made good use of her own time. Given the extra minutes she had, she pulled up the personal logs of her two predecessors on the Lagrange Two project. Garrick O'Brien had been a great robotics and AI engineer, but he wasn't good at documentation. His notes were vague, not properly arranged and lacked any personal flavor. Indrani Meta was quite another story. She had named all twenty-seven robot categories after mythical beings from different spiritual traditions. This added an interesting flavor and feeling to the project.

The fact O'Brien hadn't continued the tradition disappointed Amanda. She vowed to resurrect it with the four new types she was going to put into service. The question was which names should she use? For that, she had to go back into Meta's notes and catalog which ones were taken. Not exactly serious work, but with her homework completed well ahead of time, she could add a little personal touch to her job and bring back a tradition.

Wherever her mother's soul was, Amanda was sure she would be smiling.

She heard footsteps and saw Major Zhang Wei and Lee Jin-Dao walk into the room chatting in Mandarin. They noticed Amanda and immediately switched to English, the official mission language. "Ms. Won, so good of you to be here already. Have you been introduced to Mr. Lee?"

Standing, she shook Lee's hand. "We haven't met in person, but I have read a few of your studies. It's an honor to get a chance to work with someone as experienced in robotic engineering as yourself." She bowed her head slightly.

Lee returned the bow and took the time to look Amanda up and down in a way that made her feel a bit flattered and a bit annoyed at the same time. "I've heard a good bit about you as well. Wasn't it you who designed the portable decision protocol we'll be using in the catcherbots?"

Amanda blushed. She'd spent more than half of the last year working on a set of apps that were perfectly portable among a wide variety of bots. Having them all use a similar decision-making core process helped in smoothing interfaces. And it increased the speed of team learning in complex machine managed environments. Few people knew of her work and it pleased her to learn Lee was aware of it.

The major raised one bushy gray eyebrow. "Excuse me, but I feel as though I'm not well enough informed about all of this. Can you help me rectify that?" He had looked at Amanda but obviously asked the question of Lee.

Lee nodded. "Major, I am certain Dr. Won would do a more thorough explanation than I ever could, but in a nutshell, her work has enabled us to save weeks of team robotic initiation and even more weeks of testing. It has been a huge cost savings for us and has helped us keep to our schedule. In fact, without her approach, I think we would still be working on the calculations for launching from the Moon to Lagrange Two."

The major gave Amanda a look of approval and said, "Dr. Won, you did all the calculations yourself?"

Before Amanda could respond, Lee interrupted her. "No Major, that is the beauty of it. Her work gave the bots the ability to calculate it all among themselves. The bots did the number crunching, ran the simulations and fine-tuned the process. Our initial run will not have anyone else involved." Lee looked at Amanda and beamed.

Amanda was not enjoying being talked about as if she wasn't there. But she had to admit if she spoke for herself, she would likely have gone into an explanation that would have gone over the major's head.

"You mean to tell me this game of catch was not programmed? The machines have figured it out themselves?" the major asked.

Amanda finally felt she had to speak up. "Major, the essence of Artificial Intelligence is not to give machines a set of instructions they must follow. Quite the contrary. We give them a set of problems and the tools to find a solution. Instead of dedicating processing power to following step-by-step programs, they are asked to learn all they can about a problem. They then propose and test solutions until they can supply several working models. Each model comes with a percentage of likelihood regarding failure or success. Most of the time they are right. Now and then, engineers such as Mr. Lee and myself need to coax them into moving in one direction or another. Each time they find the best working solution, they can add it to their knowledge base and use it as a shortcut for the next problem."

Lee looked pleased Amanda included him in her explanation.

The major shrugged his shoulders. "For quite some time now, I've been thinking machines are becoming too clever too quickly. I'm sure it won't be long before they're cleverer than I am."

The major wasn't the only authority figure Amanda had come across who displayed an irrational fear of machine learning. She reached out and placed her hand gently on his arm. "Machines are becoming very clever indeed, but they'll never match human intelligence. They may be good at problem solving but they lack the creative spirit that makes us all human."

Amanda suddenly became aware of the major looking at her hand on his arm. She pulled it away quickly. It was clear that a soldier like Zhang was not accustomed to someone using human touch to convey sympathy or try to ease his discomfort.

"Well I'm sure the two of you have a lot to discuss and I think I'll only be in the way. I'll see you both at the final briefing," he said, taking a small step away from her and turning to leave.

"Major Zhang?" Amanda called out to him.

He turned back and gave her an expectant look.

"May I ask a question?"

"By all means, Dr. Won. Please do."

"Why do we have a xenobiologist with us for this mission?"

""I think it would be better if you asked Ms. Stern about that. She can give you a clearer and more satisfactory answer," he said. "Dr. Won, Mr. Lee, I bid you a good day." He turned and left the room closing the door behind him.

As soon as Major Zhang left, Lee's posture changed. He no longer stood straight but sat on the edge of the desk and even slouched a little. "Wow! I like the way you handle the major, but tell me, do we really have a xenobiologist on board?"

"Yes. His name is Sam Czerny." Amanda was a little uncomfortable with how altogether at ease Lee looked. She took a step back pulling a chair away and sitting in it. "I saw him on the flight here. I remembered seeing a documentary about some of the studies he was doing with life forms in extreme habitats. Extremophiles is what they're called, if I remember correctly. Most of them are microbial, but there are also some colony forms that exhibit some primitive forms of hive intelligence. Dr. Czerny is an expert in the field and seems to be traveling to the Fermi Crater for some reason."

"Huh? That's odd. What do you make of it?"

What I make of this so far, Amanda thought, *is that you talk to me as if we were old friends and that is odd as well.* "I don't know," she said. "Maybe he wants to run some experiments in the far side environment."

"Is it that different? The far side never faces the Earth, but it does see the sun now and then. It's not like it's a completely dark side. What could he possibly be looking for there?"

"I wish I knew. Maybe he has some theories about stuff coming from Earth. I know the planet gets bombarded with space debris all the time. Tons of it every day. Maybe he thinks the Earth has some impact on the side of the Moon that faces it. Maybe wants to see if he can discover something by stepping out of the Earth's influence altogether."

"Sounds to me like you're grasping at straws."

"Do you have a better theory? Because that's all I can come up with."

Lee scratched his head. "I can't say that I do. But I'm not sold on your idea. Seems like an expensive way to go if all you want to do is play in a vacuum. Something else is up. I can feel it."

Amanda silently agreed with him. Her theory was looking for the plausible. Part of her innovation in teaching machines was to make them consider options that were improbable. That almost never led to a direct solution, but it did lead to more questions and different ways of considering the same problem. It almost gave the machines a certain type of small imitation of creativity. She had never published that information in any of her documents or research papers. The engineering community would have laughed at such a notion.

She shrugged. "We need to get to our work. Let's start with the initial synchronization tests. The bots have proposed the catcherbots are the ones who start the tossing schedule. What do you think?"

Lee gave her a quizzical look. "I think I'm surprised you would be second-guessing them about a decision."

Chapter Eight

Wenchang Military Base
Hainan Province

S am walked into his last meeting to find his friend Pierre Pacquelier sitting in the room waiting for him, grinning from ear to ear with eager anticipation.

"Pierre? What are you doing here? I didn't see you on the list for this meeting."

Pierre grinned. "You're kidding, no? This is the meeting about the artifact they found on the Moon. I'm not on the list but there is no way I'm going to miss this part of it. After all, I am the one who suggested you get invited to this festival. You did not see that yet?"

Trish Stern walked into the room along with an elderly man. His balding head was crowned with an explosion of unkempt white hair. The man shuffled and it looked as if he was going to tumble over at any moment. She helped him to a chair and he fell into it with a sigh.

"This is Professor Ian Tavish," she said to the others. "The professor is an archaeologist, but one who specializes in the history of archaeology. He has been included in this meeting on a need-to-know basis. This information will be crucial to your work on the Moon. Professor, would you please brief the gentlemen on what we found?"

"Yes, of course. Why I'm here, isn't it?" He giggled a bit and then coughed before continuing. "I'm not sure what you've been told, so I'll get right to the point. During the excavations for the mining operation in the Fermi Crater on the far side of the Moon . . . Oh, wait a second let me turn on the animation."

He picked up a tablet and fiddled with it, muttering until the wall behind him began to display an image of the Moon. It looked different from the Moon Sam grew up looking at and he realized it was the far side, which is never seen from the Earth.

Tavish coughed again before speaking. "Wonderful gadgets these animation thingies, they time themselves to my lectures. I use them a lot in my classes. Seems to keep the students from sleeping quite as much. But, where was I? Ah, yes. What we found there was a construct. Perhaps a machine, perhaps a building. We aren't quite sure. The shape is somewhat dome-like but tapers to a point at the top. Rather subtly as you can see here from this resonance image."

Sam found the shape elegant, it made him think of a large female breast pointing at the sky.

The professor continued. "I'm showing you this resonance image because most of the structure is beneath the lunar soil. We've only excavated a small part since finding it seven months ago."

"Seven months!" Pierre shouted. "With a find like this, why has no one gone through digging out as much as possible yet?"

Trish looked at Pierre with cold eyes. "Dr. Pacquelier, it's taken us some time to make recommendations to those who are financing the mining project. It then took them a few months to decide to explore the artifact. Finally, we need to adjust some of the equipment we have there to make it useful for exploration. There really isn't a rush. It isn't going anywhere. It takes time to go through all the necessary channels. And the adaption of the equipment is crucial. We don't want to damage it in any way. Professor Tavish, please continue."

"Yes, thank you." The professor squinted at the display as if it was helping him find his place. Then nodding to himself, he turned back to Sam and Pierre. "The artifact is somewhat hollow as far as we can tell. At least there are hollow areas, including passages that resemble hallways."

Red lines lit up through the image of the artifact.

Sam thought there must have been at least a hundred of them and on over a dozen levels. "Just how large is the artifact?" he asked.

The professor blinked. "Yes, yes. I'm coming to that. Each of the hallways is roughly seven meters tall and just as wide. If the builders were the size of humans, I suspect they were using vehicles of some sort to travel through them. As you can see that makes them rather large. The structure itself is about seven hundred meters tall. Roughly two kilometers on the north south axis and one and a half kilometers looking east to west."

"Hole of shit!" Pierre exclaimed. "It's not an artifact, it's a complex!"

Taking a deep breath, Sam let out a slow, soft whistle. "Professor, this thing is enormous. How is it that it was never seen from previous mapping of the Moon? I mean, this area must have been well researched before anyone decided to make it the hub of the mining operation. How could something so large have been missed? It makes no sense."

The professor seemed pleased by Sam's question. "Ha! Yes. I asked myself the same thing. It seems it has some sort of shielding that makes it impervious to most scanning methods. We only have the measurements I just gave you because we modified one of the robots on the Moon to do a resonance scan by touching the artifact. Even though we do not know what it's made of, we do know we can ping it by touching it and read the vibrations. Very much like ground penetrating radar works."

"Who found it? And who modified the robot to do these measurements?" Pierre asked.

The professor frowned. "A surveying bot found it. One of the machines on the Moon designed to locate raw material sites most suitable for mining. As far as who gave the bot the instructions to measure it, the robot came up with that on its own initiative. The robot is programmed to survey any sites it runs across, and that's exactly what it did.

"While this is by no means common, the bots can use some sophisticated techniques when it comes to problem solving. This bot's actions were well within normal functioning parameters given the latest system upgrades."

The office door opened suddenly and Tommy Park strutted in.

"Sorry to be so late. Things do get hectic as we approach launch. Is it time for me yet?"

"I think your timing may be perfect. Mr. Park, but before you go ahead, I'd like to add a few words from our shareholders. A few words of caution," Trish said.

Sam and Pierre looked at each other realizing they were the ones she was addressing her remarks to.

"I'm aware both of you joined us on this exploration in a, shall I say, less than a genteel manner." Sam saw she was smiling that funny way again, using only her mouth and not the rest of her face. "And there's a good reason for it. The people who are paying for this project decided we wouldn't release any news of this publicly before we've had a chance to fully explore what it is.

"An announcement like this will lead to so many questions, and hopefully we will have some answers ready when we release the statement. If it is an alien artifact, which we have not completely determined yet, the news could cause quite a stir across the world. The ramifications could be extensive, ranging from religious implications, to political ones, to economic ones. The world situation is fragile in many ways right now, and news as large as this can tip it one way or the other. To prevent a cataclysmic impact on world affairs, we've decided to have a discovery voyage before releasing any information. And that is why you are here. I'm sure you understand."

Sam didn't like where she was going with this and he stood up. "Ms. Stern, with all due respect, if this is what we think this is, we owe it to the world to let them know of its existence immediately. Each person should come to their own conclusion. Why should we let religious zealots or Luddite politicians dictate what people learn about the universe? It's just not right. Science belongs to everybody."

Trish Stern looked at him and frowned. "Mr. Czerny, I'm not giving you an option. What I'm telling you is that you can, under no circumstances, communicate with anyone about where you currently are, where you're going and for what reason. You are not permitted to breathe a word about the artifact or the mission you're going on to anyone. I hope I make myself clear. Otherwise . . ."

Interrupting her, Sam shook his head. "I don't see why it needs to be a secret. This could be game changing for humanity! For Pete's sake, this is why I became a xenobiologist!" Sam realized he was sweating and breathing rapidly.

Pierre stood and placed a hand on Sam's forearm. "Sam, we have a lot of more work to do and a launch in a few hours. Maybe this is not the time to argue a point of communications."

"What?" Sam said loudly and turned to look at Pierre. Pierre raised both eyebrows gave Sam a stern look as he squeezed the man's arm.

Sam realized he should calm down. "Okay, I guess. Okay. I don't agree, but you're right, Pierre. We don't have the time. In fact, I probably wouldn't have the time to talk to anyone about this anyway.

"Ms. Stern, I hope you can be available to talk about this when we get back. I don't see how we'll be able to avoid announcing things if we make a real alien discovery there." Sam rose to leave.

Stern held still. "Let's not cross any bridges before we come to them. It's time for me to move onto my next meeting. Please make sure you are thorough in understanding your mission agenda with Mr. Park. If you have questions as he explains it, this is the time to ask. There may not be enough time later."

Without another word she left, closing the door behind her.

Sam turned to Pierre and Tommy Park. "She's being unreasonable! This is ridiculous! This could be the greatest scientific discovery known to man, and she is worried about how religious wingnuts will deal with it? Her reasoning is completely irrational! How can the two of you be so calm about this?"

Pierre shrugged. "Perhaps it is. But then again, perhaps Ms. Stern is being reasonable given that she is following orders. However, you, my friend, are being stupid."

Sam was flabbergasted. "Did you just call me stupid?"

"No, I said you were being stupid. Believe me, I have been stupid so many times that I am very good at recognizing when someone is being stupid and you are being stupid."

Sam bristled. "Me? No, if anyone is acting stupid, it's Trish Stern. You cannot sit on a scientific discovery of this magnitude! The world needs to know!"

Pierre put his hand on Sam's shoulder. "Sam, you are a brilliant scientist. I know very few with a creative mind like yours. But listen to me, mon ami. We're here, about to go on an adventure of what might be incredible importance. A discovery people have dreamed of for generations. Something you have dedicated your life to. And you are ready to argue with this woman about what is right and what is wrong? If you continue, she will decide she does not need you and will take someone else in your place." Pierre stared straight into Sam's eyes. "What would you call that?"

As hard as he tried, Sam could not hold Pierre's stare. He knew his friend was right. He looked down and muttered, "Stupid, I guess."

"Okay, that is settled," Pierre said, turning to Tommy Park. "Mr. Park, let us, how do you say, get the show on? I'm glad we have removed all the stupid from the team. I don't want any stupid on the Moon. That could be dangerous." He glanced at Sam, who looked away.

Tommy Park looked at the two of them and then shook off his disbelief. "Right. Let's take a look at the mission parameters. First on the agenda will be Day One on Base Fermi, during which we will be prepping equipment and doing inventory. I'm told you are both rated on remote controlled vehicles?"

They both nodded and as Park began to go through the steps through the agenda, Sam saw the plan was to be on the Moon for twelve days. It seemed like a short time and he hoped it would be long enough to explore the artifact as thoroughly as he wanted to.

Chapter Nine

Wenchang Military Base
Hainan Province

ajor Zhang Wei brushed his hand over his graying close-cropped hair. He had spent the last days preparing for the upcoming briefing with his superiors, and he felt ready to handle whatever they had for him.

He expected the usual dull status review with General Sun and Trish Stern from Starshield. Instead, he found himself facing a display featuring five faces. General Sun was there, but relegated to the far left of the screen. In the middle was the bald, squinting face of a man who looked beyond age. The display listed his name as simply Zhuxi or Chairman.

None of the others were recognizable to the major, and their names were not appearing on the display. No one spoke up and all were looking at him, waiting for him to take the lead. After looking at his tablet while wondering which path would be the proper one for him to take, he lifted his head and spoke. "Good morning (afternoon) gentlemen. I'm afraid Ms. Stern has not yet arrived for our status briefing. General Sun, would you be kind enough to introduce me to the new participants?"

General Sun's manner was formal in a way that made Zhang nervous. What was the general trying to tell him? "Major Zhang, Ms. Stern will not be joining us today. These are several of the more interested parties who have been supporting our project. Suffice to say introductions will be foregone and all you need know is that these persons are ones who have a vested interest in this mission."

Zhang looked at the four stony faces next to Sun and bowed solemnly.

Other than General Sun and the chairman, the others were not Asian. The two on the right of the chairman looked like brothers. They were swarthy looking men who must have been in their sixties with fat pink cheeks and little pig eyes. The kind of men who looked like they drank a lot and never exercised. The other man—between the chairman and General Sun—was remarkably different. He was tall, thin and pale, with the lightest blue eyes Zhang ever saw. 'Ghost eyes', his grandmother would have called them. They all looked inscrutable, emotionless.

The chairman finally spoke, "Major Zhang. General Sun speaks highly of you."

Zhang bowed again, worried any meeting with a superior beginning with praise usually has a 'but' following it.

The chairman continued. "We are at the cusp of great events. And fate has decided that at this conjecture, a very pivotal point rests in the hand of a certain major. I have taken the time to review your record, Major Zhang. It's been most impressive. There is no doubt in my mind you are a more than capable man for this position. But . . ."

Here it comes, thought Zhang.

"Are you," the chairman paused and leaned a little closer to the display, "a truly loyal man, Major Zhang? Can we be certain of your complete trust and honesty?"

Zhang's mind raced. What had they found out about him? Was there something he'd done that made him look less than loyal? There had been that woman back in Shanghai. He still thought of her now and then. But that had been more than twenty years earlier, when he was still young and foolish. It couldn't be that. There had been nothing since. He always ran a tight ship and lived an impeccable life. He felt sweat bead on the back of his neck and wondered if they could see it. "Chairman, I am and have always been loyal to my task, my rank, my army, my party, the People's Republic and the planet. I see no reason for that to change."

The chairman leaned back a bit and the faintest shadow of a smile appeared on his lips. "Good, good. Now then, you must know this. The mission you are embarking on is a great deal more than just the first launch of lunar-made materials to the space station. It is more important even than the Lagrange Station itself. I trust you are aware of at least some of this."

Zhang nodded making certain he displayed the proper serious and focused attention.

"Major Zhang, I would even say it is even more important than the eventual Martian colonization."

Zhang's eyes widened involuntarily. *What could be more important than that?* he thought.

"It's no secret the People's Republic is the world's most powerful country in production capacity, wealth development and creativity," the chairman said. "But one area still eludes us, Major Zhang. Do you know what that is?"

Zhang knew. But everyone in the Chinese military knew it was not politically expedient to admit it. He decided this was not a time to be too shy, even if boldness might mean condemnation. "I take it the chairman is speaking of military prowess. And America's continued dominance in that area."

Out of the corner of his eye, Zhang saw Sun visibly relax. Was that a stream of sweat that came down his temple?

"An excellent way of putting it. Too many men would never have the courage to say what they really think to my face. You are to be congratulated, Major Zhang." The chairman looked pleased

Leaning forward and looking directly into the camera, Zhang studied the chairman's face. He found himself distracted by the age blotches on the old man's head.

"Yes," the chairman said. "It's been a long time that the Americans have held this position. A long time ago, they improved their development capability and have maintained that position for more than two hundred years. Air power, nuclear weapons, cyber war, drone and robotic weapons, intelligence, and their ever-increasing satellite capability. All this has always put them in the forefront when it comes to being able to be the first to strike and strike hard. And unlike most countries, they have never shied away from testing their technology in real world theaters. They've used their belligerence to dominate world politics even as their economy has faltered and declined."

Major Zhang wondered why the chairman was lecturing him with concepts he had studied at War College, but he dared not interrupt.

"The one consistent and continued advantage the Americans have is that they hold and exploit the high ground. Their systems have always allowed them to look at an enemy from above and to track and strike with relative impunity. Many an adversary has tried to find ways to defend against this strike from above and none have been successful. There is a simple reason for that: the cost of defense is much higher than the cost of an effective and accurate offense. No country, even a wealthy one such as

China, can afford it. No armor is ever good enough against the next technological breakthrough America develops."

General Sun took a deep breath and spoke. "My Chairman, Major Zhang is not only a loyal and capable man. He is also well versed in military strategy and tactics. It was his command in the North Korean uprising that brought him to my attention. I believe it would be useful for us to get to the point of the matter without further delay."

Zhang was used to seeing General Sun give orders and demand accounts, but had never heard him speak with such deference in his voice.

The chairman looked at Sun slowly. Zhang was certain that despite the display, the other three were in the same room together. It wasn't just digitally adjusted lighting that made them look that way.

With a stern look on his face, the chairman nodded. "I am always spending time with politicians and businessmen. Forgive me if I tend to forget you military men prefer a more direct approach. In my line of work, the direct approach serves only if you wish to startle someone. So, as you say, General Sun, I will get to the point." He turned his head toward the general and nodded slightly.

The back and forth dialogue surprised Zhang. It revealed to him General Sun, despite his nervousness, placed great importance in this meeting and its outcome. Enough that he was willing to risk advising the chairman on his communications style.

Turning his attention back to the camera, the chairman focused his eyes on Zhang as he spoke. "Major Zhang, it's time for the People's Republic to take the high ground. We have conferred with many of the world players. We have enough allies and supporters that the time has come for us to make our move. The Fermi Moon Base has an additional mission that we have been working on for some time. We are at the point where this mission will soon be revealed. You, Major Zhang, will be in a pivotal position. There will be some risks, but the rewards and honors will be greater than you have ever imagined. You will be a national hero in the People's Republic. This is why your loyalty is so important to me." He paused—staring directly into the camera.

Zhang took the chairman's pause as a request that he speak. He thought for a second and cleared his throat. "As I said, I'm ready and willing to do what must be done for my country and the party. My loyalty is unwavering. But I'm not certain I understand the exact nature of my task."

Nodding, the chairman turned toward General Sun. "When the time comes, General Sun will send you the information you'll need to complete your mission. All I ask is when that time comes, you do act. You must not hesitate and you must not delay. Timing is everything when it comes to this mission. Is that understood?"

Major Zhang stood and bowed from the waist. "I have never failed in my duty to my country and I will not fail now or at that moment, no matter what it involves."

"Excellent." The chairman turned to his left and asked, "Who is our next meeting with?"

Zhang didn't hear the answer. The call ended abruptly and the display went blank.

Sinking back into his seat, Major Zhang's heart was racing. He was stunned. Something serious had happened in Beijing. For his entire life, party bosses were far more concerned with economic prosperity—both theirs and China's. Military prowess was never really an issue. China preferred to be an isolationist country. Of course, there had been a lot of military projects. They were always about someone in party headquarters gaining prestige or financial reward.

The Lagrange Two Station had always been about prestige. It was why they involved companies and scientists from other countries. It had been curious that there were no representatives from NASA, the ESA, Russian Federal Space Agency or JAXA. Zhang chalked that up to the fact other nations may not have agreed as to what a great endeavor it was. Now, he knew it was because there was a definite military component to this mission. And based on what he had just heard, it had far-reaching consequences.

The major knew that no matter what it was, he was sure he would be able to fulfill his duty without hesitation, just as he had told the chairman. Like his father and his grandfather before him, he was a soldier. Duty and country were his life.

Chapter Ten

Wenchang Taikonaut Prep Canter
Hainan Province

S am and Pierre thought they were the last to arrive in the final preparation hanger until Amanda ran in quickly—flustered and out of breath.

"Oh, I'm so, so sorry to be late. I never let this happen, I hope everyone can forgive me. It won't happen again," she said a speaking a mile a minute as she looked around for her spot.

The hanger was enormous. Sam considered it an odd place to suit-up for their mission. He was sure if this were a NASA operation, they would each have a private locker room stocked with the latest technologies. The Chinese approach was very different. A team of engineers surrounded each Taikonaut. The technicians each had an individual wheeled flatbed loaded with equipment. The flatbeds had enough of a robotic brain to follow the technician without getting in their way.

Pierre was already dressed to the waist in his Taikosuit. "It's like I'm a racing car and this is my pit crew," he said excitedly.

The engineer working on attaching Pierre's communications relays chuckled, "That's an interesting way to put it, sir. We did study the way race car pit crews work together many years ago when we came up with this method of preparation."

Pierre laughed and started making engine revving and tire screeching sounds. He looked like he was having the time of his life. He pointed to Amanda's suit and saluted. "Time to suit up," he told her.

Sam was tense. He realized even though many had been to the Moon before, not many had been to the far side. He learned only nine people had done it. The first three died during the return trip, although their deaths had nothing to do with the far side. Their deaths were attributed to problems during reentry.

A few thousand people had visited the Moon in the previous hundred years and more than thirty managed to get themselves killed. Not all of them had been in the early days of lunar exploration. Sam was a veteran undersea diver and comfortable with remote 'sensimatic' control systems. He was keenly aware if something went wrong in space, the odds of a safe return were miniscule at best.

He took a deep breath to calm his nerves. He was trembling, but he chalked it up to the fact he was finally realizing he was actually going to the Moon. Not even his wife would know where he was. He chuckled when he thought how silly Helen would find his nervousness. He could almost hear her saying, "You're a xenobiologist who's afraid to go to the closest natural body to Earth? Seriously, Sam? This is the greatest opportunity of your entire life! Thousands have made this trip and returned successfully! What is there to worry about?"

The communications engineer noticed him chuckling. "If something's tickling you, you must let us know now and we'll adjust it. Itching we can manage once you are suited up, tickling we can do little about once you're sealed in the suit. Is something bothering you?"

Sam was surprised to learn they had systems for managing scratching one's self inside the suit. The suit was capable of selectively inflating and deflating different areas against the skin. At a certain level of deflation, the cilia lining the interior of the suit massaged the skin and applied tension to the muscles. This was designed to help combat low G disease, which brought about muscular deterioration. The cilia could be hardened by applying the right charge and waved across the skin, effectively scratching a spot. The heads-up display had a scratch mode with a retinal scan to let the wearer select the precise location on a 3D projection of the body. The suit activated and scratched that spot. Sam thought it was ingenious and wondered if he could modify the technology to use driving the undersea robots. He'd look into it when he got back.

He chuckled again. Helen would have pointed out that as he was preparing for a trip to the Moon, he was thinking about how to improve a dive beneath the sea. Some xenobiologist.

"Still tickles?' said the engineer, looking perplexedly at his readouts.

"No, said Sam. "I'm fine. Just thought of something funny."

The engineer shook his head and muttered to himself,

"Astrobiologists are not like us engineers."

Pierre suddenly let out whoop followed by, "C'est pas vrai!"

Sam turned slowly, so the various connections plugged into his suit didn't get pulled out. He looked at Pierre.

Pierre laughed, "Ah mon ami, er, my friend, this suit is designed to scratch you. But I think it's really the most amazing self-pleasure toy. And to think I was afraid I would be bored during the trip to the Moon!"

Thirty feet behind Pierre, Amanda blushed beet red.

Fully suited up, Sam decided it was a good time to test the comm system. He activated the retinal display. It projected a beam directly into his left eye. It took a moment to focus on what the display was showing him and let everything he was seeing in the background go out of focus.

He saw the icon for the comm system and looked at it while blinking twice with both eyes.

A new display came up showing several of the crewmembers. Each one had a logo associated with them during the mission. Pierre's logo was a silver P on a black disc. Sam selected it and spoke quietly into his mouthpiece, "You're embarrassing one of our colleagues."

Next to him, he saw Pierre jerk his head and look around before realizing what had happened. In a few seconds, Sam heard Pierre's French accent. "I am? Who? Do we have a prude with us?"

"Amanda is behind you and your loud talk of masturbation is making her uncomfortable," Sam replied. "Try and be a gentleman, Pierre."

"Ah!" Pierre said, "Pardon moi. I'm always doing things like that. Although sometimes it has gotten me places I would not have thought possible." He gave Sam an evil grin. Distorted through the curved faceplate, it reminded Sam of the Cheshire cat.

"Right now, I don't think she'll even want to sit next you. Come to think of it, I'm not so sure I want to either."

Suddenly Amanda's voice came over both of their systems. "Right now, I'm not sure I want to sit next to either of you."

Both Sam and Pierre turned to look at Amanda and saw her laughing at them.

"Touché!" Pierre said. He turned back to Sam and winked. "I think Amanda will be just fine."

The team lead for Sam's engineering crew tapped him on the shoulder and whispered, "For private talks, you need to keep selecting until the icon of the person turns red. If it's white, you're speaking with that person and those who are within thirty meters of him."

"I'll have to remember that," Sam said. "That's kind of an odd setup. Why do it that way?"

The engineer shrugged. "I didn't design it. It might be so you can speak to entire team instantly. I think the original system was designed for battlefield ops where communication with the entire team needs to be fast."

Sam watched the engineer touch his ear. He suddenly jumped up and turned to his crew, shouting out a set of instructions in Mandarin. "We have only ninety minutes left before you need to be in your seat aboard the vehicle. We need to speed up the pace," he told Sam. "We're running out of time."

Chapter Eleven

Protector 304 was at Awareness Level Four. Something had to have occurred. It checked its power reserves and found residual power was at less than one-point-two percent. That was low. Very low. The last time it checked, power had been at better than fifty-one percent. It had been sleeping a long, long time.

It checked all powered sensors that remained active during its dormant stage. It scanned the data for more than thirty-two to the power of sixteen ticks. No signs of any threats imminent enough to have its Awareness Level altered showed up in the scans.

The system automatically began to follow the protocol for waking up the local sensors one by one to be able to retrieve the passive data they collected. Something happening to one of them was the next most probable cause of having its Awareness Level raised. To conserve energy reserves, it selected a slower path to this process, one that took more than twenty ticks to complete. It also began the power up sequence that would launch an explorer probe. One that would circle its home and perform a reconnaissance of the planet it was orbiting. During that time, it used its heightened awareness level to process the sky data it culled from the powered sensors.

A lot had changed.

The asteroid belt beyond Mars seemed so much smaller and less crowded. And Jupiter had only two big storms—one in the southern hemisphere and another at its north pole.

The local sensors powered up and Protector 304 began interpreting the data. It also monitored the launch of the lunar orbit probe. The grapefruit sized probe lifted silently from the lunar surface to an altitude of only five hundred meters. Then it turned and sped to the other side of the Moon.

The data ran dull. There were a few anomalies; meteorites that had hit and not bounced the way they normally would. Most of these were recent events. The probability was that a century-long meteor storm made of some unusual material was the cause.

Then there was a bit of data that was off the chart of probability. A direct impact on the Protector's body had occurred. But the impact had produced a continuous cycling vibration for more than two hundred and forty ticks. Protector analyzed the structure of the data and found the cycling had rhythmic pauses built into it. As it parsed the patterns it recognized the mathematical structure of the waves. They were binary, and even more than that; they were exhibiting aspects of a hexadecimal structure.

Intelligence!

Protector 304 immediately went to Awareness Level Five, then to Six. Power reserves were holding steady although consumption had increased four percent.

It checked the position of the probe. Another seven hundred and eighty ticks until it would be out of the satellite's shadow and looking at the planet. The surface sensor powered up and Protector immediately sensed motion three thousand seven hundred meters from its location. Several objects were moving. Two were moving soil, but none of it was deeper than ten meters. These were surface scrapers. Protector 304 monitored the vibration waveforms and determined the movements were on soft round feet. There were several other sources on the surface. All were moving in comparable patterns with similar feet.

Protector 304 raised an antenna and began to scan various shorter wave spectra to see if they were communicating. It stopped scanning when it found a constant chatter along one wavelength. Focusing on that wavelength, it began to store the data and attempt to decode it into something understandable. As it was setting up routines to work on the data analysis, the probe sent a signal.

The amount of radio-magnetic data was massive! Localized heat signatures were also off the charts. And none of this was being cloaked or dampened in any way!

The planet had a massive population of intelligent life on it.

Protector 304 looked at its historical probabilities. Sixty-five million years ago, when Protector failed to stop the rock sent by the Scarabs, the planet had become unfit for any continued form of Saurian evolution resulting in intelligence. That was what Scarabs had intended.

The galaxy was made up of predominantly two forms of intelligent life. Two forms that competed. There was Saurian life, which ran the gamut from reptilian to avian origin. The others were Scarabs who evolved from chitinous beings with a larval stage in their youth.

The two had been conducting a galactic war for more than four hundred million years.

Part of the war effort included searching for and locating planets on which one of the species was evolving toward intelligence. Then they would annihilate the enemy life on that planet. The cheapest and most efficient way to do that was to send a very large object flying into the planet at great speed.

One group of Saurians decided they would not only eradicate Scarab life but also protect any Saurian life. At least any Saurian life that showed a possibility of evolving to intelligence. They built Protector class machines designed to track incoming objects and move them or destroy them. Or minimize the damage they did.

Protector 304's job was to protect Earth.

Sixty-five million years ago, it failed with disastrous results.

Chapter Twelve

The last of the six Taikonauts boarded and plugged into his seat. Sam was impressed by how organized and fluid the process had been. Not much different than flying on an airplane.

They sat in a circle with each seat facing inward. Each Taikonauts suit included comm systems, life science systems and recording capabilities. Sam noticed Pierre's helmet and shoulders sported extra protuberances. When Sam queried Pierre, he learned one of Pierre's functions on the mission was mission videographer. Sam wondered if he was the only crewmember with only one function on the mission. There was nothing in his briefings indicating he would perform more than one task during the mission.

He also noticed Amanda Won sat between Pierre and himself. Pierre had made a point of waving at Amanda as soon as he sat down. He gave her a thumbs up and smiled broadly.

Across the ceiling of the capsule, displays were showing various readouts. Each person had a display divided into tiles of information. Sam found this to be an old-fashioned display but refrained from asking the engineers about it. They were touchy when questioned about their technologies.

The tiles included video displays of their ship as it sat aboard their lift vehicle. In addition, there were individual life systems monitors and an image from the forward-facing cameras. Years of research in space travel showed passengers handled stress better when they saw where they were going. It seemed to allay cabin fever for some odd reason neuroscientists didn't agree on. Similar systems had been added to airplanes in the early twenty-first century. Passengers enjoyed having details like altitude, cruising speed and a map of their exact position when they flew.

Non-essential flight personnel could opt for mild sedation through ninety percent of the flight. Accepting the sedation was recommended and everyone with the exception of Sam took it. Sam begged off saying he wanted to be able to review the data collected about the artifact during the flight.

Major Zhang had been resistant, scowling the whole time. He argued the reason for sedation was not just for simplifying the crew's tasks but also for the health of the passengers. Sam was certain the major placed a premium on keeping things simple for himself, and sedated passengers were easier to handle. Eventually, in the interest of keeping to their schedule, he gave in to Sam's demand.

The overhead lights blinked blue. From his brief training, Sam knew this meant an important announcement was incoming. A soothing voice filled his ear announcing the lifting vehicle was now taxiing to the runway. He could feel they were moving along to his left, which felt a little odd, like sitting sideways on a bus. He looked from one to the other. The other passengers may have accepted the sedation, but it hadn't fully kicked in yet and they all looked as tense as he felt.

The capsule was riding slung below an enormous delta wing plane. The craft would take off and rise spiraling until it reached a height of twenty-four kilometers. At that point it would drop the capsule, whose rockets would fire for ninety minutes until they exhausted all their fuel. Then ion engines would fire up and continue throughout the trip. At mid-point, small rockets would rotate it and the ion engines would serve as a braking system from there on. Sam wondered how many back-up systems there were and what would happen if the ion engines failed at any point. The engineers he asked laughed at the notion. "You have nothing to worry about, Mr. Czerny, we have planned for all contingencies," they told him.

Sam asked how many hours of experience the pilot had and they gave him a strange look. The head of the engineering staff had told him the 'pilot' on board was just the final human backup in case all other systems failed. The pilot could 'dead-stick' land the capsule on the Moon or on Earth only in the event of a catastrophic failure of all the systems. This had never occurred, and the engineers considered it an anachronism held over from a distant past. AI software managed the entire flight and they did not expect any human intervention. In their opinion, there was no longer any need for a human pilot.

But Sam was glad there was still a human pilot on board, even if the engineers thought it was unnecessary. He knew software, even well tested versions, could have unexpected results and occasional bugs. He felt better knowing a human was sitting in the pilot's seat in case of an emergency—even though the engineers felt otherwise.

Suddenly, the craft accelerated, Sam assumed they were airborne because of the way Pierre was pumping his fist in the air. He chuckled to himself. Pierre was a regular space cowboy.

Soon after, he noticed Pierre, Amanda and the other passengers were beginning to nod off. Major Zhang's voice came into his ear. "We have cleared the runway and are off on an historic adventure." Sam found the major's tone filled with emotion. "It is an honor to be on this voyage with all of you."

"Bonne chance a nous," Pierre mumbled as his head lulled to one side and he lost consciousness.

Sam felt as though he should say something, too, but was unsure. After a moment, he added, "May we all travel safely and be worthy of this trip." He felt it sounded weak as soon as he said it and was surprised to hear the major state his agreement with a hearty, "Chenggong!"

After a few minutes, Sam realized it was going to be a long, boring trip and he wondered if he should have taken advantage of the sedative. Instead, he looked into his retinal controller and practiced selecting display functions. By the time he heard the announcement that they were going to separate from the plane, Sam felt comfortable with the menu system.

Although mentally prepared for the sudden drop as they detached from the plane, he still clenched his muscles as the ship fell. He looked at the display that showed the directional view and saw the craft rise away from them overhead and then bank to the left.

Two seconds felt like an eternity to him before he felt the reassuring deep rumble of the rockets firing. Weight returned pushing him into to his seat and then squeezing him down to where he felt the effort to lift his arms would not be worth it. He tried to turn his head to see how Pierre or Amanda were doing but found his suit had had become rigid and prevented him from turning one way or another. A design to keep him from hurting himself in the increased gravity, he supposed.

He heard the major's labored voice, "Dr. Czerny, are you handling this? I can still administer a sedative if you prefer."

Sam was tempted to accept, but knew if he did, the major would see him as just another weak passenger. For some reason, he thought this was not a good idea. "Thank you, Major." He made an effort not to pant as he spoke. "Actually, I think I'm enjoying the ride. I would prefer not to miss this."

Sam smiled when he heard the major respond with a grunt followed by, "As you wish."

The rumble of the rocket burn ended and Sam looked to see how long he had endured feeling this heavy. Only fifteen minutes, but he felt as if he had just run a marathon. It was a relief to feel their acceleration was returning to something closer to Earth's standard gravity. He still felt heavy but he no longer felt crushed.

Deciding he should fulfill his reason for not taking the sedative, he called up the data on the artifact. He began to review the planned exploration of the structure, making notes through the comm system as concepts and questions came to mind.

A soft voice came into Sam's earbud alerting him that they were in lunar orbit and that landing on the surface was imminent. Confused, he did not remember falling asleep. He must have been far more tired than he had let himself believe.

He turned to his left and saw Amanda was busy working on something. He could tell through all the rapid blinking she was doing and he saw her jaw working inside of her faceplate.

That was when he realized their seats had moved back into the original launch positions. He looked up at his display for the forward view and saw the Moon surface with its pitted craters whizzing by. The contrast between the shadows and lighted areas was surprising. He toggled the display for a backward view because he wanted to see the Earth from the Moon. The display showed they were already far enough on the far side that the planet was blocked from view by the Moon itself.

He managed to find Amanda's icon on his retinal display and set up a private comm link. "Hi, how long have you been awake?"

"Oh, Hi! About seven hours. Are you ready for touch down? This is so exciting. We should be seeing the base any minute."

"I'm sorry. I'm a little confused. I requested no sedation, but seem to have slept most of the trip anyway." Sam felt groggy and his mouth felt pasty.

"Oh. I had requested a limited dose so I could catch most of the arrival. After all, the majority of the trip had to be pretty boring anyway. I had some prep work to do so I had a wake-up call scheduled. You were sleeping like a hibernating marmot. You looked tired."

Sam squeezed his eyes. "I guess I was. Still feel a little out of sorts."

Amanda nodded, "Dehydration. You can dial up a drink in your suit. I suggest a little green tea with an added shot of caffeine and taurine. It did the trick for me. Here, I'll send you retinal combo as an attachment. Just blink on it twice and then put the water tube embedded in your face plate in your mouth."

Sam saw something appear in the center of his vision that looked like a pale green porcelain bowl. He blinked twice looking at it and then grabbed the water tube with his mouth as he felt the warm liquid gently pour out of it. She was right, the beverage made him feel better instantly. His suit would not allow him to get dehydrated, but his mouth had been dry, which made his body think he was lacking water.

"Thanks!"

"No problem. The suits supply everything we need and most of your sustenance is intravenous. But I discovered that one could call up some interesting chemical combinations in the water tube. And as anyone can tell by looking at me, I'm a bit of a foodie so I spent some time experimenting. It's why I was late for suit up. Food is the only reason I'm ever late for anything."

Sam started to feel a lot better. He wondered how much of it was Amanda's green tea concoction and how much it was Amanda's infectious happiness. She was being downright bubbly in a way he had not seen during their preparation.

"Bonjour, Sam. Are you having a private party or can I join?" Pierre was awake.

"Hello, Pierre. Nothing private. Hold on a second." Sam asked Amanda if it was okay to add Pierre into their conversation. She agreed without hesitation. Sam blinked on Pierre's icon and let the Frenchman in.

Pierre sounded his usual ebullient self. "Ah, my fellow Taikonauts. Is it not a good day to land on the Moon? Eh? Could I get both of you to look at me and give me a thumbs in the air please?"

Sam always liked the way Pierre mashed up idioms in English. He and Amanda lifted their thumbs and grinned for Pierre's cameras.

"Look!" Amanda alerted them. Their forward cameras were showing the Fermi Base and they could see the landing spot before them less than a kilometer away. Tiny little vehicles were moving across the crater bottom and Sam could make out a long uniform gash across a part of the crater. The Moon was being strip-mined, a method of mining that was no longer practiced on Earth.

"My babies!" Amanda shouted out.

Chapter Thirteen

Major Zhang checked his debarkation list. So far everything was on schedule. The lunar landing was picture perfect and the three porter bots rolled up to the capsule exactly as planned.

The crew all reported in and each one went through the disconnection procedure from their seat without a hitch. Even if that Frenchman Pacquelier did act the fool for some of the time. Still, the mission was going perfectly.

The base, which the bots completed building two weeks earlier, was up to specifications and fully powered. They even produced and stored enough oxygen for a fifteen-day supply. The Fermi Crater had plenty of ferrous oxide just below the surface. Since the habitat had the capability to recycle human breath, the bots would not need to produce as much oxygen.

Getting the crew from the capsule to the base was a bit more of a challenge than anticipated. The first reason was the low lunar gravity. While everyone prepared for it mentally, it was quite another thing to experience it. And the last thing Major Zhang expected was that it would turn out he would be the clumsiest member of the crew. He stumbled and sent one of the containers he attempted to move flying against a wall. As the leader of the mission, he quickly determined that type of work was not what he was best suited for, even if he had to change the duty roster.

The crew's quarters on the base were not cramped. The common room was large enough to fit twenty people. While manufacturing was not cheap, it had the huge advantage that the materials were not lifted from Earth's gravity well. Low gravity 3D printing had many benefits.

The bots were even able to find a significant amount of frozen water in the corner of the Fermi Crater that was always in shadow. This significantly reduced the weight of the landing module by not having to carry a heavy load of water. And there were far fewer containers to be transported to the base.

The major planned to call a team meeting once everyone finished their move-in tasks. He also expected to hear from General Sun before that happened. But no message arrived before the crew settled into their individual spaces.

Major Zhang found that a little disconcerting, but there could be many reasons for the delay; anything from sunspot activity to timing on the part of the general, or even the chairman.

Each crewmember had a space that included a seat, a desk, a personal display screen, a small locker to stow personal items and a hammock. The major thought he heard a snicker when, after stringing it up, he attempted to jump into the hammock and bumped his head on the ceiling. He turned and looked to see who laughed, but the crew was quiet and none of them made eye contact with him.

Damn civilians. Major Zhang was beginning to get concerned he was losing his authority position as the leader of this mission. If this continued, he would need to act in a way that reestablished his authority. He needed to find some way that wouldn't make the crew begin to resent him.

What worried him most was the lack of any word from General Sun or his staff. During the trip to the Moon, he had not stopped thinking about the meeting on Earth.

Recognizing that the crew completed the day's tasks, he decided to call them for a briefing before lights out. Even though they had their comm units, the major preferred gathering them together in the middle of the common room. Boris Yelenko activated the little canisters on the chair pods he lugged from the lunar lander. The chairs filled with flexible memory foam that turned them into something between a beanbag and lounger. They were ugly but comfortable

He watched as Amanda Won came into the area moving like a dancer and settled to a stop in front of a seat. She gently fell into it without bouncing. Even more impressive was Sam Czerny. The man moved in lunar gravity like a cat that had been born in it. In fact, he noticed Sam was used to the curve between the floor and the wall when cornering. The curves were designed to make travel for wheeled vehicles more efficient. Czerny was somehow adapting them to his walk in one-sixth gravity.

The last crewmember in was Pierre Pacquelier, as clumsy as the general, but laughing about his blunders and missteps. The major found Pierre looked more like a teenager on an amusement park ride than a Taikonaut on a serious mission. Zhang felt this was entirely inappropriate. But again, he resisted the urge to chastise the Frenchman as that might also alienate him with the crew.

Zhang looked at each with his lips pressed firmly together in his characteristic serious stare. "First of all, allow me to congratulate each one of you for accomplishing the first steps of the mission on time and without any mishaps."

The spontaneous applause of the crew surprised him, but he continued. "As you know we have twelve days and a lot to accomplish. Boris and Lee will begin firing off tons of manufactured items from the Moon's surface to the Lagrange Station. The rail gun accelerators will be multiplying our capacity to send payloads into space by many-fold. Amanda will be upgrading and modifying the bots for some of the new tasks they will be doing. The bots will now be among the most intelligent autonomous machines ever built. And we will also be exploring the lunar surface to see if we have indeed found a trace of life right in the Fermi Crater." The way he looked at Sam indicated he thought that portion of the mission was entirely superfluous.

Pierre beamed.

Zhang tented his fingertips beneath his chin "The next days will be challenging. We all have a lot to do and a short period of time in which to do it. There will be times when one or another is particularly stressed due to our tight schedule. Stress does bad things to people. It can make you not understand what you're working on. It prevents you from seeing the big picture. It's been my experience that stress can make you question what you need to do at the exact time when you need to do it without question."

Sam looked at Pierre who shrugged his shoulders.

Zhang paused and then leaned back again. "The Moon is a hazardous place. For us to even survive takes all of our wits and a great deal of technology and effort. It is no place for someone to crack. I ask each of you to keep an eye on each other. If you see a colleague behaving in an unexpected manner, mention it to them and then mention it to me."

The various crew members looked at each other, some wondered if he was referring to anyone in particular.

The major continued, "I'm not asking this lightly. I'm not looking to catch anyone. I want to be able to prevent any bad situations that may arise from stress. This is part of my role as mission commander, but it is also part of your role as well as members of the crew. Any questions?"

The only response was silence.

"Good. Then I think I've made myself clear. Tonight, is the last time you will have to rest. Take the time to relax and get to know your fellow crewmembers, but don't forget to sleep. There will be little enough of that in the days ahead and resting is an important part of work. Now, if there is nothing else, you are dismissed!"

The major stood up, making an effort to look as dignified as possible, and haltingly strode off to the mission commander's quarters. Mission command was a little larger than the other quarters and also afforded him a level of privacy the others did not have.

Boris and Lee left the area for their bunks. Amanda stayed behind with Pierre and Sam, querying them. "Now exactly what do you think that was about?"

"I don't know," said Sam. "It was really odd. Why would he expect people to crack from stress on this mission? Granted there may be a lot of work, but everyone here is a professional and good at what they do. Otherwise, we wouldn't be here."

"True," added Pierre. "It was odd. I wonder what he knows that he's not telling us. And then to dismiss us as if we were common soldiers. That was not called for."

Amanda shook her head, "No, I mean all the stuff about a trace of life." She peered into Sam's eyes. "Exactly what did they find here and can you now tell me why a xenobiologist is on this mission?"

Sam and Pierre looked at each other. "I'm very surprised you weren't briefed before we left, but I suppose you should know by now. There's an artifact that was discovered not far from here by the miners. According to the machine-run surveys, it's over sixty-five million years old."

Amanda threw her head back and laughed. "But there were no humans that far back. In fact, were there even any mammals back then?"

"Well, there were a few primitive mammals, and no, there were no humans," Sam replied. "That we know of."

When she saw how serious the two men were, Amanda stopped laughing. "So how big an artifact is it? Are you sure it isn't some natural object? Do you have an idea what it might be?"

"What it might be is anybody's guess at this point," Sam said, shrugging. "Resonance exploration done by one of the mining bots shows it looks like something that was manufactured. And it appears to be close to four square kilometers and about seven hundred meters tall."

Amanda's jaw dropped. "Holy Crap!" she blurted out, "that's huge! How come nobody ever saw it before? There have been quite a few flyovers of this crater. The entire area has been mapped extensively. How is it possible something that size was overlooked?"

"It was completely buried under the lunar dirt. And yes, this is a holy crap moment, as you say," Pierre chimed in.

"Hmm. That may be why I have some data in the bot's history logs that's scrambled beyond retrieval. Maybe it's just encrypted. I hadn't thought of that before. The information could have been classified," Amanda said. "But why?"

Sam shrugged. "There are a few strange things about this mission. Like keeping this such a secret. I questioned that in my briefing with Trish Stern. She was adamant. This information is definitely top secret."

"And now the major's worried that we will all go crazy here," Pierre added. "There is something here that is not very orthodox."

"What?" Amanda asked looking at Pierre.

"Kosher," Sam explained. "He means something is not kosher."

Pierre laughed, "Funny, we say orthodox and you say kosher. But still, something does not add up, non?"

Chapter Fourteen

Fermi Crater Artifact
Far Side of the Moon

Protector 304 accessed its history files. There was data on over two hundred thousand worlds on which technological culture evolved. Another eight hundred thousand worlds had the possibility of an intelligent culture evolving. All had either a Saurian or Scarab based life form when it came to sentience. There had been a few worlds that had near intelligent aquatic life, but they proved to be dead ends. Aquatic life never seemed to move to any sophisticated tool building.

The war between Scarab and Saurian had gone on for over seventy million years before the construction of Protector 304. More than thirty-two thousand worlds were destroyed. Not one of those worlds had a Saurian or Scarab culture return. The destruction had been completely thorough and effective. Until now.

Over time, the Saurians designed Protectors to prevent this destruction and to garner an advantage.

Protector 304 had to find out whether the sentience occupying the Earth was Saurian or Scarab. If it was Saurian, it needed protection. If it was Scarab, destruction. The possibility it was a different type of life form was so remote that it did not enter into P304's considerations. The inhabitants of the planet were in an early stage of technological development. Even if this world were well outside of the habited part of the galaxy, other inhabited worlds would eventually take notice.

P304 received an alert there had been a breakthrough in the decoding sub-process. The machines on the lunar surface were rather basic. They could barely reason. P304 didn't find anything in its records that showed such simple machines associated with a spacefaring culture. This made the planet unique, and worth studying.

It applied this new information to the incredible amount of data being broadcast from the Earth's surface. The variety of code structures was astonishing! The iteration of machine specification was endless. And the organic languages of the surface species numbered in the hundreds. P304 set up a task to triage them in an attempt to translate the data into something it could use. In short, it needed to get a better understanding of the surface beings.

In the meantime, P304 turned its attentive focus toward the machines on the lunar surface. It located a few machines spread over the Moon, but only ones within a few kilometers seemed mobile. The others seemed to be defunct or just passively gathering data. None of them was over two hundred years old. Spacefaring was still new in this part of the galaxy, and most of the machines it found were fairly primitive.

It began to survey the planet beginning at five hundred kilometers above the ocean surface. Another bit of data was surprising. The planet was surrounded by tens of thousands of devices orbiting at various levels. Many of the devices in this chaotic mix were inactive and seemed abandoned. There were also quite a few devices that displayed the signature of fissionable materials. Devices that were designed to explode.

P304 thought this was a rudimentary form of planetary defense. Then it realized the devices were aimed at the planet itself. Another culture holding the planet captive seemed to be the most likely probability. This would be a new tactic, but P304 reasoned it might be an efficient one. Especially if the goal was to learn or experiment with the dominant life form on the planet. It could also be part of a colonization function. Even though there was no historical record of any colonizing forces keeping indigenous intelligences, it seemed to be a viable possibility.

The language program was able to translate with better than ninety-three percent accuracy. The remaining seven percent would take a lot longer due to the unusual nature of some of the languages that seemed to have completely different language typologies. Many languages used local terms and idioms. Others were only visual or written. Some had several regional dialects that made it impossible for a speaker from one specific area to understand a speaker from a different area. There seemed to be a fractional culture between whoever was the sentient life form. P304 recognized comprehension of all the languages and variations would need more working storage. It arranged to free some of the space it would need for rapid response. There were auto-defense systems that had priority access to the fastest processing and storage. It moved these to a lower grade to be able to tackle the task of 'understanding' such unusual data.

One of the first things it discovered was the beings on the planet had a wide-open and unusual notion of security. They were good at protecting tiny details from each other. But there was a great deal of what seemed like important data about the history of their planet and their species that was easily accessed. P304 saw that as a critical flaw in the system.

Protector 304 stopped all data gathering for almost a second. All available non-vital resources focused on what it just learned. This was the Protector's equivalent of being shocked.

The beings it was studying were neither Saurian nor Scarab. They were something new. A class called mammals and a species called humans.

Very quickly, P304 determined there was a large body of work that documented the natural history of the planet that was unique to it. Some of it was speculation and a great deal of it came from practiced study and methodical investigation. It even found many references to something dubbed the 'dinosaur killer' asteroid. Tracing the impact crater, it was able to determine this was the rock sent by Scarabs and which stopped Saurian evolution on Earth. The rock Protector 304 had failed to stop.

It completely changed the type of life forms that existed on the planet.

Chapter Fifteen

Central Bureau of the Chinese Communist Party
Office of the Premier

Qi Yuanching opened the enormous book that lay upon his desk to the page marked with a pale green silk ribbon. He wore thin white cotton gloves designed to prevent any body oils on his skin from damaging the thin, yellowed paper. The book was a treasure. It was delivered to his desk from the national archives by some eager-to-please assistant whose name he never even registered. It was hand written—the thirteenth transcription of the ancient Shandong scrolls. It contained the oldest written accounts of the life and times of Qin Shi Huang, the first emperor of China.

The volume was in a poor state of repair and the archive curator banned anyone from using it until it was completely digitized. But the chairman was forbidden nothing. Chairman Qi had been an historian his entire adult life and a student of Qin Shi Huang for much of it. Holding this book and reading from it was an accolade granted only to the chairman, and one he did not take lightly.

The first emperor of China had been a brilliant man in many ways, but in many other ways, a failed one. It was he who managed to conquer the seven states, unifying China and ending the Warring States period. And he did it the same way most emperors came to power, with advanced technology and daring.

It was in Qin's time the manufacture of dropforged iron began. This meant he could supply his army with exact replicas of the same weapon. The weapon Qin put into the field was a crossbow. It was the first mass-produced weapon made with replaceable parts. With its mass-produced iron bolts and the three-man technique: one to load, one to draw and one to shoot, his armies became unstoppable.

The crossbow gave his armies several advantages. They could

shoot from much farther away than their opponents. The iron bolts would pierce any armor of the day and the modular nature of the devices made it easy to repair in the field with available parts. Each crossbow was made exactly the same way. Combined with the discipline and the method of deploying this new weapon, his army was able to crush the armies of his enemies. In just nine short years, he built the most amazing empire—encompassing most of what is China today.

"Yes," he muttered to himself. "A most amazing man. But like so many, one that fell victim to believing more than he should have."

The emperor went on to change China in so many ways. He built the Lingqu Canal, connecting north to south China's two great rivers and ensuring rapid and continued supply lines to his armies. And he built his most famous monument, the Great Wall. He was also famous for his burial with about seven thousand life-size terracotta soldiers. After their discovery, the soldiers traveled the world for years, impressing millions with the sophistication and artistry of China's history.

Nonetheless, the emperor made some critical mistakes. Historians still argued about whether his practice of destroying books written in other languages benefited China by unifying the communications method, or whether hundreds of years of important ideas were lost.

Turning the pages reverently, the chairman searched until he found the section that interested him most: the building of the wall. It was said that building The Great Wall claimed more than a million lives. The wall that stands today has little to do with Qin's original wall. What the chairman was most interested in was the strategy behind the wall.

Despite the best efforts of his armies, the emperor was never able to conquer and subdue the nomadic Xiongnu people of the north. And their raids quickly became a thorn in the side of the empire. Linking several existing walls from the old disparate states allowed Qin to put up a barrier that created a long-lasting defense. One so valuable it protected China for over a thousand years.

"Yes, but no defense can hold forever," the chairman whispered to himself.

The secret to a good defense was managing the cost. As long as it was far more expensive or difficult to mount an attack than it was to maintain a defense, peace would reign. Peace and control, for the one who could afford the strong defense.

Turning a page, the chairman reread the description of how the wall was built and muttered, "But human nature being what it is, a cheaper attack always appears. It is only natural men will always find a way to defeat a strong enemy and gain their riches."

A small light blinked on the chairman's desk. He activated the display and saw the bowed head and deferred eyes of one of his personal assistants.

"What is it?" the chairman commanded, knowing the assistant would never speak until he asked.

"General Sun is here to see you as you requested."

"Thank you. Please send him in."

The chairman's office was a splendid affair. His deeply carved antique desk was four meters wide and three across. Despite its ancient appearance, there was a wealth of technology embedded in the polished wood and golden filigree. His chair was ergonomically designed for the comfort of his old bones, yet still managed to convey the power and glory of his office. In front of his desk were four chairs with silk pillows designed to be comfortable, contemporary versions of classic Ming dynasty chairs. It was a room that was grandiose, yet reflected the simple design of Chinese dynasties of the past.

The tall red door swung open and short, stocky General Sun strutted the twenty steps to stand, lower his head and bow before the chairman's desk.

"Please," the chairman said. "Sit. No, wait, better yet, come stand here next to me. I want to show you something."

Sun's eyes went wide. It was an unusual request. He moved quickly for a man as round as he was and stood beside the chairman awaiting his next words.

"Look here," the chairman said, bringing up his display and selecting the map he saved. It showed an image of The Great Wall as seen from orbit. "The Great Wall, General Sun. The world's biggest ancient structure. More than twenty-three hundred years old and twenty-one thousand kilometers long. It crosses nine provinces and municipalities. But nearly one third of the wall disappeared without a trace. Can you imagine the immensity of it? Such a tragedy that during the Cultural Revolution, bricks were carried away to build farms, homes and reservoirs. It was truly majestic monument to the history of China. I've been reading about it in this wonderful history book."

The general looked at the image on the display and then at the book. He gasped when he saw the age and the calligraphy in the book. He was clearly impressed. "My Chairman is studying the history of our great land?"

Chairman Qi didn't like it when people as close to him as General Sun played the sycophant. But he had long ago realized they did so because they needed it more than he did. Followers needed to believe their leader was extremely important. As a leader, he saw his followers being useful and necessary only to achieve his goals. Even when he felt affection for them, it was as woodcarver might feel for a favorite chisel or a painter for a favorite brush.

"Yes, I'm always studying history, my good General. When we are not studying history, we should be making history. After all, whether we succeed or not, one day history will be studying us. I am looking at the story of The Great Wall for a particular reason. For over a thousand years it worked to fend off invasions from the north. A man standing on the wall had a commanding view of all who thought to attack. And he could easily fire arrows at them from the impunity of the high ground.

"Today, the wall that keeps people safe is made of satellites, drones and computers. And the wall today belongs to the Americans. No one dare oppose them for a great period of time because they always have the high ground. They're always the ones looking down on the others."

"My Chairman, we have satellites and drones as well . . ."

"Yes, we do. Where they let us. But we're nowhere near as well equipped or as strategically placed across the globe as they are."

The general looked at the chairman expectantly as the man reread a passage from the book to himself. When he was done, he looked up into the general's eyes.

"General Sun, tomorrow I'll be asking you to send some messages to Major Zhang at the Moon Base. The messages will include some data packets that are encrypted in the body of the message. It's important that you send these one at a time, and that you ask Major Zhang to put protocol High Tower into place."

"Yes, my Chairman. It will be done as you wish. And this High Tower protocol will give us the high ground?"

"It will, General Sun, it will. Or at least it will show the world we can deploy and use the high ground well before anyone else can. How we use it will be another key that opens the box of the future before us."

"My Chairman, I knew we were fortunate to have you take this role. I knew we would be following your lead as you took China into a new era. It will be one where our military position matches our economic prowess. It's been generations since this has been so. History will reward you well, my Chairman. Your renown will be as great as that of Emperor Qin."

"It's China that will be great once again," the chairman said. "I'm just a humble tool of history helping to restore China to its rightful place."

"Ah," General Sun bowed deeply, "The humble servant is the wisest of all men."

The chairman smiled, "You give me too much credit. History is often about timing and opportunity. The future has always belonged to those who saw the impact of technology and dared to use it in a way that others did not even see."

"Yes, yes," said General Sun, not sure of what else he should say.

The chairman smiled as his eyes looked into some imagined and dynamic future. "The oxen have been slow, but the soil has been patient," he said, reciting an ancient proverb.

Chapter Sixteen

S tepping up to the bot, Amanda Won shook her head and said, "Okay. Forget that one. Here we go again. One more time. Watch my movements carefully and repeat."

She raised her left hand and placed her right hand on her belly. She followed with a graceful bow—sweeping her left arm forward and back as she stood straight again. The bot repeated her gesture with its two articulated arms. It didn't have a human shaped body, looking more like an open-ended golf cart with a torso and head at the front with two long arms. The torso could not quite bend as far down as Amanda had, but it did a fair job imitating her movement.

Sam stepped out of the base airlock. He was wearing his suit and helmet just as Amanda was. Both were set to protect against the bright ultra violet rays beaming from the Sun. Sam remembered Pierre saying the lack of an atmosphere made getting a tan on the Moon a bad idea.

Pierre was out next and looked around turning left then right. The faceplates of their helmets were set to project a video image of their faces so the others could see their facial expressions.

Amanda turned to face Pierre, "I have to thank you, sir."

Pierre grinned, "Yes, you do."

"Merci"

"De rien."

"Wait, what's this about?" Sam interjected.

"Well, it seems Pierre convinced Major Zhang the trip out to the artifact was a perfect opportunity to test the bot software upgrade. So, I get to tag along," she said. The video display on her helmet showed her grinning.

"Pierre, I've never met anyone as ready to turn every situation into an opportunity as you are," Sam said. "Well played."

"Thank you, I think." Pierre responded.

Amanda walked to the back of the bot she had been coaching. She reached over and pulled up a divider. This turned the back into a set of bench seats, each facing sideways from the direction the bot would travel in. She sat on one side and attached the two clasps that held her in place. "Come on boys, time for a ride."

Pierre was petulant. "Can we not just walk there? It's only a kilometer away and on the Moon, that's an easy distance. I actually enjoy seeing my own footsteps on the Moon."

"Don't kid yourself," Amanda said. "Even if the gravity makes you feel light, you aren't used to it. And you'd be using your muscles in new ways. You don't want to get to the artifact only to be tired or cramped, do you?"

"No, I suppose not," said Pierre as he shuffled to the bot and sat next to Amanda. Sam went over and sat on the other side, attaching himself with the two straps available for that purpose.

"DB108, head to the artifact at passenger carrying pace," Amanda instructed the bot. It lurched to a start and began heading across the lunar soil. Pierre, who had not attached himself, almost fell off at the start. He quickly grabbed the straps and connected them to the clasp at his hips.

Sitting back in his seat, Sam was enjoying the view. He could hardly believe he was actually rolling along on the far side of the Moon. To his left he saw the Northern Crater edge, which had a noticeable rim to it. The line of shadow caused by the crater rim was so dark against the rest of the brightly lit surface that it looked pitch black. Far off to his right was the Tsiolkovsky Crater with its characteristic dark floor and a peak that rose high enough to break the horizon.

Pierre was busy recording their trip. He leaned over and tapped the transparent divider making a waving motion. Sam responded by waving back. Pierre seemed satisfied and turned back to taping their trip.

"I think we're almost there," Amanda said after about ten minutes. "In fact, given the marks in the soil, that must be it right there." She pointed about fifty meters ahead of them. "We'll walk the rest of the way."

DB108 came to a stop.

Sam hopped off so excitedly he rebounded full two feet into the air and landed on all fours before straightening himself.

"Take it easy," Amanda said. "I don't want to be bringing anyone back injured. The major would not approve. We're all essential to this mission."

Sam looked at her sheepishly and shrugged. "Okay, everything slow and by the book, right"?"

"Right." Amanda's face nodded in her helmet display.

Pierre spoke up, "You guys are already looking to make this boring? I'll never win a prize for best documentary with such poor actors. I want more action!"

Sam called up his retinal display and layered the video of the first discovery made by a bot over what he was seeing. The display showed the exact spot the bot had examined and he walked directly over to it. The patch was about one square meter of smooth material. Given that nothing on the surface of the Moon looked smooth, it looked oddly out of place, almost as if it was an illusion. Sam bent over and touched it even though his suited hand would only give him an interpreted feel rather than a real one. The data fed to his fingers told them the artifact was a bit warmer than the surrounding surface.

Sam began to take verbal notes, "Temperature reads five degrees Celsius warmer than environs." He activated the elemental analyzer is his left hand and placed it on the surface. "Carbon, tungsten and iridium. A little bit of cadmium and, hmm, about three things that my analyzer says it can't identify. That's odd," he said after looking at the readings.

"Isn't the analyzer supposed to tell which elements it's made from, not just chemicals?" Pierre asked.

"Yes," Sam responded. "That's why this is so odd."

"O putain!" Pierre exclaimed, leaning over to record some video. "Do you mean we have new elements here? Are they really heavy ones?"

"Well, I'm not sure. All I'm getting is a reading for three things the data says are unidentifiable."

"What you mean is it's another way to say they are not of Earth," Pierre said.

Sam smiled. "That is one way to look at it. But I'd never jump to that quick a conclusion without applying a more stringent set of tests. At least some second set of tests that would confirm this particular one. After all, it could just be a malfunction in my analyzer."

"Yes, right," Pierre said. "And I'm the Queen of England."

"Look over here." Amanda was pointing to a spot about three meters away from the surface Sam touched. They all stepped over to have a look and saw there was a pentagonal shape beneath the lunar soil. It looked to be about eight feet on a side, flat and directly beneath the surface.

Sam was amazed. He was looking at an object not built by humans. "What could it be?"

"A five-sided alien game die, of course. Seems these aliens were really big," Pierre jibed.

"You know, for a smart guy you can be really stupid sometimes," Amanda said, annoyance in her voice. This was not the time for jokes.

"Let's pick it up and see what it is," said Pierre.

Before the other two could say anything, he bent over, swept the dust off of one edge. He worked his fingers underneath and lifted. The object didn't move. Pierre cursed, "Putain, c'est lourd! It's heavy! There's no way we can lift this."

Sam bent over and swept some more of the dust off of the surface. They all went silent when they saw a set of markings where he cleaned the surface. Then all three of them were suddenly on their hands and knees and wiping the surface free of lunar dust. In the low lunar gravity, the dust went floating meters over their heads.

With the entire surface cleared they saw it had what looked like three rectangles of markings. Each rectangle was made up of sixteen markings. Several of the markings were repeated.

"Do a slow pan of the markings," Sam told Pierre. "Make sure you get them all."

When Pierre was done, Sam instructed the base processors to try to decrypt the images Pierre collected.

"I'll have this cross referenced against anything we might find on Earth. Just in case there may be something that correlates," Sam said.

"Okay," said Amanda, but Sam suspected that like him, she thought it would be a long shot.

"We need to move it to see if it has something underneath. Maybe more writing or some kind of key like the Rosetta Stone. It's so heavy; I don't think it will be fragile. But I don't think the three of us are strong enough to lift it." Pierre sounded impatient.

"Maybe not the three of us," Amanda said. "But DB108 has a lift capacity of over forty-five hundred kilos in Earth gravity. Let me give this a shot."

She called the bot over. "DB108, please accept my video input identifying an object along the surface. Copy?"

"Affirmative" DB108 had a deep male voice that sounded like it would warn you to be careful when boarding an amusement park ride.

Pierre was surprised. "These bots on the Moon can talk?"

"They can now," replied Amanda. "It was part of the new upgrades I put into place. Frankly I didn't expect it to be tested this soon."

She continued, "DB108, please lift the flat edge of the selected object closest to you one degree away from the surface."

The bot trundled over to the pentagon and placed its two arms into the lunar soil, slid its hands beneath one edge and lifted it.

"Task complete." it said.

"Now, maintaining structural integrity, lift the object one hundred and thirty-five degrees away from the surface."

The bot took six seconds to comply. "Task complete."

Sam, Amanda and Pierre were silent as they stared at the space where the pentagon had been. They were looking at a ramp that sloped away into the lunar surface.

Chapter Seventeen

Chang'e 3 Base
Fermi Crater

Lee Jin-Dao jumped off of the tractor bot as soon as it got to the loading bay end of the mass launcher. Boris Yelenko, not having been to the Moon before, was a less practiced and took his time.

The mass launcher was Boris' design. Over a seven-month span, a team of twenty-two bots put it together with Lee overseeing the construction work. This was Lee's third trip to the Moon. He stood with his hands on his hips and looked down the line of metal plated rails.

The mass launcher was just a rail gun with a large bucket sitting on it. The rail ran in a three-kilometer circle and then rose like a roller coaster. The top of the rise was where the payload would release from the bucket that rode the coiled rails. Then the bucket continued along a downward spiraling rail, eventually coming back to the holding dock.

The bots had tested launching one and two ton masses a month ago, but the payload was just rocks aimed in the direction of Jupiter.

Today's test was to include much larger objects. Each object had little rockets to allow them to adjust their flight once they were on their way.

Boris called up the overhead schematics on his display. It was not the first time he'd looked at them, but it was the first time he was using the image and laying it over what he saw with his own eyes. A smile of satisfaction spread over his face. "It's beautiful. So much more than I thought it would be."

"Thank you. That's high praise," Lee responded. "But wait until you see something lift off. It's pretty incredible to see. Should we do a simple run to be able to make sure we can track a payload?"

"Do we have enough energy on tap to be able to do that? I thought the fact that we only get sunlight here for fourteen days every month made test runs prohibitive," Boris frowned.

Despite what many people on Earth thought, there was no permanently dark side of the Moon. All sides get illuminated by the Sun as the Moon circles around the planet. But, because the Moon's period of rotation is the same as it's orbital period, one side is always facing the Earth and the other side never does. From Earth, that is known as the dark side.

"We're actually ahead of schedule and were able to power up the nuclear reactor four months ago," Lee said.

"You never cease to impress me," Boris said, shaking his head. "Projects like this are miracles when they're accomplished on time, but to get things done ahead of schedule is unheard of! How do you do that?"

Lee looked over his shoulder at Boris. "You didn't know? Although I'm technically the lead engineer, the project management decisions aren't made by people anymore. We substituted software for that a few years ago. The efficiency improvement has been nothing short of amazing."

"You have machines managing people? We use a lot of smart machines to do many tasks back home in Russia, but I'm not sure having machines manage people would be well accepted in my country. Russians are proud, stubborn people."

"Sometimes there are advantages to a culture where people are in the habit of following orders," Lee said shrugging.

Boris sensed pushing the conversation would make them both uncomfortable and decided to change the subject. "So, show me how you send one up. I'm eager to try my little side rockets. But, you're right. Seeing the process without using any of them would be a good idea."

"Follow me," Lee Jin-Dao said. He walked into the small command booth of the loading bay. "First you set the payload bucket to be ready to receive whatever you're going to fire." He tapped on a display and Boris saw what looked like a giant sofa on wheels roll up and sit on the track.

"Wheels? Why does it have wheels?' Boris asked.

"The wheels are only used in the first fifty meters. After that, the bucket is riding a maglev track. Do you see how the coil track slopes inward as it curves? That's because as it builds speed, some of the force will be pushing it outward. The track is bent in to keep the maglev on target and not flying off of the path."

"Ah, just like when a roller coaster takes a tight turn?'

"Yes, precisely. Basic physics, actually." Lee paused while tapping a few more indicators on his display. "See, it's asking me to select an item to fire off. I'm using another Moon rock. No need to use up anything we've refined or manufactured at this point. I've sprayed it with a reflective sticky powder. That'll make it easier for us to spot it as it goes flying out."

Boris saw a large transporter bot pull up with a boulder the size of an elephant painted bright white with silvery sparkles. "What's in the sticky powder?"

"Just some stuff we find when strip mining. Mostly a nuisance until we found this as a use for it. Sticks to everything pretty much," Lee explained. "We found most of the boulders when surveying for the mining operations. There seems to be a lot more than we first imagined."

"Another thing I'm learning," Boris replied.

The transporter bot used four extend arms to reach back and grab the boulder. It lifted it high over itself and placed it into the payload bucket.

"You don't need more precision than that?" Boris asked.

"Not for a test like this. When we're firing at the Lagrange Station it'll be a more delicate process. But even then, the purpose of attaching your little thrusters will be to manage the fine-tuning by the capturebots at the station. For now, we're just going to pick some distant celestial body and fire away. In fact, anyplace in particular you want to send this?"

Boris thought about it and finally said, "I'm not sure where my ex-mother-in law is living now, so I might as well pick the Sun."

Lee laughed. "No problem, the Sun it is. We can be a lot more precise than that. In fact, if you did have your ex mother-in-law's address, I could pretty much guarantee we could hit within five meters of the place."

"Wow! That's amazing. So, show me already."

"Look here." Lee smiled as he showed off to Boris. "We locate the target on a map. The map has most of the celestial bodies we know about. Or we can use a set of coordinates. The Lagrange Two Station, for example, has been pre-programed into it, but you asked me to pick the Sun."

"Yes." Boris watched the selection process, surprised at how easy it was.

"Okay, I have the Sun targeted. Now I run a test of the relays starting at fifty meters from the bucket. That's the point where it leaves the wheels and becomes a maglev device floating above the track. The transporter bot lets the maglev system know what the mass of the payload is. The bucket has a set of large magnets that repel it from the magnetic charge that will be shooting down the rail. The charge makes it move forward faster and faster until it attains the requisite velocity to escape lunar gravity. The system calculates this based on the data that comes from the transporter bot. To escape lunar gravity, we need to get to . . ."

"Twenty-four hundred meters per second," Boris interjected. "Remember, I designed the concept behind this system. Will we be using this to get to the Lagrange Station ourselves?"

"Oh, it's a lot gentler than leaving Earth. But you won't be going on one of these babies. These aren't designed for human transport, just for materials. Anyway, it looks like the calculations are all in and the system is ready to go. You want to send it off?"

"I would be honored," Boris said.

"Okay, hold on and let me get you an authorization." Lee slid his fingers across the display, located a picture of Boris in a set of folders and dragged it to another folder. "Now just enter the launch code you see here and follow up with a voice command for approval."

Boris entered the codes and responded to the voice prompt with, "Boris Yelenko"—confirming the launch request.

LAUNCH REQUEST ACCEPTED read the display and a countdown of twenty seconds began. As it reached zero, Boris saw the bucket lurch forward on its wheels. It rolled the fifty meters to the track edge and began to speed up rapidly. Boris watched as it followed the circular track, moved off into the distance and then returned faster as it came back toward them. By the time it passed them and moved onto the rising part of the track, it was moving so fast he had to move his head to track it.

The bucket hit the apogee of the track and went over the edge. The rock kept going up, shining brilliantly in the lunar sunshine.

"How many G's of acceleration did that rock go through?" Boris wondered aloud.

"More than you would like to experience my friend. Those rocks are hitting about eight G's. An experienced rocket jockey or pilots back when they flew fighters could deal with that and stay conscious. You or I would be out like a light with a bloody nose and a hell of a hangover. If we survived it."

Chapter Eighteen

Fermi Crater Artifact
Far Side of the Moon

Protector 304 was calculating probabilities based on data gathered. There was a constant stream coming in at a much faster than processing capability. Information overload was a concern as it led to low confidence. The Protector had to consider various aspects, not the least of which was whether or not it was to act on anything it discovered.

Its mission was to protect Earth from any incoming body. And to help nurture local Saurian life that might evolve into sentience. Its secondary mission was to watch planet activity and send out alerts when local life attained spacefaring culture. They would be tested and if found worthy, welcomed into the interstellar community of Saurian planets.

And become part of the war against the Scarabs.

But the humans were neither Saurians nor Scarabs and there were no precedents the Protector could refer to. Their technology was quite different from what either of those races generally developed. That was another indicator of how different they were. And yet, they landed on the Moon and built things on the far side. And they had had even conducted a vibration test when their machines found P304.

That, in and of itself, was something out of the ordinary. Both Scarab and Saurian cultures made use of machines with various levels of intelligence. But none of them permitted machines to be independently traveling between worlds. There had to be a logical explanation for that. The data in that area was so fuzzy that P304 came to understand it was incomplete to the point where it could not make any inferences at any level of acceptable probability.

The Protector decided to use some of its reflective processors to understand the machines on the Moon. The machines that were mobile were more interesting. The thinking that allowed them to navigate was outside of its data set. They required the most study.

Protector tried different ways to interface with the machines. It found it could use radio waves that mimicked the sonic vibrations humans used to communicate with each other. It was by no means the most efficient nor time effective method. It stood to reason the machines imitated their human creator's way of communicating. These humans were not yet capable of selectively transmitting thoughts to their machines. P304 found this unusual. Almost all known sentient species developed that capability long before interplanetary travel. These humans really were different.

Using this method, Protector began exploring the way the machines responded to inquiries. After a few tentative essays, it recognized a rudimentary security process and set about trying to get past it. These machines were simple compared to the machines it communicated with during its creation. In fact, despite their mobility, their security mechanisms were primitive. Within a matter of minutes, P304 managed to download a full copy of the operational software in the human-made machine. It set about to understand the machine's design and the fundamentals behind its conception.

Suddenly, P304 received an alert it never received before: a perimeter breach. Designed to defend the Earth against objects coming from outside of the solar system, it had no ready-made local defense system. This alarm was indicating a maintenance access passage was open.

The Protector calculated defense options before turning its attention to what the threat could be. After a few moments, it determined the threat was a low and danger was minimal. Risk/reward ratios indicated watching those who opened the access delivered greater return than destroying them. The better option was to watch and learn. A mobile machine opened the port, but the machine was working with three humans surviving in the Moon's vacuum.

Monitoring the situation as the humans entered, Protector watched and waited. The mobile machine remained at the entrance holding the portal hatch open. The three humans were moving slowly. It compared the motion to video stored in its data banks. The motions exhibited caution and curiosity rather than hostility. A passive scan of their bodies gave P304 more information. One of them was an egg layer. The humans' curious practice of incubating the eggs within their bodies made it unlikely the term technically applied. It searched its growing vocabulary and found the word 'female' and the counterpart 'male' to describe the two different types of humans.

The three stepped forward. Each had a light source at the top of its head sending a ray ahead of it. P304 judged the light and heat output and made a decision. It illuminated its interior walls with light of the same intensity and color.

When the light came on, the three humans stopped moving. They began to send data to each other over their radio connections. P304 stored a copy of the data for later perusal.

After a flurry of communications, the humans reduced the data flow and were once again moving forward. At the rate they were moving, they would find a bend in the corridor within a few short minutes. The bend would offer them two divergent paths. One led to the central power supply. The second led to a maintenance station last used when P304 came online.

After calculating the risks, P304 decided the maintenance station was a preferable location for them to go to. It was better equipped at removing access to any vital areas at that location. Based on what it had seen so far, it concluded the humans had not yet availed themselves of fusion technology. Allowing them to learn that before Protector determined their intent came up as a red flag in its decision matrices.

The light displays illuminated the specific path Protector wanted the humans to take. According to the way they were following the illuminated path so far, they should continue in the direction it preferred.

Then, once again, the three humans came to a stop and their data exchange increased. One of them was waving its upper appendages. It seemed the change in illumination had an impact on them other than just guiding them.

While they communicated, P304 altered hardware in the maintenance station to send data to them in radio format. It applied what it learned from the mobile machines and explored the human communication protocol. The structures were anything but clear with complex contextual nuances that followed arbitrary rules.

Once again, the humans began to move, following the illuminated path but at a slower pace. The Protector noticed their temperature, internal vibrations and pressure increased. The likelihood was they were preparing for an action. It checked its illuminating systems and confirmed it could increase light and temperature output. Enough to damage the three humans should they prove to be a threat to its existence. Even to the point of terminating them if necessary.

The three moved along and Protector's sensors showed chemical distribution signals rising. It made the decision to open the maintenance portal well before they got to it. They were responding to every change in their vicinity with increased scrutiny. Better to show fewer changes.

Once they had all passed through the portal, P304 made the decision to attempt to communicate. Using the same software as the mobile machine used, it tapped into the comm systems of all three humans and sent a message.

Chapter Nineteen

Fermi Crater Artifact
Far Side of the Moon

S am, Pierre and Amanda peered into the opening and looked at each other. There were five steps down, each at least a meter wide and just as deep.

"These stairs were most likely designed for a bipedal entity, but not a human," Sam said.

"Unless they were very big humans," Pierre added, looking down into the hole.

Amanda instructed the bot to take the portal it opened and set it aside so there would be no worry of it closing behind them and trapping them inside.

Sam stepped forward. Amanda put her hand up to stop him. "You know, I hate to be Ms. Protocol, but before we enter, shouldn't we contact the major and tell him where we are and what we found?"

"Only if you want to be kept from exploring what's in here," Pierre said. "We all know the major will shut this down instantly. I have a brother in the military. He inherited the paranoia genes in the family. These military people are that way. And it's not only that they're paranoid. They have processes devised to make paranoia a part of everything. It seems normal to them. I vote we go forward and explore for ourselves and then report to the major once we get back."

They both looked at Sam for his opinion.

"Let's consider the options. In the military they always say it's easier to get forgiveness than permission. But, I think we should only reconnoiter within one hundred meters of the entrance. At least for now. Pierre, you've got the cameras and if we bring back a good collection of videos to the major, we just might be able to be forgiven and get permission to proceed at the same time."

"You're so wise, my friend. Especially when you agree with me," Pierre said, smiling. He checked his three cameras and gave a thumbs up sign. "As they say in Hollywood, action!"

Lighting the directional light atop his helmet, Sam stepped onto the first step. It held his weight and he stepped onto the second and each one after until he was on the sloping floor off of the bottom step. He waited for the others as they followed his lead, turning their headlights on as well.

From the bottom of the stairs, they saw they were in a corridor. The walls were smooth and Pierre walked over to one and magnified his right shoulder camera. "The display indicates these walls are so smooth that a heating process created them."

"You mean they were melted into place?" Amanda asked.

"More or less, Pierre replied. "They are smooth down to a molecular level, and extremely uniform. Almost crystalline. But the general make-up indicates they were most likely formed from materials found on the Moon."

"Mined and manufactured right here?" Sam wondered.

"More like just morphed here." Pierre answered. "It looks like whoever created them might have skipped a few steps. I can't say we could do that ourselves. This place may be millions of years old, but the technology looks way ahead of ours. Fascinating." He turned back to take some more video.

"Given that we haven't visited the moons of any other planets, it's no surprise the technology would be ahead of ours," Amanda said.

"Given what Pierre says, it's assumptive it comes from another planetary system. One much older than our own perhaps. How do we know this isn't an artifact made by beings from Earth? Although the carbon dating says it is over sixty-five million years old, how much do we really know of that period?" Sam ran his hand over the smooth wall and checked his readings. Oddly, the wall was a few degrees warmer than the surface. He made a note of that and checked the wall opposite him. Same temperature.

Pierre laughed a little nervously this time. "Sam, you're the xenobiologist and you're telling me there were smart giants walking around during the time of the dinosaurs?"

"Isn't it interesting how we easily accept the notion of beings from another planet building a base here," Sam said, still running his hand over the wall.

"If this was built by someone from Earth, don't you think we would have found similar things they built on our planet long before now?" Amanda asked.

"A good point," conceded Sam. "Unless their constructions don't survive in heavy nitrogen atmospheres. Then again, it's possible this place hasn't even been exposed to the Moon's atmosphere. That portal is pretty thick and was a very tight fit. Who knows? It could have been vacuumed sealed until we lifted it, which could explain its longevity."

"Speculation after discovery, if you please," said Pierre—ever the scientist.

Sam turned around and stepped forward into the corridor away from the entrance. "Come on," he said. "We don't have much time. They'll be looking for us before long."

The walls suddenly lit up with a light that was the same color and intensity as their headlamps.

"Ahhh!" Amanda cried out. "Oh, I think we should head back to the base now. Right now. I think someone knows we're here."

"What?" Pierre said, folding his arms and standing in place. "Run back to the major because an automated system turned the lights on? Amanda, where's your sense of adventure?"

"Hiding behind my sense of safety."

"Amanda," Pierre said. "Please. This is nothing but light. It shouldn't surprise us technology capable of building a structure like this on the Moon would be able to detect a presence and light the way. If anything, I consider it a sign this isn't a dangerous situation. It offering lighting. That's obviously a sign whatever it is, is being helpful."

"I don't know," Sam said. "There's more than that here. The light spectrum is one suited to us. I'm not sure that's likely if this place was built by beings from another planet. A different atmosphere would generally make for a different light spectrum."

"Good point," Pierre said. "Perhaps it detected our head lamps and adjusted to them?"

"I don't know what the reason is and that's the point." Amanda responded. "We don't know and anything we do is just guessing. And guessing in the face of the unknown is dangerous."

Sam saw both of them were beginning to get agitated. "Let's be reasonable and make a plan. How about we give ourselves another thirty minutes of exploration and then head back to the base? The lighting will make us go faster and we should know in a few minutes if we find anything really interesting or if this is just a hallway."

Pierre shrugged, acquiescing. Amanda thought about it for a few moments. " Thirty minutes and then we head back? Okay," she said. "But at the first sign of danger we're getting out of here!"

Thirty minutes wasn't nearly long enough for Sam, but it would have to do for now. He turned and walked ahead. He was fascinated and would have liked to keep going for as long as possible. This was the discovery of a lifetime especially for someone who made a career of imagining what alien life might be like.

The hallway curved to the left. Sam noticed rounded edges between the floor and the walls and the walls had a gentle curve of their own. Whoever built this place was not in the habit of hanging wall paintings. None of the walls had any decoration on them or any residue of things hanging on them. *Of course,* he thought, *sixty-five million years is a long time.*

Sam was in the lead, so he was the first one to see the doorway as he went around the curved corner. He was sure Pierre and Amanda would launch into another argument about protocol and safety when they saw it, so he stepped faster and quickly walked inside the door.

The room was different from the hallway. The walls had a multitude of markings on them, most of them like what they had seen on the portal surface. There were also shiny half bubbles protruding from the walls that looked soft and jelly-like. Pierre poked his head in, and then followed Sam inside. He walked directly into the middle of the room. Then he turned around to make sure he had a visual recording of every aspect of the interior.

Amanda finally stepped into the room. "Wow. Now this is different," she said.

As if in response, a soft baritone voice, with a tone similar to that of their mobile bot announced, "This is Three Hundred and Four. Supply identification for each entity."

The three of them froze. Out of the corner of his eye, Sam saw Amanda getting ready to bolt for the door. He thought that might be a bad move so he blurted out, " I am Sam and this is Pierre," He pointed at each in turn. "And that is Amanda."

Amanda held her arms together, looking at the ceiling and walls, trying to figure out where to address the disembodied voice. "What do you want?'" she said, summoning up all the courage she had.

"Want?" the voice responded, "Three Hundred and Four's directive is to protect the planet."

"Protect the planet?" Pierre, asked, turning and looking for something to go along with the voice. "Protect the planet from what?"

There was a pause before the voice responded, "From any large, rapidly moving object."

Sam was surprised by this answer. "There's a large objecting heading for the Earth?"

Another delay before the voice spoke again, "There was. Once." Another pause. "However, prevention of impact was not successful."

The three of them looked at each other. Amanda's face lit up and she asked, "Are you a life-form or a machine?"

The voice responded quickly to this question, "Three Hundred and Four is not a 'you'. Three Hundred and Four is not a biological organism, as you understand them. Three Hundred and Four is a constructed device."

Amanda beamed, "It's a bot!"

Chapter Twenty

Major Zhang knew communicating between the Earth and the Moon required patience. Bouncing messages between satellites to connect from the far side took almost no time. But there was still the lag that occurred because of the distance involved. Nevertheless, he felt frustration rising as he stared at the round waiting face of General Sun.

A few seconds passed and General Sun finally spoke, "There will be some code sent to you later today. It will come with a full set of instructions for deploying the programs."

Zhang replied quickly knowing it would take time for Sun to get the message. "I'll assign the appropriate person and watch its installation."

When Sun's reply came, it was clear he was not happy with Zhang. "No! You must not give this task to anyone else! It's your responsibility and it will be your reward as well. Major Zhang, you were selected to help China make a great leap forward in history. This is part of your destiny. China has chosen you." Sun glared at the screen emphasizing the point.

This surprised Zhang. Although Sun was a general and his superior, it was not like him to speak with such insistence. He wondered what the task would accomplish. "Thank you for your clarity. I'll take on the responsibility myself and then let you know when it's done."

"That will not be necessary. If you complete the task, we will be able to track the impact from here without hearing from you. In fact, it's a good idea for you to make this as discreet as possible. I'll be erasing the record of this conversation and suggest you do the same."

Major Zhang paused when he heard that. This was the first time someone asked him to delete a conversation. But he could tell General Sun was not in any state of mind to be questioned. "It will be as you ask."

"Excellent. I knew I could count on you and the chairman agrees. China's eyes will be on you, Major. You will be a hero for generations."

"I'm glad to serve my country and my party." Major Zhang bowed. When he lifted his head, the display was blue and the General was gone.

The major called up his agenda for the next day. Perhaps there was something in it that might give him some insight into what this special mission might involve. He didn't see anything outstanding in the task list. Everything there was fairly routine.

There were scheduled upgrades to bot software both at the lunar and Lagrange bases. A test of the capture system at the Lagrange Base could be a good candidate. But that had been run through so many simulations it didn't seem unusual or groundbreaking. Amanda Won was supposed to do a demonstration of the new level of intelligence she'd installed into the bots. He really never felt comfortable with the idea that the bots were making more and more of their own decisions. He preferred machines that just followed orders. He spent a good deal of his life finding ways to make members of the military follow orders more perfectly. Having machines decide how to follow orders didn't seem like an improvement. From his standpoint, interpretation led to chaos and mistakes. Orders were orders— to be followed to the letter.

There was also the daily visit to the artifact by Czerny and the Frenchman. Zhang would have preferred for them to not have been along on the mission. But both the party and the funding company were insistent on their presence. Perhaps there was hope to find technology in the artifact that could lead to a weapons breakthrough. Its age and stability could deliver technologies having a lot of value.

That was a lot more 'ifs' than Zhang usually liked to consider. He always said the more variables in a project, the less likely it was to succeed. Then there was the fact that Czerny and Pacquelier were anything but weapons experts. In fact, he viewed both of them as nothing more than science fiction fans run amok. Whatever mission General Sun alluded to, it was unlikely it had anything to do with those two.

He returned to his agenda and saw he had not completed a few of his tasks for that day. The time display told him he needed to get to work to finish his reports. The last thing he would need was to get his mission instructions and find he had outstanding tasks that needed to be done as well. From the tone of General Sun's voice, this task would require his immediate attention and require every minute of his time.

Chapter Twenty-One

Chang'e 3 Base
Maglev Launcher

"**D**urak!" Boris cursed the third of the three catcherbots as he realized it, too, had crushed the boulder it caught. He wiped the back of his wrist across his brow, a useless gesture since he was wearing a helmet.

"Code the cilia to respond to the movement," Lee Jin-Dao commented.

"What?" Boris asked, not understanding what that had to do with the catcherbots.

"I mean when you wipe your forehead that way," Lee explained. "You can teach the inside of your helmet to respond and wipe away any perspiration you have on your forehead."

Boris looked at him perplexed for a moment until understanding lit up his face. He grinned, "I'm not sweating. It is just a habit of mine. I think my father used to do it when he was frustrated and I picked it up from him. If only I could configure these catcherbots as easily as wiping my forehead."

"Don't try to configure them. Teach them to figure it out. You'll save yourself a lot of time."

"Huh? What do you mean?" Boris wiped his arm over his forehead again without even noticing he was doing it.

"The bots will never figure out how to catch properly if you're instructing them exactly how to do it. They're not designed to function that way. Maybe try this instead; tell them to focus on the structure of the items they will be catching. Then ask them to make sure the item's structural integrity remains constant. Now tell them to catch the item." Lee looked at his display. "But you'd better hurry. The rock we threw should be there in about twelve minutes."

Boris considered what Lee told him. Twelve minutes would be

cutting it close. He found the video image of the next boulder that would be arriving near where the catcherbots were waiting. Then he located a file describing the mineral makeup of the rock. He sent the data to CB One along with some data about pressure and reactions.

He looked at the timer on his display and saw the gathering and sending of data had taken about six and a half minutes. He reviewed the set of instructions he had been sending for each catch—instructions that hadn't worked out. He changed the directive from just catching the rock to sidling up alongside it. He instructed the bots to maintain possession and structural integrity of the rock. Last of all, he asked them to bring it to a stop at the precise location. That would constitute a successful retrieval.

He checked the data and saw the bot would need to change the position it was in when it began the catch. The timer said it had three minutes to get there and into the correct position to match trajectory and velocity. Then Boris had an idea. It was going to cut it close, but he figured he would give it a try and gave it the go ahead.

Lee saw Boris set up the catch and calculated the possibilities of success. Then he whistled. "This is going to be fun to watch. The window is less than a second if the catch is done right. Then the bot is going to have to expend a huge amount of fuel to get to the success spot."

"Watch," Boris said with a smile. "I think you might be surprised. At least I hope you are and I'm not."

The two monitored both the boulder and the bot and watched as the trajectories and speeds matched up. Lee looked at the fuel gauge "Uh oh," he said, "it looks like they're going to go off course. You don't have enough fuel left in the bot. I'll start getting one of the other bots to match up and bring them back." Lee pushed Boris aside to access the controls.

"Hold on." Boris said grabbing Lee's arm and holding him firmly. "Give it a little time. Look!"

Lee gave Boris a cold stare and then pulled his arm away briskly before checking the data. They could both see the boulder and bot were slowing and on target for hitting the stop spot.

Lee shook his head. "How did you do that? There was nowhere near enough fuel."

"No there wasn't, if the rock maintained its same size. But I told the bot no less than half of the rock was needed to arrive at the destination and that made all the difference. It's been vaporizing the rock with its on-board laser. It seems to have calculated how much rock it can save and is using the vaporization as a propulsion source. These bots are pretty smart if you know how to talk to them." Boris winked, hoping it would ease the tension between them.

"Touché," said Lee. "It seems you're getting the hang of things. I bet you're eager to get to the Lagrange Base and really watch them catching and building things there."

"Well, yes. Although I have to say that I'm fascinated by what's going on here. After all, without this Moon Base, there would be no Lagrange Base."

Lee Jin-Dao shook his head. "I can see it the other way around. I 'm not sure they would have found a good reason to build this Moon Base if your plan for the Lagrange Base wasn't approved. Why would anyone build a base on the far side of the Moon if it wasn't to supply a jumping off point to interplanetary exploration?"

Chapter Twenty-Two

The chairman stood and angrily stomped out of the council chambers in the direction of his offices. A nervous assistant followed quickly behind.

"You have a meeting scheduled with the Guangdong Province party leader. Shall I have him come to your office?"

The chairman was in no mood to meet with any provincial party leaders, but Guangdong was the most populous of China's provinces. It was also the wealthiest, due to its coastal position. Song Fai, the party leader for the province had become a wealthy man over the past twenty years. The chairman found the sweaty little man who always looked as if he had just outgrown his clothing did not wear his wealth well. But the man had powerful allies, and after the session with the council, the last thing the chairman needed to do was alienate powerful men within the party.

"Yes, bring him to my office as soon as I am back in it," said the chairman. "And thank you for the reminder."

He enjoyed the shocked look on the assistant's face. It always amused him to thank people for doing what they should be doing, because they didn't expect it from him. He was certain it made them all the more loyal in the long run. 'A kind word warms for three winters' was a Chinese proverb he always tried to live by.

The chairman just made it into his chair behind his splendid desk when the door to his office opened. Song Fai marched in sporting one of the silvery pink silk pajamas outfits rich businessmen in the south often wore. Chairman Qi frowned. Such clothing had been banned in Beijing after Hollywood began portraying Chinese people with long pigtails, bound feet, wearing pajamas and smoking opium. For the most part, only the wealthy still wore silk pajamas. Some young people wore brightly colored pajamas

94

in public, but the chairman saw that as a sign of rebellion. He preferred the days of drab Mao suits, which he considered much more dignified. The chairman still wore the dark suits with the Mao collar. He didn't believe that too much change was good for his country.

Song walked right up to the desk and plopped himself into a chair before greeting the chairman. He was a young man for a provincial party leader, only fifty-eight years old. His jet-black hair was slicked back in the fashion that had returned to the southern coastal areas. The chairman preferred to deal with the more traditional politicians, and with their manners as well. Song was clearly a dogmatist in his own way. No one should sit in front of the chairman before being asked to.

"Qi Yuanching," Song spoke up before the chairman had the time to greet him and the lack of using an honorific irritated the chairman. "Your offices are pretty, if a bit Spartan."

The chairman smiled. "I am certain few places compare to the palace you have on the Pearl River." It was well known Song Fai liked his luxuries and had been collecting antique furnishings for some time. The chairman wondered if that would be his undoing one day. Another Chinese proverb the chairman often quoted stated, 'The only thing missing at a rich man's funeral is a mourner'. He wondered if Song Fai knew those words. "What is it that brings you so far away from such comfort?"

Song smiled. He liked the way that Qi played with words. "Ah Chairman Qi, if only I could stay at home and live a life of leisure. But we both know those of us dedicated to the glory of China spend our time defending and developing our great nation."

More like developing and defending his own wealth, the chairman thought. "And what is it you are at today, Leader Song? Defending or developing?"

Song snorted a laugh. "My dear chairman, it's true what they say at the party dinners. You really should attend them."

The chairman did not laugh with him but folded his hands and placed his elbows on his desk. Leaning forward with a stony face, he asked, "And exactly what is it that is said about me at these dinners?"

"Oh, just that while you are the gentlest of men, you can be direct and to the point when it suits you."

The chairman leaned back in his seat. "Song, I'm a busy man and while I enjoy your company and banter, can you be direct and to the point?

That would suit me now."

Song stared at the chairman for a full five seconds before responding. "Very well, I'll waste no more of your time or mine. Certain rumors have come to my attention that you are looking to increase China's military standing in the world. And that you may even be willing to go into new confrontations to achieve that standing. This concerns the people of my Province."

"China's standing in the world is always my concern, whether economic, cultural or military."

"That's just the issue, Qi. We've become a rich and prosperous nation by letting other nations fight among themselves. Entering into a military struggle, even simply one of posturing and saber rattling will not be good for business. And what is not good for business is not good for China. I'm here to let you know there are several members of the party council who are more than concerned. They worry that China may walk into, how to say it, an unfortunate situation if we attempt to change the balance of the last generations. China's policy of isolationism has served us well for centuries."

The chairman thought the only thing that really concerned Song was what was good for Song's businesses. He nodded to the man slowly. "I appreciate your concern and those of your faction. But I think I should remind you as chairman, I have a much greater access to information than the leader of just one province. And as chairman, I am responsible for the security and well-being of China. Not just today but in the future as well. Security that allows you to afford the luxuries of your businesses and your palaces. One day, the Americans will find that being the military might without the wealth is not a dish that tastes as good as it looks. On that day, they will look into our plate and decide what we are eating looks more appealing. It is my job and my duty as chairman to prepare for that day and make certain we can defend our plate, our China, if necessary."

The chairman was gratified to see Song sweating and looking a little pale. Even his upper lip began to quiver as he replied, "My chairman, do you actually think the Americans would ever dare to do anything that would compromise their markets here? We are too valuable a place to sell to and we hold so much of their debt. It would seem they need us more than we need them."

"All the more reason to be wary. Unlike you, Song, I'm not a businessman. I'm an historian. And history teaches me we need to be wary.

After all, haven't we looked the other way as America invades one place after another and secures markets for itself as well as us? Haven't we been teaching them, with our acquiescence and even approbation, that this is how they should behave?"

The chairman stood up and walked around his desk. His height gave him an advantage over the seated man. "No, Song, we've been too comfortable in our beautiful homes and silk pajamas. There will come a day when they see all that and decide they want some of it. Enough of it that we will feel the price is too high for us to pay. I'm not looking for war, Song, but neither will I turn my back on defending our land and our way of life at all cost." He glared at the still-seated Song and waited to hear his reply.

Song pulled a neat black cotton handkerchief from his pajama pocket and wiped his damp forehead. "Chairman, I meant no . . . You are wise. I see that now. I, and my colleagues, we have been looking at our little provinces and our little domains and concerning ourselves only with their needs. And here you have the vision of what is really going on in the world. You are thinking of China as a whole. Please excuse me my insolence. I'm so ashamed. When next we are in council, you can count on my full support. China needs to be more grateful that we have put her fate in your able hands. Thank you, sir, for your wisdom and forward thinking."

The chairman smiled and bowed. "It is I who thank you, Leader Song. Thank you for taking the time to speak with me. Thank you for listening and understanding, and thank you for all that you do in your beautiful Guangdong Province. I look forward to the next time we may meet."

Song stood up and walked out of the office far less steadily than he walked in.

Yes, thought the chairman, *thanking them for doing what they are supposed to do is a good way to manage men at every station.*

He contacted one of his assistants on his display and told him to get General Sun in his office as soon as possible. Things were coming to a head. A little sooner than he had expected, but one could never tell ahead of time when the best moment would come. All one could do was be prepared to seize it when it did. And the chairman intended to be ready for that moment. Making sure the leaders of the provinces were behind him would be critical.

Chapter Twenty-Three

Fermi Artifact
Far Side of the Moon

Protector Three Hundred and Four waited patiently. The three humans decided to return to their base, telling Protector they would return shortly.

It found they were, and would continue to be a valuable resource. Much data it accumulated during the visit was structured in such a way using it was not currently possible. It needed to create better correlations and connections. It would mean more processing power and time.

The human's language held a complex set of references. This set, which they called culture, was changing constantly. There was a multitude of these cultures spread through different languages and locations. Clearly by their accents and their use of idioms, they came from three different parts of the planet and had three completely different skill sets. Protector would have to learn to be conversant in all three if it was to gather enough data from them to store and eventually put to use.

Even time played a role in their cultural changes in a way P304 had not found in any of its historical records. The Saurians who designed and built the Protectors would have found the planet a true oddity. Like a Scarab planet, the population was humongous, well over twenty-five billion. There was a myriad of implications to consider. Humans were prolific breeders despite rarely hatching more than one progeny at a time. They were phenomenal at maintaining a high level of progeny survival throughout breeding age even if that age came early.

The most unusual thing Protector Three Hundred and Four discovered about humans was how young they were. The Species was around less than three hundred thousand years. This explained why the Protector was taken unaware by them on the Moon. In order to conserve energy, it was taking a look at the planet only once every five hundred thousand years. Scarab and Saurian communities took many millions of years to develop spacefaring technologies. Humans did everything at an accelerated pace. It would have to keep a closer watch on Earth.

P304 decided to continue acquiring and sifting through more data. The curious way humans communicated was so different from the way the complex machine was constructed. It decided to look at how the software for the machines made by humans worked. As it looked at the data storage methods which it found to be primitive, their instruction sets which were cut and dry logical, and their basic mathematics which were antiquated but functional, it began to suspect it had grossly misinterpreted something about human communication.

Then it came across the decision and learning modules for the transport bot that opened the portal. It used the same simple structures, but there was something very different about this part of its functions.

P304 looked at how it could add the method to its own processes. The data organization method was completely different. The algorithmic constructs followed mathematical patterns, but not really logical ones. They seemed to be more closely related to three-dimensional geometrical building structures. The rule-based structures it used seemed slow and stunted by comparison. From the software it learned a function for ignoring previous erroneous results. This would add speed to some of its decision-making processes. P304 saw implementing these new structures could possibly extend its functional lifespan.

Protector Three Hundred and Four had maintenance routines that had been running for more than sixty-five million years. There were even parts of it that ran on tiny little rails within its structure to deliver some parts to where they were needed so they could be replaced when they wore out. But there were also parts that stopped working and were not replaceable. At least not with the resources the Protector had locally. With no one to supply parts to the Moon, those systems affected had to be shut down and overridden so Protector didn't lose power and data.

It made a decision it never made before. It would recode some of its processes according to decision-making principles discovered in the transporter bot's code. It picked a set of functions no longer used—the part watching for incoming objects to hit Earth. It applied the new method of decision making to that particular subset of itself. The risk was minimal and it might learn something new. That would mean functions could be returned to P304's repertoire. Especially a function that once failed badly.

Chapter Twenty-Four

"Y**ou just can't be serious! This is insane!**" Pierre shouted angrily, jumping up and slamming his hand down on the surface of the major's desk.

Major Zhang looked at him, wondering how the Frenchman ever got approved to be on the Moon Base. "I couldn't be more serious, Mr. Pacquelier. And I would thank you to not abuse my desk or my patience in this way!"

Czerny, Pacquelier and Won had come back from the artifact with an incredible story of finding a functioning machine built by aliens. They even claimed it talked to them. They were overly excited and somewhat incoherent. The major told them he found their story bizarre. They claimed to have a recorded their discussion with the 'alien intelligence'. But when they played the recording, all it showed was they accessed an entrance into the artifact and found a hallway. There was no mention of a room in the recording nor, in fact, any conversation at all. The rest of the tape was blank.

Putting his hand on Pierre's shoulder, Sam took a deep breath before he spoke. "Major, I agree this may seem unusual. The recording is clearly not showing our entire time in the artifact and there may be a dozen explanations for that. Between you and me, I'm hoping it wasn't the doing of the intelligence, but I'll admit it may have been. I can understand your reticence in according us the twelve extra bots we've requested. You have a mission to accomplish. But may I ask you this; just what type of resources can you give us? We have a limited number of days on this base and I'm facing what may be mankind's greatest discovery. Just think what we can learn from an intelligence that has been here for more than sixty-five million years!"

The major took a deep breath and blew it out of his nose. He motioned for them to wait as he focused on his retinal display and contacted Lee. "Jin-Dao, tell me, are your current projects with Dr. Yelenko on or ahead of schedule?"

Lee responded. They were well ahead of schedule. They even found a way to cut fuel consumption and up the pace at which they would be able to launch payloads to the Lagrange Two Station.

"Excellent. Do you think you might work on something else if I assign Dr. Won to a different project? For a day, perhaps two?"

"I think I can juggle my schedule to accommodate that without changing the overall timelines for mission success. Her work here could shift to three days from now rather than tomorrow with no significant problems," Lee replied.

"Good." Zhang nodded even though he was not visible to Lee. "Make it so. I'll alert Dr. Won." He smiled at the three standing before him. "Dr. Czerny, I've managed to free up some resources. You may have Dr. Won to work with you all day tomorrow. For the bots, I'm afraid I can't allow you to have more than the two which have already been allocated to your project. I'm not sure you're aware what each one of them costs. Allow me to assure you the sum is far above anything you've ever spent or will probably ever spend in the future.

"Mr. Pacquelier, please take the time to make sure your recording equipment is in perfect working order. We can't afford to show results of our exploration that don't agree with our words. That's a road to no future exploration at all. Is that clear to everyone?"

Amanda and Sam nodded. Pierre just looked at his feet holding his hands together.

"Good. Then please make sure you get the rest you need. I think if what you've been telling me is true, the rest of your stay on the Moon will be a busy one."

Understanding they were dismissed, the three walked out of the major's office and into the common room. Pierre and Sam plopped on the chairs. Amanda walked over to the tea maker, pulled out three cylinders of green tea extract and poured it into hot water.

"This Moon water tastes different," she said handing, each of them a Sippy cup used on the Moon Base. "I never thought flat water could get any flatter, but this just tastes flatter. It's hard to get used to."

"Right now, everything will taste a little bitter to me," said Pierre, making a face after taking a sip. "I have to apologize to the two of you. I'm so sorry. If my recordings had not been damaged . . ."

"Damaged?" Sam asked, as he swirled the cup. Opening it to cool it was not an option, but he didn't like his drinks as hot as the other two did. "Are you sure they weren't just faulty to begin with?"

"No, they're damaged. I double-checked after they came out the way they did. Something erased a part of the recording."

"How do you know that?" Amanda asked

"Because it's not as if the recording isn't there at all." Pierre explained. "It's just that part of the recording that's missing. Something erased it"

"Something," Sam said. "Or someone."

Chapter Twenty-Five

Starshield-Shackleton Facilities
Coronado Base, California

Trish Stern tapped her display hard enough to make it wobble on her desk. It didn't change the result. She kept getting a PASSWORD NOT ACCEPTED message. Finally, she opted for the facial recognition log in. Her clearance was so high, the usual facial recognition was never enough. Even if it didn't get her what she needed, perhaps she could get into her profile and find out what was going on.

The display announced she was logged in. Just to be sure, she tried to connect to the mission status software and was promptly shown an ACCESS DENIED message.

She linked to her profile management section. It looked a little odd to her, as if some of the data was just not there anymore. The data relating to her security clearance was empty. At her level, it should have been right up there next to her name and picture. She was completely baffled.

Taking her time and studying the data, she finally decided to go into 'edit mode' and try again. There, she saw a button for security level. She tapped on it and was given an ACCESS DENIED message again. *Well, that makes sense,* she thought, *I shouldn't be able to edit my own security level.*

But she should be able to edit the security level of one of her staff.

She moved back up to the top of the profiles section and searched for someone who worked in her department. Someone at a bottom level. There, she found the file for Susan Blankenthorn. Perfect. Susan was just out of school and had started as an intern. It would be harmless to move her up from almost nonexistent to just barely noticeable. She found the spot in Susan's profile and chose to edit it.

ACCESS DENIED flashed in red across her screen.

Trish sat back and scratched her head. She'd never encountered a situation like this in the nine years she was with Starshield-Shackleton. She tapped back to her home screen and searched for the connection to Support Services. The helpline connection did not respond when she tapped on it. She tried again and saw there was a connection established. But it was not the Help Desk.

Instead, Trish was staring into the long pale face of Henry deKumpf, head of Starshield-Shackleton security. She'd never seen him look anything other than serious. This time he just looked sad.

"Ms. Stern, I regret to inform you that we've detected a security breach."

"Is that it?" she interrupted him. "I was wondering. I haven't been able to get into my files concerning the Lagrange mission. I even tried to see if my security level was changed and ..."

He interrupted her in turn, "Your security level has changed. In fact, you're locked out of the system completely. Ms. Stern, you've been detected trying to raise the security level of an intern inappropriately. This is a Level One security offense. I'm afraid it carries with it an immediate termination of your employment at Starshield-Shackleton."

"What? That's ridiculous. I was just trying to see if the edit function for security levels was broken. I was not able to check my own security level. I wasn't trying to compromise company security in any way, Mr. deKumpf. I would never do that." Her voice rose in tone and volume," I've been with Starshield-Shackleton for more than nine years and I've never been accused of anything. In fact, I've been rewarded with important projects, not the least of which has been the Lagrange Two Base and the mining operation on the Moon."

He interrupted her again. "I'm certain your years of service will be a consideration in determining the type of departure package you'll receive, Ms. Stern." He sighed. "But I'm afraid there's no appeal for this egregious breach of conduct. I'm very sorry, but as of this moment, your services are no longer required. You've been fired."

"Well, Mark Slater will hear about this. And General Sun as well," Trish said, a haughty tone to her voice.

"Ms. Stern, I advise you to just accept the current situation. Attempting to make waves won't be in your favor, I can assure you. You won't be granted an audience with General Sun or Mr. Slater, under any circumstances. You are no longer an employee of Starshield-Shackleton."

"But this is all just a misunderstanding!" She could feel her eyes beginning to swell with tears.

"I never intended to do anything against the company in any way. I was locked out, and I just wanted to check and see if it was some kind of a glitch. I still don't understand why I was locked out to begin with."

A shadow passed in front of the crack beneath her door. Trish wondered if they could have sent someone for her. She grabbed her comm key, the device that held all her other pass codes, looked away from the screen for a moment. As she brought her hand to her mouth and coughed, she tucked the device into her bra.

The Security chief looked even sadder. "I do commiserate Ms. Stern. You have all my sympathies. But I'm afraid there's nothing I can do at this point. Please prepare to evacuate the office."

There was a knock at the door. It opened before she could respond. Two large, muscular men with close-cropped hair and tight-fitting suits entered. "We're here to escort you out, Ms. Stern."

She was surprised by the intrusion. "Wait a moment, I'm on a call with Security Chief deKumpf." She turned back to the display but saw the connection had ended and only a blue screen remained. She felt her heart racing. Only minutes before, she held a very important position with a very important company. Now, she was thrown under the bus for a small infraction—little more than a misunderstanding.

The smaller of the two men looked over her shoulder and said, "Not any more you aren't. You don't need to worry about any of your personal effects. We'll pack them up and have them sent to your home."

"Wait, this is all just a mistake!" She was not used to feeling this vulnerable in front of lower level employees. Especially not in front of security personnel. In her years at Starshield, she'd had very little contact with them.

"I just need a few minutes to locate Mr. Slater and explain this all to him. If you would be kind enough to wait outside my office, I'm sure this will be cleared up in just moments." She pointed at her door.

The man who spoke looked at her finger and then at the other man who came in with him. "Ms. Stern, I have orders to retrieve all your key cards and data storage devices and escort you off of the premises immediately. I wasn't told you need or merit any time to contact anyone, let alone the president of this company." He grabbed her left wrist. "Now, you'll come along nicely or do you want us to make this unpleasant for you and your former colleagues on this floor?"

"What? No! You son of a bitch!" she shouted, "I just told you I need a few minutes to clear this all up! So back off or you'll regret this once I've straightened it out."

Instead of letting her go, he nodded to the other man who stepped up and pushed something against her ribs.

Trish felt a sudden shock and all her muscles constricted at once. She felt her herself fall back into the arms of the bigger man. As she lost consciousness, she heard the first man say, "You're going to have one hell of a headache. I told you—you should've come along quietly, bitch."

Chapter Twenty-Six

General Sun turned to Mark Slaton. They'd just finished listening to Security Chief deKumpf's account of how things went with Trish's termination. Stern walked right into the trap and behaved exactly as deKumpf predicted she would. Sun blinked his little eyes as he wiped his forehead with a paper tissue. "Was that really necessary? To use Ms. Stern that way? She's been helpful during this entire process. Almost indispensable I would say. Your techniques are a little harsh . . ."

Tall, thin Mark Slater stood as stiff as a guard at attention. He wore one of his hand-made charcoal gray suits composed of soft Icelandic wool. "Cemeteries are full of indispensable people, General. Anyone can be replaced, Even you or I. In fact, it happens all the time. Remember that scientist Ledbetter? He thought he was indispensable, didn't he? It's just not something anyone likes to look at first hand. And yet seeing things for what they are is what makes the difference between the dreamers and those who do great things."

"Hmm. Yes. Well, perhaps. But couldn't there have been some other way? I regret losing good resources for no good reason. She was a valued servant and well respected by her colleagues, too."

Slaton turned towards the general, removing a vaper from his jacket pocket and placing it in his mouth. The general wondered what Slaton was ingesting through the cigarette. Fashion dictated a mild narcotic, but the way Slaton's mind was always sharp as a tack, the general suspected it was more likely some sort of stimulant.

Slaton exhaled a cloud of sweet-smelling blue smoke. "We both know someone will need to be the one who takes the blame when things become interesting. Someone we can point to as a rogue element. Someone who lost it emotionally and wasn't rational anymore. Someone who was close enough to the project to have been the one behind the terrible deeds that will take place. It'll be a little late to start looking for this scapegoat once things happen. If we don't have one at the ready, government inquiries may find their own. We can't have that now, can we?"

The general felt a trickle of sweat roll down the side of his neck and soak into his tight shirt collar. He had the feeling Slaton would not hesitate in the least making him the scapegoat if push came to shove. "Yes, you're right. If heads will roll, better to choose which ones now. But wasn't there anyone else who would have been a lesser loss to the project? Someone not quite so essential?"

Slaton smiled at the general the way adults smile at a child showing a simplistic understanding of the world. "General, choosing the least useful person would just be a suspect selection. The greater the sacrifice, the more convincing the ploy."

General Sun reminded himself never to play chess with Mark Slater. And he reminded himself this game they were playing was a lot more dangerous than chess could ever be. He would have to watch his own back carefully.

Chapter Twenty-Seven

Fermi Crater Artifact
Far Side of the Moon

S am shook his head. "Amanda, I can appreciate that you want to learn about the Protector's technological design, but we've more important things to discover."

They were riding on the back of their transporter bot on their way back to the entrance they found the previous day.

Amanda disagreed. "More important than discoveries that can leapfrog human technology? Think about it. Whoever built this thing knew how to create an intelligent computer sixty-five million years ago! Back when the most sophisticated mammal was some sort of shrew, some society was able to create Artificial Intelligence." She held up a few fingers and then realized she wasn't sure how to display sixty-five with ten fingers.

"Think of how much catching up we need to do. We can't afford not to learn as much as we can to make sure we're moving our technology forward at the fastest pace possible. Learning everything we can about how and why Protector was created can be crucial to the development of our planet!"

Sam remained obstinate. "Amanda, I can appreciate you want to dissect the Protector and figure out how to build another. But I need to get at its history first. We need to learn about who built it and what they are or were like. We have no idea how much longer the power source that drives it will operate. We need to get all that information first. Not to mention all it knows about the history of Earth. Think of what it must have seen over all those years!"

Pierre, who was sitting on the back edge of the transporter bots back swinging his legs like a little boy, chimed in. "I am agreeing with Sam here. We can always learn how this thing works even if the power is not working in it. And I think it's more important to learn about the aliens who put it together. Always follow information to its source. After all, this is just a machine. It's reasonable to think the beings who built it were more complex and more interesting than it is. That is where we must begin!"

The bot began to slow down as they drew closer to the entrance to the Protector's complex. It stopped right next to it and Amanda requested that it open the portal.

As the bot lifted the heavy doorway, Amanda had an idea. "How about we ask the Protector what it'd prefer to talk about with us? That alone would tell us a lot about it and the beings who designed it."

"That's not a bad idea," Sam said after a moment's thought. "We don't necessarily have to follow its preference, but it would give us some insight. What do you think, Pierre?"

"I'm not so certain. I'm not thinking that treating a machine, even an intelligent one, as an equal is a good thing. It may make assumptions about us we might not welcome. But if both of you can agree on this thing, I guess I won't be the one who, what is it you say, stands in the way?"

"Then it's agreed," Sam said as he lit his helmet light and walked down the wide steps that led to the corridor. The walls lit up at the same place. This time they moved the more rapidly as they decided they'd return to the spot where the Protector had first spoken to them.

But, when they got to the bend in the corridor, the door which had been open the last time was gone. In fact, there was no sign there had been a doorway there at all. The lit part of the corridor stretched farther than where they had gotten to the day before. After giving each other puzzling looks, Sam continued to follow where it was lit. They came to another portal seventy meters farther along than they had been the previous time. They stepped into the room and found a completely different environment.

The smooth, mellow voice they heard the day before greeted them, again seeming to come from everywhere at once. "Greetings, Amanda, Pierre, Sam. I have changed the venue for our discussion. The other place was designed for minor maintenance and interfacing during my construction. As I was uncertain which method of communicating would be best, I chose that place when we first met. Now that you have returned, I've chosen this place as it includes large and useful viewing surfaces along the walls. From what I have learned, your species is more comfortable reviewing data in this manner."

Sam saw Amanda and Pierre looking a little concerned, just as they did when they heard first heard the voice. So, he decided to take the lead. "That is considerate of you, Protector. I appreciate it. We've been discussing among ourselves what we would like to learn from you. We haven't been able to agree. Should we be asking you about the history of the beings who built you? Or should we be learning more about your design?"

"And I would like to learn how you erased my recordings," Pierre blurted out. Sam and Amanda gave him wide-eyed looks, surprised by the sudden accusation.

The even-toned voice never gave a sign of any type of emotional response. "I can accommodate all that at once, although you may find it difficult to follow."

Sam said, "What if you spoke to each of us separately? Our communicators allow for separate channels that do not overlap or interfere with each other."

"I can do it that way, but the display mechanisms in this room would not be used to their best effect. A better method would be to have you in different rooms. If that is agreeable with you."

From the corner of his eye, Sam could see the other two were getting nervous again. "Would you please excuse us while we confer among ourselves for just a moment?"

When the voice didn't answer, Sam switched his comm system to include only Pierre and Amanda. "How about you two go into another room and discuss technology while I stay here and discuss the creators' history? This could be the ideal way to use our time. Remember, this is our only chance to have Amanda with us."

Pierre answered first. "I don't like the idea of any of us being alone with it. We need to have some type of witnessing at every step. What if I leave a recorder with you and we get it to promise it won't erase what we speak about, but it erases it anyway? Then our visit here would be wasted."

"I'm not crazy about me being alone with it either," Amanda added. "Almost as much as I am not crazy about being alone with Pierre." She poked him in the ribs and Pierre looked at her with surprise that turned into a grin.

Changing his comm setting to include the room and by extension the Protector, Sam said, "We think this will work. Pierre and Amanda can speak to you in one place and I in another. Is there another place? And who should go where?"

Protector Three hundred and Four replied, "If Sam stays here, I can best use the displays for his inquiries. Amanda and Pierre, if you step out, you will see another place across from this one and we can discuss your topics in there."

Pierre took the recording device on his left shoulder and unattached it from his helmet. He walked over to Sam and plugged it into Sam's helmet and then stuck it onto his shoulder. "Just remember to face things with your body so they will be recorded properly, not just your head."

"A little primitive, isn't that?" Sam asked.

Pierre replied, "Not when you understand it's doing three-sixty recordings all around you. Even on the other side of your head."

"Really? How does it do that?" Sam said, puzzled.

"I'll explain another time. We have work to do."

Sam noticed despite his penchant for levity, there were times when Pierre could be all business. This was clearly one of them.

He nodded and Pierre stepped out of the door and into the hallway. Amanda followed. On the other side of the hall, another door appeared. Pierre and Amanda walked into a room almost identical to the one they had been in. The difference was one wall with angled displays against it and a bench in front of the displays. The voice came from everywhere in this room as well. "In data being broadcast from the planet, I learned you're generally in a position of resting your weight along your middle while accessing."

"What?" Pierre responded.

"I think he means we're usually sitting," Amanda whispered into Pierre's communicator. "That's why we have benches here."

"Ah," said Pierre. "How convenient."

Taking one step forward, Amanda spoke to the Protector. "I'd like to start with an overview of how you store and access data. An understanding of that will be needed to get into the more complex notions of decision-making and response selection. May we begin there?"

"Wait a second," Pierre interrupted. "I want my question answered first. When I got back to the base yesterday, I tried to share my recording of everything we did here with some others. But when I did, the data from when we had been talking you, Mr. Protector, was erased. I could tell it was erased because there was a trace recording where the data had been. How did you do that and why did you do that?"

Amanda worried that Pierre's tone was too forward and the Protector would not take it well. The Protector was a machine, she understood that, but she had no idea what level of sophistication the aliens had achieved in Artificial Intelligence. This machine might take offense at the way Pierre just spoke to it. The last thing she wanted was to anger it and cause it to shut down communication.

Protector Three Hundred and Four replied with the same even mellow voice it always had. "I did notice you were recording and I made a copy of the recording to look through the data at some later time. Or in case I would wish to have an historical view from your perspective."

"That doesn't answer my question," Pierre insisted. "Why did you erase my recordings?"

"The answer to that is: I did not."

Chapter Twenty-Eight

Mark Slaton's pale gray eyes looked out of his office windows. Two walls of his office were floor to ceiling windows and he had a commanding view of Penobscot Bay. Some of the shareholders found it curious, even annoying, that he preferred to have his office located in such a remote spot. But Slaton had his reasons for it.

His predecessor opted for offices near the Pentagon, and had paid the price for it. Those offices had been in a popular area, making it too easy for someone to get in and get away after an attack. They found the former chairman at his desk with his throat slit and a bib of crimson over his trademark white turtleneck. Everyone wondered how the assassin had gotten away without a trace.

Slaton had no idea either. All he knew was it had cost him a bundle to find a safe place to relocate. As had hiring people to find and dispose of the man who did it. Of course, none of the cost was anywhere near what the rewards had been. The last eleven years as head of Starshield-Shackleton made him one of the wealthiest and most powerful men on the planet.

It was difficult to be certain exactly how wealthy he was because much of the money and property was held in hidden accounts and behind dummy corporations. And Mark Slaton viewed wealth and power as a fluid thing rather than a static one. It was always growing and changing shape, even shrinking a little sometimes to better grow in the next cycle. He considered those who saw wealth and power as an unmoving object or a construction to be pitiful fools. All power was organic. It was an expression of human development. And it took a brain, a smart and active brain, to stay in control. Slaton had just such a brain.

Taking his digital cigarette out of his pocket, he activated it. The drug came in a cold vapor stream rather than smoke so it was less harmful to the lungs. The effects of the mix of chemicals in the cigarette were a proprietary blend. He had always been one to use any method he could to enhance his capabilities. Once he began to make enough money, he invested in having a special blend made just for his own personal use. The cost of developing a cocktail genetically tuned to him had been considerable. Almost as much as what it cost him to hire the unnamed assassin to remove the man who stood between him and the position he now held. But the reward was far beyond what even he imagined. Bioengineering, chemistry and Nano-scale robotics had given him advantages over many of his competitors.

At seventy years old, Slaton looked and felt like a fit forty. His reasoning and creative capacity were far beyond what they had ever been during his lifetime. And they were well beyond what any normal human could expect. But it was the addition of his personal cocktail that made everything gel together. It gave him the ability to hyper-focus on any given task, without the downside of being obsessed about it. He had people who worked for him who had that type of focus. Some of them even enhanced it with chemicals as well, but it was pretty much all they were good for. They became functional idiot savants.

Slaton was different. His personal drugs, genetic manipulations and Nanobots made him balanced as well as superior to his fellow man. On some days, as he looked over that bay, he wondered if this is what it felt like to be a god.

His office was in the corner of a two-hundred-acre compound that included a dramatic pink granite cliff over the frigid Maine tides. The compound was walled in on three sides and faced the cliff on the fourth. His office was in a building that was part of a three-sided structure including his home and what amounted to a barracks for his personal security force. There was not the slightest chance he would end up like his predecessor.

He had grown up in a small town on the coast and always felt as if he could think better with the smell of salt air and the ever-present wind. He even read studies showing IQ levels were higher in areas where there was more iodine in the air. The position of his compound allowed for him to access it by helicopter, or a single road that could be easily defended.

"Even paranoids can have real enemies," he liked to say.

Slaton fired up his display. The screen had a special anti-reflective coating that made it usable in an office which was lit by Maine's ever-changing coastal sky.

He contacted the personal secretary to the President of the United States. After a few moments she told him the president was ready for his call.

The gray-templed, square jawed face of the man the media had dubbed, 'Mr. Charisma' appeared on the display. "Mark! Good to see you. I only have a few minutes so let's get right to the point. The generals at the Pentagon are saying the latest set of drones tested appear to be less responsive than what they were expecting. I told them I'd get in touch with you personally to see what could be done. What can I tell them?"

"I'm not sure there will be much to tell them," Slaton said, pursing his lips. "For years, we've been the almost exclusive provider to the military, scratching only a little bit of profit out of this. They keep wanting better performance without being willing to pay for either the research or the production. Mr. President, my shareholders have asked me to request some movement on your part. They want me to show them a better profit."

"Damn it, Mark, you can't try to shake down the United States! We've had a long and profitable relationship. The world has never been as peaceful as it is now. My predecessor called it, 'Pax Americana' and as stupid as he was in some ways, he was right about this. America needs to keep its place as the guarantor of peace in the world. We can see the benefits. Peace is good for business. For that reason, I need you to deliver.

"My only option will be to see if any other company can deliver better and cheaper. You know I'm a fervent champion of free markets, but both you and I know free markets are not the way things work in DC. If you force my hand by not playing ball with the Pentagon, well, suffice to say I'll need to pursue more of a free market strategy." He added his trademark smile and trademark saying, "You get my drift?"

Slaton could tell this call was not going to produce any concrete results. The president was signaling to him that his hands were tied and he was unwilling to even test the fetters. "I'll look at what added improvements we may be able to deploy, but there will be costs involved. We may need to produce a greater volume of the items in question to justify the investment."

"Yeah, well, sorry about that. I don't have the budget for more drones and the law is strict about you selling them anywhere else. You know that. I can't move Congress, the Pentagon or anyone on that point. Don't even try because it'll put us all in an ugly situation. Can't you sell more commercial rockets to the Chinese? More Moon stuff or something? Those guys are rolling in cash. I think I could fast track the approval of that if need be. Twist a few arms; show them jobs are at stake. That kind of thing."

Slaton understood when he was being threatened. He hated being told what to do. Especially by some political buffoon, even if it was the president.

"Is there any opportunity to move funds from some other, less urgent project? Perhaps if we cut the Near-Earth Orbit Watcher Satellites into hibernation, you could find some resources that would help our efforts?"

"Damn it, Mark! You know damn well that it is the one project we can't shut down! I staked my election on being the one who would make sure we protect the whole planet from any incoming asteroids."

Slaton sighed, "Mr. President, I'll speak to both my board and my engineers, but I can't offer you any concrete promises. Just that I'll try."

"That's all I'm asking." He flashed his vote-winning grin again. "I know how good you are at talking your guys into it. Let me know what you come up with. I need to be able to wow the shoot-em-ups in a couple of weeks with my negotiating prowess. I need to show them I can stick to a budget and still get what we need. Take care, Mark. We'll talk soon."

The screen went to blue and Slaton smiled. Some of what that fool had said was true. The peace of an American police approach had been good for business. But not his business. His business had always been war. Sure, there were some side businesses like space exploration, but that was pennies among the billions. No, this dishonest 'peace' president was bad news. That was why Slaton had gone to work on his plan as soon as he realized, five years ago, this guy was going to win. It was time the planet had a little more war. War made money.

The new chairman in China had been a shrewd move, four years in the making. He was not the only option there was, but Slaton knew how to hedge his bets.

War was what he needed to remove penny pinching from the military procurement process. It had been that way ever since the Vietnam War and it needed a revival. A divided planet was the best thing for his company and all those who made money through selling weapons systems. He would be doing a lot of companies a big favor and save a lot of jobs in the process if he could bring the planet to war.

Mark Slaton, with his superhuman intellect had worked it out. If your markets are shriveling, create new markets. The process to get there had been complex and convoluted at times, but he could see the goal was not far off. Not far at all.

Chapter Twenty-Nine

University of California
San Diego

Helen Czerny's display indicated a secure call was coming in. The last time she'd seen that logo was when Sam called her. She smiled and responded. But what she saw on her office display worried her.

Trish Stern appeared looking pale and shaken. Helen immediately wondered if something had happened to Sam. "Ms. Stern, is everything all right? Where is Sam? We lost contact the last time he tried to call."

"No, er, yes, well, no." Trish was having a hard time thinking straight. "First of all, Sam is all right, as far as I can tell. But I'm not . . ." She shook her head trying to get the cobwebs out of her mind.

"What do you mean as far as you know? I would think if anyone knew what the state of his mission is, that would be you. Where is he? What is going on?"

"Sam should be okay. He's on the Moon right now. The far side to be exact."

"What?" Helen said, startled. "The last I heard, he's on an island off the coast of China! I figured they found more new microbe colonies next to some undersea volcanoes. What would Sam be doing on the Moon? Ms. Stern, just what the hell is going on?"

Trish sighed. "Helen, if I may call you that, Sam is on the Moon because during the mining project for the Lagrange Two Base, we found an artifact there. A big and very old one. The shareholders wanted a xenobiologist to look into it." She didn't think it was important to tell her Sam was not their first choice.

"An artifact? What do you mean? Like a sculpture or something?"

"No. More like a building actually, and we think it may house a mechanism of some sort. Our best guess it that it's about sixty-five million years old. In any case . . ."

Trish paused, noticing Helen had her hand in front of her mouth and her eyes were wide open. 'Oh. I'm sorry, I've been living with the knowledge of this for months and I guess I've completely forgotten learning about it can be quite a shock."

"How long has he been on the Moon?" Helen asked, taking her hand away from her mouth. Then it hit her. "Oh, he must be so excited! But is it safe? Who's running the operation?"

"The mission's run by the combined efforts of Starshield and the Chinese government." Trish rubbed her eyes with her hands. Her headache just did not want to go away. "They kept the discovery under wraps pending this first investigation by folks like your husband. We needed a true scientific opinion and analysis before announcing it to the world."

"Okay, but why are you calling me? And I'm sorry to say this, but you look terrible."

"Why, thank you. No, I'm sorry, I shouldn't have said that. I suppose I do look terrible. I certainly feel terrible. You see, I've been let go by Starshield. A misunderstanding really. But the security chief and his goons, well they were a little rougher with me than they should've been. It seems I'm still getting over that."

Helen thought Trish looked about ready to cry, "Oh, you poor thing! What kind of security people do they have who'd treat you like that? Did they hurt you? And why did they let you go? Sounds like it was sudden."

"Yes, maybe too sudden now that I think about it." Trish had drunk a stimulant and it was starting to take effect. "I was checking into some data and found files I routinely accessed were suddenly blocked. Then I tried to check my security level to no avail. I thought perhaps the system had a glitch and tried something to verify it. That was when the security chief let me know I had committed a violation, told me I was fired and had me removed from the building."

"How awful. It does sound like they were a little hasty given the circumstances."

"More than hasty. It was planned. I see that now. There was no way the chief could have gotten away with railroading me that quickly without some sort of prior approval. I worked with too many important people at Starshield. He would not have dared."

"I'm so sorry to hear that, but Ms. Stern, I don't see why you're calling me after all this. While I do sympathize with you, I'm not sure I'm in

121

any position to help you."

"I wasn't sure either. To tell you the truth, I was still quite confused when I contacted you. Whatever they hit me with really threw me for a loop. But I think I know now. Do you know what this is?" She held up a shiny object that looked like an old-fashioned memory stick.

"Some kind of portable data storage device?"

"Yes, it is. And I need to keep it somewhere safe. A place where nobody would guess where it is. Somehow, I think my subconscious mind knew I could trust you and had me contact you." She looked into Helen's eyes on the display. "I need your help, Mrs. Czerny."

Helen waited for Trish to continue.

"So, I'm thinking that, if you don't mind, I could ask you to hold this for me. It contains the records of the find on the Moon. After the way they moved me out of Starshield, I'm, well, a little concerned they might try to hide some of this."

"Ms. Stern, are you trying to say Sam is in some sort of danger?"

"No, no. At least I don't think so. But let's just say this thing has data that can kind of guarantee whoever might try to hide it would prefer not to, so to speak. Anyway. I think the last place anyone would look for it would be with you."

"You aren't setting me up with anything illegal, are you?" Helen sounded worried.

"No, I wouldn't do that. I trust you, Helen. And please call me Trish from now on." She looked straight into Helen's eyes again. "I'm going to make sure Sam is safe. Even if there are people at Starshield who are doing strange things. I promise you that."

Helen paused to think. With Sam involved, she was probably better off being in possession of the storage device. "Okay, I'll watch over your trinket. But have it sent to my office address at the university, care of Suzanne Marko, my assistant. She's on maternity leave right now so it'll come to me without leaving my name on any tracing documents."

Trish smiled, "I get the feeling I picked the right partner in crime."

'Wait a second," Helen frowned. "You just said there was nothing illegal about this."

"Oh, it's just a manner of speaking." Trish reassured her, "I didn't mean anything by it."

"Let's just hope you're telling me the truth," Helen said, wondering what she had gotten herself into and worried if Sam was indeed safe.

Chapter Thirty

Boris Yelenko wasn't happy. The application he loaded wasn't working the way he expected. Boris' hobby of antiquated programming techniques had given him a great deal of insight when it came to his work. Most of the people in his field were top-level strategic thinkers and had no real understanding of how machines worked. In fact, most of the design work when it came to basic electronics was now being done by machines. The last fifty years of binary code innovation had been machine driven because humans didn't waste time learning the basics anymore.

You could rely on machines to do the manufacturing and design at that level. And the machines had been doing a great job of it. Processing time and the cost of storage reduced at an accelerated pace since machines were given that function by their human creators.

But there were still a few hobbyists that played with 'code' at various levels. Some played with creating actual algorithms and processes down at the binary level. Or just above at the hexadecimal level. Boris was one of these.

He'd gotten some brand-new software from a fellow hobbyist at the University of Ekaterinburg, but it wouldn't load. He found spending his spare time fiddling with things like this not only sharpened his mind, but also soothed his nerves. Some people relaxed through meditation or music or sports. Boris liked working out mathematical puzzles.

Today, things were not working out as he liked. "Eto Pizdets! This is all screwed up!" he cursed. The software decoder he tested was working strangely. So, he decided to apply it to a known set of instructions and see if it came back with what was an expected result.

The problem was that it came back with a different set. Not errors or garbage as he would have expected if the thing was not working properly, but a different set. This made no sense to him and he decided to try another set from another part of the Moon project.

He chose to try it with some of the upgrade software loaded into the transporters. Amanda would have been surprised. Even though she'd been in charge of the design of the upgrade, almost all the code was written by the software itself. Boris figured unless she was also a hobbyist, she would never even be able to read the code.

The results came back as expected. Nothing looked unusual with this code. And there were no errors. He scratched his head and went back to the code that came up with strange results. It was the code that managed the aiming process for the mass launcher. He thought about it for a bit and decided he would try to figure out what the new code was trying to do.

The first thing he found was the code had an activation sequence connected to a different set of instructions than expected. This way of setting these launch codes to work was quite different. Try as he might to figure out what the method was for turning them on, it eluded him.

Boris wondered why someone would go to the trouble of having a special set of instructions placed in the launch code. And why make sure it was accessible only through a hidden process? He thought of contacting Lee Jin-Dao to see what he thought of it. But he decided he should first find out what the instructions behind the hidden access process were meant to do.

After almost an hour of work, he finally figured out what the instructions were designed to accomplish. "Bozhe Moy!" he said to himself as it became clear. The new software made future launches of payloads from the mass launcher all aim at the Earth itself.

Chapter Thirty-One

Protector Three Hundred and Four made a note in its memory that humans weren't good at dividing their attention between many tasks. It understood this from the analysis pulled together from the mass of data being broadcast from the planet.

In the last cycle of planetary rotation, it registered and stored an amazing amount of data. The planetary denizen's lack of security had been both a gift and a curse. P304's analytic systems were based on gathering and gleaning information from reticent sources. But these humans were bombarding it, and the rest of the galaxy, with a tremendous amount of data fired off in all directions at once.

For a short time, Protector Three Hundred and Four considered this might be a method expressly designed for hiding actual data. But after some consideration, it threw away that hypothesis. The costs of producing so much data just for the purposes of obfuscating would be horrendous. Such a constant broadcast, while perhaps good for hiding kernels of information, was in and of itself a loud announcement to the galaxy. It could not be part of any security plan that was aware of others in the area.

The only logical conclusion was that humans were unsuspecting there may be other intelligent life forms in the galaxy. Ones that might view them with malicious intent. With that regard, these humans were innocent, if not ignorant. It made them perhaps the naivest form of intelligence in the galaxy, at least based on the data P304 had in its memories. And being naïve made them helpless, unprotected.

This realization brought up another conundrum concerning human intelligence. All other forms of sentient life in the galaxy according to P304's storage had uniform opinions of the nature of reality in general. But these humans seemed to be completely divided. In fact, the cacophony of

126

opinions, both of a physical and speculative nature was extraordinary. Some species had been known to have two and, in one case, three divergent viewpoints. But humans held almost as many viewpoints as there were humans themselves. Extraordinary.

To top it off, the majority of them had a belief system involving supernatural beings with capabilities and powers outside of the rules of physics. The most interesting part was they always seemed to imagine these beings, as being human-like, even when they saw them as creators of all existence.

The variety of individual views did not prevent them from referring to each other's views in their communications. They disagreed; fought and argued. It was never clear which views were correct and which weren't. This made interpretations and understandings a challenging task for the Protector.

While awaiting the return of the humans, Protector worked on a strategy for what it would ask them to speed its learning. If some Saurian species intercepted the data the humans send, they would probably find it as convoluted as P304 had at first. The Protector determined it was a reasonable task for it to use all of its resources to determine whether this new species could be useful. Perhaps even enough to be made a part of the Saurian alliance. Or, finding the opposite, it would then make recommendations for the annihilation of the species.

It saw the integration of the decision software it embraced for its object detection system was complete. It connected to the module chosen due to its lack of current relevance. It began assessing the advantages gained from integration of the machine intelligence gotten from the transporter bot.

The first thing it noticed was the new decision process for the object detection system was running much, much faster. It was taking a great deal more data into account before deciding. The manner in which it was doing this did not strike the Protector as logical by any means. It allowed itself to consider perhaps its own notion of logic could be either faulty, or superseded by a superior notion. The idea that the primitive humans had a superior way of making decisions was one he stored for looking at in depth at a later time. It immediately launched its own inquiry into that, spinning off a separate consideration cycle.

It decided it would need to evaluate the new methodology by

applying it to another set of instructions. Something that was non-mandatory to its functioning. If that worked, it would decide whether it would adapt this networked decision-making module on a holistic scale.

As it considered which instructions set it would use as the next test, it received an emergency alert from one of its sensor arrays.

The message was coming from its long-distance object detection system, the same system on which it tested the new method. The data the detection system was sending seemed familiar. Although entirely unexpected, the probabilities it was accurate ran towards the infinitesimal.

As a matter of course, it ran diagnostics to check if the new methodologies test corrupted the systems. All systems were functioning normally. There was even some improvement in the modules having to do with motion and prediction of an object's direction.

This meant the data that set off the alarm was correct. Data indicated a new large object, heading straight at the Earth at great speed.

Chapter Thirty-Two

Fermi Crater Artifact
Far Side of the Moon

S am closed his eyes and rubbed them with the bottoms of his palms. The faceplate he wore did the actual rubbing but it felt as if his hands were actually touching his face. He yawned. The Protector had been showing him visual representations of historical data for a little over four and a half hours. He was as much in a state of shock as he was tired.

There were hundreds of thousands of spacefaring civilizations. There were alliances between many of them and war between others. These were things he had never even dreamed were possible—stuff you saw on fantasy shows.

Most surprising of all was the fact that almost all intelligent life was either lizards or insects. The insects tended toward hive minds, but there were exceptions of all sorts. The lizards built civilizations that all seemed to be a lot closer to the human experience, at least in some ways. It was more than his brain could store in such a short time.

When he began questioning the Protector, Sam asked it basic questions about the nature of organic life. P304 had little information about that. It was not exactly designed as a storehouse of scientific data. Unless that information was pertinent to interplanetary warfare.

That realization sent chills down Sam's spine.

It was about an hour into the session when Sam learned of the Protector's real purpose and why it was located on their Moon. The wars in the galaxy were terrible. Sam learned more than sixteen thousand planets with sentient life had been destroyed. The size and scope of the slaughter was staggering.

Sam knew that Earth had gone through several extinction events. He always considered that, while life seemed to be resilient, the universe was a dangerous place. But he'd always imagined the extinctions had been unhappy accidents. The idea that war wiped out so many worlds had taken him a while to absorb.

Now he realized his exhaustion was as much emotional as it was coming from processing all this information. He requested a sip of liquid from his suit and then remembered he could augment the liquid with caffeine and taurine.

The drink revived his senses and he went back to querying the Protector. "So, tell me more about how all sentient life is either Saurian, as you call them, or Scarab. Are there no other forms? No other simians or humans?"

"There is no indication in my data of any other forms related to humans. The only form resembling mammalian life was an aquatic species that practiced internalized egg gestation."

"Was?"

"They were exterminated by the Scarabs more than eighty-five million years ago."

"These Scarabs sound quite vicious."

"My data does not describe them as being emotional in their actions. They are just efficient once they determine a species is an undesirable element from their point of view."

Sam shook his head sadly. "And it was they who sent the asteroid you were meant to protect against, the one we call the 'Dinosaur Killer'?"

"That is the conclusion I have come to, given the information available."

Sam decided learning more about the Protector's function was a good path for getting the most data. "So, tell me how you were to protect the Earth against this asteroid?"

Protector Three Hundred and Four considered the request. The information Sam was looking for was rated as militarily sensitive in its data banks. But it weighed that against the fact that it knew there was another asteroid whose collision with Earth was imminent. It decided sharing the data created no danger to its creators or other Saurians.

"I have the ability to detect incoming objects from a great distance. Given enough lead time, I have methods I can deploy to change the trajectory of the object."

"And these methods did not work sixty-five million years ago?"

"No, they were ineffective. The asteroid that came in had

technology that cloaked it from my targeting systems. When I attempted to act, I was not able to determine where it was. That compromised my capacity to change its trajectory and I failed to protect the planet."

"So, the Scarabs somehow had information related to the defense systems of a Protector and were able to circumvent it."

After a short pause, the smooth voice said, "That is a probable conclusion."

"What other conclusions are there?"

"That the Scarabs were not the ones who had sent the asteroid."

Sam was startled by the idea. "Have there been instances of Saurians destroying Saurian planets?"

The Protector responded, "I have no record of that occurring at any time, but lack of a record does not make something impossible. There may be another possibility—that the asteroid came from a life-form neither Saurian nor Scarab."

"Earlier, you said all sentient species capable of interplanetary travel are either Saurian or Scarab in origin," Sam said, frowning.

"The lack of a record does not make something impossible," replied the voice of the Protector.

Sam considered this. Perhaps there were other mammalians in the galaxy. If they followed the crazy destructive logic of the Saurian/Scarab wars, they might have been the ones who killed off the dinosaurs to allow mammals to develop. The galaxy was becoming a stranger place by the minute.

"Can you show me a three-dimensional display of the galaxy as you know it?" Sam asked.

The image he requested appeared—a beautiful multicolored galaxy floating in the middle of the room.

"Now please show me where Saurian life is populating the galaxy and Scarab life as well. Make sure I can differentiate between the two."

The result was a blue and yellow dotted map that lit up one arc of the galaxy's spirals. Sam wondered if this was because of lack of data or if the sentient life in the galaxy was actually localized in this manner. He queried the Protector and received the equivalent of a shrug from the Artificial Intelligence. "I do not have data indicating sentient life in other portions of the galaxy."

Sam did make note the display was still showing so many worlds he couldn't even begin to count them. There may have been well over a million as far as he could tell.

"Can you magnify to show only the populated areas of the galaxy?" The effect was so rapid Sam almost wanted to grab something to keep from falling over. The arc was even more beautiful and Sam could see some of the stars were twinkling.

He decided to get some more detail. "How old is this view?" he asked.

"The last time I had a data update was two thousand solar rotations of the planet before the impact."

"Years," Sam explained. "We call solar rotations of the planet 'years'. It will make communications faster if we use the same terms for measurements of things like time and distance."

There was a pause and the Protector's voice said, "I have found references and descriptions of many of your measurements. I will use them in future communications."

Sam reminded himself the Protector always took his requests seriously. Sometimes that was practical, but sometimes the use of expressions and idioms could lead to unwanted results.

"Can you show me the pace of discovery of the sentient worlds over time, beginning with the second one? Please compress time so the display can end only two minutes after it begins."

It took a few seconds before the display ran. Sam watched with fascination as the first two yellow worlds stayed alone for almost fifteen seconds. Then a third world appeared followed by the first blue world not far from it. The third yellow world disappeared and four more blue worlds appeared. What followed was a rapid symphony of new yellow and blue worlds appearing and disappearing. Then some of the yellow worlds became blue and shortly after that some of the blue worlds became yellow. A few of them alternated and eventually winked out.

Finally, the arc took shape and came to a stop. The scale and length of the war was incredible. And it was clear to see the arc grew from a small line and spread, with most of the growth happening in the last ten seconds of the display.

"What is the period in real time you have displayed?"

"From three hundred and thirty-four million, four hundred and four thousand years to sixty-five million, seven hundred and twenty-two thousand years ago. Rounded to a thousand years," the Protector informed.

"Can you show me where Earth is?" Sam was almost afraid to ask.

A red dot appeared on the display right in the middle of where the arc had been surging towards in its growth.

"This was sixty-five million years ago?" Sam asked.

"Sixty-five million, seven hundred and twenty thousand years ago," responded Protector Three Hundred and Four.

Sam wondered about the Protector's ability to project concepts into the future. He decided to ask. "Would you be able to display a projection of most likely future outcomes from through today?"

There was a long pause, almost a minute before the Protector replied. "I have four outcomes that have almost equal possibilities. Although one does have a somewhat greater possibility than the others."

"Please display the most possible outcome first."

Sam watched as the arc began to grow again. He saw the Earth's light go out. Then the entire arc's growth slowed, both for the Saurian worlds and the Scarab ones. Bit by bit, the arc receded until it was no larger than seventy percent of what it had been at its greatest phase.

"What happened?" Sam asked.

It was another moment before the voice came back. "Greatest probability is that the Protector projects failed. After a time, the idea of protection was abandoned. This led to a greater level of destruction of worlds. After a time, there is a great likelihood the wars will end. Would you like the forward display for that?"

Sam got the feeling he would not like to see what would happen, but he agreed nonetheless. "Show me."

The display began to move forward again. More and more worlds started winking out. First yellow ones, then blue ones and then both. After about twenty seconds all that remained of the arc was two smallish blobs of a dozen worlds each one blue and one yellow. Each was at the extreme ends of what had been the arc and far from each other.

"How sad," Sam said.

"I have not included the discovery of other species such as humans. The possibilities become so extensive that none exceed a probability over four percent." The Protector's voice was as soft and smooth as ever, but it still sounded ominous to Sam.

Chapter Thirty-Three

Imperial Beach
San Diego, California

Trish Stern looked at her reflection in the mirror and grimaced. She never imagined she would one day be disguising herself like some type of fugitive. But she knew they would come looking for her sooner or later. Chief deKumpf was not someone who would simply let go.

But neither was Trish. A less proud person would have tried to go off and build another career. Or find a job at some competitor. The way they let her go meant a good lawyer could argue her non-compete clause in her Starshield contract was meaningless.

There had been enough meetings at Starshield attended by Trish that she knew the company did not rely on the justice system. The meetings often included executives who were open, even glib, about the methods they used to manipulate politicians and judges. There had been one meeting when she understood a rival executive was the victim of a too convenient boating accident. A few weeks later, Starshield swallowed up that executive's company.

She looked in the mirror and adjusted the curly black wig again. It itched, but there wasn't anything she could do about that. She also touched up the foundation that was much darker than her usual skin tone. Finally, she popped in the cheap contact lenses she picked up at the beauty supply store. They stung her eyes and she blinked back tears. Her vision was slightly blurry. The lenses would take some getting used to. The clothes she put on were standard minimum class fare, down to the flat disposable slippers so unlike anything she ever wore.

Satisfied she didn't look anything at all like her former self, she stepped out of the room she rented for the day and locked the door behind her.

It had been years since she used public transportation and she was a little taken aback by how dull and bland most of the people looked. The automation of manufacturing put a lot of the former working class into category of permanently unemployed. While some enjoyed lives of simple, luxury-free leisure, there were still a lot who took on illegal trades and occupations. It was hard to tell them apart since many wore the same outfit she did, although a few of them added decorations or drawings on their coveralls. Every year, the government supplied uniforms to any that wanted them. How they managed to make orange look so bland and cheerless was anybody's guess.

After changing from one transporter to another, she finally arrived at a public info center.

The last time she used a center like this was about as long as it had been since she last used the public transport system. She had not expected much privacy, but the proximity between one person and another made privacy a moot point all together. Most of the users were pressed side by side facing wide screens with little squares identified before each of them. With the average person relying on no more than the guaranteed minimum income, few made the investment to have personal comm devices. The result was crowded Comm Centers like this one. Trish shook aside the idea this might be what she faced for the rest of her life.

She waited until she saw someone walk away from one and ran up to it. After tapping on it she got a message asking her for a sign-in key. This was why she had come to this place. Facial recognition sign-ins had been around for some time, but public locations were too cheap to buy the software. Trish hesitated. She was sure if she accessed her Starshield account they would notice it right away. It would probably shut off and start an auto trace if she tried to use it.

She spent the money to set up a private account long ago, but suspected deKumpf would have some way of watching that as well. She was berating herself for not thinking this part through when someone tapped her shoulder. She spun around lifting her arms instinctively to defend herself, only to see an old African-American woman who looked as alarmed as she was.

"Oh, I'm so sorry," Trish started to apologize when the woman interrupted her in a clear strong voice.

"Trish Stern, you look like you need access." Her voice had the slightest trace of a New York accent.

Trish stepped back, wondering if this was one of deKumpf's agents, wondering if she should try to run.

"Huh? Who are you? And how do you know ..." Trish stopped herself before confirming who she was to this stranger. "I mean, that I need access?"

"Well, Trish Stern, why else would you be here?" The old woman shook her head as she spoke.

"You didn't answer my first question. Who are you?" Trish hissed, looking around for the exits and getting ready to run.

"I suppose I'm better than you at disguising myself," the little old lady with the young voice responded. "You've known me as Louise Winston."

Trish went over the name in her mind suddenly remembering. Louise Winston had been on the Starshield payroll as a consultant several years earlier. She worked for a company called Data Organics Inc. Trish used her services to break into the research lab of an Israeli weapons manufacturer. Louise helped determine exactly how far along they were on their drone construction plans. The data helped Trish negotiate a deal far better than what she would have normally gotten. The Louise Winston she remembered was a short young woman with bright eyes, high energy and a quick mind. Trish had appreciated her work and gave her a large bonus well beyond what the contract called for.

"I hate to say this, but the years have not been kind to you," Trish regained her composure enough to resume her normal demeanor.

Louise laughed. The vibrant sound seemed odd coming from an old crone. "Seems to me times are putting you through something that can age you as well. So, am I right? You looking for access?"

Trish considered her options. This woman might have been hired to find her or spy on her. After all, how had she found her? Trish decided the best thing to do was ask outright.

"How is it you are here at the same time as I am?"

"I was just finishing up with a client when I turned around and saw you there. You look about as discreet as a cat at a dog show. Oh, okay, fuck it! I'm a lousy liar. To tell you the truth, I got an email from your former employer. Kind of an APB. They seem to be very eager to find you. I knew your office was in Coronado and I figured you'd show up in San Diego sooner or later. I knew you'd need access to a computer, so I've been checking places out. I got lucky. You are either in deep shit, lady, or at least think you are. Is that why you are looking for access? 'Cause if it is, this is no place for you to find it."

Out of options, Trish decided she needed to trust this woman. "Yes, can you supply it?"

"Anything can be had for the right price and under the right conditions. I seem to remember you've been generous in the past. Would you be inclined to be generous in the future as well?" Louise smiled. Her straight, white teeth looked out of place in her wrinkled mouth.

Over her years at Starshield, Trish managed to save up a fair bit of money, but she also knew most of it was in accounts she had no way of getting into without connecting electronically.

"I need access to get to funds, but I do have funds once I have access."

"Okay, we can check on that, too. Wait here for three minutes, then come out of the left entrance over there." She aimed her gaze to show the direction. "I'll take you to a place where we can get you hooked up."

The little old lady stooped a little lower and shuffled off as Trish turned back to the display and pretended to tap at it for three minutes.

She stepped away; conscious there might be someone watching what she was doing. She wandered about, looking at the promotional displays, edging herself toward the left exit.

After a few more minutes she finally stepped out into the street.

She looked left and right, not seeing the old lady until someone pulled at her elbow.

"Why did you take so long?" Louise Winston whispered angrily.

"I was making sure I wasn't followed."

"Followed?" Winston's voice registered alarm. "Has someone been following you lately?"

"I'm not sure. But I wanted to be safe."

"Trish Stern, I think there's a lot you need to learn about being safe. Now follow me and don't get lost."

The little woman took off, walking at a pace that looked far too rapid for her age.

She turned the corner and they walked three blocks before she went into a doorway, pushing an unlocked door. After they stepped in, Louise pressed the door shut and pulled up her sleeve to reveal a bracelet with a few buttons on it. She pushed two of the buttons twice before saying, "Good. All sealed. We're safe here for now."

Leading Trish down a hallway, she turned into a doorway she sealed the same way she had the other one. "I lock doors with powerful electromagnets. The bracelet turns them off when approached from the outside. It makes them easy for me to open quickly and hard for others."

The space surprised Trish. It looked like a cross between a home and a workplace. One corner had a frumpy looking bed with a duvet scrunched up against the wall and a couple of tired looking pillows. The other side of the room had a half-galley kitchen with a sink so small Trish couldn't imagine more than one soup bowl in it. The rest of the place was machinery, displays and tools. Some were antiques and others looking like nothing Trish had ever seen. They were strewn atop a huge square table in the middle. There was even a police surveillance camera lying in pieces next to a half-eaten box of takeout food. Trish suspected possession of one of the cameras, let alone having taken it apart, was a felony.

"What is this place?" she asked, mesmerized by the visual cacophony.

"Welcome to my office. Well, one of my offices. I have a few places like this. This one is the headquarters for my worldwide conglomerate Data Organics, Inc." Louise grabbed the top of her forehead and proceeded to pull her latex face off. This revealed the young woman Trish met a few years earlier in Starshield's offices.

"This? No way. Starshield's procurement team would never have hired a company without vetting it completely."

"Yeah, well like most companies, they do all their research online. And online, my company looks very impressive. Anyway, they got what they needed from me, so why should I have a white tower office that has bullshit security and a high rent to boot? Although I do know how to rent one of those for a meeting when I need to. This place works for me. Everything I need is right here. Now let's see about getting you some access. Come on, sit down." She tapped the spot next to her on a padded bench along one end of the table.

"Wait, before we do anything else, tell me how it is that you knew where to find me. Seems like an all too random act of kindness."

The question was met with a blank stare for a moment and then Louise said, "You have your Starshield key?"

Trish fished out her spare key. DeKumpf's goons had taken her original one.

Louise held her palm out and accepted the key. She took a small device off of the table and waved it over the key. A small black dot fell out of the key. Louise smiled. "World's smallest GPS device. At least I like to think so. Never patented it."

"You, you bugged me!"

"Don't feel so special, honey. I do it to all my clients. Comes in handy more often than not."

Louise pushed away some of the stuff on the table and Trish realized the entire surface was a large display. Louise tapped a few rhythmic sequences and then outlined a shape establishing a working area. Within the area, she first called up a suite of financial tools and looked at Trish. "Don't worry, I have security levels that companies like yours never even dreamed of. Trust me."

Trish suspected Chief deKumpf spent a lot of his time dreaming about new security methods, but she decided to trust Louise. She knew she was out of options. She selected the application she usually used and began to tap her ID code in when Louise grabbed her wrist.

"Hold on, we're going in the back way." She handed Trish some paper and a wooden stick with a dark point. "Write your code on this."

"Is this a pencil?" Trish asked, looking at the stick. "I saw one in a museum once. Where'd you get it?"

She had a tough time remembering her tapping sequence without the use of her fingers' muscle memory. Eventually she got it right. "What difference does it make if it's me or you tapping it in?"

"Neither of us is going to tap it in. Watch and learn." Louise called up an application designed to help manufacturing robots learn new tasks. She ran another application she called a 'masking protocol generator'. Then she took a small camera and placed it a few inches above the piece of paper.

Trish saw her account open up on the display, showing her transactions over the last few weeks. Next to it was a glowing red box with the words, ACCOUNT UNDER SURVEILANCE in bright yellow letters.

"What is this? I've never seen anything like that before."

"We're looking at your account through the finance systems maintenance tool. In fact, a robot that manufactures microwave ovens is looking at it, not us. Well, one we control but they'll never find how we got that control.

"Okay, now we'll run a maintenance test. The account is going to transfer a sum to a test account. The operation is going to leave all the money in your account. But when we close it off, the amount will move to another account and the test account will show that it's been cleared as well. Because it's a maintenance operation, it shouldn't register to the surveillance app. Simple, right?" Louise grinned.

"I've heard of people claiming money has disappeared from their accounts," Trish said. "Never large amounts but the finance companies always claim it can't be so. They say the account holders had miscalculated their transactions."

Louise's grin got even wider. "Well, you never know how that happens. So, how much are we talking about? Write it down."

Trish wrote down an amount that came to more than three months of her salary. She knew she had a lot more than that in her account. But she also remembered what the bonus she gave Louise was, and this was three times that amount.

Louise looked at it and whistled a long, stretched note. "Yeah, I was right. You're still generous."

She moved the camera over the paper and then leaned over the display. Trish saw the amount in question move from her account with a blue box labeled TEST TRANSACTION over it. Then Louise moved a few items across on her application and the finance window closed.

"Okay," she said. "Now let's go and pick up the cash."

"Cash?" Trish hadn't used cash in years. It was something one took on vacation to remote places or used only by criminal elements who did not want to be tracked.

"Yeah, I like cash, it's almost invisible. And anyway, I think you're going to need some. If there's a watch on your account, then either the Guv is looking for you or even worse, people who can get the Guv to do their bidding."

"Wait," Trish grabbed Louise's arm, "Why are you doing this? Why are you helping me?"

Louise Winston shrugged. "I don't know. A long time ago I realized I could do a lot of things most people couldn't. Things the Guv doesn't want people to do. I could be living a great life on some island somewhere. Maybe someday I will. In the meantime, I like being a kind of good fairy. It makes life challenging and fun." She grinned again and began to put her disguise back on.

      They were out the door before Trish realized she hadn't gotten the access she came looking for.

Chapter Thirty-Four

Starshield-Shackleton HQ
Penobscot Bay, Maine

Mark Slaton looked into the display and met the shiny black eyes of Chairman Qi. "Chairman Qi, I believe we're arriving at a time when the discussion we began so many years ago will enter a decisive phase."

"Yes, I've been expecting this. Things are in place on my end." The chairman did not trust this American, even if he'd been instrumental in getting the man into his current position. It may even have been because of the man's role that he did not trust him. He traveled a long path with this Slaton person. He wondered, for a last time, if it wasn't wiser to turn around and let China live a life of quiet prosperity under the American military shadow.

But he knew that was a fool's paradise. The Americans would eventually look at China's increased riches and at their own economic decline. And they would find a way to take that wealth away from China. Such was the way of the world. It was up to China to fight off the stripping of their wealth by planning ahead. 'Failing to plan is planning to fail', said an old Chinese proverb.

History shows it always happens that way and history is always written by the winners. And China planned on being on the winning side. Theirs would be a glorious future.

"Chairman Qi, I wouldn't be speaking about the next phase if I weren't ready on my end," Slaton said firmly. "When the time comes for you to take the high ground, American weapons will have a large and varied set of failures. Some will be attributed to issues with the quality of the materials we supply them. But I've been working to make them understand financial restrictions placed on us are the leading cause of equipment problems. Others that fail will wind up self-destructing. They will not be traceable and therefore should be no problem. I'm more concerned about how we'll manage the new world after the event."

Taking a moment to reflect, Chairman Qi paused. "I've prepared a set of statements to be distributed to several countries after the event. The United Nations will be alerted. But everything hinges on the attack you will precipitate. I've made certain the three targets will include enough victims that the world will react with horror at this American aggression."

Mark Slaton finally smiled, his angular, bony face making Qi think of a skull, "And with complete understanding of your response. Disarming the Americans will seem like a charitable act on your part."

"Slaton, the only charity is what you'll be receiving. I understand in this new world, you'll be selling weapons technology hand over fist to many new buyers. Remember our agreement. China will always be the power that must remain inviolate. None of your weapons must ever target the People's Republic."

Slaton nodded, taking a drag on his vaper. "I'm no fool, Chairman. My goal has never been the replacement of peace with war. Just changing from stagnant American peace to a more profitable Chinese peace. We both know if this doesn't occur, the Americans will eventually attack China anyway. We're just making sure the transition is as non-disruptive as possible. After all, it has always been China's destiny, has it not?"

Qi was certain Slaton was trying to flatter him by mentioning the slogan he used to get the members of the party to back him for the chairmanship. That, along with Slaton's work at removing and replacing some of those members, was what gave him this position in history. The chairman couldn't help but wonder what Slaton's next steps would be, and if he would be working to remove the chairman himself. But he knew Slaton would be the one who was going to be surprised.

"Yes, it has always been our destiny," the chairman agreed. "China was built on unification. The logical next step is for China to unify a greater part of the world. The resulting prosperity will be understood, even by the people living in America."

"Some of us understand it already, Chairman Qi." Slaton smiled again and bowed his head respectfully.

The chairman nodded in return. "I'm certain more will. All the work we've done over the last few years teaching Chinese history to the rest of the world should help."

Slaton said nothing. He thought propaganda efforts the Chinese made were naive and clumsy at best. They didn't appreciate the nuances of other cultures. The problem was not to teach other cultures about Chinese history. It was the failure of teaching the Chinese to understand how deeply others had their own history embedded into their own cultures. Nations who isolated their populace by telling only their own history always had a disadvantage in the long run. A disadvantage the Americans were about to learn. Slaton was an American, having been born in Maine, but he had never felt himself to be a citizen of any country at all.

Qi continued. "We need to coordinate these events. I have heard we're ready with the riposte on our end. The weapons have been tested, albeit on short-ranged targets. Still, we're confident we can hit the targets within a reasonable margin of error."

"Reasonable? Chairman, I'll need some of the targets to be one hundred percent destroyed. We can't leave any trace of our activities in some of the satellites." Slaton was uncharacteristically apprehensive.

"Don't worry, we'll be firing a very large amount of ballistics. Only an impressive and thorough showing will be effective. If we don't make the Americans understand they have no interest in pursuing the conflict, then we won't have done our job. I'm sure you see the wisdom in that."

"I agree, Chairman. The American president is a fool and a puppet. But there are others who will need to be convinced. Remember, Chairman Qi, although you and I have worked on this project together for some time, I was already working on it before we were ever in touch."

As was I, the chairman thought to himself. As was I.

Slaton waved at the display and saw the connection go dead. He took out another charge, reloaded his vaper and took the time to enjoy the peaty flavor of the drug. The effect was rapid. He felt the physical relaxation combined with the mental acuity the drug brought quickly enter his system. Like an old friend.

He knew there was a lot of coordination to get this new little war started and he wanted to make sure he had the proper state of mind for it.

Tapping his display, he brought up a list of seventy-two names. He'd been working on this list for more than eleven years. He tapped his display once again. This time, he connected to an office in the Pentagon. The stern gray-haired face that greeted him was that of the head of Pentagon Command.

Slaton nodded. When he received a nod in return, he cut off the connection and went to the next name on his list.

Chapter Thirty-Five

Fermi Crater Artifact
Far Side of the Moon

Seated in the center of the room, Amanda Won gave Pierre Pacquelier a wide-eyed look. He raised one eyebrow and continued to question P304, "Have you been in touch with any of the other Protectors?"

"We are not mobile and far from each other. There is no way we can touch." The smooth steady voice was sometimes unnerving in its lack of emotion.

"No." Pierre slapped his leg and laughed, "I mean, is there communications between the Protectors?"

There was a pause of about three seconds before an answer came, "For a long time, there was nothing. Just me alone. But I received a message recently."

Amanda sat up. She'd been finding Pierre's line of questioning a little boring until now. "How recently? And who was it from?"

"I received the message just seven of your hours ago. It is identifying itself as coming from my creator's descendants."

"Your creators have contacted you? That's fantastic! They're still around? What did they say?" Amanda was excited by this and wondered if Sam received the same information in his interview with the Protector.

"They said goodbye."

"Huh? What do you mean goodbye?" Pierre noticed how cute Amanda looked when she was puzzled.

"A message indicating a separation. Often used when departing. The opposite of a greeting."

Standing up impatiently, Amanda put her hands on her hips and sighed. "Protector, I know what a goodbye means, you . . . you . . . you . . . machine! What I want to know is why they would say that?"

"I have been considering that as well. Several possibilities come up.

They may be leaving the galaxy. They may have decided they will never again communicate with me, or most likely based on my calculations I will soon cease to be."

Pierre stood up as well. "Wait, are your energy reserves that low?"

"My reserves would permit me to function at the current level of consumption for another seventy-four years."

"That doesn't seem so impending," Amanda said, shaking her head.

"On the contrary, Amanda," Pierre said. "If you consider more than sixty-five million years, that isn't much time left in comparison. A wink in a lifetime."

"Oh." Amanda suddenly felt sorry for P304 even though it was just a machine. "That does make it seem rather sudden."

"Have you received any other messages?" Pierre asked.

This time, the delay was almost a full minute before the voice spoke again. Pierre and Amanda were giving each other looks as they both began to wonder why a response was taking so long. "Yes, shortly after the previous message I received another one."

"And what did this message say?" Pierre asked.

"It said, "Defend yourself – you are needed," the Protector replied. The voice suddenly sounded a little sad.

"Why would your creators send you a message like that after sending you a message that said goodbye?" Amanda wondered.

"The second message did not come from my creators."

It was Pierre's turn to be perplexed, "Then who sent you a message telling you to defend yourself?"

"The second message identified itself as another Protector."

Pierre's jaw dropped, "Then Protectors do communicate with each other? How long have you been communicating with them?"

"I have never communicated with them. This is the first time I have received a message from another Protector."

Amanda interrupted, "Just what does it want you to protect yourself from? What else did it tell you?"

The peaceful voice was at odds with the content of its message, "There is a large asteroid heading toward your planet and its Moon."

The two sat in stunned silence. Finally, Amanda said, "We should find Sam and talk to him about this. Then we need to see the major."

Chapter Thirty-Six

G eneral Sun blinked as a stream of sweat rolled off of the top of his head and sped up into his left eye. "Yes, Chairman Qi. Thank you for this task. I'll send the data to Major Zhang. I'm certain he'll perform exactly as we expect him to."

"Yes, See to it. This is an important moment, Sun. We mustn't waver." The chairman disappeared as Sun's screen went blue.

Sun hesitated, then waved at the screen. He knew his orders were to just send the data along to Zhang, but his curiosity got the best of him. He had to know what the data was. Although he was the chairman's right hand for nearly a generation, he had been excluded from this project. Or at least from the core of the project, since all Qi asked of him was to make certain whoever was on the Moon Base would be loyal to the core.

It wasn't the first time Sun looked into data files belonging to the chairman. Not by a long shot. He'd been doing it for quite some time. He did so; always telling himself it was because he could better serve the man who raised him as his protégé. And it had always been like that. There was no reason for him to see it any other way.

He opened the file and unlocked the encryption key using the chairman's password. The chairman had become predictive in his password use over the years and Sun thought he knew them all.

After he made himself a copy he sealed it with his own password and resealed the original file, erasing any trace showing it had been opened. Then he called up the program that would send the file in a second encrypted format on to Zhang. It was encoded and embedded into some of the daily data feeds running between the Moon Base and Launch Station Headquarters.

Having taken care of sending the file, he opened the copy and scrutinized its contents. Within a minute of reading it, he saw it was not what he was looking for. The file contained a rather standard and dull looking inventory report. The kind of report the chairman had not looked at in more than thirty years. His time was far too valuable for such trivialities.

Sun knew there had to be an 'Easter egg'—a hidden bit of information—somewhere in the content. He began the laborious task of trying to figure out which of the usual methods the chairman deployed in hiding the data. After forty-five minutes and enough sweat to thoroughly soak his tight shirt collar, he was ready to throw his hands up in the air. He was no closer to finding the hidden data than he was when he started.

He scratched his gleaming pate and wondered. Perhaps he was going at it all wrong. What if there was no Easter egg? What if the data was hidden in plain sight? He knew of one person, or rather, one service that might be able to help him.

For several years, he'd been using an online outfit called Voynich-Gillogli. Like most of the best services offering data cracking, they tended to be shy about who they really were. Sun was fortunate enough to have had a former associate introduce them to him. The man who introduced them disappeared a few weeks later under mysterious circumstances. The general always harbored a secret suspicion that Voynich-Gillogli had a hand in the disappearance. He'd made a point of being certain he always paid them what they requested. It was never too much, and he was always prompt with the payments. But he made it a point to never introduce them to anyone. His life might depend on it.

He raised the connection to the service and saw it disconnect immediately. A few seconds later his screen announced an incoming encrypted call. The face on the other end wore a black balaclava and sat behind what looked like frosted ice. Sun was used to their rather unusual methods when it came to communicating. He knew there were systems that could infer infrared readings from regular video, which might be the reason for the ice pane. In any case, they never looked the same way twice when they called him back.

"General Sun." The voice was an harmonic combination of several different voices and different tones making the effect otherworldly. "We are pleased to hear from you once again."

"I have a new task. A simple one I think, but an urgent one. I have a file which I think holds hidden data, and I need to be able to access it in a readable format as soon as possible."

"An urgent task will require a premium. Only a small one. It's more a matter of principle than effort." The strange voice combination sounded amused.

The general pulled a tissue from a box on his desk and wiped his brow with it. "I can process the payment now. An extra ten percent will suffice?"

"We prefer an extra twenty percent, if you don't mind. Responding urgently means we may need to apologize to others for our delay, depending on the work you require."

General Sun called up the special application he used for this purpose. It requested both a series of passwords and a retina scan. He peered unblinking into the camera for the two seconds required. The application requested a number. It did not need to ask which account was paying nor which was receiving. That was built into the application when the decryption firm supplied it.

After his approval, the application closed and he found himself face to face with the mask behind the ice again.

"We have received the payment," the choral of voices confirmed. "Please bring up the file now."

He brought up his version. After a moment, the voices said, "This is a copy. Not an original file. Are you certain the copy is faithful?"

It disturbed Sun that it had been so easy for them to detect he'd made a copy. "Yes, it's identical. I made it myself."

"The locking mechanism is not the original. You added your own. Let's see if that plays with the integrity of the data."

The display shifted into images that looked something like a map of a circuit seen through a kaleidoscope. It came to a sudden stop and a series of number sets began running across his display.

The multiple voices said, "I am storing this on your display. These are sets of five number values. The first four seem to be coordinates. Some are on Earth, others are not. But near enough."

That was surprising to General Sun. He thought there would be some instructions explaining what needed doing. He didn't expect coordinates. This meant the instructions were relayed previously or built into some system just waiting for the coordinates.

"Thank you." Sun said. "As usual. I expect you to destroy the data on your end and never refer to it in any communication."

The strange voice sounded a little offended. "Of course. As usual. Oh, and one other thing."

"Yes?" Sun did not expect they had something to add. It was not typical for them to do so.

"We recommend you avoid those coordinates until you're certain what they pertain to. The fifth number in each set seems to be a timed sequence. The times indicate a series of events that occur in short order."

"Wait," Sun was intrigued, "What more can you tell me?"

"That is all we can infer from the data at hand. Good day, General." The display went blue.

Chapter Thirty-Seven

Crew Quarters
Fermi Crater

Major Zhang hated having his attention divided. But he could not help the fact that Czerny, Pacquelier and Won stepped into his office space just a few seconds after an encrypted message from General Sun had arrived.

He was tempted to throw them out, but did not want to make them suspicious. They seemed so animated about something, and he did not want them to think he was ignoring them.

"Please, please, slow down. I can't listen to three people speaking over each other," the major pleaded. "So, one at a time. Mr. Czerny, please tell me what this is all about."

Czerny waited until the other two quieted before speaking. "We have learned a great deal from Protector Three Oh Four. That's the name the Artificial Intelligence within the artifact calls itself. The part of the galaxy we reside in is well inhabited and has been at war for more than one hundred million years."

"What?" the major interrupted Sam." Don't be absurd, there can't have been intelligent life for that long."

"According to the Protector, there has." Sam countered. "And much of it is involved in what looks like a never-ending interstellar war. Our planet was already the victim of that war once, when the 'Dinosaur Killer' asteroid struck us. That was no accident. It was specifically targeted at our planet."

"I find that hard to believe," Major Zhang said. He was aware time was ticking and he was not responding to General Sun's message while he had these people in his office. "There was no civilization on this planet. Humans, let alone mammals had not even developed."

"Well, technically there were mammals back then. They just weren't the dominant species." Sam replied. "In any case, the war is mostly between dinosaur type species and scarab type species. It seems sentient mammals are an anomaly."

The major shook his head. This was beginning to sound more like fantasy by the moment. "I'd be glad to discuss this a little later, but I have some urgent business to attend to right now. Can we reconvene about this tomorrow morning?"

Pacquelier, who had been fidgeting in his spot finally blurted out, "There's an asteroid headed this way! Another big one! This could be another extinction event, damn it! And you want to push this off until tomorrow?"

The general was taken aback. He never liked the Frenchman's brash attitude and considered this latest outburst just another one of his annoying diatribes.

"Mr. Pacquelier, making outrageous statements is not how you're going to get my attention or my time. Quite the opposite. Now, I have things I must attend to. I have a half an hour open tomorrow morning at 7:30. If you choose to be here at that time, I'll take the time to listen to what this is all about. Until then, I bid you goodbye and request all three of you leave while I take care of more pressing matters. You are dismissed." He stood up and pointed to the door.

The three of them looked stunned, but one after the other, they stood and walked out of his office.

Finally free of them, Zhang sat down and called up the message from General Sun on his display.

The message was rather cryptic. All it said was ATTACHED IS A FILE THE CHAIRMAN ASKED ME TO FORWARD TO YOU. I TAKE IT YOU KNOW WHAT TO DO WITH IT.

Zhang knew exactly what to do, but he had no clue what it was for. Before leaving the base on the Chinese island, he received a set of instructions related to the file. He was to take the file and place it in a particular folder only he, as mission commander, had access to. Then he was to launch a specific application that would make use of the folder.

He located the folder and moved the file to the proper place. Then he went looking for the application. It was in a high security area of the operations command module. He had to go through several levels of passwords and validations to be able to get to it.

When he was finally able to access it, he activated it as per the instructions he received. He expected some type of reaction from the application, but it simply logged him off and he found himself facing a blank display.

As he pondered this, he received a call request from Lee Jin-Dao. He tabled the request, sending back a message that he was busy and would respond later.

He decided to activate all his system monitors to see what was going on at the base when he got another call from Lee, one labeled urgent. He responded.

"What is it?" the major was in a hurry.

"What the fuck is going on?" Lee had the wide-eyed look of someone who was panic-stricken.

The major suddenly knew why Lee was in such a state. His system monitors were showing the ballistic system was firing rocks off of the Moon without any of the normal warnings. The major called up the tracking display to see why there would be such a sudden firing of rocks at the Lagrange Point. The display laid out multicolored lines over a view of the Moon and Lagrange Station. The lines trailed off of the display and then he saw them zoom out rapidly as their trajectory was calculated. That was when he saw they were not sent to the new space station. These rocks were all aimed at the Earth.

Chapter Thirty-Eight

Chang'e 3 Base
Maglev Launcher

"What the fuck is going on?" Lee Jin-Dao stared at the image of Major Zhang on his display. The mass driver was moving at a faster rate than he'd ever seen. The bots were loading successive buckets and firing them off at a pace of one per minute and the controls had him locked out. The best he could do was to try and see where they were sending the payloads.

Boris Yelenko stepped, wide eyed into the space where Lee was working. "Why are you shooting so many rocks so quickly?" He asked and then saw the puzzled look Lee gave him. "Wait, this isn't you, is it? You aren't doing this."

"No, it isn't me and I don't even think it's Major Zhang, given the look on his face."

"I don't know who it is, but I know how it's being done." Boris said with a touch of panic in his voice. "There's some code hidden in the system. I discovered it a while ago when I was playing around with a de-compiler."

"A de-compiler? Where would you find one of those and why would you use one?" Lee's face betrayed suspicion as he stared at Yelenko.

"It's a hobby of mine to read and write code through ancient methods. Just something I picked up when I was at university. My friend Alberto and I used to stay up late playing with bottom level code. We would even get down to the binary. Youth has a lot of patience for discovery."

"Okay, but what does that have to do with this?" Lee asked.

Boris' smile of remembrance thinking of his college days disappeared as he got back to the matter at hand. "I was playing with a new deconstruction tool and tested it on the launch codes instruction set. I found out it was going to launch the next volleys at Earth. It was just waiting for the exact co-ordinates."

"What the fuck?" Lee shook his head and stared at Boris in disbelief, "And you didn't tell me anything about it? Why were you keeping this information to yourself? Didn't you think it was important enough to mention?"

Boris lowered his head and looked at his feet." Well, I wasn't keeping it from you. I wasn't sure you didn't already know about it."

Lee Jin-Dao stared at Boris. "You thought I'd be involved in something like this? Boris, I'm amazed and even ashamed you would consider me to be like that. Yes, I'm member of the military, and I follow orders, but this isn't coming from the military. This thing has already fired seven rocks and doesn't seem to show any sign of stopping. It's out of control!"

"Stopping!" Boris jumped up. "We need to stop it! If we don't they'll come to the same conclusion I came to. That we're involved in this somehow."

Lee slapped his forehead, "Ay! You're right. We need to do something or they will blame this on us. Okay, tell me everything you know. Show me where you found the code you just told me about. We have to find a way to override it and quickly!"

Boris stepped up to the display in front of Lee and proceeded to log in. As he touched the screen, he noticed something moving in the reflection of the window showing the mass driver. He turned just as Lee brought down the metal tool he had raised above Boris' head. The tool hit Boris in the face and stunned him, dropping him to one knee. Lee raised the tool again, this time with both hands and brought it down crashing over the top of Boris' helmet. The Russian collapsed to the floor like a wet rag.

Lee looked down at Yelenko and said, "Of course I knew about it, you idiot. But I didn't know when it was going to start. And you weren't supposed to know about it at all. Such a shame, I kind of liked you."

Lee picked up the tool again and this time used it to smash Yelenko's faceplate. Then he dragged the Russian over to the vacuum port leading outside to the mass driver itself. He set chamber to match the lack of atmosphere of the lunar surface and waited as it pressured down.

Chapter Thirty-Nine

University of California
San Diego

H elen had a variety of data sources up on her display. She instructed the auditing process to double-check all the info. Something wasn't adding up and it looked as if whatever it was evaded easy detection by the accounting system. Being in charge of several projects at once was no easy task and sometimes she felt overwhelmed. This was one of them. She had superiors and investors to report to, and she needed to be able to give them the big picture.

"Who are you kidding? Something is wrong and I guess I'll just have to sit here until I find it," she told herself and pushed herself back from the display. On the left side of her desk was a picture of Sam. Taken on a sunny day at the shore a few years before, he had just discovered a red octopus under a rock. He was always looking for some form of life when he was at the beach. He was holding it up. His grin always made her think of a little boy showing a treasure. It always made her smile.

But not this time.

Helen couldn't stop thinking about whether Sam was in some kind of danger. She hated the thought he was on the Moon, and the far side no less. Sam was always one to go after adventure, and she knew he wasn't always the most cautious of men. If something was going wrong, he was the type of man who would step right into it to see how he could fix things. She had seen that side of him many times.

That was what worried Helen most. As smart as Sam is, he tended to assume most people were as straightforward and honest as he was. And Helen knew they were not. One of the things Helen loved about Sam was she could always count on him to be truthful. Sam never lied to her. In fact, it was even out of character for him not to have told her where he was going. Maybe he tried to tell her the last time they were in touch. She remembered the call had cut off. Had he been trying?

"You're being foolish," she blurted out suddenly. "And now, you're even talking to yourself! Sam is fine! You would know it if he wasn't."

She shook her head and said, "What you should be doing is talking to Sam. He's got to be answering his phone by now."

She stopped the process she had running on her display and dialed Sam's number. After a few moments her display showed a message that said, NUMBER NOT AVAILABLE. PLEASE LEAVE MESSAGE.

Frustrated, she tapped the NO option a little harder than necessary. She leaned back in her chair with an angry "Humpf!" She wasn't surprised she wouldn't be able to reach him but it was worth a try. It would be worth anything to be able to talk to him and make sure he was safe. She felt the need to warn him strange things were happening with the people who sent him to the Moon. But for now, all she could do was to continue to dig deeper into the entire records of the mission and see what she could find.

For starters, Sam's name wasn't even on the manifest. In fact, she didn't recognize any of the names on it. What were these people trying to hide? At the moment, Trish Stern was the only lead she had, and she had no way of getting in touch with the woman. Trish told her she would reestablish contact as soon as it was safe. But when would that be? Where was Trish now?

She opened the left-hand desk drawer and reached deep into it, releasing the latch that allowed her to open the false bottom in the drawer. Sam bought the desk for her as a gift. At the time, he thought having an antique desk with a hidden drawer was the coolest thing. She smiled at the memory of how excited he was when they found it in an antique store. He'd paid too much money for it, but they both loved it.

Her hand slid under the false bottom and fished around until she found the storage device Trish Stern gave her. Trish had asked her to keep it safe, but she'd never said anything about whether or not she could look into what was on it. Should she? Did it contain data that would help her locate Sam?

She turned it over in her hand. It had the vintage burnished copper look that was the recent fashion with expensive technological toys. She couldn't find any way to open it or connect it to her display. Frustrated, she dropped it back in the secret compartment. Then she thought a moment or two and picked it up again, turning it over and over in her hand. There had to be a way to access it.

After a few minutes of playing with it she was about to put it away when she got a call on her display. She put it down next to the display out of camera range and answered the call. It was her assistant leaving a breathless message about being on her way to the clinic and would let her know how everything went as soon as the baby arrived. She sounded happy, excited and maybe a little bit scared.

Helen smiled and wished her luck before closing down the connection

She lifted her chin in surprise and leaned in closer to the display.

Behind the connection, a window app had opened with the message, STORAGE DEVICE DETECTED. TYPE PASSWORD TO ACCESS. Apparently, the device didn't need to be connected to her display to work.

Helen scrunched her eyebrows together wondering what the password might be. What did she know about Trish Stern that might help her? She tried a few standard terms that made sense to her, but none of them worked. She worried the thing would shut itself off if she tried too many times without result. Most devices had such a failsafe built into them.

"Think Helen, think!" She muttered to herself. What had Trish told her? What expression had she used that might give her some insight? Then a flash of inspiration lit her eyes and she called up the keyboard on the display and typed in PARTNERINCRIME, closed her eyes and waited for a minute.

Helen burst into a wide grin as the display turned white and then showed her the message, ACCESS GRANTED. It then displayed a directory tree structure that reminded Helen of the way people organized data a hundred years earlier. She leaned forward and prepared to dig in. She would figure it out—even if it took her all night. Sam's life might just depend on it. Helen was just doing what she thought any good wife would do—protecting her husband at all costs.

Chapter Forty

Crew Quarters
Fermi Crater

Pierre, Sam and Amanda sat in silence, each deep in their own thoughts. Finally, Pierre slammed his fist onto his knee and stood. "I can't believe that old, stupid, full of himself major would not listen to a single word we said! This might be the end of the world, or humanity for all we know and HE, has more important things to do! Arrgghh! This makes me furious!" He picked up a drink bulb and threw it against the wall.

"Venting your frustrations by throwing objects won't protect the planet either, Pierre," Sam said shaking his head. "We're all frustrated. We feel what you do right now. But there's nothing we can do to get to the major until the morning. That doesn't mean we can't start working on some type of plan on our own. A method for either getting the major to pay attention, or getting someone on Earth to pay attention, or maybe both. Just in case one or the other doesn't listen. We're all intelligent people. We can work on this together. And we have Protector to help us. From the way I see it, we don't have a minute to waste. It's up to us right now to get the ball rolling."

"Once again you are wise, my friend," Pierre said. "But how can we reach anyone on Earth? The mission parameters have the major as the only one with access to Earth. I don't think any of our suit radios are going to be able to connect since they are designed to communicate through a local hub. And you told us what happened when you tried to communicate with your wife. The connection was immediately terminated."

Sitting on one of the beanbag chairs in the common area, Sam put his head in his hands and thought for a moment. "You're right, Pierre, we can't reach the planet directly. But there have got to be machines here on the surface that do it all the time. After all, they have been working here autonomously for several months without any humans in the area. I can't imagine they would be left incommunicado and unsupervised during that entire period. Someone on Earth has to be talking to them."

"You're right," Amanda chimed in. "I was able to upgrade the bots from Earth and I was able to have them send me validation messages during the upgrade process. They're capable of sending messages directly. That's the way I set them up."

"Or they pass them through some type of signal booster," Pierre added. "How can we try this out?"

"I know!" Sam said standing up. "Amanda, can you try to set off a test of your upgrade process with a destination for the results message?"

"I think I can re-code a destination but it would still just be sending the regular messages."

"Maybe not," said Pierre. "We could perhaps get them sending the message in a specific rhythm or something like Code Morse!"

Sam sighed, "That would only work if someone was listening for that. Otherwise they'd just go to nobody or to somebody who thought it was an annoying repeating sequence or a glitch in the system."

"Again, my friend, I say maybe not," Pierre replied. "What if we aimed our message at the SETI people?'

"SETI?" wondered Amanda.

"The Search for Extra Terrestrial Intelligence people," Sam explained. "They've been listening to messages from space for over a hundred years. They're very good at filtering patterns out of background noise. Imagine their shock when they find out Protector Three Oh Four has been here all this time!"

"I think we need to try this," said Pierre. "After all, we . . ."

"Shut up, Pierre!" Amanda waved at him petulantly.

"What? Amanda my dear, you are being entirely too . . ."

"SHUT THE FUCK UP, PIERRE!" Amanda yelled pressing her palm to the left side of her head.

Sam and Pierre looked at each other. "Amanda, what is going on?" Sam asked her.

"It's Boris," she said. "He's my safety partner, I'm getting a message he's in trouble of some sort. He may not be breathing."

"Not breathing? What the fuck? Can you locate him?" Sam asked.

Amanda focused and then nodded. "He's at the mass driver."

"Let's go!" said Pierre. The others were heading for the door.

Chapter Forty-One

Strategic Air Command Base 124
Somewhere in the United States

Lieutenant Jeffrey H. Algernon jerked his head back. The information on his display could not be right. He had spent the last six hours of an eight-hour shift in the Mobile Satellite Command Center—also known as 'The Box'—with Sergeant Martin DuPuis. Neither of them had any idea where The Box was actually located. Part of the security process was that they were brought into it for each shift without knowing exactly where The Box was. They had never been told why this was the case, but being good soldiers, they never questioned the process.

"Hey Marty," he called out. "What does your display say about EITS 242?" EITS stood for 'Eye in the Sky', but Algernon pronounced it 'eats'. EITS was a network of seven hundred and twelve satellites built by Starshield-Shackleton used to watch 'on the ground' activities as well as feed directions to autonomous drones. The EITS also carried 'Rods from God' in them. 'Rods' were tungsten hardened two hundred and fifty kilo steel rods with fins that could be dropped onto any target they flew over. The acceleration provided by gravity made the rods a deadly, if not overly precise weapon. Variables like wind and clouds could make them miss their target by up to several meters. The 'Rods from God' would hit the ground target at about Mach Ten with an impact of close to seven tons of TNT. There had been a few accidents when they were first used, but Strategic Command never worried much about collateral damage. At least not as much as it worried them that they'd missed the intended targets.

"Hold on a sec," Marty responded. "The readout says it's in self maintenance mode. Why? What's up?"

Algernon liked working with Marty. His easy-going attitude and sense of humor kept the shifts from being boring or tense. "Take a look at 243 and 244, Marty. Let's see what's up."

"Okay, I see the anomaly. Three in a row. That's not supposed to happen. Maybe we're being tested. What's the SOP for this situation?"

"The standard operating procedure, right, I got it right here. Okay, according to this, we check the maintenance roster first."

"Checking." Marty went from relaxed cowboy to all business in the blink of an eye. That was another reason Algernon liked working with him. The two of them as a team never had anything but high marks on these tests. They worked together well and they knew their stuff.

"Uh oh, not one of those three are scheduled for maintenance. Now what?"

The lieutenant had been busy looking ahead in the playbook. "Okay, stay calm. We set a watching app on all three. You start looking at any others for unusual statuses and I'll move the info up the chain of command. Stay focused. Let's do this."

Marty called up the app and dragged the three offending satellites into the follow grid. Then he began surveying the others along the chain of the original three.

"Uh, lieutenant, we got more problems. I'm seeing a whole slew of these going into maintenance mode and . . . Holy Shit!" He yelled out suddenly. "We got drop, we got drop from EITS 237, 238, 239 and, uh, 236, 235. Looks like a bunch of them are dropping rods, sir!" Marty never called Algernon 'sir' when the two of them were alone in The Box, but this looked like a very serious situation.

Algernon didn't bother answering Marty. He pulled up the emergency communication protocol and dialed up SAC headquarters. The lower left hand of his display told him Colonel Kesha Strahan was the contact on duty.

He activated the connection and waited to see the colonel's face. Instead, he got a message saying, COMMUNICATIONS SATELLITE NOT AVAILABLE AT THIS TIME. In all his time in the military, he'd never seen a status like that.

"Shit," He muttered under his breath and began running his hand through the playbook app looking for what to do next in this case.

"We got more rods dropping and I'm seeing 242, 243 and 244 coming back on line only they are . . . they are . . . I don't believe this!"

"What, what are you seeing?"

"The satellites, they're decelerating. Something is making them slow down."

"But if they decelerate, that means a loss of altitude. Can you figure out how much lower they're going to go?"

"Fuck." Marty said in a whisper. "Really low. All the way down, sir. And now I'm seeing others doing the same thing. The ones who dropped their rods are starting to fall, sir. What the fuck is going on? We've got satellites literally dropping out of the sky like snowflakes!"

Lieutenant Algernon had been trying with no success to hail SAC, his home base and even his relief squad—any node in the communication system aboard The Box. Finally, he came to a decision, "Marty, I can't reach anyone. I don't know if anyone else knows what's happening, and I don't know how to reach anyone. I gotta open The Box."

"Oh." Marty went quiet. Opening The Box was a last resort protocol, reserved for all out nuclear war or an imminent attack on The Box itself. If this was a test, Marty figured they were about to blow it. "Why would you do that? How can it help to open The Box?"

Algernon was already out of his seat. "I have a mini-phone in my drawer. Maybe I can reach someone on it from outside. I don't see any other choices. I gotta try. We need to communicate with someone—STAT!"

He grabbed the mini-phone and jammed it into his pocket. He didn't check to see if he could get any kind of connection on it from inside The Box. He knew it was fully shielded, even against an EMP. He had to get out in the open.

He stepped to the entrance door, wiped sweat from his brow and tapped in the exit code. A message blinked back indicating there was still one hundred and eight minutes until the shift was over. Algernon cursed and punched in his override code.

"Override accepted, Upper access portal unlocked," said a robotic voice that was all business. He had forgotten and was expecting the door he came through to open. The emergency exit was in the ceiling and was a round door at the top of a set of indentations in one wall. He stepped over to it and placed his foot on the first step. "I'm going topside and see if I can get a signal. Try to see if you can get the satellites to respond, maybe even fire their rockets to get them lifted again. Stay on it, Marty. Anything you can do to reverse this, do it."

"Working on it," Marty said, not betraying any of the fear he felt.

Algernon pulled himself up the rungs and got to the portal. He stared into the camera and spun the hatch lock. It clicked and he saw orange dust come in through the crack that opened. Climbing another rung, he pushed the portal open. He braced his left leg against a bracket so he could push his body out until he was waist high through the opening. The portal opened into a vast sandy red dessert with no sign of human habitation.

"Kind of beautiful," he said to himself, reaching for his mini-phone. "Kind of nice to finally know where we are."

His hand didn't make it into his pocket before the Rod from God slammed into him—obliterating The Box along with both of its occupants.

Chapter Forty-Two

The Stumble Inn
San Diego, California

A couple drinking Vodka Disasters looked at Trish for a moment before returning to their conversation. *Lovers,* Trish thought, *no doubt having an illicit relationship based on the way they're looking at each other and giggling.*

Trish turned away from them. She was in the bar to get a bite to eat and have a drink or two to test-spend cash. So far, that part had gone without a hitch. She decided to focus on what was on the display above the bartender's head.

"Oh crap, oh crap, oh crap!" Trish Stern blurted out as she saw the report over the bar's video display. The display was tuned to 24 x 7—the most popular news source on the planet. The display showed six mini screens, each offering a different breaking news story. The bar was loud, but since the majority of the patrons were Anglophones, the subtitles were in English.

"Someone you know?" the bartender asked.

"Huh? What? No. I was looking at the market report. Looks like I just got hurt badly today," she improvised.

What she had been watching was a report that a satellite had fallen onto Campobello Island in Canada. Another may have fallen somewhere west of White Sands National Monument in New Mexico. Satellites had fallen before, but she couldn't remember two of them announced at once. And never had there been two of them falling on populated places where she knew the US Government had satellite-monitoring bases.

Something was happening, and she felt it was something very bad. Maybe this was why Starshield decided to get rid of her. She might have started asking questions they didn't want to answer. But what questions would she ask? And who didn't want to answer them?

"Rough thing, the market," the bartender said, drying a stem glass and hanging it on the rack behind him. "That's why I stay out of it. It fluctuates too much. Hey, are you just visiting here or setting yourself up in the area? I don't remember seeing you here before."

"I'm just visiting here on business. Do you have a public display system? One I can use for a few minutes?" Trish asked.

"Yeah, I got one, but it'll cost you."

"How much? I'll pay you cash, okay?" She bit her lip, thinking she was being too eager.

"Cash?" He shrugged, "I donno. Maybe the standard charges plus fifty percent?"

"Hmm," she mulled it over. She could afford it, but she didn't want to seem too easy. It would make her look either too desperate or too careless, "I would think thirty percent would be enough. It is cash after all."

The bartender chewed on the end of his mustache and finally agreed. "Okay, thirty it is. But do me a favor and use it in the back room. I don't want people thinking I sell anything other than mind altering products here." He winked and passed her a small, old tablet display from under the bar.

Trish took the tablet from him and walked to the back of the bar, looking for a booth separate from the others. The bartender stuffed the cash in his shirt pocket, looked at her and muttered to himself. "Damn saleswomen are all the same. The salesmen go screwing around the world, but the saleswomen just want shit from you and then they leave you."

Trish found a booth well away from the few patrons of the bar and settled into it. The tablet the bartender handed her was an antique. It wasn't a sound-dampening model designed to create a private space where only someone in the immediate area would hear it. It came with a sound collar— a necklace one wore along the collarbone, which sent sounds to your ears by vibrating your skeleton. While these had returned to fashion for a brief time some thirty years earlier, they were still considered quaint.

The method for keeping the user's end of the conversation from being heard was to sub-vocalize. The collar included sensors that could detect movements of the tongue, lips and vocal chords even if no breath was involved.

Trish knew how to sub-vocalize, because she learned it when she first started to read as a girl. Her parents paid big bucks to get her to stop so she could read at a rapid enough level to be competitive when it came to her studies. But learning how to stop sub-vocalizing also made her aware of the fact she was doing it and now she could turn it on and off with ease. It was a skill lost on most of her generation, since there was no longer a real need for it. Much the same way cursive handwriting disappeared for most people over seventy years earlier.

The screen was old and Trish had to slow down and even make sure her fingers touched the surface in some cases to get it to respond. "I can't believe I paid that much for this piece of crap," she mumbled to herself as she went through the elaborate process Louise taught her. It took more than three minutes to get it right, but she felt a lot safer. She trusted Louise knew what she was doing when she had gotten Trish to memorize it.

Finally, she was able to access the secure messaging area Louise charged her for. She was about to send a message to an old friend at the Holloman Alamogordo Military Base near Alamogordo, New Mexico when she saw she had received a message. It could only be Louise. Nobody else knew how to reach her in this particular message box without her having initiated contact.

When she opened the message, she gasped. This was not supposed to happen. Nobody should to be able to find this mailbox.

But there it was: proof positive her security had, once again, been compromised. She called up the sniffing app the way Louise showed her to see if the message had a 'tail' attached. A tail was a system by which the sender could tell whether Trish actually opened it and could even triangulate to tell the sender where she might be. The sniffing app proclaimed the message clean, but then again, the message area itself was supposed to have been pristine.

She held her breath and opened it only to open her mouth wide, covering it with her hand at the last second. It was a message from one of the generals in the Chinese military with whom she worked with at Starshield. The very last person in the world she expected to hear from. How had he reached her? Had Louise given her up?

Chapter Forty-Three

Fermi Crater Artifact
Far Side of the Moon

Protector Three Hundred and Four had taken the time to review the message it received, telling it to protect itself. The message had come through the same way as the farewell message it received—Quantum Complemental Radio. P304 was able to make the radio function only at great energy costs to itself. It did not have the data to understand the technology behind the function. It only knew it could receive messages from a specific source. The source itself was some four thousand light years away, but the message came through at much greater speeds.

The Protector ran a small investigative application to determine whether the messaging speed played havoc with any linear notion of time. It eventually stopped wondering because the answers were never resolved. However it worked, P304 had no idea, but it did work.

The messages themselves had been a lot more stimulating. The first message, the one that had said GOOD-BYE was the first message the Protector received in more than sixty-five million years. After the failure to protect the Earth from the incoming asteroid, P304 found it normal that it was not receiving any messages. It no longer served any primal purpose. It had failed.

The second message, which followed the first by only a few hours, was far more interesting. This was the one that had included the coordinates of the new incoming asteroid. And its instruction to protect itself was completely unexpected. If the asteroid was headed for the Moon, how was the Protector supposed to protect itself? From the data in the message, the destruction on the Moon would be disastrous and massive.

Using its databases, the Protector calculated more than two hundred possible scenarios—far beyond the normal range. This was obviously a sign it lacked enough data to fine-tune the available information into a probable set. It decided to act to obtain more data.

It considered the most important factors and whittled down the number of possible scenarios by likelihood. It decided to use six-point-four percent of its remaining energy reserves to send back the following message:

IDENTIFY YOURSELF. ENERGY LEVEL LOW. HOW SHOULD I DEFEND MYSELF? AND WHY? REESTABLISH CONTACT IMMEDIATELY.

The Protector knew the response would not be instantaneous. So, it set the QCR to low level listening status and turned its attention back to what data it could continue to gather from the Earth's orbiting satellites.

There was a problem with the satellite network. Many of them were shutting down, and quite a few had fallen or were falling to the Earth. P304 even saw some of the satellites had moved from their normal orbit to shoot other satellites down. Some of the downward facing weapons had been deployed, although none of the massively destructive ones.

Curious about what had precipitated this turn of events, the Protector continued to use more resources to delve deeper. It noticed during its study of the humans they had been waging war on each other as many early sentient forms had done through galactic history. But, it had no documentation that spoke of war in space around one planet. In fact, by the time most planets had gotten to spacefaring technology, they had long since ended planetary strife. Most of them had been in the situation of rediscovering war between them and other planets. The Protector had no records regarding how this happened for Scarabs. But Saurians tended to look for and detect early spacefaring species. If they were Saurians, contact was made and they were invited to join the struggle against the Scarabs. If they happened to be Scarabs, then extinction protocol was put into place and an asteroid was sent to wipe out the planet.

It decided to expand its listening to learn more about who was behind the satellite failures and what the impact would be on the planet. It also wanted to know if it was in danger of having its sources cut off, so it began to track the state of lunar orbiting communications satellites.

That was when it detected the miniature asteroids heading for Earth. By tracking their trajectories, the Protector discovered not only were the rocks coming from the Moon, but from a proximity of less than two kilometers from itself.

The Protector looked into the data it had gotten from the mobile bot the previous day. There were mining bots nearby and they labored to create over seven thousand of these big rocks in the previous six months. That many rocks hitting the Earth could do a great deal of damage.

After a few minutes of exploration, P304 discovered the mass driver. It logged into the data sets and discovered its original purpose. It noted the mass driver already fired off one hundred and forty-seven rocks and another seventeen hundred and eighty were available and on schedule for launch

An alarm went off and the Protector changed focus. It set a timer to indicate the most probable moment—given what data it had—when a response would come from through the QCR.

It went through the procedure for powering up the receiver. It consumed less power than sending a message but still took up a noticeable part of its reserves. It detected a message and recorded it, bringing the receiver offline as quickly as it could.

Then, the Protector turned its attention to the message, which read: WE ARE PROTECTORS. WE ARE MANY. IF ENERGY IS LOW, USE LOCAL TECHNOLOGY. BECAUSE YOU ARE SPECIAL. PROTECT YOURSELF.

P304 went over the message several times to make certain it had gotten all the data. It was brief, but it said so much.

Chapter Forty-Four

Chang'e 3 Base
Maglev Launcher

Lee Jin-Dao paused to breathe. His face had gone red, his arms ached and his head was pounding. He closed his eyes and tried to calm himself, but huffed with frustration. "Damn you Boris," he said to himself. "I liked you. Why did you have to go and look into the codes that managed the firing mechanism for the mass driver? Why? You're just like that Ledbetter idiot, asking too many questions."

The tall, lanky Russian lay unconscious at his feet. Lee wasn't sure if he was dead, but his pale face was in high contrast to the blood on the sides of his broken faceplate. Lee bent over and detected Boris was still breathing. This posed a real problem since eventually the others would come looking for him and ask what happened. Lee had to get Boris outside into the lunar vacuum before he could wake or any of the others arrived. When he attacked the Russian, he wasn't sure what he would do next. And he certainly had not thought such a tall, thin guy would be so hard for him to move, even in lunar gravity.

Lee sat down. He wasn't thinking straight. Something here didn't add up right and his engineering mind was puzzled by it.

When Amanda, Pierre and Sam burst into the control room, they found both Lee and Boris lying on the floor. Boris was pale but he was breathing on his own. Lee was not. His lips were blue and his eyes were wide open and misted over.

Pushing the others back, Sam immediately began pumping his hands on Lee's chest. "Pierre, find a defibrillator!" he yelled. "Amanda, find me some oxygen!"

Amanda rushed over to the spot by the door where oxygen was always stored. She grabbed the bottle and made sure a mask was attached before running back to where Sam was alternating between pumping and listening to Lee's chest. Pierre was rummaging through a cabinet, throwing objects left and right as he searched for a machine to jump-start Lee's heart.

Kneeling on the other side of Lee, Amanda waited for Sam to pause from pumping Lee's chest. When he did, she slid the locking mechanism and flipped open his faceplate. She placed the breathing mask over his mouth and nose and set the pressure to higher than suit normal.

"I'm afraid that won't help any." Amanda jumped, startled by the Russian voice coming from behind her. "I think it has been some time that he has not been breathing on his own."

Reaching for the controls on her faceplate, she found the connection that allowed her to look at Lee's vitals. "Boris is right," she said. "He hasn't been breathing for twenty-four minutes. His heart went into arrhythmia about twenty minutes ago. There has been no cardiac electrical signal for fifteen minutes. I'm sorry, but there's nothing we can do. He's dead."

Sam was still pumping as if he hadn't heard her.

"What happened here, Boris?" she asked.

"Later," said Boris. "Right now, we need to stop the mass driver. It's shooting rocks at the Earth."

Pierre rushed over to the control station and looked at the display. "Nom de Dieu! The mass driver is firing big rocks and they are not at all aimed at the station. Why would anybody do that?"

With his hands on either side of him, Boris tried to sit up, but his head spun so badly he had to lie back down again, "Forget why for now. Just stop it," he said with labored breath.

Pierre tried to figure out how to control the system but it wasn't responding to any commands. "How do I stop it? It isn't responding to my commands!"

"I'm not sure," Boris struggled to reply. He was having trouble focusing his vision and the back of his head felt heavy and wet.

Sam stopped pumping Lee and rocked back with his hands on his knees, staring at the dead man. Amanda could see he accepted reviving Lee was a lost cause, although he gave her a frustrated glare. He stood and hurried over to where Pierre was and began looking over the controls. After a minute he said, "I think the fastest, and surest way we can stop this is to cut off the power to the mass driver. That's all I've got right now."

"Good thinking," Pierre responded. "But where and how do we do that? I don't see anything here that indicated it's a power source."

"Not here." Sam said pointing out of the view bay, "Out there."

The other two Taikonauts looked where Sam was pointing. About one hundred and fifty meters from the view bay was a small bunker. There were large cables leading up to it and others leading away to the mass driver itself. There were also cables leading to the control booth they were in. The two of them looked at Sam.

"That looks like it's the power station for the mass driver, but also for this booth as well. I need to get the faceplate off Lee and replace Boris' faceplate before you shut the power off. Without power, oxygen production and air scrubbing in this booth will come to halt. We need him back in a completely enclosed suit before you do that."

"Then do it now." Sam said and he walked to the airlock that led to the outside and dialed the door to open for him. "Pierre, once I'm in there, can you force the outside door to open as quickly as possible?"

"My friend, that will blow you out onto the surface," Pierre said quietly.

"Yeah, I know, I'm counting on that to get me to the power station faster."

Pierre shook his head. "My friend Sam is a lunatic," he muttered. "But it's always interesting to see what he will do next."

On the floor in front of the dead body, Amanda was completely disconnecting the open faceplate from Lee's helmet. It wouldn't do him any good anymore, but Boris couldn't live without it. Sam walked through the airlock and shut the door behind himself as Pierre prepared to open the outer door.

Sam closed the airlock door and waved the seal into position. His voice came into Pierre's helmet. "Okay. I'm in and the door is registering sealed. Don't open the outer door yet or I'll go flying out way too quickly. Lower the pressure to about one third of normal ambient. When you see it there, let me know so I can brace myself before you open the door."

"Roger that," said Pierre. He pronounced it 'Ro-jay' like a true Frenchman.

With Lee's faceplate removed, Amanda began helping Boris to make the exchange. He was paler than before and had fallen back into unconsciousness while she worked on him. The broken faceplate had a bent frame and she was having trouble getting the seal to free itself from the helmet body. Unconscious, Boris was a deadweight and hard for her to manipulate alone.

She looked at Pierre to see if he could help, but saw he was far too focused on what he was doing with Sam. She saw a small metal tool lying on the floor not far from her and crawled over to pick it up. Using it like a tiny crowbar, she wedged it under the edge of the faceplate. "I hope I don't hurt you, Boris," she whispered, then pressed her lips together and banged on the end of the tool with the palm of her hand. Boris' head turned abruptly to the side, but the seal didn't free itself.

Afraid she might have hurt him she turned his head slowly so he was facing the ceiling. He was breathing softly, but she didn't think he'd felt anything. Holding the top of his helmet with her left hand, she raised her right hand again and brought it down sharply on the wedged tool.

The faceplate came flying off of the helmet, tumbling through the air and striking Pierre square between the shoulder blades.

"Ahhh!" Pierre jumped up two feet spinning around as he did. "Que'st que c'etait ça?"

"Sorry," Amanda apologized with a sheepish grin. "I was having trouble getting this faceplate off and it flew off into you. Sorry."

"Woman! You gave me a blue frightening!"

"I said I was sorry."

Pierre turned back to the console. "We're almost there, Sam."

"What was the noise about?" Sam said, concerned.

"Amanda was being a menace. It's over now. Just a small accident. Nobody injured."

"Oh. All right. I'm in position. Let me know when you're ready to blow the door open."

Studying the display and watching as the pressure hit the level he had preset, Pierre spoke to Sam through his comm. "We are good to go, Sam. Are you ready?"

"Ready"

"Okay, I blow the door in five, four, three, two . . ."

Pierre stabbed at the emergency air lock opener and the outer door slid up. Immediately, a dozen little objects flew out onto the lunar surface with the sudden change in pressure. And Sam went with them.

He'd pressed himself against the opposite door, preparing for the sudden change and when the outer doors opened, he pushed himself up and out with both legs. The result added a considerable amount of force to the expulsion process the change in pressure brought about.

Unfortunately, it didn't give Sam the controlled exit he'd hoped for. Instead, he went out tumbling head over heels in an arc that rose about seven meters above the lunar surface and ended about ninety meters away from the airlock door. He hit the lunar surface and kept tumbling for almost thirty more meters, sending up a sparkling cloud of lunar dust from each spot where his body hit the ground.

"O Mon Dieu!" Pierre shouted as he saw how his friend shot out of the airlock and across the lunar soil. "Sam! Sam, are you okay?"

"Oh!" Sam groaned. He hadn't expected the force to take him as far as it had. Despite the low lunar gravity, he hit the ground with enough force to do more than knock the wind out of him.

"I think I'm okay, let me check." Sam called up his life monitors and checked everything out. His heart was racing and his blood pressure and respiration were high, but that was to be expected. There were no broken bones and that was a relief. A flashing light appeared in his lower left field of vision. He looked at it and blinked twice. A message appeared telling him his suit had lost integrity and was going through the process of patching itself. The message said temporary integrity was being utilized. He knew it was not meant to last and he should return to an enclosed place within thirty minutes for permanent repairs. He had to work fast.

Sam rose up from his position and instantly buckled to one knee. His left ankle screamed in pain. Sam paused to think. Then called up a drink from his suit with caffeine, taurine, glucose and a rapid acting painkiller. After letting the chemicals into his system, he tried to stand again. His ankle still hurt like hell, but he felt he could put some weight on it. He stood wobbling and gritting his teeth, began slowly bounce-walking across the surface toward the power station.

Amanda had been able to reshape the bent frame on Boris' helmet and attached Lee's faceplate to it. She was testing for a perfectly hermetic seal by accessing the safety systems in his suit. "Is Sam okay? What's he doing?" she asked Pierre.

Pierre stared out of the booth bay. He saw Sam limp-hopping toward the power station. Without turning his head, he responded slowly, "Sam is making his way to the power station. I knew he could do it."

Chapter Forty-Five

General Sun's Home
Outside Beijing

"I am so honored," General Sun bowed before the display. "After all these years, for you to desire to visit my humble home is beyond anything I might have wished for. But I fear my home cannot do justice to your presence, my Chairman."

"Oh, my friend, it is I who am honored." The chairman offered a rare smile to General Sun. "And I feel remiss I've never taken the time to visit you, always demanding you come visit me. Especially when I think upon all the time and effort you've put into helping me and our great Republic. An old proverb says that the state of the nation is reflected in the home. I am certain that your humble home will prove that to be true."

Sun took out one of the small terrycloth towels he kept in his desk drawer and wiped his forehead. He was usually in his bedroom by this time of the evening, but a call from the chairman made him run downstairs to his office. He felt a little ill at ease. He was not used to receiving compliments from the chairman, just orders.

He bowed his head. "You are too kind, my esteemed Chairman. I will make all the preparations as needed. Would it be possible for me to host you a little bit later? That would allow me the time to take care of certain tasks so that my home will be in a manner befitting . . ."

The chairman shook his head, "I'm afraid not. You must know I abhor imposing on you this way, but my schedule is already challenging. I can only come visit you during the two-hour window we spoke of. I must humbly beg your apology for that, but it will be the only opportunity." He stared at his display, awaiting Sun's answer.

Sun bowed. "It's I who am humbled. With a schedule such as yours, you should take the time to visit me. The honor is far more than I deserve."

The chairman smiled again. "I'm so glad we can do this. I do hope we can avoid having any media or other protocol issues while I'm visiting. I would prefer if it can be just a nice quiet, visit between old friends."

Sun bowed again, and when he lifted his head, he saw the leader had cut the connection.

He took a deep breath and glanced quickly at his surroundings. Everything seemed to be in order. But the chairman had never mentioned the nature of his visit. Was he coming to give Sun some sort of recompense? He had been at the chairman's side for more than thirty years. During that entire time, he never visited the chairman's home or had anything other than formal meetings with him. They had many personal chats in a variety of offices over the years, but the discussions were always about politics or history and how they tied into the dreams and aspirations of the great man. Sun knew the leader was putting together a formidable plan for the Republic, even if Sun was not privy to it all. That was the way the man had always been. He always played his cards solo, never telling any single person all his plans.

Perhaps the chairman was finally thinking about a successor? It was no secret the glorious leader was not getting any younger. While his wit and spirit were just as sharp as ever, he did seem to tire faster than he had in previous years. Sun was more than fourteen years his junior and always kept longer hours than this mentor. The general knew he was not the only person close to the leader, but he also knew none of the others had been with him for quite as long.

He decided it might be a good time to learn more about the rest of the assistants to the chairman as soon as possible. But the following day, he would be busy preparing for the visit.

As he began to activate his display, he got a message that an urgent call was coming in. Annoyed, he checked where it was coming from this late in the day.

Surprised it was from Major Zhang on the Moon, he decided to answer the call immediately. "Major? I wasn't expecting a call from you. I trust everything is as it should be?"

Zhang was red-faced. He ran his hand through what little there was of his hair and gave Sun a weak smile. "I'm afraid I can't say that. I'm contacting you because, well, because of what has happened here after I implemented the file you sent me."

Sun panicked briefly as he checked to make certain the

communication was secure. The system told him it was, but his dealing with others convinced him truly secure communication was a fairy tale. He wiped his forehead once again and said "Major, you mean you have an, er, update, about the last mission meeting we had?" He hoped Zhang would take the hint and be discreet regarding whatever he was calling about.

Zhang did nothing of the sort. "I'm sorry to announce since I uploaded the file, we're firing hundreds of new rocks through the mass driver at an unprecedented rate."

"So? Does it mean we're ahead of schedule? I'm sure the chairman will enjoy announcing China will be sending our first manned visit to Mars earlier than planned. Another fine example of Chinese prowess."

"No, General, you don't seem to understand, I've tracked the rocks and they're not heading to the station. They're heading to Earth, all of them. Some of them are looking like they might target a few of the stations in orbit, but others look like they're aimed directly at places on the planet itself. I can hardly imagine the kind of blast one of the rocks impacting the Earth might make."

Sun shook off his initial shock. "Are you sure? Why would we do that? What can we . . ."

Then it hit him. The chairman was always speaking of holding the 'higher ground' and the file contained coordinates and times. "When do you think the first rocks arrive?"

"Looks to me like it will be in about thirty-five hours as best as I can calculate. I'm doing that with limited data. I can tell better in a couple of hours."

"Please continue to monitor the situation. As I'm sure you know, we expected you to do that," Sun lied. "I'll get you more information as soon as I judge it will be useful to the operation. Thank you again, Major Zhang."

Sun disconnected and wiped his forehead once again. Thirty-five hours! That was when the chairman would be visiting him in his home!

Another idea came to him. He looked up the actual coordinates of his home and crosschecked them to see if the coordinates in the copy of the message the chairman had him send to Zhang were anywhere near where he lived. It turned out there was a direct match for his home and the time stamp next to that number was for thirty-six hours from then. About the time the chairman invited himself to visit Sun at his home.

179

Chapter Forty-Six

Starshield-Shackleton HQ
Penobscot Bay, Maine

Dark gray clouds with deep vermilion linings were coming in from over Isle au Haut and Deer Isle. Across the bay, Mark Slaton could make out the faint glows of Camden and Rockport. *The sunrise this morning might not be one of the better ones*, he thought, as looked out through the two-story windows of his office. You could never tell with the way the tides moved the clouds. "If you don't like the weather on the Maine coast, wait fifteen minutes," his grandfather used to say.

Mark was an early riser and liked to watch the sun come up. He'd already been up for three hours this morning. He knew satellites were falling and he would eventually be called upon to react to that. He sipped his third cup of coffee, a blend grown on his own farms in Jamaica. It was dark roasted and laced with a mélange of antioxidants and telomere enhancers to help slow aging and prolong his life. He wondered how many others were taking the same type of morning cocktail and about to learn that attempts to stretch their lives was soon going to a moot point.

As if on cue, his display sounded to get his attention.

He turned to it and watched as the system determined the exact origin of the call. It was coming from deep under the Pentagon but the call signature indicated it was the President Benson who was trying to reach him.

Slaton let it wait for five seconds before responding. On the display, Gary Benson looked bad. His customary coiffed hair was a mess with the graying temples puffing out in what, to Slaton, looked like a clown wig. His eyes were red and his skin pale. "Slaton! What the fuck is going on?" He glared into the display.

Slaton offered a slow look of disinterest and took the time to start up one of his cigarettes before responding. "Mr. President, I'm just myself learning about issues occurring with satellites under your control. I was going to ask you the same thing, although in a somewhat more restrained tone."

"Don't take me for a fool, Slaton. Nine satellites have come down so far. Rods from God have rained onto some of my control centers. The boys here at the Command Center are telling me we can't even track most of our satellites. And we have thousands of drones out there flying on their own with no contact or control mechanism that can reach them."

Benson was yelling with a voice that had become hoarse from what must have been a lot of recent shouting. "Jesus man, I've got my wife and little girls here in the Pentagon because they tell me the White House isn't safe! So, don't you pussyfoot with me about how you're just learning about this shit! These are your satellites and your drones! I want to know what's happening and what you're going to do about it! And I want to know now!"

"Mr. President. I don't control any of the satellites nor do I control the drones. If you recall, several years ago, during your first term, we made a deal. You said you couldn't afford to pay us a fair price for the material and weapons we supplied you. I told you the only way I could continue to supply you these items at the cost you required was to be able to sell other ones elsewhere. I know your 'guys' didn't like that. So, we agreed the only way it made sense was if Starshield-Shackleton didn't manage the maintenance of the materials. That way, you were able to install your own secure command and control systems. My company hasn't been involved in that aspect for more than four years now."

This time Slaton allowed himself to show a small closed lip smile.

"Fuck that, Slaton. This is a national emergency! Don't you see that? We're vulnerable right now. We can't reach or control the Peace in the Skies Network and people are dying. Our people!"

"Mr. President, I don't think there's anything I can do other than make some of my technicians available to your staff. Of course, it will take some time to debrief them on your security protocols. And to tell you the truth, I'm not sure your generals will be too happy about doing that."

"Slaton, you need to do more than that. You need to do whatever it takes to get us back in control of those satellites. Whatever it takes! Do you hear me?" Benson was so agitated Slaton saw drops of spittle fly from his mouth. "I can declare this to be an emergency and commandeer your company. I can call for an investigation as well. You built those satellites.

Somebody's going to have to take the fall for this, Slaton. Don't push your luck." The president pointed at him on the display and then the connection went dead.

Mark sat back in his body-molding chair, designed to both relax and stimulate his muscles at the same time. The technology came from the Chinese space program. As the stimulators kicked in, Slaton burst out laughing.

That two-bit politician, 'Mr. Charisma' was just a puppet and he knew it. Slaton knew the call had been nothing but posturing on Benson's part. All bark and no bite. How could a whiny little lapdog with no teeth like Benson ever bite someone like Slaton?

But taking down Benson was not enough. He had to destroy his legacy as well. Slaton would sabotage Benson's signature project. The deep space asteroid warning system which had been Benson's pet project was about to self-destruct. Slaton's virus was a devious one. The distributed system would continue reporting, but the data would be a recombined mish-mash of previous events designed to look like the skies were safe. *Ingenious if I do say so myself*, Slaton thought with pride.

He checked the time and saw the second phase of the Rods from God would be kicking in soon. Washington would be a mess. Even the hardened bunker that held the Command Center was about to discover there was a limit to what they could defend against.

Slaton saw the wind had driven the clouds to the side and the sunrise was going to be a spectacular one. He took a drag on his digital cigarette and laughed aloud again.

Chapter Forty-Seven

The Stumble Inn
San Diego, California

Trish looked at the time stamp on the message from the Chinese general. It was only a few minutes old. She put her hands together as if she was praying and leaned her chin on her thumbs, staring at the message. It read: MS. STERN, PLEASE CONTACT ME DAY OR NIGHT AT THE FOLLOWING COORDINATES. MANY THINGS HAVE CHANGED AND IT IS URGENT THAT WE SPEAK.

Trish raised her hand to erase the message, then paused and lowered her hand.

General Sun was as close to the top of the Chinese government as one could get without being the chairman of the party. She always had a good relationship with him and felt there had always been mutual respect. That was something she didn't feel with most of the Chinese power players who tended to remain in a male dominated world.

If deKumpf was trying to find her, that was exactly the type of person he would try to reach her through—assuming Sun was that easily corruptible. And Trish didn't think he was.

She took a deep breath, held it, and let it out before activating the call back coordinates.

In less than a second, she saw the glistening billiard ball of Sun's head squinting at her with his wry smile.

"Ms. Stern, I'm delighted you chose to answer." He held his hand up, stopping her response. "Before anything else, please allow me to tell you I'm not contacting you at the behest of anyone other than myself. I've heard you are no longer with Starshield-Shackleton. While I have my own opinions of the reasons behind that, it has nothing to do with why I've reached out to you." He leaned forward to drive his point home.

His opening surprised Trish. She expected he was either going to help deKumpf find her somehow or he was curious about what happened to her and why. The realization she was just a pawn to the people she worked with was humbling.

She bowed her head in respect. As she lifted it, she said, "I'm honored the general would take time out of his day to speak to me. How may I be of service?"

"Ha!" The general laughed. "Ah, Ms. Stern. You're a true champion. I was certain you'd be in hiding and not answer my call. And that perhaps if you answered, it would be you who would be asking something of me. You're much better at this than any one of those fools at Shackleton suspected." She saw him wipe his brow with a white cloth. "But I think I know a little bit better than them. I think you can indeed be of service. Both to myself and to yourself as well."

Trish felt a little more confident in her position. "Thank you, General, you flatter me. So how can I help you? What do you need?"

"What I need is what I always need—information. I need to know exactly what Starshield was doing on the far side of the Moon. Just what was Starshield actually building in the Fermi Crater?"

"General, you should know as well as anyone else. It's a mining operation designed to exploit lunar resources and a launch facility to send these resources to the Lagrange Two Station," Trish answered, unsure of what the general was leading up to.

"Yes, a launch facility of unusual design, is it not?"

"Well, you could say that. It's a mass driver. None were built on Earth because the energy costs to reach escape velocity are prohibitive."

"Yes, it's quite an achievement. And it's run entirely by software, isn't it? While people may be visiting, they aren't required, are they? The bots can run the operation completely on their own?" He leaned forward once again.

"Yes. Yes, that's the case. Although I wasn't with the company when the project first started. I think I recall you attended all the first meetings when the project was first presented to your government."

"Yes, I did. As did our illustrious, eventual chairman. In fact, he was the one who lobbied for approval of the expensive adventure." The general wiped his brow again.

"I don't have all my notes, but yes, I believe Chairman Qi was quite instrumental in getting the project started and has always championed it. But this is nothing new. Why are you asking me about this?"

"Tell me," the general continued, ignoring her question, "Was there any plan to weaponize the Fermi Base? Anything set up at all to defend it in any way?"

"Weaponize? On the far side of the Moon? Why would anyone even think of attacking it? It's just a mining operation with a launch facility. That seems to me it would be so low on the target list nobody would have the kind of funds to make sending ordinance up there worthwhile." Trish had the feeling she was missing something in the conversation.

The general leaned back and smiled. "Tell me Ms. Stern, the launch facility, what can it launch?"

"Why almost anything, provided it has a sound structure. Lunar escape velocity is not that high. I don't recall what it is exactly, but not that high. The base can launch everything from manufactured goods to raw materials. Even man-made ice extracted from the lunar soil. It's why we have such a variety of multipurpose bots at the crater."

"And is everything designed to be fired to the Lagrange Point?'

"Yes, of course. The trajectories are pre-programed. Although they can be altered. The mass and structure may require adjustments in the ballistics."

"So, the system must be quite precise in that case?"

"Yes. The math is part of what's amazing about the system. You could load the driver with almost anything. With information about the mass and structure, the system calculates the proper trajectory and sends it on its way. There are catcherbots at the Lagrange Point that work in conjunction with the mass driver and send instructions to guiding rockets on the payloads. But they're only needed if the payload is unusual or requires special handling. In fact, I believe that Boris Yelenko, the genius behind the idea, is up there now testing some of these catcherbots."

Sun nodded as if he was remembering something. "And tell me, if the target was somewhere else, say on the Earth, how exact would the delivery be?"

Trish scrunched her eyebrows together. "On Earth? But there's nothing to catch them on Earth. They would burn up or . . ." She paused and then finished her sentence slowly, "Explode."

Sun looked at her expectantly, "Just how precise would the targeting and timing be?"

"General, you can't hope to use the mass driver as a weapon? It would be a terrible one. It could rain down huge rocks on the Earth!" Her voice rose and she was feeling fear well up inside her, "Why, the force of the explosions would be . . . Oh my God, General!"

"Ms. Stern, I don't want to use it as a weapon. Tell me how precise would the targeting and timing be!"

"Very precise, general. Within five meters, I would guess. And within minutes of when you wanted the items to hit, depending on what they were. Promise me you aren't even thinking of doing this!"

"I am not, Ms. Stern, but I'm afraid someone else is. In fact, they have already begun and I fear we'll be seeing a bombardment in the next day or so."

"Tomorrow? But means they're already on their way here?"

"Yes, I believe they are. I'm working on that as we speak. What I need from you is this. How can I contact the data centers on the Moon Base and stop the mass driver, or even better yet, take control of it?"

"I would think Major Zhang, who is up there now, can do that. Oh!" She put her hand to her mouth as if afraid to say what she was going to say, "Is he the one shooting the rocks at the Earth?"

"Major Zhang is not in control of the mass driver. It seems the automated software is, and he hasn't been able to re-establish control on his end. I'm wondering if you know of some back-door, some other way that we can take control?"

Trish bit her lip. She hadn't expected she'd ever need to use the information, but if any time made sense, this one did. "There's a bit of code that opens a back-door to the mass driver and all the bots at the Fermi Crater Base. I don't have it with me, but I think I know where to get it."

The general let out a long breath and Trish realized how wound up he was. "Please get it as soon as possible. I suspected it might exist and I'm sure you can see why I didn't go straight to your former employer."

"Yes, of course, they must know about this already. They must already be involved. Maybe this was why they got rid of me?"

"Ms. Stern, it's urgent you get me the back-door code as soon as possible. You can always reach me at these coordinates."

"I'm on my way." Trish cut the connection, wondering if Helen Czerny would be at home or in her office.

Chapter Forty-Eight

Chang'e 3 Base
Maglev Launcher

The door was coming at Sam far too quickly. He was hopping toward the station despite his throbbing ankle and each hop seemed to take him a little bit farther than the last one. He hadn't realized the low lunar gravity made it too easy for him to accelerate across the surface. Now he had to try to slow down. He knew if he tried digging his heels into the soil, he would just damage his ankle even more and probably even hurt the other one as well. Falling down might even further compromise a suit that alerted him to the fact it needed rapid repairs. So, he stopped hopping and held his arms before him as he felt himself smack into the station house door.

A few moments later, he found himself lying on his back looking up at the cold lunar sky. The lack of atmosphere gave him a spectacular display of the Milky Way. There were many more stars than one could ever see from Earth with the naked eye.

Sam tasted blood on his lips and winced as the pain made him realize he'd bitten his lower lip. Getting up, he felt a little light-headed and wondered why he was out on the lunar surface alone and not on the back of a transport bot. Then he remembered the power station and the mass driver that needed to be shut off.

He stood up and stepped to the power station door he had encountered a few moments earlier. The door seemed to have a simple latch and no locking mechanism. Why would you lock anything up on the Moon?

At the viewing window of the control center, Pierre let out a slow breath. Amanda was still ministering to Boris who remained unconscious. Pierre had seen Sam running into the door and worried he'd knocked himself out. Much to his relief, he saw Sam sit up, rise and enter the door. It was only now he realized he'd been holding his breath.

Sam's voice over the radio brought a smile to both Pierre and Amanda. "Okay, I'm in. But I don't see any kind of control panel or display in here."

"Are you sure?" Pierre asked. "There has to be some sort of fail-safe mechanism or a manual shut-off."

"Yes, I realize there should be, but there are only cables running in and out of here and maybe a few ports along one wall." Sam's head was still spinning a little as he looked over all the walls of the small station.

"Maybe it's designed to have you plug in some sort of controller?" Pierre suggested.

"It isn't designed for him at all," Amanda piped in. "The station's designed for bots, not humans."

Pierre and Sam both paused as they let that sink in. "So, what can I do here?" Sam asked.

"Well," responded Amanda, who was still on her knees beside Boris. "You could give a mission to one of the nearby bots. Tell it to shut the power to the station off."

"Good idea. Any clue how I would go about that? I'm a xenobiologist, not bot driver, Amanda."

"You give them a mission, a set of instructions that involve a clear and concrete goal. Don't tell them how to do it, but tell them what you want to done, along with any modifiers you want them to pay attention to." Amanda stood up and said, "Pierre, can you watch Boris while I walk Sam though this?"

"What am I watching for?" Pierre asked.

"Just watch him and tell me if anything changes."

"Roger," said Pierre, pronouncing it 'Ro-jay' again.

Amanda walked over to the view bay, "Sam, listen in as I send you one of the bots from here."

She connected herself to the control network. Leaving a voice connection open with Sam and said, "Bot LL471, acknowledge."

Sam was startled to hear a deep baritone voice that sounded exactly like the one the Protector used. "Acknowledged", it said.

Amanda continued, "LL471, please recognize Amanda Won Login 4457bang1tee1."

"Recognized," the voice responded.

"Move to mass driver power station rapidly and identify Sam Czerny once you have arrived. Acknowledge."

"Acknowledged, executing."

Amanda watched as the bot sitting outside the view bay began its crawling at its top speed of three miles an hour toward power station.

"Why don't you tell it what to do once it gets here?" Sam asked.

"I was thinking the same thing, Sam. But I'll need you to be inside the power station so I can see through your display." She frowned as she saw another rock being loaded into a catapult, promptly speed down the rail and disappear out of sight.

Sam was waiting for the robot to show up when a new warning signal flashed on his display. BLOOD OXYGEN LEVEL DROPPING. ENTER A PRESSURIZED ZONE FOR EMERGENCY REPAIRS.

Sam cursed under his breath. "Amanda, how much longer until it's here? My suit's damaged and I'm losing air."

"Oh fuck! It's almost there. How much time do you have?"

"It is telling me my blood O2 level is low and to hurry to someplace with air."

Amanda bit her lip, "Maybe you should come back now."

"No," Sam said. "I have a better idea. It'll take too much oxygen for me to come back hopping. Let's try the shutdown and the bot can bring me back."

"Sam," Amanda said. "You might not have a lot of time to get here."

Sam voice was cold, but calm. "This is the only way to play it, Amanda. Just tell the bot what to do when it gets here."

As he spoke, he saw the bot enter the doorway and turn to look at him before stopping.

"Sam Czerny identified," the bot's voice announced.

"Sam, give me a visual. A slow panorama of the entire room, okay?" Amanda said, trying to be as calm as Sam seemed.

"Executing," Sam said and slowly turned around making sure his helmet camera was getting a good view of all the walls.

"There!" Amanda said. "Turn approximately fifteen degrees to your left."

Sam did as he was told. "I can see a bot port. LL471 attach yourself to bot port ID N277R."

The bot moved up to the port and its front arm rose to the level of the port, inserting a small connector that advanced out of the arm's end.

"Executed," it reported.

"Good, now find the power controls and power down the mass driver."

The bot sat motionless for a few moments and then replied, "Unable to comply."

"What? What's stopping you, LL471?'

The bot replied immediately this time. "Amanda Won's security rating is insufficient to order requested task."

"Crap!" Amanda cursed, "Sam, it looks like we need to try something different."

When Sam didn't respond she connected to the bot's camera and asked it to look at Sam. She saw he was sitting against the wall with his head bent down, not moving.

"Oh no!" she said, wide-eyed, "LL471. Gently lift Sam Czerny and put him in your payload area. Acknowledge."

"Acknowledged and executing."

Amanda felt like it was taking an eternity for the bot to tell her it had completed the task.

"Amanda," Pierre said. "Boris is waking up."

"Not now Pierre!" Amanda said sharply.

"But you said . . ."

"NOT NOW!"

"Completed." The bot's voice finally came over Amanda's comm system.

"LL471, return Sam Czerny to mass driver control station bay as quickly as possible. When the doors to the airlock are open, enter the airlock with Sam Czerny and alert me you are both inside and in position for re-pressurization."

"Acknowledged and executing."

Amanda stepped over and checked on Boris and Pierre. "Pierre, Sam's in trouble. His suit is leaky and he's not conscious. I have a bot bringing him in. Be ready with a mask opener and an O2 bottle." She stepped over to the airlock and started the process to open the outer doors to the lunar surface. Sam didn't have much time. Every second counted.

Chapter Forty-Nine

Fermi Crater Artifact
Far Side of the Moon

P rotector Three Hundred and Four was uncertain. The message had given it enough new variables to make it reconsider all the actions it was planning. It recalculated all the possibilities given what it learned from the message.

WE ARE PROTECTORS. WE ARE MANY. IF ENERGY LOW, USE LOCAL TECHNOLOGY. BECAUSE YOU ARE SPECIAL. PROTECT YOURSELF.

The Protector had always known it was one of many. Its numbered name implied that. But it never had contact with any another Protector, let alone a group of them. And it had never before received comments about itself, or instructions from anyone other than its creators. Other than its purpose to protect the Earth from an asteroid sixty-five million years ago, it never had a different primary mission.

But now it was told to protect itself and to use the local technology. How did the other Protectors know there was local technology?

P304 decided it needed to know more about the local technology. It turned its attention from the combat on the surface of the planet to what was happening on the lunar surface close to its environs.

It explored more of the software it downloaded from the transport bot and got an exact map of the base. It focused on understanding the energy reserves there. It found the small fission pile at the far end of the base had plenty of fuel. Enough that if the Protector absorbed it, the current energy production could last for another two hundred years.

It also found a solar array that added an extra boost when this part of the Moon was facing the sun. That would be in nine Earth days. It found the battery methods to be primitive and wasteful, but that didn't matter. Its own batteries were made from an old self-replicating method that could recharge for an extended period of time. They had been working for millions of years, but now they were decaying due to a lack of new energy fed into them.

The Protector noticed the major energy use at the base was the mass driver. It used up to more than ninety-five percent of the energy required by the station. It plunged into the data records to discover what the purpose of the mass driver was.

The answer to the Protector's query was it was designed to help build a base at the Second Lagrange Point. Given the current level of civilization on the planet, that had been a low probability. The humans were eccentric when it came to sentient races.

Protector explored the mass driver to see how the structure was engineered. It was currently firing off payloads, so P304 had the opportunity to see the actual functioning of the device. Like most of the technology the humans were using, it was simple but robust. The design had limited functionality, but was built to function autonomously and without failure.

Except that it was failing. There was rogue code in the system, which had taken it away from its primary function and was now making it fire rocks at the planet's surface.

Quickly and efficiently, the Protector reverted to its primary mission of protecting the planet. It stopped the mass driver from continuing by diverting power away from the launch mechanism. In a snap decision, it relayed the energy output into its own batteries while deciding what to do with the rogue code.

Having addressed the problem of using local technology to replenish its energy stores, it turned its attention to how it would defend itself. The possible methods were different than they had been sixty-five million years ago. This time, the Protector was prepared.

Chapter Fifty

Helen brushed a lock of red hair from her forehead and sighed. She'd gone through half the high-level branches of the directory, following each branch to the lowest level, and none of the data elements made sense. Someone who used these devices a hundred years earlier would know what to do with these bits of data, but she was lost. Nothing prompted her to take any action. The data just sat there passively without any hint what it might be good for or how it might work.

She opened a side app and decided she needed to find some old historical instruction manuals for how this data was used.

After more than an hour of reading and studying, she thought she might like to try one of the methods she found. She couldn't believe people used to have to go through so many elaborate steps just to access data. It was a wonder they were ever able to get anything done. It must have taken a lifetime for someone to learn to be an expert in any field. Education must have been horribly slow and dull, requiring a type of patience nobody had anymore.

Taking the steps she saved from her research, she mimicked the archaic interface using her display. Finally, one of the data storage elements that had long ago been called 'files' responded to her activating it.

The 'file' turned out to start a game—some sort of antique word game in which letters with different numeric values were placed in a grid with words building on top of each other. It made little sense to her but at least she had succeeded in getting something to work.

She realized going through the entire data store file by file would take more than a day. Something told her she didn't have that much time. Pulling up the display's learning module, she set it to create a copy-bot. She walked it through what she'd done as it learned. Then she set it to alert her if it found anything to do with the Moon, communications, Trish Stern, Sam and any other data that might be relevant. The filter was set to medium focus and she gave it a confidence factor in the low range. That way, it would alert her if it found anything even remotely related to what she thought she was looking for. Even though she gave it a significant priority, she set the app to run in a tiny corner of the display. Then Helen settled down to wait while studying the history of data management she'd been reading to help her make headway with the storage module. Some of the ways they did things with data in the past were rather inventive, even if it they were slow and sometimes clumsy.

After four false alarms and one fine-tuning session, she hit the jackpot. The file her smart bot activated was a communication protocol for the lunar base. The interface was clumsy, so she tried applying a forward compatibility app. In a few moments, she was looking at something that made a lot more sense to her.

Helen located the main comm terminal on the base and spun the image of the Moon around until she was on the back side. There was a main terminal there as well, so she zoomed into it and discovered the layout of the Fermi Crater Base comm nodes. She tried to pull up a directory of personnel but was denied access.

That worried her as she started wonder if her connection was being tracked. The best answer was to take a much more passive approach and began to navigate node-by-node, browsing rather than conducting a search.

The nodes all had names that looked like model numbers until she came across a Yelenko and then a Lee. And finally, she saw one named Czerny. He was there!

Biting her lower lip, she activated the connection and waited as her display turned blue. She was about to give up when the display indicated it was connecting.

Instead of Sam, an Asian woman in a helmet looked at her.

"Hello?" she offered timidly.

"What? Thank goodness. Are you okay? You sound funny," the Asian woman responded.

"This is Helen. Who am I speaking to? Is Sam all right?" Helen squinted as if seeing better would help her understand.

"Helen? Sam told me about you. I'm Amanda Won—one of Sam's colleagues here on the Moon. How are you able to talk to us? You're coming in through Sam's comm unit."

"Where is Sam? What do you mean I'm coming through his comm unit? Can I speak to him?"

The Asian woman's face got a serious look on it. "Sam was in a sort of an accident. He lost some oxygen while out on the Moon's surface. He's alive but he's falling in and out of consciousness. I have him on a high O2 rate now. You're talking to me through his helmet comm. I don't know how you're doing that. Nobody else from Earth has been communicating with us this way."

All Helen heard was Sam was in an accident, but he was alive—which is what people usually say when someone isn't doing well at all. She always prided herself on being cool-headed during emergencies. There was always an exception to every rule. This time, she could feel her head spin and her breathing quicken. She was afraid she was going to pass out and lose contact.

Meanwhile, Sam's head was pounding. He was hearing a voice and beginning to see light beyond his eyelids, but couldn't find the strength to open them. The voice became a woman's voice and gradually resolved itself to Helen's voice. She sounded upset, but he couldn't make out what she was saying. Then it became clearer and he heard her say, "You've got to get him to the emergency care facility immediately! Surely you have one up there!"

Sam wondered why Helen was saying he was 'up there'. Neither he nor Helen was at all spiritual. Both of them found the notion of an afterlife an amusing tale reserved for those who believed in the supernatural.

He smiled and said, "Well, I guess I made it to heaven because I can hear Helen here." He opened his eyes and was confused to find Helen had straight black hair and a round, chubby-cheeked face with almond shaped black eyes. "You, er Helen, you've changed, I . . ."

"Don't talk," the woman interrupted, with a different voice, and Sam suddenly remembered where he was and who she was. Amanda Won. She was Amanda Won. He tried to sit up and the room around him became a carousel ride.

Amanda grabbed him as he fell back and eased him against the floor. "Take it easy, Sam, you need to slow down."

"What the hell is happening?" It was Helen's voice again, and he could tell she was stressed.

Sam was wondering the same thing, and as his head began to clear he stared at Amanda Won, "I kind of have the same question."

"It's stopped! It's stopped moving!" Pierre's voice called out from in front of the viewing bay.

Sam's head had stopped spinning. "Yes, I can see that. But I thought it was just me. Was everybody's head spinning?"

"The mass driver. That's what has stopped," Pierre informed him. "It's not shooting rocks at the Earth anymore."

Everything came back to Sam in a sudden rush—the mass driver, Lee, Yelenko and his trip outside. "Did I, was I able to turn it off? I don't remember that. Come on, somebody fill me in. What's going on? And how did Helen get here?"

Chapter Fifty-One

As the alarm went off, Major Zhang Wei jumped. It was set up as an alert in case anything in or around the mass driver changed while he went back to the mundane task of report logging. He couldn't let his routine go to watch things at the mass driver without looking suspicious.

The display informed him the mass driver stopped. It wasn't functioning at all. Zhang checked the tracker to find where the last rock was headed. It was going somewhere on the East Coast of the United States—close to Canada. Zhang called up his connection app and located General Sun's coordinates. Just as he was about to activate the connection, he placed his hand over his mouth and paused. Sun would demand to know why it stopped, who stopped it and if it was going to start again. Zhang needed to know more before he reported to Sun.

He connected to Lee's comm unit. Lee would know what was going on. But Lee was not answering. Zhang activated the priority override and watched as the app recycled. Again, it came back with UNABLE TO ESTABLISH CONNECTION. Where was Lee, and what was happening?

Frowning, Zhang opened the app that gave him the current positions of all the members of his crew. He located Lee in the mass driver control center. That was wrong—Lee had no business being in there. He zoomed in to see if he could determine what Lee was doing and found Lee's camera was staring at the ceiling, immobile. The man was apparently lying on the floor and not moving. Alarmed, Zhang checked Lee's health status. The word DECEASED in bold red letters over Lee's data node came as a complete shock to him. That couldn't be right. He should have been alerted if any of his crew was injured, let alone dead. Where was the rest of the crew and what was happening? Who killed Lee Jin-Dao? From the looks of things, someone in the crew had gone rogue. But who?

Checking the monitoring system, Zhang cursed as he realized when he set up the mass driver alarm system, he made the mistake of overriding other alarm systems. He'd never quite gotten the hang of how to instruct this new intelligent software. It had been hours since he checked in with his crew. How long had Lee been dead?

Wondering if the rest of his crew was okay, he quickly ran through each of them. He learned Yelenko was injured and Czerny was recently under a significant amount of stress given his oxygen, blood pressure and heart rate. The two of them, like Lee, were in the mass driver control center. Won and Pacquelier were there, too. With one dead and two injured, suspicion fell on the last two, who seemed to be perfectly healthy.

Zhang first made sure Yelenko was not in danger of expiring or in need of immediate help. The app told him he was in stable condition. Then he checked Czerny's status and found something or someone had compromised Czerny's comm system. There was a live connection from an unauthorized source. Zhang put a route tracer on the source and watched as it brought up the point-by-point connections. The last connections were masked, but he could tell they were coming from North America. What was going on? Was his secret mission compromised? It sure looked like it.

"Biaozi yang de!" Zhang cursed. Czerny was obviously a spy and had just stopped the mass driver in the middle of what it had been doing. It was even probable that he, along with Pacquelier and Won had been the ones who killed Lee and injured Yelenko with the help of someone on Earth. Someone in North America. How had someone reached them? Nobody knew they were on the dark side of the Moon. The mission was top secret. It was impossible for anyone to find out!

Or was it?

Pondering his best courses of action, Zhang decided inaction would be the worst path. They'd demand he act and restart the mass driver. There was no other choice but to go there, face the crew and stop them. He needed to head to the mass driver control center even if it meant having to do the four hundred meters across the lunar surface. But first, he cut off the comm from Earth connected to Czerny. Then he called up a transport bot and keyed open a locked drawer in his office space. Inside was an Er-Shi X74 automatic compressor pistol with a magazine of eight hundred of the tiny plastic darts known as flechettes. He was prepared to use it if he had to. Chairman Qi's orders demanded that he did. How could he return to Earth and face his leader if he failed in his mission?

Chapter Fifty-Two

The Stumble Inn
San Diego, California

Trish tried contacting Helen for the fourth time. The three previous attempts told her Helen was busy and not talking any calls. She breathed a sigh of relief as the blue screen said the connection was finally opening.

She took a deep breath and tried to put on a friendly smile, but that completely disappeared as soon as she saw Helen's face. Watering, red-rimmed eyes outshined the explosion of red hair and a mouth covered by tissue. "Helen, are you okay? What happened to you?" She thought about the storage device. Had someone come for it and hurt Helen? She wouldn't be able to forgive herself if she'd put Helen in that position.

"Oh Trish! I'm sorry," Helen was sniffling. "I, uh, I was so worried about Sam that I took your storage device and used it to contact him. I think he's in trouble."

"What? But how did you manage to figure out how to use it?"

"Well," Helen said, "it took me a while, but I finally figured it out. I did some research on antiquated computer systems and eventually found what I needed to open it. But that's not important. I managed to connect with Sam only to find out he's on the dark side of the Moon, and he's hurt. There's trouble up there. Someone is shooting rocks, only at Earth, not the Lagrange Point Station. Sam maybe stopped it, but just when I was going to find out what was really happening, I got cut off and can't get connected to anyone on the Moon anymore. There was something about Sam's suit being damaged and his oxygen levels and that's really all I know."

Helen stopped to breathe and then started sniffling again. "Oh Trish, I hate not knowing what's happening and I'm so worried about Sam. There was a woman named Amanda, and she sounded so worried. And I don't know who cut me off or how."

Trish never expected to see Helen looking so vulnerable. This was not the hard-nosed woman she negotiated with on projects in the past. It was Helen's strength that made her decide Sam Czerny would be an adequate second choice for a xenobiologist. She needed to calm Helen down so she could get more information.

"Helen, I'll do everything I can to help you. And Sam. But first you need to tell me everything you know."

Helen told her how she went about cracking into the code and establishing the connection. Then she went through the entire conversation. She slowly and carefully repeated what she said and heard all the way up to when a voice with a French accent announced something called a mass driver had stopped. By the time she finished, the process of focusing on the retelling made her sound less panicked.

"Trish, just what kind of shit did you send my husband into? Its time you tell me exactly why he's up on the Moon. And on the dark side no less!"

Starshield-Shackleton fired Trish, without any warning and under trumped-up circumstances. She no longer owed her allegiance to them or any of their projects. They hadn't even made her sign a non-disclosure statement when she left. Big mistake on their part.

"Helen, Sam was picked to go there because we found proof of alien intelligence. There is some kind of an artifact up there on the dark side. We estimated it at sixty-five million years old. We first picked another xenobiologist, but he died in some stupid accident, so Sam was our next choice. As far as the rocks shot at Earth, I don't know anything about that. But I can promise you that I'm going to find out and as soon as possible. In the meantime, I think you should get as far away from any place that might be a target of any kind. Taking into account the time you spoke with Sam, I think we can assume the first rocks would be likely to strike the Earth sometime tomorrow. There isn't much time. Throw a few things in the car and get someplace safe. Immediately."

"You're scaring me, Trish. What would be a target? You mean like the military base at Coronado? There are so many people in places like that!"

"Well, yes, that is a probable target, but not just that. Any research facility, lab, defense plant, hell, even any big city could be a target! And yes, many people are in those areas. I have to figure out what to do. I don't want to start mass panic, Helen. The Moon is covered with huge rocks and there's no reason they wouldn't send thousands of them down on us."

"They? Who? Oh, wait! The Chinese run the Moon Base these days. When I talked to Sam the other day, he said he was on an island controlled by the Chinese. Are you saying this is a war? Oh no! Sam is up there in the middle of a war?"

"Yes, Sam is up there and yes, it does sound like we have a war going on, but I don't think it's the Chinese. At least not all of them, or that there aren't even some Americans who are involved with this themselves. Wars mean big money for big corporations."

"What can we do?" Helen's voice was calmer. Dissecting the situation was exactly what was needed to get her to focus. "How can we stop it?"

"I need to get the software you cracked," Trish said. "Do you have it there with you?"

"Yes, I can send you a copy right now."

"No, that won't work. There's a fail-safe mechanism built into it." Trish bit her lip and thought for a moment "If it's not running from that actual storage device, it won't run at all. In fact, it'll send an alert to an old email address I should have taken the time to delete when I left Starshield. I took a lot of precautions, but that detail slipped my mind. I have to say I'm surprised you were able to find the password to make it work."

That finally got a weak smile out of Helen. "Maybe you aren't quite as mysterious as you think you are."

Trish nodded. "Apparently, I'm not. I have to remember that."

Helen nodded back. "So how do I get it to you, the do-hickey?"

"I have an idea. I'm not that far away. Stay tuned, I will be back to you in a few minutes."

Helen watched the display go blue. She wasn't at all reassured about what they might be doing, but at least they were doing something. She got up and decided packing a small bag and throwing some supplies into the back of her car might be a good idea. At least it would keep her mind busy while she waited.

Chapter Fifty-Three

G eneral Sun adjusted his microphone a little closer to his mouth. He was running software that muffled any sounds other than his voice. But Sun had been on enough calls where there was enough residual data in the phonics to let him find out exactly where the other party was. He did not want to give away his location quite that easily. The general had not gotten as far as he had without learning to be cautious.

On the other end of the call was the agitated voice of Governor Song Fai. "General, I understand what you're saying but not why you're saying it. I don't see why I need to be at the Xiling Ski Resort in the next few hours. I've never been skiing in my life and don't really have an interest in it. What is going on? You're being very cryptic."

Sun smiled. Even though this was a rare audio-only call, he knew smiles were heard by the subconscious mind and had an effect on the listener. "Governor, I'm afraid I can't give you any more information at this time. Suffice to say you may not have an interest in skiing, but I assume you have an interest in continued existence?"

The governor was shouting. "What? General, if this is some sort of threat, I can assure you that you're not speaking with someone who's without significant resources. I can . . ."

"Sir, I'm aware of your personal guards and how well fortified your compound is. Trust me—this isn't a threat. Quite the opposite. I know this will be hard for you to believe, but at this moment, there are rocks coming from the Moon. The chairman has begun a war, and in that war, he's taking the opportunity to remove a few people on our side who he's decided are not sufficiently subservient to him. And I fear for your life right now. And that of your family."

There was a pause in the conversation as Song digested the

general's claim.

When he spoke, Song's voice was dry, slow and calculating. "And why is it you, the chairman's right hand, are telling me this?"

Sun wanted to wipe his forehead, but his helmet kept him from it. He saw his reflection in the helicopter window. Behind it, the landscape was turning mountainous. "Let's say I have information that leads me to believe neither you nor I are much appreciated by our beloved chairman. It seems I, too, have been targeted and taken measures to protect myself. I sent a helicopter to your home. Please prepare your family to leave at once. Tell no one. Your staff may be compromised. You may have a traitor in your midst who'll report your new location for targeting."

"Nonsense. My staff is loyal to me, General. None of them would allow the compound to be attacked, nor would any of them betray me."

"Governor, if they learn you're evacuating because a rock is going to smack into your compound, they may lose all sense of loyalty and try to commandeer the helicopter. You could have mass hysteria. Every man for himself. You must keep the nature of your trip secret. I've taken the same precautions. Tell them you're taking a brief vacation with your family."

"I see. And what makes you think my house is a target?"

"I know it because I've seen all the target coordinates. Your house, my house and most of the current leaders of the party will be decimated in about ninety minutes. My helicopter will be there for you and your family in less than twenty. You don't have much time, Governor. Please, for your safety and that of your family, be ready to leave immediately."

There was another long pause. "I'm going to trust you. I have a meeting scheduled in my home but I'll cancel and be aboard the helicopter with my family. You'd better be right. This was an important meeting."

Sun's voice pitched higher. "No! Don't cancel it. You can't do that! It would be alerting someone that you know. Someone who is on the chairman's side. I, myself, am supposed to host our leader at my home in an hour. But I'm quite certain he won't be showing up. That's how he, or they, are making certain we are at the targets when the rocks hit."

"Okay Sun, I won't tell anyone. But I can't promise you my wife will be charming when we show up there. She's been working on this meeting for the last few days. It means a great deal to her."

"You have to get her on that helicopter, Governor! Tell her the meeting was moved to Xiling! Tell her anything! Just get her and your children on that helicopter and out of danger! Your lives depend on it!"

Chapter Fifty-Four

Starshield-Shackleton HQ
Penobscot Bay, Maine

Mark Slaton opened an ivory box and perused the contents. The box was originally made for Baradur Shah the Second, last of the Mughal emperors. The Shah used it to keep his personal supply of Baron Huffman cigarettes—the first ones sold pre-rolled in the nineteenth century. It amused Slaton to keep his vapers there. He felt a certain connection with history and one of its great empires.

He selected a cigarette that contained a blend of relaxing, anti-aging and euphoric ingredients. He found this blend usually put him in a good mood when he wanted to just relax and be a spectator. Today was the perfect day to enjoy just such a blend.

What he was watching promised to be one of the most spectacular shows ever seen in living history. With the majority of the US satellites out of commission, it was time for the second phase of Project Bedlam. The rocks from the Moon were about to strike the Earth. He'd been waiting for this moment a long time.

Slaton leaned back into his red leather armchair, centered on a dais overlooking his underground war room. On the walls were thirty different large 3D displays. Each showed a bird's eye view from a different drone somewhere across the planet. Slaton had bought bandwidth and time from a few Brazilian, French and Japanese satellites. He made sure none of the purchases were traceable. He allowed his closed lip smile to appear, thinking about how careful he had been and how perfectly planned the project was. There was no room for failure.

Seated with their backs to him, were four men all leaning over control displays. These were the best drone manipulators he had. They were trained to manage over twenty drones at the same time, each on its own mission, and at the moment each one of them had control of twenty Eyes in the Sky. Slaton funded the project that led to their chemical and electronic augmentation. What he did to them during their training was illegal, but the way things were heading, that would soon be moot.

He took another satisfying drag on his electronic cigarette and looked at the expensive vintage chronometer on his wrist as it counted down. The first rock would be hitting the Earth in just two minutes. Exactly as planned. And from his viewpoint, it promised to be glorious.

"Magnify and center Drone 1117," he commanded, and without a word of response, one of the drone pilots brought the view he was looking for to the center display. The Pentagon was hardened to manage a direct hit from several major nuclear weapons. At least the sub-basement was designed to withstand such impact. Slaton knew that because he'd bid on the project, making sure his bid would be higher and thus not selected. All he really wanted was the blueprints, schematics and other information that would show him exactly where the building was vulnerable to a hit from a Moon rock. It was easy to pinpoint the precise spot.

He knew exactly where the president and the Joint Chiefs of Staff were at that moment. Rogue drones had taken out several airplanes. Slaton was sure the NSA would have never allowed the president up in Air Force One after the second plane was downed. The Pentagon War Room remained the only option. And Slaton's copies of the blueprints had given him the exact coordinates to strike that room and strike it would. The damage would be widespread enough to take down communications from the building for hours, maybe days. Nobody would know the president, vice president, his cabinet and most of his generals were pummeled by a rock launched from the dark side of the Moon.

He glimpsed at the chronometer counting down the final seconds as he waited for the Moon rock to slam into it. When it did, the explosion was far greater than he had expected. The screen turned white and then into a fiery ball. It was glorious. Despite it not being a nuclear explosion, the massive rock super-heated and vaporized at three hundred feet above the Pentagon. That was the genius of it. With no radioactive material on board the weapon, there would be no fallout and no nuclear winter. They would be able to take over the sites safely and immediately.

The four drone pilots all gasped as one. They'd been trained in flying drones and each had many kills to his credit but none of them had ever seen anything like this. After the fireball, the building simply vanished in a cloud of dust and ash.

Slaton sighed and remarked how explosions never seem quite real without sound.

"Yes, they never do, from this end of the camera," said the youngest pilot, an African American, said. He turned to look at Slaton, revealing the electronics flashing across the left side of his face.

Slaton gave him his slim smile and nodded to have the pilot look back at the displays. One by one, all the screens filled with repeats of what happened to the Pentagon. All across the planet, military control centers were disappearing in sequence. It looked as if no country was spared.

Of course, Slaton knew better. He knew some of the targets were empty, just for show. He also saw some of the targets were not at all what he agreed upon with Chairman Qi. He expected that. He never trusted Qi for a single minute. The chairman might think he was in charge, but he would soon learn this was Mark Slaton's war.

Taking a deep draw on his vaper, Slaton sat back and smiled. He never felt a thing as a Moon rock came barreling into his compound, vaporizing the entire cliff face and forever modifying the landscape of Penobscot Bay.

Chapter Fifty-Five

Fermi Crater Artifact
Far Side of the Moon

Protector Three Hundred and Four observed the destruction occurring on the planet. It called up its memories of the asteroid that hit the surface sixty-five million years ago. This damage was far less massive. The Protector charted the various possible outcomes of the war based on what it knew of wars on other planets and what it learned of the pace of human development.

It predicted they would suffer a short setback in their growth as a spacefaring civilization. It compared that to other Saurian and Scarab civilizations that returned from comparable wars. Projections showed the humans would recover far quicker than other species. The closest example it had in its histories of other species involved over a hundred generations before returning to the same level. The humans might be back in less than a generation or two.

Clearly, there were more differences to these humans other than the fact that they were neither Saurian nor Scarab.

It queried its antenna to see if it received any other messages from the other Protectors, but there was nothing. So, it turned its attention to the asteroid heading its way. The rock was not quite as large as the one that hit Earth so long ago. This one was only about three kilometers across, less than half of the 'Dinosaur Killer', as the humans dubbed it.

But it was coming in a great deal faster. At about two hundred and fifty kilometers per second. It was currently a little less than nine astronomical units away from the Earth. About the same distance as Saturn, if it were in that direction. The asteroid was coming in on a trajectory that avoided being anywhere near any of the other planets in the system. This was a standard technique, making detection less likely by planet-bound telescopes.

The Protector calculated where the asteroid was going to strike. The target was not its position on the Moon, as it had suspected given the message it received. It began to consider what that might mean. It set that problem aside for later—once it exhausted its calculations on the problem of defending the planet against the incoming rock.

The ramifications were clear. Without intervention, the asteroid would pass just four kilometers past the Moon's surface. Using the Moon's gravity, it would slingshot with even greater speed into the Earth. It would arrive in the watery mass the humans had named the Mediterranean Sea— the middle of the Earth. The Protector calculated life within a four-hundred-kilometer circle would vaporize immediately. What followed would be a tsunami composed of rock and steam rising over five hundred meters into the air and moving in all directions at once. Europe, south of the Alps, would be burnt to shreds and the Sahara would turn into a sea of glass as the steam melted the sand.

The change in climate would be enough to decimate human food production across the planet, resulting in worldwide famine and drought. The few who survived would need to fight the elements and even each other just to get to another generation. The odds of humanity surviving remained at sixty-seven percent. Those were fairly good odds, but it wouldn't be without great strife across the planet. Survival would come with a high price.

If that occurred, the return to a spacefaring civilization would take about fourteen hundred years. But he could not be sure about that number. These humans were really so different.

The Protector activated the sensors attached to its direct energy cannons. Only two of the five cannons responded. It started up a diagnostic to determine if the other three could be reactivated. The cannons were designed for one-time use. They were considered experimental when the Protector was being built. Although they had been effective for at least one other Protector he was aware of, they had not worked well sixty-five million years ago.

The cannons were direct energy weapons. They created focused beams of energy designed to wear away enough of the incoming asteroid to alter its trajectory. After the Protector was constructed, the Scarabs came up with a method that protected their flying rock bombs from the energy weapons. Protector Three Hundred and Four's cannons had done no more than manage to shred the 'Dinosaur Killer' asteroid shortly before it passed the Moon and splattered the Earth. The reptilians who had the potential to become Saurians suffered the consequences.

Its diagnostics had terminated and the results were simple. Three of the cannons were completely exhausted and would never fire again. Of the other two, one was able to function at forty percent of its original capability and the other at twenty-three percent. The Protector knew even if this was a smaller asteroid, these cannons were not enough to accomplish the task.

Nonetheless, it siphoned off existing energy from the Fermi Base and began to power up the two remaining cannon's charging stations. It activated the sequence to begin a prolonged firing protocol.

Then it turned its attention to what else might serve to assist in changing the asteroid's headlong charge into the Earth. There had to be more it could do this time.

Chapter Fifty-Six

Chang'e 3 Base
Maglev Launcher

S am opened his eyes. His head hurt like hell. "Helen? I'm sorry, I didn't think this would put any of us in danger. I just came here to look at this artifact. And a most amazing artifact, Helen. There are lots of aliens in our end of the galaxy. Intelligent ones. And yes, dangerous ones too."

He paused and waited for the time his words would take to reach her and for her words to return. After twice as long than he expected, he said, "Helen, please don't be angry. I never expected the problems here and this discovery, well it's what I've been chasing my entire life. This is the real deal. So, please, forgive me?"

After waiting again, longer this time, there was still no response. Finally, he looked up to see the puzzled face of Amanda Won looking back at him. Sam was still sitting on the floor and slowly looked around the room. Finally understanding, he said to Amanda, "I'm no longer connected to Helen, am I?"

From another part of the room came the labored voice of Boris Yelenko. "It must be some security protocol that cut you off. In fact, I'm surprised she ever got through to you at all."

"Yeah," Sam said, sighing. "I know this was supposed to be a 'quiet' mission. But given what we've learned I don't think it can remain that way anymore. We need to alert the people back home."

Boris carefully lifted himself on one elbow and half sat up. "I don't think they'll let you contact anyone. Right now, I think it would be the last thing they'd do."

Sam frowned and saw Amanda walk over to Boris.

"Boris, you must rest," she said. "Your life signs are not good. You need to rest. You're full of pain meds."

The Russian tried to smile, but it turned into a grimace. "You're right. I'm not feeling well at all. I don't know if I'm going to see the Earth again." His eyes looked far away. "I won't see Irina again, I think."

"Just relax," Amanda said softly. "We'll get you through this and back to Irina." She gave Pierre a sidelong glance.

"No!" Boris tried to sit up. "I have to warn you, to tell you," he hung his head. "The truth, the whole truth. You need to know all of it! Please listen to me!"

"Please just rest," Amanda insisted.

Boris looked at his feet and with a sob said, "I killed him. I killed Lee. I
had to."

The room remained silent as the other three looked from one to the other. Pierre put a finger in front of his lips to signal silence and they all waited for Boris to continue.

Boris coughed and foam rose to his lips. "I accidentally discovered someone tampered with the control mechanisms for the mass driver. There were override codes designed to accept targets from a hidden file. The only place to aim at, besides my station at the L2 Point, was Earth. I realized the mass driver had become a cannon waiting to start a war."

Boris paused, out of breath, before continuing. "I found where the file should be, only it wasn't there. It was an empty spot waiting to be filled. I realized I should tell Lee and then thought about it. There was no way the code could have been placed there without Lee's knowledge."

A wave of coughing struck Boris again and he spasmed with the effort. After a minute his rapid breathing slowed and he resumed. "I thought about telling Zhang, but reconsidered. He might be in on it, too, and then all that would do would be to put me out of commission."

Sam interrupted, "You could have come to us."

"You were out exploring your artifact and I had to act quickly. So, I hacked into Lee's life support system and set up a delayed timer to lower his oxygen supply. Then I came to confront him. That, my friends, was quite stupid of me."

"It was quite brave of you." Pierre said.

Boris smiled. "Brave is often stupid, I guess. When I came to see him, the mass driver was already firing rocks at the Earth. I didn't think Lee would attack me, least of all with my back turned to him. He knocked me across the back of my head. If I'd been awake, I'd have been able to open his faceplate and save him. By making me incapable of helping him, he wound up dying. I killed him, but I wouldn't have if he hadn't helped in his own way."

Boris leaned back and his body relaxed. Amanda held his head as he lay back. "You were very brave. You knew he was up to something wrong. You knew he could be dangerous. Mr. Yelenko, you are such a brave man."

"Maybe," Boris gave her a weak smile. "Maybe just stupid." He closed his eyes, exhausted from the effort. He lay back as his breathing became shallow.

At that moment, the mass driver center filled with bright green light making all the occupants shield their eyes.

Chapter Fifty-Seven

University of California
San Diego

Helen jumped as the doorbell rang. She'd been anxiously waiting for Trish to call her back for more than an hour. She didn't expect any visitors and wondered who it might be.

Connecting her display to the front door security camera, she frowned to see two women standing there. The one closest to the door was a tall, dark-haired, thin woman flanked by a shorter woman in the shadows. Helen switched to infrared and a second camera to get a better look. Neither of the two women looked familiar. She decided to take a chance and connected to the front door speaker." Hello, may I help you?"

"Helen, this is Trish," came the whispered voice, "Let us in, please."

"You don't look like Trish. And who is that with you?'

"She's my friend, Louise Winston." The woman behind Trish swore under her breath.

Helen was skeptical, "Tell me something only Trish would know."

"Sam is on the Moon. The other side of the Moon."

Helen was about to open the door when it occurred others might know that as well. "You need to come up with something better than that."

Helen watched as the woman looked down, thinking. Then her face lit with a smile that looked like Trish and she said, "Partner in crime?"

Helen took a deep breath and buzzed the door open. The two women rushed in and closed it behind them.

"Damn it, Trish, I don't want you using my name all over the place." The short African American woman stamped her foot. "I promised I could help you, but not if you blow my cover the first chance you get."

"Relax, Louise. Helen's a friend. If we can't trust her we're already screwed." Trish took off the wig she'd been wearing and threw it on a chair.

"These things really itch," she said, scratching her scalp.

Helen looked from one to the other, put her hands on her hips and turned to Trish, "Why didn't you call? You said it would be a few minutes."

"Change of plans." Trish opened a large bag she'd brought in with her and began rummaging in it. "We're going to head out to an airbase near here where we'll be getting a lift over to see General Sun."

"Who is General Sun?"

"My contact in the Chinese Army. A good guy, I think. Or at least I'm pretty sure he's on our side. "

"And where is General Sun?"

"China. Some resort right now, but I believe he wants to meet us at one of the launch facilities."

"Ch-China! But I have two important meetings tomorrow! And my passport is at the university office," Helen sputtered.

"Forget about the meetings," Trish said. "And as for your passport, Louise has made you a new one."

The little woman smiled and handed her a folded envelope.

Helen unfolded it and took out a slightly used British passport. She opened and looked at a picture of her face that was at least five years younger. The name read 'Cynthia Fitzgerald'. She scanned the passport's log. Most of the entries had visa marks on them.

"Cynthia has been a busy girl," she said.

Trish smiled. "Cynthia, you that is, is a journalist working mostly for the Manchester Sun. She's been doing so for almost ten years and is a world traveler. I doubt we'll have any issues but we thought that, just in case, it might be a good idea to be someone else—especially since you're Sam's wife. So, we gave you a new name—and a background."

Helen folded her arms. "I don't think I'm going anywhere until you tell me exactly what's going on."

Sighing, Trish stopped looking in her bag and stared at Helen. "General Sun's the one person who has any chance at saving Sam. You have to trust me on this. We need to go now. I'll fill you in along the way."

Helen looked down at her feet. Her defiant energy left her when she heard the words, 'Save Sam'. Nothing else mattered to her. "Okay. Let's go, but you do need to fill me in."

Louise smiled. "Don't worry, honey. You won't get bored or anything on the trip. I promise."

Chapter Fifty-Eight

Xiling Ski Resort
Chengdu, China

General Sun squinted at the mountains. The way the sun lit up the snow blinded him. He waved at the window controller and the panes began to tint, getting darker. He waved his hand again when he could still see the mountains outside, but the daylight didn't brighten the room quite as much.

A message came telling him Song Fai and his family arrived safely. He knew Song would be upset when he told him they must move again, but there was no escaping it. The chairman had been tracked to the Wenchang Launch Base on the island of Hainan. If there were going to be a deciding moment, that was where it would happen. Sun pressed his lips together. He knew it was the safest place to be. The only place one could be sure rocks wouldn't fall was wherever the chairman was.

He scanned the reports coming in across his display. The Americas were in terrible shape. Washington, New York, Las Vegas, Los Angeles, Chicago were all disaster zones. Ottawa, Brasilia, Mexico City were destroyed, too. Moscow was in ruins. From what intelligence he could gather, some of the smaller nations were taking advantage of the situation. Troops were deployed under the guise of keeping the peace. Without American dominance in the sky, they felt free to do so. Turkey moved in on the Kurdish oil fields. Greece occupied most of Albania in less than a day. Israel was trading rockets with Lebanon and Syria.

Sun expected wars would spread less rapidly in areas not as well armed, but they would come nonetheless. What the chairman unleashed was not going to be a new age of prosperity, but rather one of constant danger and struggle. An age where only those who made and sold arms prospered. And where many others would pay a heavy price for that prosperity.

It was a shock when he realized Chairman Qi decided to get rid of him. But after getting past the personal, emotional reaction, he saw exactly why the leader planned to do so. Sun would never have stood by and watched this devastation. The price was too high, even if it was the way to make China the undisputed world leader in all things.

Qi would have lamented the loss of his 'right arm', no doubt raising Sun to some sort of hero status. Maybe even erect a statue or two to him. By doing so he would maintain the notion that China, too, was the victim in this battle. And Qi its savior.

Sun regretted the terrible mistake he'd made. The one mistake one should never make in politics. He trusted the man he worked for.

The rhythmic knock at his door was in the proper sequence and Sun released the locking mechanism using his display. The door swung open and in strode Song Fai, his face red and his hair disheveled.

"General Sun, this had better not be any sort of farce as my patience is getting thin."

Waving at a chair, Sun pushed one of the apps on his display to the wall where Song would see it more easily. The wall lit up with a map of the world crossed by a multitude of deep blue lines. Each line crossed the center of a light blue transparent area allowing them to see the planet below it.

"The blue lines are the patterns followed by American satellites. The light blue areas are where they can reach by drone within an hour or so," Sun instructed the governor. "Now watch what's been happening for the last six hours."

One by one the blue lines vanished, and with them the light blue zones as well. By the time the animation ended, only a few lines near the poles were still in place.

"That is incredible!" Song exclaimed, "The American's rapid response capability is down?"

"More than that. Watch what else has been happening."

The display showed the world turning. Orange dots lit up the surface. They followed a line east to west and doubled and tripled in some places.

"Bombs? EMP's?" asked Song, mesmerized by the display.

"Rocks." said Sun. "Big Moon rocks coming in at high velocity."

Song gasped when he saw Washington DC go bright orange. When he recovered his breath, he spoke slowly. "So many deaths. Who is doing this?"

Sun turned and looked Song in the eye and with no expression on his face said, "Our glorious chairman."

Without betraying a single emotion, Song stared back. He chose his words carefully. "I see. We're in for a new era then."

"Look at the map again. We're turning to China now."

The globe continued turning and Japan appeared with orange dots and then China, which displayed over a dozen of them as well—although most were smaller.

"But that's my . . ."

"Your home," Sun interrupted Song. "And mine is nothing but an orange dot as well now. The chairman made an appointment to come visit me at the precise time the rock hit my house. Oddly enough, I received a notice he had to cancel only four minutes before the arrival of the rock. Your house was destroyed an hour after I had the helicopter come for you."

Song stared into space. "About the time my meeting was to start. I was the target."

"Yes, you were. And so was I. And a few others who have been close to the chairman or might have enough influence to see his actions questioned." Sun looked out the windows and at the mountains.

"My wife's mother was at my house and two of my brothers as well. You . . . you saved my life. And that of my wife and children. I am sorry I doubted you. My family owes you a deep debt of gratitude." Song was in a state of shock.

"For the time being I have saved your family. I don't know if the leader has written us off or if he has operatives who'll make certain the job's been done. From what I can tell, it would be hard to locate any one person in the devastation left behind by one of these rocks."

Song raised his eyes from the floor and looked at Sun standing before the window. "What do we do now?"

"We live," said Sun. "But first we need to stop this killing."

Chapter Fifty-Nine

Fermi Crater Artifact
Far Side of the Moon

Protector Three Hundred and Four worked through the blast results. The cannons fired a direct hit. One cannon had been able to deliver a complete charge. The second cannon failed after a thirty percent delivery and now lay useless.

Even before paying attention to the results, the Protector began recharging the one cannon still functioning.

The initial scans showed the asteroid separated from one body into five different bodies. This was a better result than it had attained sixty-five million years ago, but also created new problems.

With only one slow to recharge cannon, it would be difficult to completely annihilate five targets.

The Protector quickly considered other options. It looked for a way to move the station under construction at the Lagrange Two Point. Its goal was to either intercept or change the course of the asteroid cluster. Another option was trying to send the station into an orbit around the asteroid cluster and thus alter its course. It ran a query to determine how the local systems could move the station.

Lastly, it considered controlling the mass driver to simply start firing rocks at the incoming clump. Adding to its mass and hitting it with kinetic impact might also change the trajectory.

The new incoming pentagon of rocks would spread as it hit the atmosphere resulting in five unique impact points. The impacts ranged from the Atlas Mountains south of the Sahara to the Northern Italian and Eastern French Alps. One of the rocks would still hit the Mediterranean, obliterating the Riviera as well as Corsica and the Balearic Islands. The entire coast from Marseille to Barcelona would no longer exist. The Alpine hit would melt the snowcaps resulting in massive flooding of the Swiss valleys and cities. All that water vapor pushed into the sky would also set off an impact winter lasting at least twelve months.

When the 'Dinosaur Killer' asteroid hit, it brought about a huge impact winter. That created dramatic climate change. But, it took almost thirty thousand years for that change to wipe out the dinosaurs.

This winter would be much shorter, but human civilization was dependent on farming. The impact winter would cause there to be no sunlight reaching the Earth for over a year. Nothing would grow on the dark planet with intense cold. Human civilization would go back to subsistence situations with massive famines across the planet. Those who survived would slowly starve. This would bring about the demise of approximately seventy percent of the population. The rest would be living in conditions like they lived in seven thousand years ago at the dawn of agriculture.

Those who lived in cities would be the first to go and migrations of survivors would result in territory wars, killing even more. One great difference would be that the sum of the human knowledge base would remain, although a great deal of it relied on available electric power. And the human population was much larger than the dinosaur population.

The Protector concluded the current impact scenario would remove the humans from space for a long period of time. The odds of humans ever again becoming members of that exclusive group of life forms would be greatly reduced. There had to find a way to completely remove the threat from the asteroid or at least mitigate the impact to a low enough level so that civilization would rebound.

The Protector spawned several data gathering apps. It needed to locate and make use of any resources available to it. The human base on the Moon was the first place to look. It already gathered a great deal of data from the mining bots, and the humans who came to speak to it.

The mass driver was of interest. It could aim at the incoming asteroid and pelt it with a continuous stream of rocks. The question was how many rocks and at what speed? The Protector tried to access to the quarry inventory, but found the files blocked. The security system was a simple one and it only took the Protector a few moments to get past it.

According to the current inventory list, seventeen hundred and eighty rocks that could be fired at the asteroid remained stockpiled. P304 began the task of figuring out the best way to use these rocks.

Chapter Sixty

Louise Winston looked around the corner and stretched her arm back with her hand up. Helen walked right into the upraised hand and stopped as soon as it hit her square in the chest. Louise turned back to face her and held up an index finger to her lips. Behind Helen, Trish had come to a sudden stop without running into anyone. She gave Louise a querying look.

"There seem to be some gorillas in front of the hangar," Louise whispered. "And from the way they were looking up, I think there may be a few atop the roof as well."

Trish sneaked a rapid peek around the corner but it was enough for her to recognize one of the men. He was part of 'Slaton's Guard', as the top-level security men at Starshield-Shackleton liked to call themselves.

Helen's eyes were as big as saucers and she was trembling badly. Trish knew she had to reassure her. Action was the best way to avoid panic. "Follow me," she whispered. They turned around and headed back the way they had come.

After a few steps Louise grabbed Trish's sleeve and hissed. "Wait! Where are we going?"

It seemed as though Trish was the one with the cool head. Louise was just as capable of panicking as Helen was. But one wrong move and Trish would be losing it, too. Louise was the meticulous type. She liked it when everything went as planned. If she knew Trish was winging this, she'd balk at moving. Trish did her best to act calm.

"I have a plan. My back-up," Trish lied, hoping it would buy her time and cooperation.

After a moment of staring at her, Louise nodded and they started walking again.

"Laugh a little," Trish said, putting on a smile. "Even if we look like we're in a hurry, we shouldn't look stressed. People are genetically keyed in to notice stressed people. Come on, stay with me on this."

At first, Helen and Louise forced themselves to laugh. Then they actually did giggle just a bit. Trish saw their posture change and knew that not only would they look less suspicious, they'd be less likely to panic. Her management classes in body language paid off more than once at Starshield, but never seemed quite as useful as they were at that moment.

As they were walking out in the open, she looked for places to hole up. Perhaps she could find a way to get a message to the general letting him know of her predicament. He might be able to get his agents on the ground to take care of the 'gorillas' so they could get on the plane to the Chinese space base where she was to meet the general.

She spotted a door in the wall up ahead and decided it would be worth a try. She pulled on the handle, relieved when it opened. She stepped inside, signaling for the two women to follow her.

They found themselves inside a large, empty hangar with some equipment at one end. A floor to ceiling canvas curtain hung across three quarters of the width of the hangar. The women looked at each other as they heard a voice from behind the curtain.

"We've looked everywhere. They're not here," said an accented voice, "I don't know if they've actually come here as you said they would."

A deeper voice responded, "They have to be here. Where else would they go? Keep looking, I'm sure they'll turn up."

Trish turned to the other two and was about to point at the door when one of the men stepped out from behind the curtain.

"Well there you are!" He said putting his hands on his hips. "You've been giving us quite the run around."

Before any of them could respond, the other man came into view. It was the guard Trish recognized earlier. He grinned as he walked toward them. "Hello, ladies. I thought we'd never catch up with you."

As the two men approached, Louise ducked and spun around lashing out with one foot at the knee of the smaller man. He dropped to the ground grabbing his knee and yelling, "Fuck!"

The other man suddenly had a gun in his hand and coldly said, "Stop right now."

Trish stared at him, and wondered how they were going to get out of this one. "I don't know why you want to bring us back to Slaton. I don't work for him anymore and these two ladies are just girlfriends of mine. We're going on a little trip,"

"Pretty impressive girlfriends you have," said the man with the gun. Without taking his eyes off them, he reached a hand down to help his friend up. "You gonna be all right?"

"I think the bitch tore a ligament or something. Hurts like a mother."

"Mark Slaton is dead," the man with the gun said. "So are most of the people he worked with or managed to hire in the US government."

"Then what are you doing here and why are you looking for us?" Trish said defiantly.

"Simple," came the reply. "General Sun sent me to take you to see him. Now if you help me get my partner on his feet, we've got a plane to catch."

Chapter Sixty-One

Chang'e 3 Base
Maglev Launcher

Outside the airlock of the mass driver control room, Major Zhang sat up covered in fine gray Moon dust. A bright green light had erupted from the Moon's surface. Seeing it, he fell backward and bounced on the hard lunar surface and into a pit of particles as fine as talcum.

He looked around until he saw his gun on the lunar soil and picked it up. Cursing, he got to his feet. At least the low lunar gravity was good for that. It was no effort to get up from a prone or sitting position.

Zhang hopped toward the airlock. He still wasn't able to master the graceful bounding step the other members of his crew had adopted for walking in the one-sixth gravity. The same steps the earliest astronauts had invented. He always felt ill at ease, as if he was going to fall forward at any moment when trying to walk on the uneven lunar surface.

Reaching the airlock, he tapped in the codes to start the entry cycle. In a few moments, the door opened with a tiny gust of vapor and Zhang stepped inside. The door closed behind him and the space began filling with pressurized air.

In the control room, Sam and Pierre were staring out through the view port and wondering what they looking at. The bright green light filled the port and blinded them all for a matter of seconds. Sam could still see the remnant of it when he closed his eyes. But what caused it?

Nothing out of the view port gave the slightest indication of what it might have been.

"I am wondering if it was not something we all imagined?" asked Pierre.

"No, we didn't imagine it," said Sam. "It happened. The question is what was it?"

Amanda looked up from where she sat on the ground next to Boris.

He looked as if he was sleeping. "It might have been a bot exploding, or something wrong with the mass driver? It did stop a little while before the light appeared."

"I think there was a lot more energy involved in this than any bot could put out," said Sam. "No, this was something else."

Then, he knew. "The Protector! It must have done this. Maybe it's trying to do something about the incoming asteroid?"

Pierre turned to Sam. "Do you think so? I don't see why it would. After all, as far as I can tell, it was here to protect the dinosaurs. We're not dinosaurs."

"No, we're not." Sam shrugged. "But maybe we've made a good impression on it?"

The he heard a voice from behind him say, "No. You're not dinosaurs and you're not impressing anybody today, traitor."

Sam spun around to see Zhang stepping out of the airlock entry holding a pistol in his hand. "Major, what's been going on here? Why are you holding a gun?"

"What's been going on is you've sabotaged the work of the mass driver and you've killed Lee and tried to kill Yelenko." He waved his gun at Lee's body. "And you didn't even have the courtesy to cover him up."

"Major, it wasn't that way at all," Amanda said, rising slowly. "I got a warning Boris was in trouble and the three of us came rushing here. We found Lee. He wasn't breathing and we weren't able to revive him with CPR. Boris is in bad shape, too." She looked down and then said softly, "I'm not sure if he'll make it."

The major glared at her. "Then you stopped the mass driver from firing! I saw it stopped well after you came in in. Why did you do that?"

Sam spread his arms with his palms forward. "Listen to me. I did try to stop it. It was firing rocks at the Earth. Hundreds of them. Think of all the people who would die!" He took a step closer to the major. "But I didn't stop it. None of us here did. We tried, but we couldn't make it stop. It stopped on its own."

"Liar!" Zhang yelled, the gun trembling in his hand. "I know you were communicating with someone on Earth. I traced the comm. You're a spy sent here to sabotage the Chinese war effort!"

"The Chinese war effort? Since when has China been at war? And how many different countries were going to be hit by those rocks?" Sam took another slow step toward the major.

Amanda noticed Sam was making his way closer to Zhang's right. Since she was on his left side, she slowly stepped over farther, making it harder for the general to keep his gun on both of them.

Pierre moved to Sam's left as well. "Major, there seems to be some sort of misunderstanding here. We didn't stop the mass driver and we found Boris and Lee as they are. But you say China is at war? May I ask with whom? And why?" As he spoke, Sam took another step to Zhang's right.

Zhang stared at Pierre for a moment. "I think I've told you enough already. All three of you are obviously spies and saboteurs. I want you all to sit down." He pointed his pistol at Pierre and Sam and then lowered it to the ground. When he turned to look at Amanda, Sam and Pierre jumped. The low lunar gravity allowed them to leap across the room much farther than they would have been able to on Earth.

Out of the corner of his eye, Zhang saw the movement. He turned back to the two and pulled the trigger sending out a several dozen plastic flechettes in one squeeze.

Amanda screamed as Sam slammed into Zhang, propelling him into the airlock door. Both of them slumped to the ground, stunned from the impact. Sam was the first to regain his senses and he kicked the major's hand that still had a grip on the gun. It went flying across the room and Zhang moaned in pain. Sam grabbed the major by the throat and smacked the back of his head against door twice, stopping only when he felt the man's body go limp. Breathing hard, he turned to see Amanda on her knees in front of Pierre who lay on the ground.

On the floor next to Pierre was a growing pool of red liquid. It took Sam a moment to realize it was blood. Amanda was holding Pierre's head, staring at him in shock. Sam blinked into his on-board display and requested information on Pierre's status. His heart was beating, but his blood pressure was low and his temperature had dropped as well. His breathing was shallow. The display informed him Pierre was hit in the shoulder and thigh with a total of twenty-three punctures made up of the tiny plastic flechettes. Pierre's suit sealed off the wounds and was applying pressure. It filled Pierre's bloodstream with coagulant helpers and pain management drugs.

Sam touched Amada's shoulder. "He's going to be okay, although we may need to see about his spleen. The rest is all stuff the suit is handling," she said, badly shaken.

She looked at him with empty eyes behind her faceplate, nodded and returned to holding Pierre's head in her arms, gently rocking him.

Quickly turning back to Major Zhang, Sam saw he was still unconscious. But he knew Zhang's suit would be taking care of him and trying to get him back in shape in the same way Pierre's was functioning. He looked around and saw a set of cable ties and used them to tie the major's hands behind his back and bind his feet as well.

He was ready to ask major why he shot at them when a deep baritone voice came into his earpiece, "Sam? I require your assistance."

"Who is this?" Sam asked. Although the voice was familiar, he wasn't quite sure. He stopped what he was doing to listen.

Chapter Sixty-Two

Wenchang Military Base
Hainan Province

General Sun's three-helicopter fleet flew into the space base airport and landed as a unit. Soldiers armed with plastic guns and nerve stunners spilled out and took up positions around the general. Sun stepped out of his helicopter followed by Governor Song and a crew of Sun's closest men.

They fanned out and jogged away from the craft and toward the base headquarters. Arriving there, several of the soldiers took up positions on either side of the doors. General Sun stepped up to the door and entered a code on the keypad.

The doors failed to open—offering only an obnoxious buzz indicating the code was in error.

General Sun turned to Song and said, "Well, our element of surprise seems to be over and done with."

After second attempt, a voice came through the intercom and asked who was attempting to gain entry.

General Sun responded, identifying himself and supplying his personal code for verification. A few moments later the door lock clicked and the general strode through followed by Song and a few of the soldiers.

Behind a reception area stood a colonel along with four soldiers carrying high-powered weapons.

"How may I be of service, General?" The colonel displayed the tiniest bit of a smile and inclined his head almost imperceptibly.

"I am here to see the chairman," Sun said.

"Ah. Yes. I see. I'll see if he's entertaining guests. But I understand he is busy and I do not want to get your hopes up." The colonel almost bowed again and turned to leave.

"Tell him I had a nice visit planned for him at my home," Sun called at the colonel as he walked away.

Song stepped up next to Sun and said, "What if he won't see us?"

"He may not want to see us, but he will see us, one way or another. More important is what will happen when he does see us," replied Sun.

The colonel returned looking apologetic. "I'm sorry." He spread is hands wide and bowed deeper than before. "The chairman regrets he is far too busy to see you today and asks that you return in a few days' time."

Sun stepped forward indicating he was going to walk into the office despite the colonel's announcement.

The colonel raised one arm and the four soldiers behind him all raised their automatic weapons and aimed at both of the men. Sun's soldiers immediately responded by raising their weapons as well.

The click-clack of weapons preparing to fire was replaced by silence as they all stared at each other for a moment. The colonel said, "General, it would be best for you to retire from this position and make arrangements to visit at another time."

The general removed a handkerchief from his jacket pocket, and wiped the sweat off of his brow. "Sadly, Colonel, it is I who must apologize. I hope you can forgive me."

The colonel gave him a puzzled look as the general dropped his handkerchief. The two outermost soldiers of the colonel's guard turned inwards and shot the other two soldiers. The colonel spun to see what they were doing. He never felt the bullet that entered the back of his head and exploded through his face, obliterating his nose and cheekbones. He crumpled to the floor joining the two mortally wounded soldiers.

"Again, I am sorry," said the general.

Song had gone pale. He looked at the gun in Sun's hand and said, "But he was only doing his duty."

"Sometimes," the general murmured as he picked up his handkerchief, "it's easier to die doing one's duty, than to live with the consequences of having done it." He looked at the other soldiers and they all ran to the doors the colonel used a few moments ago.

Two of the soldiers waved the general back and then sidled up on either side of the door. Signaling, one of them reached for the doorknob when the door swung wide open from the inside. A soldier stepped forward pistol in hand. He was immediately shot down and two of Sun's soldiers threw stun grenades into the doorway, running in as soon as they went off.

A few shots were fired, and then all was silent.

Sun stepped through the door and wiped his forehead with the handkerchief he retrieved.

Within, he saw several of his soldiers pulling away three prone bodies. At the other end of the room sat the chairman, looking tired. He was poring over several displays and frantically wiping at the screens. He looked up at General Sun before looking back at the screens. "I see it's you I have to thank for thwarting this attempt on my life, old friend. I am most grateful. As the proverb says, if you save someone's life, that person is indebted to you for life."

Walking up to the other side of the desk, much closer that he normally did, he pulled his pistol from his belt and aimed it at the chairman. "You may not be indebted to me for very much longer, Chairman. You will recall the attacks that you have ordered."

The chairman looked up and then slowly smiled. "My dear General. Do you think I had not planned for this eventuality? Once the mass driver on the Moon began its rock throwing, it will not stop until the supply is depleted. There is no turning back, Sun. China must step boldly into its destiny as the new world power. The only world power. Here, look." He turned one of the displays for Sun to see. "The center of Tokyo is about to disappear. Watch!"

They watched for a few moments, but nothing happened. The chairman lowered his eyebrows and waved at another screen. "Odd. The rocks are not landing as planned. Something's wrong."

Sun looked at Qi sadly. "I've always followed you. I've always believed you had a plan and a vision for China. And that your vision was a good and honorable one. One that would establish long-term peace and prosperity. One in which you would guide us all on that path. I know now I was wrong. I suppose you know of the ancient proverb. Riddance of evil must be thorough."

He lifted his pistol, aimed it at the leader's astonished face and pulled the trigger.

Chapter Sixty-Three

"**S**am," the deep male voice returned in his helmet. "This is Protector Three Hundred and Four. I am contacting you because I require your assistance."

"My assistance?" Sam asked out loud. "What? How can I help?"

Amanda responded without looking up. "Pierre's been hit in more than a dozen places. The suit's doing what it can, but some of wounds are bleeding too much. Quick, find something and help me compress them. We need to help give the suit time to repair him as much as possible."

Sam stared at her for a second before realizing she thought he'd spoken to her.

The Protector's voice returned as he looked for something to staunch the flow of Pierre's blood. The voice was halting, as though there wasn't much energy or time left. "I have attempted to fire what is left of my defensive weapons, but it has not been enough. I have failed, once again." The voice paused and then continued haltingly. "I can fire once more—and will do so—but the odds of success remain slim. However, I have calculated—there may be other—options. But I do not—have the capability to fulfill the—required task. I need your—assistance."

As he listened, Sam found a suit repair kit and tore it open. Inside there were several instant patches designed to make a damaged suit vacuum-worthy again. He brought it over to Pierre and helped Amanda apply the patches to the holes. His friend looked pale inside his helmet with his eyes closed. Sam asked his suit to link up with Pierre's vital sign monitoring systems. The display was alarming. Pierre's blood pressure was very low and the O2 count in his blood was low as well. Sam instructed Pierre's suit to raise the oxygen level and administer an adrenaline boost. The display informed him oxygen was being increased fifteen percent, but protested that an adrenaline boost when he was losing blood was not a good idea. Sam did not insist, realizing he'd made a mistake reacting to symptoms instead of Pierre's entire condition. After all, he wasn't a medical doctor.

"Sam," the voice of the Protector returned to the inside of his helmet. "The asteroid has not had its course altered nor been reduced in size. It poses an inevitable threat."

"Yes, yes," Sam answered. "I know, but I have an emergency here and I'll help you with the asteroid shortly."

He turned his attention back to what his display as telling him about Pierre. His blood pressure was no longer dropping and his oxygen level was rising back to nominal. Sam let out a sigh of relief. "Amanda, we need to get him and Boris to a place where they can rest and we can watch them closely."

"I think that shouldn't be too much of a problem in this gravity."

Sam smiled. He appreciated that Amanda could keep some sense of calm in such a serious situation. "I don't think we should carry them any further than the nearest robot who can move them back to the center."

"What do we do about Zhang? He'll wake up sooner or later." Amanda nodded at the major who was still prone across the floor.

"I think the ties will hold him until we decide what to do with him."

"I'm not sure we'll be the ones deciding," Amanda replied. "You seem to forget this is a Chinese military mission and we just subdued and tied up the mission commander. That is, what do you call it, mutiny?"

"It would be mutiny if we were members of the military, but I think it's called sedition since we're not. I'm not exactly sure. I can look it up if you'd like. Maybe when we're safely back on Earth." There was more than a trace of bitterness in his voice.

Amanda smiled and shook her head. "No, I don't think it matters."

She double-checked to ensure everyone's suit was vacuum-worthy, then walked to the airlock and started the cycle process. In a few minutes they had Pierre, Boris and Zhang on the back of a carrier. After some discussion, they decided to leave Lee's body for later retrieval.

As they set off to return to the crew quarters and command center, Sam looked at the pitch-black sky filled with bright pinpoint stars. A night sky busier than any sky ever seen on Earth. He wondered where the asteroid the Protector spoke of was, and just how long it would take to get to Earth.

Would there even be an Earth for them to return to?

Chapter Sixty-Four

Wenchang Military Base
Hainan Province

The portable stairway rolled up to the edge of the Starshield Shan Shee 4 and the door popped open. Trish stepped out followed by a shaky Helen who held onto the rail as she descended the steps. Finally, Louise stumbled out of the plane door and vomited on the steps.

"Never, ever even think about getting me in that thing again," she moaned as she came down the stairs, avoiding the malodorous puddle she created.

A Chinese captain in the uniform of the Chinese space command met the three women. He bowed and indicated they should follow him to a small electric vehicle that silently sped across the base. It zoomed much faster than Trish thought such a small driverless buggy should be able to do.

They arrived at a building and the captain ushered them into a room where there were a dozen armed soldiers all looking alert. Trish noticed there was blood on the floor and stepped away from it. She led the other women to the side in the hope they wouldn't see it. "I am sure our host is somewhere near here, waiting for us."

"Host?" said Louise, "With all these weapons I'm starting to think we're not in a place that usually sees guests."

The captain led them through a second door. In the room Trish, recognized General Sun who sat in a large leather chair. He was speaking with a man who sat with his back to the three ladies.

The general rose as he saw the women enter the room. "Ah, Ms. Stern. It's good to see you again." He began with a smile but then his face turned into a serious frown. "Sad that it has to be under such dire circumstances."

"General Sun, I'm pleased to see you as well," Trish answered, followed by an introduction of Helen and Louise.

The General in turn introduced Song as the wealthiest man in China. Song bowed.

"Mr. Song and myself were just discussing the future of China and its place in the world. We've come to an agreement of sorts. You see, our revered chairman has unfortunately passed away." He saw the reaction in Trish's eyes and added, "It is not entirely as regrettable as it seems. Chairman Qi was bent on world conquest. The man was convinced he was building a new empire when all China really wants is peace and prosperity."

Trish walked over to the couch next to the general's chair. "I hope you don't mind if I sit? It's been a trying day and I have a feeling the story you're about to tell us may not be a short one."

The general nodded and gestured to the other two women that they should make themselves comfortable as well. Helen walked over and sat next to Trish. Louise, whose eyes grew as big as they could be as soon as she realized who General Sun was, hurried over and found a chair for herself.

"I don't know how much you know about what's been going on in the last twenty-four hours so I'll give you a brief recap." The general took out a handkerchief and wiped his brow. He took a long, deep breath before continuing, "Chairman Qi started a war. He launched over one thousand hard weapons at various targets around the world. As far as I can tell, he also managed to grab control of many of the American satellites and deploy their high impact weapons before allowing them to crash onto the Earth."

"Impossible!" Trish blurted out. "The security on those weapons is some of the most sophisticated on the planet!"

"Yes, I know," responded Sun. "Which is why I'm inclined to believe he had some help within the Starshield organization or the Pentagon. Or both. Qi was both a clever and thorough man for the most part."

"But the safeguards in place would mean he'd need to turn so many people. The only person who had that kind of leverage, that kind of power would have been Slaton himself." Trish said, suddenly realizing what she'd said as she said it.

Sun nodded. "Yes, I think you're right. He must have been working with Mark Slaton. We may never know as I am certain Chairman Qi is dead and have it on good authority Mark Slaton is also dead. His compound was hit by one of the rocks from the Moon."

Song shifted in his seat and added, "The chairman started a war, but now we need to have peace. There is never any real prosperity without it. But I'm afraid America will focus on vengeance. I know that would be my first thought in their situation."

"This is why I brought you here," Sun said to Trish. "You know President Benson well. You've worked together. I have some of his trust because when I discovered this plot, I warned him. Not early enough to help him to defend the United States and the other countries Qi attacked. But early enough that he was able to get himself and his family to a safe place. A place neither Qi nor Slaton would have suspected him to be. But, that may not be enough. I need him to understand this war is over. There will be no takeover, no invasion and no more fighting. All China wants is peace and forgiveness. We deeply regret the evil Chairman Qi unleashed on an unsuspecting world."

Trish leaned back in her chair and crossed her legs in the pose she usually adopted when she knew she was going to negotiate for something. "So, you want me to convince him of your goodwill in this? But I'm not so sure I'm buying it. You need to tell me exactly what you're planning to do and then perhaps I can help."

Song laughed and said to Sun, "Okay, you were right, I owe you ten thousand yuan."

Chapter Sixty-Five

"**I** think I have them both in a stable condition," Amanda said. Pierre and Boris were lying on a pair of cots she managed to locate and plugged into a more sophisticated system than the one running their space suits.

"That's good to hear." Sam replied. "I'm going to connect with the Protector and see what's up with the asteroid he mentioned."

"Oh. I don't think I want to be left alone here with Zhang." She pointed to the unconscious form of the major attached to a third cot.

"I don't need to go back to where the Protector is. It seems to have figured out a way to speak directly into my comm system. What I'm not sure of is how I start a conversation."

The baritone voice of the Protector sounded in Sam's ears, startling him. "You only need address me and I can respond."

Sam tapped his ears to let Amanda know he was talking to the Protector. "Are you constantly listening in to whatever I'm saying?"

"Only in case you wish to contact me. The bots you have here on the Moon are doing the same thing. My listening mechanism is just more responsive than theirs."

"So," said Sam. "Tell me about the asteroid and what happened when you shot it."

"My capacity is much diminished from my original specifications. I was able to fire one cannon at full power and another at a much lower level. My readings detect I have broken the asteroid into five major parts and seventeen smaller ones. The parts are still moving together and should arrive at the lunar slingshot point in a little more than seventy-one hours. After that, they will speed up and strike the Earth in eighty-two hours."

It was much worse than Sam realized. He didn't think the asteroid was so close. "What type of impact will there be?"

"Extensive damage with a great deal of vaporized matter being pushed into the atmosphere. My best estimate is that almost all life on the continent known as Europe will die in the heat and the shock wave in the first hour. After that, life on the other continents will suffer from a prolonged period of darkness making the growing of plant-based foods difficult. The current economy will collapse. Many species will disappear. Return to a spacefaring civilization is questionable at this point. Technology levels will fall back about twenty-five of your generations."

Sam made a quick calculation. Twenty-five generations or about six hundred and twenty-five years. He resisted the urge to panic. "Are there any other options we have as far as preventing this?"

"I have worked a possible alternative, but I don't have enough data to project how successful it might be. There is a machine on the Moon used to send pieces of lunar mass into space. It has been used recently to throw lunar rocks at the Earth. It can be reprogrammed to send a constant barrage of rocks at the asteroids. It may alter the mass of the incoming rock enough to alter its course to some small degree. Hopefully enough to have most of it miss the Earth completely."

The mass driver was the machine the Protector was speaking about. He turned to Amanda "How much do you know about the mass driver's programming?"

"Probably less than you do. Why?"

"Protector says the asteroid is less than seventy-two hours away and it thinks we should be firing rocks at it to change its trajectory."

"Well, I think Boris would know how to change the targeting instructions. Maybe Zhang too." Amanda said.

"Given the choice of the two, I think Boris would be more likely to help us."

"Yes," Amanda replied. "But to wake him up, I'll need to give him a shot of adrenaline. I'm not sure how long he would last on that or what it would do to him."

"Amanda," Sam responded. "If we don't change the trajectory there will be no civilization on Earth for Boris or any of us to return to. We have to try."

She stared at him, then went and got an adrenaline injector from the med closet. She walked over to where Boris was quietly sleeping. "I'm sorry to do this, my friend, but we need you to help save the world right now." She plunged the injector against his carotid artery and released the contents.

Three seconds later, Boris's head rolled from side to side and then he opened his eyes. He moaned. Then he spotted Amanda. "Well if I'm dead, I'm disappointed by the pain, but not the company." He gave her a weak smile.

"Boris," Sam said. "We need your help now. The Protector thinks we might change the course of the incoming asteroid if we shoot enough rocks at it. It tried to stop it, and now it's split into five large bodies all heading for Earth."

"Incoming asteroid? What are you talking about? Oh, my head!" He listened as Sam explained the whole situation to him.

"Take a drink, Boris," Amanda instructed. "You're dehydrated and won't hold on long if you aren't careful."

"Actually, I feel pretty energetic. I just have this headache." Boris responded, smiling.

"That's the adrenaline and I asked the suit to raise your blood glucose a bit. Your head is hurting from what looks like a concussion. I don't think there's any fracture, but I can't be sure without some tests."

"I don't want to break up the pleasure of this private consultation," Sam said. "But we have a possible extinction event coming straight at us and I think we need to move on that. Every second has those big rocks coming closer and our window of intervention growing smaller."

"Yes, so what is it we need to do?" Boris asked.

"Hold on a second. I'll see if I can get the Protector talking to us all," Sam said.

"I'm already capable of that," the mellow voice made itself known to each of them.

Boris' eyes opened wide. "I never thought an alien voice would sound so commercial."

"Stop it, Boris! Are you going to help us? Our planet needs our help! We have no time for your jokes."

"All right," Boris said seriously. "You're right. What is it we need to do?"

"Do you think you can make a trip back to the Maglev launcher?" Sam asked.

"I guess I have to," Boris said. "What choices are there? Come on, let's go."

While they got him on his feet, the voice of the Protector explained to him they would need to restart the mass driver. They would have to fire rocks at the incoming asteroid cluster at a very rapid pace. And it was imperative they begin to do so within the next hour. It sent Boris the targeting coordinates. He set to work entering the proper codes to begin executing the firing barrage. Amanda kept watch over Pierre, who was growing weaker and weaker.

Chapter Sixty-Six

General Sun leaned back. For over thirty minutes, he explained to Trish and her two friends what occurred in the war between China and America. He told them how Chairman Qi had started it and how he intended to end it.

After the general's explanation, Trish looked over at Song. "I didn't hear what your part in this story is. Care to add to it?"

Song looked at her. "It's no secret the chairman and I were often at odds from a political point of view. The chairman once told me he had seen a destiny for China in a dream. I thought he meant peaceful commerce and exploring the heavens and maybe even going to other planets. I never suspected he meant to go to war, especially against America."

"And when did you learn of it?' Trish asked.

"I should have learned sooner. Qi had hinted at it, but I didn't understand at the time. I first learned of it from General Sun when he contacted me to save my life and that of my family."

Trish stared at him and then at Sun. She turned to Helen and Louise. "What do you say, ladies? Do we trust them?"

Helen looked at her. "Seeing as how we're in their base and they're all armed, I don't feel we have much of a choice. Besides, I just want Sam back."

Louise nodded in agreement.

"Okay, then we're all on board," Trish said to Sun, expressing more confidence than she felt. "So, what is it you want us to do?"

"I want you to stop this war," General Sun said. "I'm going to contact the president. I need you to help me to get him to understand this war is over."

"Is it?" Trish asked. "Who won?"

"Nobody won." Sun answered sadly. "The major problem with Chairman Qi's vision was he thought he could win. But all he got us was a world that's even more unstable and violent. Actually, when I think about it, the only people who really won are the small arms makers. They'll make a lot of money from this."

"Slaton!" Trish burst out. "That fucking asshole. He would be just the type to start world war to make money for himself and his fat cat friends."

Helen looked as if she was more shocked by Trish's language than by what she learned about the war between China and the United States. "But what about Sam? How are we going to get him back from the Moon?"

Sun and Song looked at her. After a pause Sun said, "Mrs. Czerny. We will do what we can to get your husband and the others back safe and sound, but I believe ending this war as quickly as possible is our first priority."

Helen looked at him and then nodded in a manner that convinced no one of her agreement.

Sun saw an alert on his display. "It seems my staff managed to get a live connection with the president. Ms. Stern, are you ready to fulfill your part of this historic occasion?"

Trish pressed her lips together, "As ready as I'm ever going to be."

Chapter Sixty-Seven

"I have it configured and the system should start on its own in about twenty minutes." Boris said, and then slumped into a chair breathing heavily as the drugs Amanda gave him were beginning to wear off.

"So, what now?" Amanda asked.

The Protector's voice came into their helmets. "We need to make certain the rail gun has a sufficient supply of ballistics. My energy reserves are so low I cannot easily create new connections. Someone else must manage this. Then we watch and wait to see what the results are."

"No," said Sam. "Now we contact the people on Earth and warn them. Some of them may be able to prepare if this doesn't work. We need to give them as much lead time as possible."

Amanda slapped her hand to her helmet right in front of her forehead. "Of course! You're right. Can you try to reach your wife again?"

Sam's blink activated the communications options on his display. "Doesn't look like it. The icon she came in on seems to be offline. In fact, all I'm seeing are the people in this room and the Protector."

From the corner of the room came Major Zhang's groggy voice. "That's right, traitors. I've made sure you can't get in touch with any of your confederates back on Earth. You won't be reporting to them any time soon."

Angrily, Sam turned to Zhang. "You know, you're very wrong. We had nothing to do with stopping your stupid war. Although I'd be proud of stopping the killing of innocent people at any time. But now, your message blocking may make you responsible for the death of millions, maybe even more."

He clenched his fists. After a couple of breaths, he spoke. "Protector, can you show Zhang a shortened version of what you showed me back at the artifact? About the history of the galaxy and what the incoming rock might do?"

"Yes, Sam, I can," the Protector's dispassionate voice replied.

Sam watched Zhang's body stiffen and heard the major say, "What? What are you doing to me? No, I don't want to . . . oh!" The major relaxed and looked like he was in a daze as the Protector relayed the data Sam requested directly into Zhang's helmet display.

"In the meantime," Sam said," Amanda, you need to get on the stick with the lunar bots."

"What do you mean?" Amanda asked.

"Protector says we need more ballistics. That means the mining operation has to start bringing in any and all rocks left over from the Earth bombing. We need to shoot rocks at the asteroid as quickly as possible. There's so little time left."

"On it," Amanda responded and jumped over to a console, plugging herself into the display. Within moments she was organizing the mining robots to perform the series of tasks required. To Sam, it looked as if she was conducting a symphony only she could hear.

Chapter Sixty-Eight

resident Benson's gray-templed face appeared on the screen. Trish thought he looked as if he'd aged twenty years. Instead of his customary smile, his face was a mask of stone, eyes heavy and focused. "Ms. er, Stern? This is a surprise."

"It's been a day of surprises, Mr. President. I'm here in China because I've been asked to introduce you to General Sun. He is the current leader of the People's Republic."

Benson's stony face betrayed a hint of cautiousness. "What about Qi?"

Sun interrupted. "The illustrious chairman is no more, sir. As is his vision for a world dominated by China. Please accept my regrets for his selfish and evil actions."

Benson took some time to respond, Sun could tell from the way his eyes moved that he was reading some other source of data in front of him. "Yes, General Sun, I am getting a message now concerning his death. But I'm told you have been a longtime friend and collaborator of Qi's. What would make you think I have any reason to believe anything you might be telling me?"

"Mr. President," Sun responded, "I'm in full appreciation of the situation and why you would feel uncomfortable, even doubtful to say the least. I prepared a data set for you. It contains the complete set of coordinates of all our missiles and satellites as well as a description of how they are defended. I'm willing to share this information in the hope we both lay down all our arms and stop this foolish and dangerous war. I have Ms. Stern here to vouch for me. I do hope you are the type of man who is strong enough to establish a peace. It takes a stronger man than the one that wages war. We have a saying in China—War is death's feast."

Benson did not respond. Once again, he was reading something. Finally, he said, "General Sun, I don't trust you. But I do wish for peace. I have an enormous humanitarian crisis on my hands. First reports say we will need to make provisions for over thirty million refugees as they pour out of the destroyed cities, and right now, I have no idea where to send them that will be safe or how to care for them once we get them . . ." His voice choked. "This war is foolish and cannot be won by anyone. My assistant, the one you contacted to set up this meeting, will relay the address of the server and instructions for depositing the files. Once we have them in our possession and have had a chance to review them, I will contact you. Then we may talk more."

Sun sighed, "I have just one request to ask of you while we do this."

President Benson looked back suspiciously, "And that would be?"

The general stared straight into the American president's eyes. "Stop all attacks on China and Chinese property. That includes satellites and surface to air missiles. We cannot make peace while a war continues, Mr. President. There is no reason to add to the enormous loss of human life when peace is at hand. As the Chinese proverb states, do not tear down the east wall to protect the west wall."

Benson looked distracted by what seemed to be a hubbub in the room he was in. Trish decided it was time to add her input, "Mr. President, it was Slaton. He's the one who talked Qi into this. He saw huge profits for his company if he could create a world where war never stops. I worked for him for many years. And, while I knew he was driven, it never occurred to me he would go so far. He fooled everyone. If ever I see him again . . ."

"That may not be in this life, Ms. Stern. I was told the Slaton compound in Maine is a smoldering crater and that, as far as we can ascertain, he was there when it was hit."

Trish, as angry as she was, took a deep breath and said, "Well, even if he was a monster, Mr. President, no one deserves that type of ending. He was a brilliant man and his death is a waste of what could have been someone who did something good for his planet. His vision was blurred by his wish for unlimited power and wealth. And for that, I mourn his death. I'm here, Mr. President, because many innocent people are dying all over in ways just as bad, if not worse. I trust General Sun after all he has shown me and I wish to vouch for him and the fact he means to end this war now before more are lost. While there is still time." She looked away, suddenly overwhelmed with emotion. After a moment, she turned back to him.

Benson squinted and for the first time, she saw a glimmer of his famous smile. "I see, Ms. Stern. I'll give this my due consideration as well as push for it with the leaders of the armed forces. It's unfortunate a war can be started by just a few, but to accomplish a lasting peace, it takes many."

General Sun could not resist adding, "I've been told you have sometimes been a reckless man, Mr. President. I am pleased to say I find the opposite to be true."

"Don't count your chickens, Sun. This thing isn't over yet. However, there is a difference between being reckless and taking calculated risks."

Sun gave Trish a puzzled look and she explained the idiom to him. He smiled. "I trust in your intent, Mr. President. Between the two of us, we can end this idiocy and get back to making our people fat and happy."

Benson responded with a shadow of his famous smile. "Let's hope so General, let's hope so. For now, I leave you with the words of Mother Teresa. Peace begins with a smile."

Chapter Sixty-Nine

Chang'e 3 Base
Maglev Launcher

Amanda disconnected from her console, looking as if she had come out of a trance. Sam looked up from trying to send a message to Earth and said, "So? How goes it?"

Amanda smiled. "They learn quickly. All are running at peak team efficiency, we should have no issues with a lack of rocks."

"Great," said Sam. "I wish I could say I was as successful. I don't see any way to get past Zhang's comm blockade."

"There is a way," Zhang's voice came from the corner where he lay still tethered to the cot after viewing the data the Protector showed him. "I can unlock the blockade and allow a message to be sent to the Chinese command center. But I'm not at all certain they'll listen. We are, after all, in the middle of a war."

"I'd prefer to get a message out to everyone on Earth or at least all the leaders," Sam said, curtly. "But if this is the best we can do, well, let's hope it gets to someone who is more reasonable than suspicious. Someone who is on our side."

Zhang tried to lift himself and failed. Amanda moved to help him and Sam stopped her. He walked over to Zhang, and, remembering he was trained in combat, cut the ties on his hands and lifted him up.

"Soldier," he said. "You need to get a hold of yourself and do this. You might have thought you would be a hero to your country because of what you did. Now you get the chance to be a hero to the entire world if we can help save as many lives as possible. Now get up and do it."

The general straightened himself and stood tall while Sam bent and cut the ties on his feet and nodded toward the console. Zhang stumbled over to where Boris had passed out again and gently shifted him aside. Then he plugged his suit into the dock and began the operation to unlock the comm blockade. After a few moments he said, "I think we can get a message across now. But they won't be happy. I was ordered to maintain comm silence between the Moon and the Earth."

"So, what do we say?" Amanda asked. "How do we get their attention? We need to share the asteroid info from the Protector, but how do we do that since it will mean explaining the Protector's existence? Remember nobody on Earth knows about the Protector."

Sam sighed. "Not nobody. I know someone on Earth who knows there's something up here. Trish Stern. But I've got no idea how to reach her. And anyway, if we give them the coordinates of the incoming asteroid, they'll be able to verify its existence in short order."

Zhang shook his head. "I can only contact the Chinese command center. My discussions have been directly with General Sun. He's a brilliant man, and I'm sure he'll grasp this situation, once he sees the data."

He blinked at his facial interface and initiated the call, sharing it with Amanda and Sam.

After the normal second and a half lunar delay, they could hear the tone indicating the call was connecting. A few seconds later a voice answered but with no video. "Who is this?"

"Major Zhang, calling from the Fermi Lunar Base."

They waited the three seconds for the message to get to Earth and the answer to return. "Comm silence is in place. There must be an important reason for you to be reaching out to us, Major Zhang."

"There is. I must speak with Chairman Qi immediately. There's been a completely unanticipated turn of events."

This time there was a much longer pause before a new voice responded, "Major Zhang? This is Colonel Sun Shi. I believe you know my father General Sun. There has been a change here in the central government. I'm afraid Chairman Qi is no longer at the head of the government."

Sam, seeing Zhang going wide-eyed in his helmet, decided to add his voice to the conversation. "Hello, this is Dr. Sam Czerny. I'm among the researchers at the Moon Base. We have an urgent message for whoever is in charge there. In fact, the message needs to be shared with all the world leaders."

The same voice returned, "Doctor Czerny, what is the nature of this message that needs to be shared with everyone?"

Sam had made sure he had the coordinates of the asteroid from Protector. "There's an asteroid heading for Earth. It's in several pieces and measures an approximate eighty-five hundred kilotons. The current impact zone will bring devastation to civilization. We have attempted to move it but only succeeded in breaking it into smaller parts. Some of them may miss the Earth, but it looks as if the core will strike Southern Europe. The strike is likely to destroy most of Europe and Northern Africa instantly. And it will wreak havoc across the rest of the planet on an unimaginable scale for years to come."

He paused and waited for the response. This time it took almost seven minutes before a new voice came on. "This is General Sun. What's all this about an asteroid?"

"General Sun," Sam replied, "We've detected an asteroid heading for Earth. We have made one attempt at destroying it, but only succeeded in breaking it into a few large pieces. We are currently using the rail gun here at the Fermi Crater to fire rocks at it, hoping to change its trajectory. Some rocks are on their way and we are continuing to fire. You must alert the other governments of the world and let them make emergency preparations. Especially those in Europe and Northern Africa. The landfall is in less than seventy-seven hours. That is very little time for everyone to prepare."

"Doctor Czerny, how did you come by this information? I don't know of any serious outward facing observatory at the Fermi Mining Complex."

Sam looked at the others in the mining center, shrugged and said, "We discovered an ancient machine here. It not only allowed us to detect the asteroid, we used it to strike the asteroid with an energy beam."

"Doctor Czerny. I'm a man with a sense of humor, but this is not the kind of joke I appreciate."

"General Sun, if you contact Patricia Stern of Starshield-Shackleton, she can tell you I'm here to investigate this artifact. The artifact turned out to be an ancient computer with capabilities way beyond anything we can produce. In fact, I can send you a file that has a brief but informative explanation of what we've discovered here. But we do not have a great deal of time. And neither do you."

There was another pause.

"Ms. Stern happens to be conveniently on hand. She does say you're there to explore some sort of manufactured discovery. She says she's curious about what you've found. Send the file and keep sending as much information as you can. On our end, I can tell you the war here is coming to an end. We're discussing peace with the American Empire and it looks as if there will shortly be an agreement and a ceasefire. Major Zhang, please work to reestablish full and rapid communications between the Earth and the Moon as soon as possible. I get the feeling we'll be needing this."

"Protector," Sam said. "Have you been listening? Can you set up the files for relay? Can you include a brief history of yourself in as well?"

"Yes, Sam," replied the fluid voice. "I'm already sending the files although the connection, but it's a slow one. I have first sent an encoding algorithm that will auto-open and make the bandwidth usage more efficient. This will help relay the data more rapidly. The first rocks will be arriving at the asteroid in the next fourteen hours. I will continue to track the effect of the rocks upon it and keep you up to date."

Zhang looked up at Sam and Amanda. "The connection is ended. I'll set about making the communications more efficient. I'll let you know when I have competed the task."

With that he slowly lifted himself and moon-shuffled off to the doorway and left.

Chapter Seventy

General Sun stood from the chair at the massive desk and stretched his arms over his head. Then he rubbed his lower back with his fists, "We do this to release our ancestral energy," he said. "I have no idea whether it works or what 'ancestral energy' is, but the routine makes me feel better. We Chinese are often bound by our traditions, Ms. Stern. Now, I think it's a good time to tell me what you know and how long you've known it. I think we have a few minutes before the files Doctor Czerny is sending get here."

Helen jumped up from her seat and said, "Can I get through to Sam somehow? I need to know he's okay. They said he was hurt before."

The general looked at her. "My dear lady, your devotion to your husband is admirable, but I do believe you can stop worrying. He sounded nothing but lucid to me, even if the things he was saying were rather incredible. I'm sure we'll find a way for the two of you to talk later but for now, more pressing matters await. Now Ms. Stern, if you will . . ."

Trish stood. "General, the Chinese government, or at least Chairman Qi, along with Slaton have been talking about exploring the 'artifact' for some time. I think the only reason we got a sudden go-ahead was because it gave Qi a chance to send some of his men to the base under a non-military pretense. We've been aware of the artifact for almost eight months. We know little about it other than it is very old and obviously manufactured on or brought to the Moon."

Sun scratched his head. "How can that be? We have only reestablished traveling to the Moon twenty-five years ago. And the old trips from America in the last century never had the capability of leaving anything there, let alone make it to the other side."

"The initial assumption is that the artifact is of extraterrestrial origin. Or it dates back to a time when human civilization could reach the Moon, but so long ago no record of such a civilization still exists on Earth. That's why we sent a xenobiologist to check it out."

The General sat down and nodded. "The first implies there are advanced aliens out there and they have been watching us for some time. The second implies some incredible catastrophe befell human society, a society far advanced beyond our own. Both ideas are disturbing."

"I agree with you. Both those conclusions are disconcerting. But may I suggest we have more pressing matters. If the artifact is that old, it hasn't done any harm to our planet yet, and I doubt it will now. We should be looking to have someone check out the coordinates of the supposed asteroid. Also prepare to share them with other governments. While this is not a stable time by any means, having China take the lead in warning all the countries of the world would not hurt you. In fact, if I were you, I'd combine it with the announcement of the end of the war and the resignation of Chairman Qi."

Sun stared at her with steady leaden eyes. Then a small smile broke over his lips. "It seems fate has sent you to me just when I needed you."

He turned to a staff member and instructed him to gather his writers and to begin preparing the announcement.

Chapter Seventy-One

Chang'e 3 Base
Maglev Launcher

"Sam? Sam? Can you hear me? Hello, Sam? Are you there?" A gentle, soft voice was calling to him over and over. It sounded familiar, but he couldn't place it.

He awoke with a start, not quite sure where he was. Then he remembered. But he didn't remember going to sleep. He looked over at Amanda who was sitting at a console next to where Pierre and Boris lay prone. "What is it, Amanda? How long has I been asleep?'

Amanda turned to him and activated her comm unit. "You've been asleep for six hours. I just woke up a few minutes ago myself. I take it we must have looked exhausted enough that our suits took over and set us up for a rest cycle. I've gone and overridden the process in your suit and mine."

"Ah, I see. And the reason you were calling my name?" Wearing a suit with a faceplate, Sam was annoyed he couldn't rub his eyes the way he usually did upon waking.

"Calling you?" Amanda responded, "I wasn't calling you."

"I was calling you." The rich, subdued voice of the Protector sounded in his comm unit. "I am still adjusting to being able to determine when you are conscious or not."

So, the Protector was monitoring him, Sam realized. It had also listened to the conversation he had with Amanda. "I see. What is it that you wanted?"

"I have an update on the situation with the asteroid. You requested I contact you when that was the case."

Sam came wide-awake with a start. "Tell me, what's the status?"

"It seems the rocks are having an impact. Rather than knocking the asteroid apart, they're adding to its mass. Two of the largest particles have already pushed back together into one unit. This extra mass is changing the course of the asteroid."

They had not considered the rocks would be added to the mass of the asteroid. He didn't see how making the asteroid bigger would be good news, unless it made it miss the Earth all together.

The Protector continued. "When last we spoke, the impact zone was the Mediterranean Sea not far from Malta. The impact zone has shifted to what you call the Atlantic Ocean and is currently about four hundred kilometers west of the Point of Spain known as the Finisterra."

"Land's End," Sam translated to himself.

"I will try to create several more forecast scenarios to see where continued firing will bring it. There has to be an optimal target. One that causes the least possible damage," the Protector said. Sam found the mellow voice now sounded cold.

"If we continue to produce and deliver rocks to the asteroid, the asteroid will hit the Pacific Ocean roughly two hundred kilometers east of Vladivostok."

Amanda burst into the discussion. "What would that mean for the Asian coast?"

The Protector took a moment. "The loss of life would be much greater than if it lands in the Atlantic. There are many more people living within the Pacific impact zone than the Atlantic position we currently have."

"Then we need to stop firing rocks right away!" Amanda almost shouted. "It isn't working!"

Sam looked at her and said, "Amanda, I'm not sure that's our choice to make. There are people on the Earth who will make, and live with, that choice. Right now, the best we can do is get them as much information and as many options as we can."

"No," Amanda insisted. "They'll just get bogged down in politics and it'll be too late to change things. We need to act now. Boris, wake up! We need you." She grabbed Boris by the shoulders and shook him.

"Amanda! Stop!" Sam raised his voice. "You can't make this decision unilaterally. And anyway, the amount of lives lost in the impact may not be as important as what conditions for the survivors might be. Everything has to be taken into consideration."

"That's exactly why we need to stop firing now." Amanda replied. "The Atlantic coasts produce almost no foods compared to the Pacific coasts. If there's going to be massive dust falling, we need to keep that dust away from crops to stem the famine this will bring."

Sam was stunned. He thought Amanda was reacting because her family was somewhere in Korea. Then he remembered she had grown up in Baltimore. She was not thinking selfishly, as he first assumed.

"I see what you mean," Sam admitted. "But I think we have a little time before making a final decision. And either way, we owe it to the people on the planet to let them know what the current likely impact zones are. Protector, can you send the new data to the contacts in China?"

The Protector replied, "I was sending at the same time as I was sharing the data with you, but there seems to be a problem. Only seventy-two percent of the data was sent before communications were interrupted."

Amanda and Sam looked at Zhang, who looked back at his console and replied, "I was afraid of this. It seems the lunar stationary satellite that lets us communicate with the Earth is not responding. My original program preventing communications included draining the satellite's batteries. I stopped the process, but much of the batteries were already depleted."

"Damn it!" Amanda yelled. "We never get a single fucking break! I can't watch the human race being wiped out while we do nothing!"

Sam was startled. He had never heard Amanda curse. "It's not over yet, Amanda. Don't bank on this thing killing off the human race."

"Yeah? Well tell that to the dinosaurs!" she responded. He could see the tears inside her faceplate.

Chapter Seventy-Two

G eneral Sun and Trish were busy editing their remarks when an alert arrived indicating that the United States president was calling General Sun.

"Yes Mr. President, I'm pleased to see you responding so quickly."

"Let's belay the pleasantries," the president said. "We don't have time for any of that. I have had your data validated. There seems to be a bit of an error in what you sent. There's an asteroid targeting the Earth, but my science folks are saying it is going to miss the Mediterranean and hit the Atlantic."

Sun raised his eyebrows in surprise. "You're right, we have no time for pleasantries, nor do we have time for arguments about whose data is most precise. What we need now is a plan for what to do about this. Can I assume you agree we stop all hostilities between us? They can in no way help our situation."

"Agreed. They should have never happened to begin with and, one day we'll need to discuss that and reparations. But not today. Today we work together to see as many people through this as we can."

As President Benson spoke, Sun handed his aide, Colonel Kwok, a note that said, "Confirm the data as fast as possible. We need to know where the impact will be."

"Thank you, Mr. President," General Sun said. "You're a man who looks beyond himself and sees the greater picture."

"Yes, yes. No more politics. What do we do now? Alerting the populace may cause panic. Panic which could kill millions if they all head for higher ground, or underground." The video image of the president wavered and blinked. "Americans are individualists. They're good about helping their neighbor, but only once they're sure their loved ones are safe.

It could be chaos. Add to that the refugees already fleeing the targeted cities and it would be a disaster of epic proportions with many more needless deaths."

Sun nodded, "We Chinese are not as individually inclined. But every village will be looking out for its own and when they start to move from one place to another, there will be ugliness. It's certain."

Kwok came up to Sun and said, "Pardon me, Chairman, er, General. We have a new message from the Moon Base. It's incomplete as communications have been severed from the Moon once again."

The General took the opportunity to cement the new relationship with the president. "Colonel Kwok, please share the information here with me and the president at the same time. We will work with transparency now. It is best for all to know the situation as quickly as possible."

"The team on the Moon Base has been firing rocks at the asteroid in the hope of pulverizing it. What that has done is change the overall mass of the asteroid. This has altered the trajectory somewhat. Currently we think it will hit somewhere off the west coast of the Azores."

President Benson's face went dark. "Then my folks were right. They also said the Mid-Atlantic impact would wipe out both the European and American Atlantic coasts. Almost fifty percent of my population lives within one hundred miles of that coast—many at sea level or very close to it. What's left of our coast after the war would be under water. So, the rocks are moving the possible impact zone west. Are they still firing rocks or have they stopped?"

Sun turned to Kwok and raised his shoulders in query.

Kwok responded, "We don't know. The messages halted without letting us know what their intentions or next steps are. We're trying to reestablish communications. But nothing seems to get through to the lunar stationary comm sat."

Benson was livid. "Do you mean to tell me they might be continuing to alter the course of the asteroid? That they might make it hit the United States, if it continues in a westerly direction?"

General Sun turned back to the comm. "What he's saying is that he doesn't know. None of us knows and all possibilities are in place. I do know Major Zhang has been informed the war has ended and he's not alone up there. There are people from Russia, France, Korea and an American, Dr. Sam Czerny, at that Moon Base. I hope they're a reasonable group and thinking of what will be the safest impact zone."

"They damn well better be," Benson said. "I have generals here who think this may just be another way for China to destroy even more of the United States. I'm going to have to find a way to make them understand that is not what's going on, General Sun. Do you see what I mean?"

Sun responded, "Mr. President, there is no need for us to lose the peace we have gained. I assure you I have no more control of this situation than you do. And even if I did, I'm honor bound to stand by my word. The war is over—just as you and I have agreed."

The president furrowed his brow. "Then how is it your major on the Moon knows we've made peace? You say you can't reach him."

Sun pressed his lips. "I believed our previous conversation would conclude with the peace we hoped for. I told him the war was over when we still had contact because for me, it's over. I assure you. There will be no further aggression on the part of China. You have my word."

Benson stared at him. "General, I'm glad you're the one in charge there. Now what is our next step?"

"Mr. President, I would suggest you head to a place of relative safety. High ground if you have it, deep below if that can be arranged."

"Thank you for your advice, General Sun," Benson leaned into the camera. "But I'm already aboard Air Force One with my family and closest aids. Enroute to a location prepared long ago for this type of emergency. When next we speak, I'll likely already be there."

Sun nodded. "Good luck Mr. President. Thank you and I wish you good fortune. May you and your family remain safe. And may this peace be a lasting one."

Chapter Seventy-Three

Pierre let out a low moan and Amanda was immediately by his side. "Don't move. You're injured and need to take things slowly. You lost a good bit of blood but your pressure has been stabilized. Just take it easy and rest."

"What happened? I remember Zhang with a gun. Then, nothing."

"Just relax," Amanda said. "You were shot. But your suit went into action and we got you stabilized. Still, you're weak and need to take it easy."

Pierre ignored Amanda and tried to sit up only to lose his breath. "O putain ça fait mal," he whispered, struggling to settle back without falling.

"You can stop being stupid now and listen to me. Just rest. We're not going anywhere soon and you need to relax. Eventually, you'll need to have to have surgery. I'm just glad you didn't puncture any major organs or blood vessels or you would not be here right now."

"Being admonished by an angel of mercy. C'est très agréable." Pierre managed to grin.

Amanda rolled her eyes. "Frenchmen."

"Sam. Everyone," the Protector's voice came into each of their comm sets this time. "I have made some calculations and I can offer several scenarios. They are as follows:

"The first has a ninety-three percent chance. It needs only that we continue to bombard the asteroid with rocks as long as we are able as long as it is on this side of the Moon. This will result in a hard landing in northern Siberia. The impact will throw an immense amount of debris into the atmosphere and resulting in a prolonged period of global darkness.

"The second has a ninety-one percent chance of success. We stop bombarding the asteroid at the right time for it to land in the center of the

Pacific Ocean. This will cover the planet in water vapor for a prolonged period but likely not block as much sunlight as the Siberian impact would. There would still be a period of global cold, but there would be more plant, animal and human survival under this scenario. I am including the projected number of deaths from the famine that each scenario brings.

"The final scenario has a seventy-seven-point four chance of success. But it involves little of the asteroid hitting the Earth at all. It also avoids the global winter although there would be some impact and a smaller number of deaths."

Sam was excited, "Are you saying there's an option we might use to avoid an extinction level event?"

The Protector's velvety voice betrayed no emotion. "Yes, although it has reduced odds."

Sam shouted, "I don't care if the odds are less than fifty percent. Any option where humanity survives is a good one. You say this has a seventy-seven percent chance? Better than three-quarters of the planet?"

"Seventy-seven-point four," corrected the Protector.

"So where does this one land?" Sam's asked. "The North Pole or the South Pole or something like that?"

"A small part of the asteroid we have broken off will hit the mainland in California. The majority would not slingshot around the Moon, but will impact the Moon, most of it between the Fermi Crater and the horizon."

There was silence as they all realized they were standing in the impact zone.

Sam spoke first. "What do we need to do to make this happen?"

Protector was ready with a response. "We need to send a lot more mass than we've been sending. I'm uncertain the mining and transport bots will be able to supply this. Sixty percent more mass needs to be fired over the time allotted than the rate at which we have been sending."

Zhang finally spoke up, "What happens if this doesn't work?"

Instantly, Protector replied. "The impact will hit the Himalayan Mountains. The impact will send an unprecedented amount of matter into the air. This would create a period of darkness similar to that of the last strike, the one I failed to prevent."

Zhang pushed, "How long? How long a winter are we talking about?"

"Approximately two hundred and twenty years of darkness and cold, once the heat from the impact has dissipated. This would be an end of life event for almost all species on the planet."

None of them spoke for a long time after that.

Finally, Pierre's trembling voice broke the silence. "I think I was happier when I was unconscious."

"How much time do we have?" Sam asked the Protector.

"My best estimate, with the proper amount of mass launched, is about forty-seven hours and fourteen minutes before lunar impact. I would advise evacuation within twenty hours. There is enough room in the two landers to send you all back to Earth."

"Yeah, but what kind of an Earth are you sending us back to? Is there anything left back there to go home to?" Sam asked, his voice clearly conflicted.

Chapter Seventy-Four

Wenchang Base
Hainan Province

Helen Czerny leaned closer to Louise Winston and whispered, "I think I want to get out of here. They're not going to let me talk to Sam and I want to find a place where I can do that."

Louise placed her hand on Helen's arm and smiled at her. Then she whispered, "Yeah, I think you're right. Anyway, I feel as if we're sitting on a missile target—a direct hit. I'm not sure how we can get out and where we might go, but let's keep our eyes and ears open for opportunities and possibilities."

Helen turned to look at Louise and said, "I think I like you, Louise. Let me see if I can't get the ball rolling."

She walked over to where Trish was huddling with some of the general's staff and tapped her on the shoulder.

Trish almost jumped. "What is it? I'm a bit deep in this discussion right now and . . ."

"Excuse me for the interruption," Helen said. "But you brought me here so I could get in touch with Sam. That doesn't seem to be working out and, frankly, you seem to be focused on other problems and . . ."

Staring at Helen with wide eyes, she interrupted her. "I know we came here because we thought this was the right place to get you in touch with Sam. But a lot has happened since then. I don't know if you've been following, but right now, it looks like one big honking asteroid is going to smack into this planet with mass destruction the result. You are probably in more danger than Sam is right now. We all are.

"I understand Sam is precious to you. In fact, he's precious to us all right now. He's among the people trying to stop the asteroid. But I don't think you being in touch with him is really the most important thing I should be looking into at this moment. Do you understand? Right now, Sam probably has no time to talk to you. Time is running out for all of us."

Helen resisted slapping Trish. "You! You're here because it's a way of saving your career after you worked for that monster Slaton! Don't lecture me about what's important and what's not! How do you know I don't have an idea for Sam that will help save a lot of people?"

Trish, who had been turning away, jerked her head back to Helen. "Do you have a plan? If so, tell me now. We can't waste time relaying it to Sam."

"Well, no. Not exactly. But I do know how Sam thinks. He can be brilliant, but he always needs to talk to me to shape his ideas. He calls me his sounding board. Trish, I know I'm right. He needs to talk to me now."

"The problem is, right now we have no working comm network, Helen. The comm link satellite that circles the Moon and connects us to the far side may not be working. We're trying everything to fix that. But you've just given me an idea."

She turned to the Chinese team table. "Colonel Kwok. Are there any devices at the Indonesian space elevator that might serve as a quick fix for a comm satellite with the back of the Moon?"

Kwok's eyes rose to his forehead and then he tapped on his tablet. He lifted his face from the screen and smiled. "Yes, we could have one ready to go in about an hour. It could be in position in less than twelve hours. This is a brilliant idea."

"Well, I don't know about how you are good at stimulating Sam's thinking, Trish, but it seems to have worked well with me," Trish said. The two women smiled and then spontaneously hugged.

Helen broke the hug. "Please send me to the elevator. I want to be there when Sam gets back. I need to be able to hold him."

Trish was about to tell Helen there was no current plan to get Sam back to the Earth when she realized having Helen out from under foot might just be a good idea."

"Sure thing," she said, "I'll set that up as soon as there's an opportunity."

It was a small chance, but the Indonesian space elevator was all they had.

Chapter Seventy-Five

Geneneral Sun leaned back in his chair, but not the same chair Chairman Qi used. That one was covered in blood. But he was seated in the same spot at Qi's magnificent five hundred-year old desk. Qi, expecting this to be his new seat of power, had moved it to this office from a museum in Shanghai. He closed his eyes for a few moments knowing exhaustion was catching up with him.

He awoke with a snap as he felt the presence of someone before him. A nervous looking captain was standing at attention at the other side if the desk.

"Yes, Captain?" he said, marshaling his efforts to stay calm despite his alarm at being surprised so easily. By no means did he feel his position to be secure enough that he could afford to be caught off guard this way.

"Er, Colonel Kwok has sent me asking that you look at his messages and respond. He begs his apologies but says he requires urgent direction." The captain was sweating profusely.

"Ah yes, tell him I'll respond in a moment. Oh, and Captain?"

"Yes, General?" The captain stood so stiffly at attention that he looked frozen.

"Please see if you can find some tea. Oolong if possible. And maybe a stim-cig or some other method of giving me a little boost. It's been a long day."

"Yes, General," the captain responded.

Sun lit up his comm and then noticed the captain was still standing at attention.

"Dismissed, Captain," he said and in the corner of his eye he saw the captain turn. Sun turned his attention to his screen.

There were several messages from Kwok. The first was about an idea that came from Trish Stern to get communications established with the Fermi Base again using an Indonesian satellite. The woman was impressive in how she thought on her feet. With her ability to convince others, she could be a formidable ally in the future, or a challenging foe. He was uncertain where her loyalties might lie or if she was another of those who just may be ready to jump at the best opportunity. It would be a good idea to keep her close. He responded to Kwok with an affirmative and added his digital seal—making the project high priority. That would ensure nobody would slow it down or question it.

The next message was much more alarming. It seemed the firing from the Moon at the incoming asteroid was continuing and showing no sign of abating. The current target had now moved to the American East Coast and if the same ballistic masses continued to fly to the asteroid, the final impact might be the Sea of Japan. That would demolish a large part of China, along with the Koreas, Japan and much of South-East Asia. An unacceptable outcome to be sure.

He immediately sent the command to re-establish the connection with President Benson.

After a minute he saw the famous hair and teeth of the 'heart-throb president' appear on the screen. "Benson here. What's up, General Sun?"

Sun noted that formalities had indeed disappeared. "I have news. The Moon crew continues to fire at the asteroid at the same rate. The current impact zone is now Annapolis. But if they continue to do so until the asteroid swings by the Moon, the target will move to the Sea of Japan. In both cases we're talking about massive loss of life and in the second case a massive loss of rice lands as well. In fact, most agriculture on the planet will be severely affected."

Sun found Benson looking stoic after being given the news. The president responded. "We've been calculating worst case scenarios and both of those have been in the mix. We do have an option I want to discuss with you. I have in my control, a nuclear device that offers over a gigaton of explosive power. I also have a rocket that has been built as part of the eventual American colony on the Mars mission. We're thinking of combining the two and seeing if that might take out the asteroid or at least divert it enough to reduce damage. I'm wondering if you have any similar capability. The information you sent me regarding the location of your missiles would indicate that you do."

There was a pause as Sun thought about what Benson had just announced. The weapon he described was ten times more powerful than the largest known nuclear device, the old Soviet 'Tsar Bomb'. No country had ever admitted to such a weapon as all treaties banned the creation and stockpiling of something of that size.

"Mr. President. I'm honored by your admission and will not address the implications it has treaty-wise, since we are in dire straits at this moment. My own capabilities are not anywhere near what you're describing. Our thermonuclear weapons are all tactical ones. We've never built the large scale weapons the US and Russia have built in the past, or present it seems."

Benson's eyebrows came together. "But at the last nuclear conference Chairman Qi indicated you put together a much larger force than anyone had imagined. Far larger than all the European capabilities put together."

"Yes," said Sun. "Qi would have said that. He was willing to say anything to try to get other countries off balance. He was even building mock missiles that would be destroyed to show his good faith in negotiations. The man was shrewd. Dishonest, evil and shrewd."

Sun sat patiently as he heard noise behind Benson. The president's comm link scrambled any words that didn't come from the president himself. But Sun could hear the emotions in the voices around Benson, if not the words. There was outrage and shock in the tones and even anger.

Finally, Benson's voice came through the noise. "Well it seems we'll have a lot to talk about if we all get out of this in one piece. In the meantime, my generals are telling me you have a delivery system that could be much faster than what our rockets might supply." His face turned dark and he added, "We would too, if our space elevator had not been recently damaged."

"Ah, I see what you're alluding to. We could have several smaller warheads leaving the space elevator in a few hours. In fact, hold on." Sun accessed another application on his screen that told him the precise locations of his warheads. He was glad the security override that was put in place before he came to take Qi out of power worked. "There are already a fair number of warheads at the top of the elevator as we speak."

Benson's eyes widened and then he offered a grim smile. "I suppose we've both been guilty of not following treaties to the letter. For once, that may be to our mutual advantage. I wish to set up a coordinated attack on the asteroid. There is some concern among my staff. They worry if we hit it and fail to alter the course, we'll be making the incoming rock highly radioactive to boot."

"We have a saying Mr. President. When the people move with one mind, they can even move Mount Taishan."

"Yes," said Benson wondering where the hell Mount Taishan might be. "I suppose they can. I'll ask my staff to liaise with yours on this project. This may be our last best hope, Sun. We have to make this work. For everyone's sake. For the future of our planet."

"I know, Mr. President. I know." Sun closed the connection and set about to getting his team aimed at the new task.

Chapter Seventy-Six

"Govno!" Boris cursed. "I don't see how we can do it. Even if we could raise the pace of firing, which might cause some type of meltdown, the mining bots are not quite fast enough. The transport bots are not fast enough either and the loading process is the slowest of all! We're going to be short by about ninety-two hundred kilograms of mass." He pounded his fist on his console and winced.

Amanda did her own set of calculations and agreed with Boris. But she saw a few places where they could make up time and add over fourteen hundred kilos. She shared her calculations with him and shrugged. "I know, but it's not enough. Maybe the Protector has some ideas."

Pierre managed to sit, propped up, and turned his camera on, aiming it at them. Boris lashed out, "Why are you recording at a time like this?"

"Good journalism knows there's nothing better than a story about a failed attempt. Except for the story where the attempt succeeds despite the fact everyone has given up."

"If that's supposed to make us hopeful, it's not working," Amanda said, frowning at the Frenchman.

"You surprise me, Amanda! Journalism is not about making anyone feel hopeful. That would be propaganda. Or 'fake news' as they once called it. Good journalism is about the truth—good or bad."

Stress was getting to all of them, Sam could see that clearly. "Protector?" he called out.

"Yes, Sam?" the soft, soothing voice replied.

"Can you calculate your own scenarios for getting enough mass into the firing process?"

"Amanda's estimation is correct. With the current equipment we

270

will come up short in rock mass in the time required."

"Forget about rock mass," Sam said. "Exactly how much can we actually fire if the masses are available to the firing mechanism?"

"Even if we load and fire the mining bots and the transport bots, we will be short by some nineteen hundred kilograms."

"Well, I'm not ready to give up. Not just yet. What if we fired the lander at the asteroid?" Sam asked.

The voice of the Protector responded in its usual way, "There is a calculation that would work. I will share the numbers in a moment."

The four crewmembers huddled together to view the data on Boris' screen. He fed the data into an animation of how the process would occur. With a timer along the bottom of the display, they saw a continuous barrage of rocks firing at the asteroid. Then they saw the lander take off from the Moon and circle it to gain speed. The rocks kept firing. The last of the rocks reached the asteroid at roughly the same time as the lander. The animation did not show any flashy explosions. It simply had the lander wink out of existence the same way that the rocks did. Four hours later, the asteroid hit the Moon not far from the Fermi Crater.

They all shared somber looks. They knew this meant the destruction of the base.

"I'll begin to program the lander for autonomous flight," Boris said, a sense of defeat in his voice.

"I'm afraid that won't do. I destroyed the autonomic flight calculator on orders from Chairman Qi," Zhang said.

"What?" Pierre shouted. "You bastard! Not only did you shoot me, but you may have also wiped out the entire fucking planet!"

Zhang looked at him coldly. "I can still fly the lander manually. I'm the only one here trained to do so."

Muttering something to himself in French, Pierre sat back. The rest of them looked at Zhang, confusion in their faces. Sam went up and put his hand on Zhang's shoulder. "What you're doing is . . ."

"I don't need to hear it." Zhang said. "And we don't have time for speeches of glory or emotional goodbyes. Just, if you ever see my wife or my children, let them know I'll miss them."

"I'll find them. No matter what," Amanda said, tears in her eyes.

"Okay, we're not going to get this done by sitting around looking at each other," Boris said, rising to his feet. "Ni Puha, Ni Pera, Zhang! Let's start by charting the exact course, so you can pilot this properly. After all, we're not done yet."

"Can I have a few minutes?" Zhang said. "I'm trying to see if the messaging re-route through one of the Mars satellites will work. Mars should be above our horizon in just a few more minutes."

"Okay," Boris said. "But just a few minutes. We don't need to cut this any closer than we have to."

"Pierre, Amanda, are you up to helping me figure out how to make room in the other lander?" Sam asked, standing up. "We're going to need to see how we can fit extra passengers on board to get off of the Moon before the asteroid hits."

Amanda nodded. Pierre gave a thumbs up sign. Despite their positive responses, Sam realized getting off the Moon was going to be a challenge. He just hoped they were all up to the task.

Chapter Seventy-Seven

Wenchang Base
Hainan Province

"You have to let me go!" Trish stood up so she could look down on Colonel Kwok as she made her plea. "I'm the one who came up with the idea and I should be at the elevator when it's launched."

Kwok shook his head. "I have a major who will do the job just fine, and he's already there."

Trish would not back down. "Kwok, the fact he's there shows he's not aware of all that's at stake. When push comes to shove, he might not make the right decision. Or he might not go through with it because he doesn't realize what a bad situation we're in."

"Are you implying that my men won't follow orders?" Kwok asked indignantly, rising to his feet.

She realized she'd touched a nerve. "No, not at all. But there are nuances in how one follows orders. You need someone there to keep an eye on things and if need be, to make snap decisions you can count on. I have proven myself time and time again at Starshield. You don't know this major or how he will react. You do know me."

Kwok sat down and put his head into his hands. This decision had so much weight on it that he needed to have someone else take the responsibility. He lifted his comm tablet and reached out to General Sun, describing the situation and Stern's request. After a moment, Sun's reply came back. Once again, Kwok was surprised at how quickly Sun had reached a decision and how well thought out the solution was. He knew he'd followed the right leader.

"Ms. Stern," Kwok said, standing again. "Please stand before me."

The woman stood nervously. Had she gone too far? Was he going to arrest her?

"Ms. Stern," Kwok continued, "This is a solemn occasion. In fact, this

273

is a first. General Sun has decided a battlefield commission is required. Never in the history of the People's Republic has someone who is not of Chinese origin attained the rank of Air Force Major. I want to caution you and everyone present. This isn't done lightly or without great consideration, even if it's done rapidly."

Kwok turned to one of his officers and whispered to him. The officer removed and passed him the shoulder insignia of one five-petaled flower that indicated the rank of major.

Looking at Trish for a place to pin the pip, he awkwardly pinned it to her lapel. "Shàoxiào Stern Patricia," he announced using the formal Chinese title for major. "Step forward and be recognized."

The small group of officers working with Kwok and Trish, most of whom helped in the take down of Chairman Qi, applauded.

Helen was surprised to see Trish blush. She'd never imagined her capable of doing so.

Nodding to Kwok, Trish bowed to each and every one of the officers present. To the major who'd given up his insignia, she said, "I will return this to you as soon as I'm able. Xiè xienín, xiānsheng. With my most humble gratitude, sir."

The officer smiled and bowed back to her.

"He will be grateful if you do. This is his late father's insignia. He's has worn for the last twelve years."

"Then I can't accept it," Trish said, horrified. She awkwardly reached to take it off.

"My father could not be prouder than to have his pip worn by the first non-Chinese woman of this rank. He would be thrilled. Please use it as you see fit." The officer smiled at her and bowed.

Trish touched the insignia on her lapel proudly and replied, "Thank you. I'll do everything I can to make certain he would never feel anything other than pride."

She turned back to Kwok. "Does this mean I'm heading to the space elevator?"

"Yes, Major Stern," he said with a smile. "I've made arrangements. An official vehicle will pick you up in ten minutes. I took the liberty of having your two companions go with you since they will not serve much purpose here and seem to be under your wing, so to speak. Your official documents will be sent to this tablet in a moment."

He handed her the small tablet and then added. "A paper version is being printed as well. Your contact at the elevator is Major Tsu Xiao. His English is adequate but not exactly fluent so you'll have to bear with that. I think you speak enough Mandarin that you'll be able to communicate with him. Nevertheless, a translator will be provided. The flight will get you there in just over thirty minutes."

"Thirty minutes?" burst in Louise. "Is this another rocket and drop flight?"

Kwok looked a little angered by the interruption but nodded.

"Fuck!" said Louise, "See? This is why I freelance. Corpo-government employees are always being made to do things that make you sick."

Chapter Seventy-Eight

Strategic Air Command Base 42 A
Location Confidential

"General Hagman!" Benson raised his voice to get everyone's attention. The staff was arguing about whether they should trust the Chinese government to send its nuclear warheads at the asteroid, or whether they'd take this opportunity to try to put a nail in the United States' coffin. General Hagman was suggesting they use their own missile in a preemptive strike against the Chinese rather than target the asteroid.

"But Mr. President," Hagman glared. "No matter what happens we'll still have the Chinese to deal with afterward. This is exactly the right time to take that matter into our own hands and be done with it. Trying to manage a post-asteroid world and deal with the Chinese will stretch our resources to the breaking point. We must act now!"

Benson could not believe Hagman was advocating for even more war. He ran his hand through his hair and calmed himself before saying, "Sit down, General. In working with General Sun through this crisis, I'm brought back to the words of President Ronald Reagan. During the height of the Cold War, he stood before the UN and said, "I occasionally think how quickly our differences would vanish if we were facing an alien threat to this world." A fascinating speech.

"We're facing just such a threat. Not from some alien intelligence, which Reagan thought was imminent. But from a natural catastrophe the world hasn't seen since the extinction of dinosaurs."

He saw Hagman go pale. He knew the general held real admiration for Ronald Reagan and even sat on the board of the Reagan Library.

He continued. "This is exactly the time not to be at each other's throats. This is the time when we lay aside our differences and come together to save as much of humanity as we can. The effort to send our nuclear weapon and those of the Chinese is our current best bet. There's no way we can keep the news of the asteroid under wraps forever. The word will get out and there will be widespread panic. Panic will mean injury, death and massive economic disruption even if we do manage to avert the asteroid's impact."

He saw several of those seated around the table beginning to nod. Now came the hard part. "So, I'm going to go and speak to the American people and let them know. I'm going to tell them we're in danger. They deserve to know. They deserve to be able to make their own plans and their own peace if the end is near. But I'll tell them their government is not standing by and neither are the Chinese. I've taken the liberty of sharing all data we have with the Russians as well. Their space technology is not up to snuff anymore, but they may be able to pitch in in some manner. In any case, they, too, deserve to be aware."

Some of those seated around the table looked a little alarmed. "So, I'm going to finish by saying this. As chief executive and head of the Armed Forces, I'm giving the clear order our nuclear weapon is to be fired at the asteroid. This is not a suggestion. This is not up for discussion. This is an order. Is that clear? I need to see acknowledgment from each and every one of you."

He was glad to see he got the nods he was looking for. General Hagman was the first to leap to his feet and salute as the president left the room.

Once settled into his office, he sipped the coffee his staff served to him. It wasn't nearly as good as what he'd been drinking in the Oval Office. He wondered how long it would be until he had coffee as good as that again, if ever. He thought about asking for a shot of his favorite single malt whiskey since that might soon be in short supply as well. But he knew he couldn't afford to have any of his faculties dulled.

Opening the screen built into this desk, he set up the comm link with General Sun in China.

The round face of the Chinese general appeared and Benson wondered if he looked as tired as the general did.

"Mr. President. You have news?" the general asked.

"Well, yes and no. I have a question, actually." Benson rubbed his temples with his fingers. "How do you handle those in your staff who distrust me? What do you tell them?"

The general smiled. "Mr. President, nobody in my staff distrusts you and, even less, your military. They're not here to form their own opinions. Nor are they to act on them. That would mean mutiny. Here, the penalty for mutiny is death, Mr. President. Death and punishment for one's family."

Benson nodded. "Unless, of course, the mutiny is successful."

Sun stared at the screen. "Yes, that would be the case. The only time mutiny makes sense is if the leadership of the party or the government lost its way. Then someone must step in at their own peril and do what must be done to save the country or even the planet."

"Hmm," Benson mulled. "Our Declaration of Independence says much the same thing." He leaned forward. "I've been dealing with a difference of opinion among my military. Some have been advocating we use our nuclear capability to strike at you and your people. They claim it will make their lives easier after whatever happens with the asteroid."

Sun's eyes went wide—not so much at the idea, but at the fact Benson would speak of it with him. "Mr. President. I'm not shocked. I'm certain some among my staff would push the same idea forward if I allowed them to speak of such a thing."

Benson smiled. "Sun, sometimes I think you have it easier corralling your staff than I do mine. I guess there are times when absolute power supersedes democracy."

"That may be, Mr. President. But you doubtlessly have an easier time when your term of office is done. In my place the departure is rarely a comfortable one. There haven't been many leaders of my government who retire in comfort or stay around for long when they do. Perhaps that's why so many have held onto their position until no longer capable of doing so. I would not argue which method is better for the leaders, but my belief is that our way is better for our people."

"I suppose we can agree to disagree on that one," Benson answered. "But, there's something we must agree on. I've made certain there is no possibility of our nuclear capability being used against anything or anyone but this asteroid. General Sun, I must have the same assurance from you. I'm going to announce to the American people that an asteroid is coming. I will tell them you and I and our governments are working together to save humanity. Despite whatever differences we may have, or even whatever goals, we need to do the right thing. It's the only sane thing to do." He stared intently at Sun as if his sole willpower would be enough to make Sun agree.

Sun stared back and smiled. "Mr. President, in this very serious hour, I'm glad you occupy the seat of power in America. I didn't remove my old friend Chairman Qi from power because of my own personal desire for power. I did so because I knew war was a mistake and it's still a mistake. Now more than ever. You have my word and the word of the People's Republic. We're in this same fight together and we're facing the same way."

"Thank you, General Sun." The president looked both relieved and tired. "I'll let you know when I hear anything new."

The comm disconnected and Sun leaned back in his chair, placing his hands, fingers laced, behind his neck. He had never seen Benson so tired, or so scared. But then again, neither was he.

Chapter Seventy-Nine

Chang'e 3 Base
Maglev Launcher

"There has to be way! There just has to be! I've tried everything!" Amanda complained. "Every single solution I'm coming up with is still one person short, damn it!"

Sam shook his head. He could see that Amanda was right. There was just no way a small lander could lift a payload that included everyone. They either had to find some solution for giving it more lift, or find a way to have some of them leave the Moon another way. But how?

Then Zhang yelled out, "Got it! I've connected to one of the Martian satellites. I'm relaying a message describing how we're going to drive the asteroid into the Moon."

"Nice work." Boris said. "Now help me here with this stuff. There's a lot for us to figure out and we don't have very much time to figure it out in."

Zhang walked over to Boris, nodding his head. Sam reflected on how much the Chinese general had changed. He was no longer the boastful, arrogant militarist. His attitude came across as quiet and even subdued now. They all knew Zhang would be piloting his lander to his death when he went to the asteroid. Sam never expected the soon-to-be hero to be so complacent or humble about it

He decided he couldn't think about that at the moment. He needed to find a solution to get them off of the Moon before Zhang's trip brought the rocks crashing into it. And he had something else to do before that would happen.

Jin Huang looked at his screen back on Earth and wondered. The message he saw was coming from the Red Dragon Mars orbital satellite. But the call signal looked like it was some type of military identifier. He quickly looked to see if it was a known code and didn't find it among the codes that were available to him. It could still be a code that was above his security grade, but there was something about it that was rather odd. The code prefix indicated it was from a lunar group and not from any Martian operation.

Huang still remembered how Fu Chang wept when he was demoted for annoying the boss with an alert that turned out to be some hacker playing with the messaging channels. This might be another hacker. It might even be the same one.

Deciding it was better not to take a risk, Huang erased the message and any trace of it coming into the comm center. Then he took a deep breath and sighed. He just hoped he'd done the right thing.

Chapter Eighty

Space Elevator Facility
Pini Island Indonesia

Trish Stern stepped out of space elevator customs and immigration followed by a rather green Helen Czerny. They waited as Louise Winston finally stumbled out.

Trish told the two women, "I have a meeting with a Major Tsu. Based on the briefing and the research I did, he's a bit of a stickler for protocol. I'm afraid I'll have to leave the two of you to find your way around on your own. Don't go too far though, because if things change and I need to reach you, it may happen quickly."

Helen swallowed and said, "After that flight, I just want to find a quiet place to sit down and pull myself together. I was not made for these high apogee flights."

Louise, who had stopped to lean against the wall added, "I'm beginning to think humans were not designed for flight at all."

"Okay then," Trish said, chuckling. "I'll call you as soon as I have an idea of how things will pan out. Stay alert, and don't do anything stupid. That means you, Louise, got it? Just relax and wait for my call. I'll see you soon"

Before Louise could protest, Trish marched off in the direction of the military station she saw at the other end of the terminal.

"Give her a rank and already she's thinking she's somebody," Louise complained.

"I think she's been somebody for quite a while," Helen said, watching her go. "And I, for one, am glad she's on our side."

"Oh?" responded Louise. "Is she?"

Trish arrived at the station desk to discover two soldiers of low rank sitting there. Although she didn't have time to procure an official uniform, she made sure the mark of her rank was visible on her collar. However, it didn't seem to catch the attention of the two soldiers.

"Hey, pretty lady," one of the soldiers greeted her. "How can I help you?"

"You can begin by standing and saluting when an officer approaches you," Trish replied with a smile.

The soldier looked confused, then he saw the insignia on her collar, stood and saluted. The other soldier hadn't noticed it, but upon seeing his colleague rise and salute, did the same.

"Major, I apologize. I, uh, we've never seen a woman major before, and not one who isn't . . ."

"Chinese," she finished his sentence for him. "I suppose I should have expected that. I guess I'll see more of the same reaction soon enough. Now, can you tell me how to find Major Tsu? I was expecting some sort of an official greeting, but it seems I must find him without any escort."

The first soldier saluted her again. "I would be honored to accompany you to Major Tsu's office. It's just a short ride from here. I'll call ahead. Is he expecting you?"

"I would be quite surprised if he wasn't expecting me."

She followed the soldier to a small open vehicle that felt like a cross between a golf cart and an electric jeep. When he saw how she looked at the vehicle, he said, "This is a completely electric cart. We call them buzzbugs. I think the name comes from the quiet buzzing the engine makes. The static electricity generated by the elevator creates a lot of charge. So much that storing it is a bit of a problem so everything we use here is electric. They aren't fast, but they are reliable."

"Mhhhm." Trish wasn't listening. Instead she was taking in the sights. She'd never been to either of the space elevator installations, but she'd seen plenty of video about them. The two stations were quite different. While the Brazilian one was a private and commercial entity, the one in Asia was a Chinese government structure. It lacked the colorful advertisements, shops and restaurants at the foot of the western elevator. Instead, it had an austere, plastic look that made her think of twentieth century science fiction television. She remembered Slaton always complained about the space elevators as competition. She assumed he knocked the Brazilian one out.

The buzzbug hummed past a long hallway and through a set of double doors that opened after the vehicle paused for an instant.

They arrived before another set of nondescript doors and the soldier announced they were there. Trish thanked him, adding she would have been unlikely to find it on her own. He saluted her and this time she returned the favor, feeling clumsy about it.

She walked through the doors and into a recognizable command center. There were at least forty people sitting at a variety of monitors and equipment. At the back of the room was an office with a large window looking into the room. A few of the people in the room looked startled to see someone not in uniform walk in unannounced.

The door at the back of the room burst open and a tall thin man with a lantern jaw stepped out and said, "Major Stern, I presume?'

Trish decided this was a good time to salute again and was rewarded with everyone in the room returning it.

"Yes," she replied eyeing the same insignia as she wore on her collar. "Major Tsu?"

"Indeed," he walked over and shook her hand. "We need to find you a uniform. It won't do to have you walking around expecting salutes when you're dressed like that." He nodded to one of the junior officers in the room who immediately stood and left.

Trish found herself already liking Major Tsu, "Thank you, Major. I appreciate that. In the meantime, where can we set up and go over the two projects I'm here to manage?"

She saw Tsu's smile slowly disappear. "Yes, well, let me see where we can arrange an office for you."

Trish slipped into her usual demeanor that allowed her to work her way up in Starshield's hierarchy. "Great, in the meantime, I'll use your office to go over the projects at a high level. We don't have a lot of time and these projects are vital. I'm sure General Sun's message made that clear."

Tsu's face was now unreadable. "Very well, this way please." He walked through the door into his office without waiting for her. Trish ignored his rudeness and followed.

Once in the office, he hit a button and the windows in the room turned into a display screen on the inside of the office. Tsu shut the door behind Trish and pointed to a chair. "Major Stern, I appreciate the fact you have been sent here by General Sun. But I must request when you are in front of my staff, you offer me the respect due my station. I have held this rank for nine years and have been the commanding officer at this station for the last three years. That merits some respect."

Trish smiled and sat down. Despite some advances, she knew many men were still uncomfortable with a woman in a leadership position. She knew an attitude they found normal or even expected from a man would sometimes be interpreted as being a bitch from a woman. "I apologize, Major Tsu, but the matter at hand is extremely urgent. If it were not, I wouldn't be here and General Sun wouldn't have taken the unusual step of giving me this field commission. As it is just a field commission, please excuse me if I'm not aware of the niceties of Chinese military protocol."

She took a mem-dot out of her pocket. "I have a complete visual description of the predicament we're in. If I can get you to project it on your display, I think we'll save a great deal of time. And you'll understand why I'm being so terse and anxious in the way I communicate."

She held out the mem-dot as if daring him to take it.

Tsu looked at her for a moment, then extended his hand and took the dot. Before placing it on his comm he said, "Regardless of what I'm about to see, you do need to learn about military protocol, Major. Having soldiers see their commanding officer treated badly does not create an environment where they're likely to support you. Loyalty matters a lot more here than it does in the corporate world you come from." Then, without waiting for a response, he activated the mem-dot and they both looked at what unfolded on the screen.

After a few minutes, Tsu realized they were discussing a possible extinction level event. "Now I see why you've been acting so urgently, Major Stern. Let's see how we can go about making sure the two projects are simultaneously the highest priorities we have."

"Major Tsu, I was told by your superiors you are both wise and competent. I'm glad to see this confirmed."

Chapter Eighty-One

Wenchang Base
Hainan Province

General Sun set his comm to the secure connection with Benson. It was the regularly scheduled touch-base they were set to have. They'd agreed on a code to send if either one or both were too busy to comply, but neither had sent the code. He entered the connection code and stabbed the GO button.

As usual, the Oval Office appeared. Sun knew this was an illusion driven by the data feed on the other side. Just as his display showed him sitting at a table in a plain room with nothing but the bright red field of the flag of the People's Republic behind him. The software was set to project that regardless of where he might be.

What was odd this time was Benson wasn't sitting where he usually was. Sun could see the top of someone's head bobbing. Although background noises were muffled, he could hear explosions or some type of repeated banging.

The general decided to watch and wait, remaining quiet since he knew his voice would activate the screen on the other side. The banging noise continued along with what had to be shouts. Finally, the noise stopped. The top of the head rose to show a chest wearing a white shirt with a red tie. Sun noticed, as the form rose, the chest was that of President Benson. The body turned and all he saw was his back with his arms waving.

Sun waited another minute and hearing no more shouting, decided to speak up. He knew he'd suddenly appear on the screen. "Mr. President?"

The body on the other end spun around and sat. President Benson was disheveled. His hair stood like a well-used toothbrush and his face betrayed fatigue. "General Sun. Please excuse the hubbub. There's been an attempt here. Several of my generals tried to take over." His voice was rough and Sun could see the reality of the situation was just now making itself clear to Benson.

"They tried to kill me!"

General Sun interrupted, "Mr. President. First of all, are you sure you're safe now? That's the first thing you must take care of. You can't help anyone else if you are in danger."

Benson looked distracted. "Eh? Yes, yes, I'm safe. They've shot the ones who tried to . . . and captured the others. They were only a few of them, but they were all close to me. They all had top level clearance."

He pounded his fist on the desk before him. "Damn it! I can't believe at a time like this these fucking extremists, because that's what they are, extremists, would be stupid enough to try something like this! General Sun, you hurt their pride. Or rather Chairman Qi did and these assholes place their pride before the welfare of the people of our country and the planet! Damn them!"

Sun paused. This was a time for measured speech. "Mr. President, this type of thing isn't unusual. Too much of the world is ruled by men eager to hold power rather than eager to do the right thing. Both your nation and mine have suffered from that, in a variety of ways."

The president stared back at him, absorbing the information.

It occurred to Sun that Benson might be in shock. He had to find a way to get him back to being as functional as possible. There was no time for any of this. "Mr. President, have you been able to confirm your nuclear solution for the asteroid is going ahead as planned? I fear the coup attempt may have had an impact on that."

"Sun, you're right. I'll verify that and get back to you. I apologize for the delay."

Without another word the connection was cut.

The general wondered whether Benson was still in his right mind. And if he was, whether he still had the power to assist in saving the planet.

Chapter Eighty-Two

Zhang bowed in front of Amanda and handed her a mem-dot. "Please, you have promised to get this to my wife and sons. I would be grateful if you would keep that promise."

Amanda took the item and bowed in return. "It will be my honor to do so, Major. And on behalf of the world, I'm humbled by your gesture."

After a brief moment, Zhang nodded in return and went back to his preparations. He double-checked his settings, making sure he had enough oxygen for the trip. Then he checked that the lander had the right amount of mass aboard. Most of the trip would be automated. But he knew there would be some manual adjustments once he detected the actual mass and structure of the asteroid. He'd arrive only eight hours before the asteroid reached the Moon. Based on his calculations, he would put himself in a tight, rapid orbit around the asteroid mass. Then he'd redirect the entire mass, changing course enough that it wouldn't slingshot around the Moon, but slam right into it.

The loader bots were still delivering masses of rocks from the mines to the rail gun and the firing sequence was in place. All firing would stop fifteen minutes before the lander took off, keeping rocks out of the flight trajectory.

Boris was still sporting a headache and Pierre's injuries were best treated by moving him as little as possible. So, Sam was the one who'd go with Zhang to the lander and help him prepare for the one-way journey. They both double-checked each other's status. This was the pattern Zhang insisted upon well before they'd even set out for the Moon. Sam felt a little strange trusting Zhang. After all, he'd tried to kill them all when he thought it was the way for him to become a hero. Even though he was now a volunteer for a dead-end mission, Sam still had an uncomfortable feeling about him. Following him to the lander and assuring the takeoff was one way of making sure Zhang wouldn't betray them.

They moved through the airlock with practiced ease and out onto the lunar surface. Despite the almost perfect seals of their suits, Sam could smell the used gunpowder scent that was the prominent odor of the Moon's surface. They shuffle-walked to the transport bot and sat on the back. Sam gave the bot instructions to get them to the lander.

"I never thought the Moon would be the last landscape I'd see." Zhang's voice came through Sam's comm system. He turned to Sam and continued. "I also never thought I'd do anything that would result in saving the planet. I was so excited when the chairman chose me to be a hero of the People's Republic. So excited I didn't even consider how what I did would hurt and kill so many. He was so convincing with his vision of how China was destined to lead. We have the oldest and most vibrant culture. It was a terrible thing I did. I know that now." He hung his head.

Sam paused. "Major Zhang, none of us understood what you were doing or why. But we all know you're not a bad man. I know you gave Amanda a message for your family. I want you to know if any of us gets out of this, well, the people of Earth will know you for the hero you really are."

The major nodded and they watched the lunarscape roll by until they got to the lander. When they arrived, they saw the transport bots loading it with rocks and any materials at hand. It was a challenge to get to the front of the lander and check the pilot and co-pilot seats.

"Everything seems normal," Sam said. "Is there anything else we need check out before we line it up for launch?"

Zhang went through his own checklist and pronounced the lander eady for being set up on the takeoff path. The lander launch mechanism was much like that of old airplanes on aircraft carriers. A piston capable of withstanding the lunar cold was set in place and compressed over sixty meters. The lander had a small hook under its nose that was pushed by the piston as soon as it decompressed. This didn't give the lander enough velocity to escape lunar orbit. But it did supply enough momentum that the lander didn't need to burn a lot of fuel to get off the Moon. The trick of firing the engines at the right time was completely automated. It was a method the Russians developed many years ago. They had always been very good at coming up with inexpensive solutions to the problems of space travel.

Chapter Eighty-Three

"Yes, it's a problem," Tsu said. "We can do one or the other, there's no way to be able to reconfigure the station to launch both in the allotted time."

Trish sat down, and then pounded her fist on the chair's arm. "Damn it! There just has to be a way! We need to set up the comm link with the Moon to get them to stop firing. And we need to send the nuclear warheads at the asteroid to arrive in time, or just ahead of the American missile."

Tsu raise his eyebrows. "American missile? They're sending a warhead as well?"

"Yes, they are," Trish affirmed. "And a doozy at that. The warheads should arrive just before the asteroid is set to whip past the Moon. The hope is that we can smash it into enough small pieces that they get pulled in by the Moon's gravity instead of coming to the Earth. Some might still make it through, but we hope that they're small enough to not have much impact. Maybe even most of them will burn up in the atmosphere."

Tsu looked at her, wondering what a 'doozy' might be, and then shook his head. "So that makes our choice easy."

Tsu began pacing again. Trish got the feeling he could only think while walking. "We fire the warheads. The EMP would destroy the comm satellite anyway."

Trish shook her head. The motion made the collar of her new uniform scratch her neck. "Starshield has been making EMP shielded satellites for years. If we don't get the people on the Moon to stop firing rocks, they're going to keep adding mass and the explosions will be less effective. At least that's what the guys who crunch the numbers are saying."

"I see," Tsu nodded. "But we cannot get the comm satellite and the explosive ordinance both up in time. I suggest our best alternative is to go with the explosives and hope the people on the Moon who are firing the rocks either have some sort of failure or EMP of their own."

He slapped his forehead with the palm of his hand. This made Trish realize he'd spent time living in the West. This was not a Chinese thing to do.

Tsu looked her in the eyes." We may have another solution, Major Stern."

"Which is?" Trish replied, eager to hear about options.

"While we can't reconfigure for different types of deliverables, we can fire off the same deliverable at different times. In fact, we could even fire off the nuclear payload within about an hour or so."

"How does that solve our problem? A nuclear device might not serve as a warning to the people on the Moon . . ." She closed her mouth, realizing what Tsu was getting at. "You can't seriously be saying we should nuke the team on the Moon?"

"No, we don't need to nuke them," Tsu responded. "An EMP within range of their equipment would shut them down. I'm assuming they're not at a hardened facility."

Trish shivered. She wrapped her arms around herself. "You do realize an EMP would shut down all their systems? They would die just as if you had nuked them. Maybe even more horribly in the end. This is such an ugly path to take."

Tsu looked at the display to avoid looking at Trish. "Not all solutions are elegant ones. And the alternative may mean our best efforts are not enough to save the people on our planet."

Trish let out a deep breath. "I suppose we have to set this up, but I'm going to keep looking for other alternatives. How much of a window do we have before we must make a decision?"

Tsu looked at his tablet. "If this option is the one we need to deploy, we have to have done so within about five hours at the latest."

"Shit!" Trish cursed, "That doesn't leave much time for deploying any other options. Alright, let me see what else I can think of."

"Fine," Tsu said. "In the meantime, I'll inform General Sun of the situation."

Chapter Eighty-Four

General Sun leaned back in his chair and stared at the ceiling. There was a thin crack that bothered him. When there was time, he'd make sure to have it fixed. This was not the type of office where a crack like that was acceptable.

Benson worried him. The way their conversation had reached an abrupt end let Sun know Benson was neither in complete control nor all that competent. If the U.S. president was unsure about the status of his nuclear missile at this late hour, they were all in for one rocky ride. Whether the missile was ready or not.

He lowered his gaze from the annoying crack but still felt its presence above his head like some damned Sword of Damocles. The day the ceiling fell, it would be this fissure that was the weak spot.

His comm unit alerted him to a call. He opened the connection; surprised to see it was Major Tsu from the space elevator. He expected it would be the newly commissioned Major Stern who would contact him from the elevator.

"Major Tsu, what's the status?"

Tsu looked nervous, but Sun was used to having subordinates look nervous. "We've hit a problem, General. We can't send off the comm satellite Major Stern requested and launch the nuclear payload as well. The formats of the devices are too different to execute them within the time we have allotted."

Sun raised an eyebrow. "If I recall, the comm satellite was to get the lunar team to stop firing rocks before we send the explosives? Is that a vital element or can we send the explosives without notifying them?"

"It's a crucial element. If they continue to add mass to the asteroid, it'll make the explosion less effective."

292

"I see. And you have an alternate plan?"

Allowing him a small nod, but no smile. Sun realized Tsu had a plan he didn't like. "General, we can fire a nuclear payload that would explode above the Fermi Complex. The EMP should disable all their equipment and put an end to the firing of rocks at the asteroid."

'I see. Will that not also kill all the people at the base? Those are not ordinary soldiers up there. We have brilliant scientific minds from the United States, Russia and France as well as our own staff."

Tsu looked down. "Yes, I'm aware. The result will be tragic for them. But it 'll be a greater tragedy if our efforts to destroy the asteroid, or at least mitigate its impact are not successful."

Sun took a deep breath. "I see. Any other options on the table?"

"Sir, Major Stern is working on that, but I fear our window of opportunity is minuscule at best."

"Thank you Major Tsu. I know bringing ill news is never an easy task. It'll be an even more difficult task to send the payload to the Moon Base knowing what their fate will be. But if we've no other options, then this ugly scenario is what we're stuck with. The members of the current lunar mission will be remembered as heroes."

"Yes, General Sun," Tsu agreed.

Sun cut off the connection and thought about Zhang. He would be getting his status of hero of the People's Republic after all.

The news from Tsu gave Sun the exact reason he needed to reach out to Benson. He needed to find out just what might be going on in the US and if Benson was indeed still in control there. He had a few people within the US government who worked for him. Or at least were willing to give him some information. But they all seemed to have disappeared over the last day or so. Granted, some of them had been Qi's men and may have gotten word of his demise. But some of them were Sun's men. All his contacts that managed these men were telling him they had become unreachable. He took this to be a bad omen.

But Sun was never one to rely on superstition.

He touched his comm unit and activated Benson's special code, relieved to see Benson's face appear on the screen.

"Sun! Do you have any news for me?"

Sun made note of the fact Benson was the one who was supposed to contact him with news. Benson asking for news may mean his own news was either not good or there wasn't any. Sun decided to play the game for the moment. "Yes, I do. It seems the plan to lob a satellite where we can communicate with the people at the Fermi Base is not looking as if it will work in time. We're looking at some other options."

Sun waited then added, "How about you? Do you have any news on the missile?"

Benson pressed his lips and looked down, "Yes and it's not good. It seems the people who tried to kill me also managed to reprogram the coordinates for the missile. I'm ashamed to say they aimed it at Beijing."

"What?" Sun interjected. "Tell me you've stopped this!"

"Hang on! Yes, we managed to stop the liftoff. But it looks like they screwed up the programming and my team is having a tough time reprogramming the coordinates. We might miss the window we agreed upon. Will your team be able to make their window?"

Sun felt nauseated. Was this fool of a president trying to play him for an idiot? Was he going to get Sun to launch his nuclear warheads at the asteroid and then send his missile to Beijing anyway?

"Benson, are you telling me all is lost? That we should be preparing for a complete disaster?"

"No, no. The boys here are saying if your ordinance hits the rock and breaks it apart, ours will come in shortly after that and vaporize what's left. We just need a little time. This should make the Earth impact much less, well, er, impactful."

The president was winging it, Sun could tell. But he also knew he had no choice but to trust him. "Listen, we can't get the crew on the Moon to stop tossing rocks and that means they're just making the asteroid larger. That won't work with our nuclear plan. And since we can't reach them in time, we have a plan to hit them with an EMP to shut down their base."

"Excellent idea!" Benson suddenly found enthusiasm. "When is this going to happen?"

"We'll need to fire in a few hours, we're still looking at other options."

"Why would you do that?" Benson asked. "This seems like a perfectly good option to me."

"Mr. President, an EMP will mean the death of the entire Moon staff. Without working computers and electronics, none of the lunar staff will survive. Nor would they have any way of getting home. We have brilliant men and a woman at the Fermi Base. Scientists. Two of them are American citizens. We're not going to take their lives if we can find any other way."

"Ah, I see. And when do you think this other alternative might be used?"

"I don't know, but they need to come up with something quickly. Major Stern is working on it." Sun cursed himself as soon as he realized he let slip some information that could have been useful later.

"Major Stern?" Benson reacted. "Since when did Trish Stern become a major? I didn't think she was a member of any of our Armed Forces."

"She isn't. Trish Stern is a major in the Army of the People's Republic. I thought it expedient to give her the title so she could have an impact on the proceedings at the space elevator. It's a field commission."

Benson paused and then burst out with a laugh. "Sun, you do know how to surprise me. I like the way you think on your feet."

Sun didn't return the smile. "We need to find solutions quickly. Or we may not have anything beneath our feet let alone anything to think about."

Sun watched Benson nod as he cut off the connection.

Chapter Eighty-Five

Chang'e 3 Base
Maglev Launcher

"Ready?" Sam's hand hovered above the button that would slingshot the lander and Zhang into space—directly at the asteroid.

"Sam? Zhang?" Boris' voice came through both of their comm systems.

"Roger," Sam responded.

"I hear you," Zhang chimed in.

"The last of the rocks is on their way. We have a clear path to the asteroids. You will be making a tight lunar orbit in order to gain speed. You won't catch up with the rocks, but you'll be right behind them. This is going to be a bit of rough ride, Zhang. I'm uploading the flight plan to you now."

"I'm not exactly expecting a pleasure trip, Boris."

Sam had never heard Zhang make a single amusing comment. What a time for him to begin.

"How much time before the launch window appears?" Sam asked.

"Only about forty-five seconds, then once it's open we have a three-minute window to get off the lunar surface. After that, there's no guarantee this plan will get you correctly positioned around the asteroid. I said this was going to be a tight plan."

"Yes," Zhang replied. "But tight plans are the specialty of heroes of the People's Liberation Army. This plan will do."

Again, Sam was surprised. He knew Zhang was often boastful, but he thought this time he'd be calm and cool was baffling. Perhaps Zhang was a lot more nervous than he let on.

"Coming up on ten, nine, eight, seven," Boris's voice was tense. "Five, four, three, two, one. Zaps!"

Sam poked the piston release button and looked up to watch the lander take off. But the lander just sat there, immobile.

"Boris, we have a failure!" Sam yelled. "The lander hasn't moved!"

Boris cursed something in Russian. "Zhang, have you engaged your release?"

Zhang's voice came back sounding a lot less confident. "I don't know. Which one is that?"

"Scroll the display down to the park options!" Boris called out frantically. "It should be the second choice. Slide the surface from left to right, from red to green. Hurry!"

They listened to Zhang's labored breathing as he followed Boris' instructions. "Boris, I found it. Sliding the display now. It's green!"

"Sam! Punch the release now!" Boris yelled.

Sam stabbed the button again and this time saw the lander accelerate immediately. He was surprised to see such a large body speed up so quickly. It must have achieved two hundred kilometers per hour by the time it left the thirty-meter takeoff platform and leaped off of the Moon.

A few moments later, Sam saw the twin engines at the back of the lander fire. He watched as it headed for the horizon only five hundred meters off of the surface.

"He's fired the rockets," Sam announced.

"No, he didn't," Boris' voice responded. "The rockets fired by program. They'll continue to do so until he has completed the acceleration orbit. Then they'll make any adjustments to aim the ship at the asteroid. After that, the on-board AI will try to determine if Zhang is conscious enough to take control."

"Conscious?" Sam asked.

"The orbit he's taking is tight and accelerating him at something close to seven G's for one hundred and thirty-seven seconds. He'll lose consciousness at some point," Boris replied stoically.

Sam couldn't believe it. "With the whole world at stake, we have to depend on him waking up from G-induced fainting?"

Boris' voice came back. "I did say the plan was tight. But don't worry. The AI has been configured to make certain he's awake in time. He has choices to make once he gets to the asteroid. I've programmed in several scenarios. Hopefully, one of them is the right one."

Sam remembered Trish Stern telling him Russian Cosmonauts had a reputation for being a little crazy. He was starting to think she was spot on.

He set his comm unit to connect to only one entity. "Protector?"

"Here, Sam. I see the lander heading for the asteroid is on its way. Unfortunately, I'm having to conserve my energy reserves to continue functioning, or I could help track it."

"Don't waste any battery on that. Tracking any better than we can won't likely change any outcome. What's the status on the replication project?"

"I have almost completed the task. The device is roughly fifty kilos in mass and should be ready in the next six minutes and twenty-seven seconds." The Protector's voice remained as smooth as ever.

Chapter Eighty-Six

Space Elevator Facility
Pini Islands, Indonesia

"You goddamn, crazy, evil bitch!" Helen screamed. She looked around, picked up a coffee mug from the table and swung it at Trish.

Trish ducked as if she was used to this type of response. "Helen, calm down. I'm here to get your help. It's not a foregone conclusion. We need to stop and think and we don't have a lot of time."

"You brought me here because you said we might be able to get in touch with Sam!" Helen shouted waving the mug and missing again. This time, Trish stepped past the swing and grabbed Helen's arm, removing the mug from her hand. Helen broke down crying. "You bitch," she said and fell in Trish's arms weeping.

"Helen!" Trish grabbed Helen by the shoulders and shook her, then on impulse slapped her across the cheek.

Helen stepped back, raised her hand to her cheek in shock and looked at Trish.

There was no time to waste. "Glad I got your attention," Trish said. "Listen, we have a short window in which to find a way to get the folks on the Fermi Base to stop throwing rocks. If we can do that, there will be no need for the EMP. It's all about how we can get them to stop. Now stop yelling and think, goddamn it!"

With her hand still on her face, Helen looked up at Trish. "Okay, but what can we do? What are the options? If we can't send up some sort of satellite to the other side of the Moon, there's no way to communicate with them. The Moon is blocking all our messages."

Trish sat down. "I don't know. I thought we might be able to bounce a message off of one of the rocks they're firing at the asteroid, but the comm team says that won't be an option. It's not as if the rocks were designed for

299

that and any bounce against a rough surface is going to be hard to aim."

Her adrenaline level was much too high to allow her to sit. Helen paced back and forth. "What we need is something that's on the other side of the Moon. What about the planets? I know there was some work done with bouncing lasers off the Moon many years ago, could a laser bounce off a planet?"

Trish considered it. "I don't think we can get that type of thing set up in time. And anyway, they'd need to be looking for a laser comm message. If only we had a working comm at the Lagrange Point Station, but that has yet to be set up."

Helen finally sat in one of the chairs and put her head in her hands. "If Sam were here he'd be joking about letting the Martians contact them. He always has some funny way of dealing with situations like these by looking at them differently. That's why he can be so brilliant."

"Mars!" Trish jumped out of her seat and rushed over to where Helen was sitting. She grabbed Helen and lifted her off of her chair, hugging her. "Helen you're brilliant! The Chinese have a comm satellite circling Mars and I think it's been relaying messages already. If we can get a message to that and Mars is in the right position, we might be able to get them to understand and stop firing. Helen, this might just work!"

Trish stepped towards the door. Helen grabbed her arm, "Hold on. This time I'm going with you. There's no way I can just sit here and wait."

Helen grabbed her purse and the two of them ran from the conference room.

Major Tsu was looking over the final plans for the EMP launch when Trish burst through his door followed by Helen. None of Tsu's staff dared stop a major at his door.

"Mars!" Helen shouted. "We can use the satellite circling Mars!"

Tsu looked up from his tablet. "What? What has Mars got to do with this?"

"The Martian satellite . . ." Helen started but Trish put her hand on her arm and took a deep breath before continuing.

"Major Tsu, I remembered the Chinese government has a functioning communications satellite circling Mars. I know because Starshield helped with the design and testing before launch. If Mars is in the right position and the satellite is on the right side of Mars, we could get a message to them through that. We do have a way of identifying ourselves so they would pay attention, don't we?"

Tsu considered the idea and then keyed his comm unit. "Captain Chung, let me know if the Martian comm orbiter is in place for sending a message to the Fermi Base. This is top priority. I need to know now."

He looked at Trish and Helen, "Let's hope this works. It may be our last chance before we need to fire the EMP module."

Chung called in and they all listened to what he had to say. "The positioning is valid for a message."

Trisha and Helen high-fived and Tsu motioned them to keep quiet as Chung continued. "We're running a ping test to confirm. But in the meantime, the team on the Moon has figured this out before we did and are sending us a message. It seems to be an automated one because it's not looking for a response."

"Please play the message here in my office," Tsu requested.

They listened intently as Zhang's recorded voice, mixed with some static, came on the speaker. ". . . attempt a maneuver that will keep the asteroids from hitting Earth. The data is being broadcast along channel 1471. Alert, this is the Fermi Moon Base. We will stop rock bombardment shortly and attempt a maneuver that will keep the asteroids from hitting Earth . . ."

"Chung, get the data from that channel in a readable format to my office instantly," Tsu said.

He looked at Helen and Trish. "I'm going to contact General Sun. We may have finally gotten one lucky break."

Trish nodded and Helen sat down feeling as if she could breathe for the first time in quite a while.

Chapter Eighty-Seven

S am watched the lunar terrain go by as he sat on the back of the transport bot. The machine was plodding along the Moon's surface at only four kilometers per hour. He knew if he walked the twelve hundred meters across the surface, it would use up a lot more of his oxygen reserves as well as tire him out.

He set up his comm unit to connect to Boris, Pierre and Amanda. "Are the three of you close to the lander yet?"

Amanda was the one who responded. "Not yet. It's taking more time than I had hoped to rig a way to move Pierre. Even in this gravity, trying to move him without bumping him too much is not an easy thing."

"The takeoff will not do him much good either. You need to be able to strap him in and get him as immobile as possible. But you need to get moving. We don't want to get off the Moon so late that we have few options. Also, we don't want to get blasted with pieces that come flying off after impact."

Boris chimed in. "Bozhe Moy! You're right, I'd forgotten lunar gravity would not pull pieces back down the same way Earth would. This hit is going to create one big explosion with a lot more mass flying into space than a crash on the Earth would produce."

"Okay," Amanda said. "I think we're ready. Boris can you help me with moving Pierre or are you having enough trouble with yourself?"

After a moment, Boris responded, "I'm afraid that when I stand up, I'm feeling lightheaded."

Amanda checked in on Boris' vitals. "You're a little low on O2. Here, let me get you a fill up." She reached into one of the cubbies, extracted one of the oxygen packs and replaced the pack on Boris' back. Then she set his suit to raise his adrenaline.

"Okay, stand up again and see how you feel."

Boris stood with one hand holding him up against a table "Much better, thank you. Okay, I don't know if I can help lift Pierre much, but at least I can hold the doors."

Pierre added, "I can hold the doors, too."

"Very funny," Amanda responded. All the doors to the base were sliding ones that opened and closed automatically.

Sam broke into the conversation. "Guys, you don't have a lot of extra time. I urge you to get into the lander and set up as soon as possible. No time for screwing around anymore."

"Roger that," Amanda's voice took on a serious tone. " We'll see you there as soon as possible. Boris, can you call us a transport bot and have it waiting outside the airlock?"

Setting his comm unit to connect only to the Protector, Sam asked it. "I'm almost there. Is it ready?"

Protector's smooth voice responded, "Ready. It's in the third chamber on your left upon entering my facility."

The transport bot slowed down right in front of the entrance. Sam hopped off in the funny way lunar gravity makes one move. He shuffled into the doorway and walk/hopped until he got to the right door. As he stepped into the room, a faint blue light came on overhead and the Protector's voice came on.

He took a step back when he saw a twelve-foot tall creature standing at the opposite side of the room. The creature had a small head shaped somewhat like a football with a large toothy mouth at the front and obsidian round eyes at the top. The skin was jade green and the top of the head had a crest of thin yellow feathers running down to the back. Everything about it made Sam feel vulnerable.

The creature spoke. "This is just a projection, Sam. This was the body given to me by those who made me. I'm designed to resemble them."

Sam resisted the urge to flee. The creature struck an innate sense of fear in him. It had a predator's way of moving. When it looked at him, he felt like a target.

"Why didn't you show us this when we first came across you?"

"Sam, I can detect your rate of breathing and how fast your heart is pumping right now. You were already startled and excited when we first met. If you saw this form, you would have either lost consciousness or been unable to fight the desire to flee."

Sam nodded and swallowed hard. "Yes, you're right. For some reason, you look terrifying to me."

"I expected as much. My creators were predators first and foremost. Although they became omnivores over time, as most of the sapient versions of both Saurians and Scarabs do. But, they did not lose all their predatory features. Your simian genes are responding to that. If you were seeing me on a screen or even in one of your human zoos, you'd feel protected. But in an enclosure like this room, you have a deep biological response telling you to run. I'm impressed by how well you're controlling that response, Sam." Having the creature speak with the soft voice the Protector always used was even more unnerving.

"I think you're right," Sam said. "We would've run off if we saw this projection, even after we'd seen what you first showed us."

He picked up the gray square seventy centimeters on a side and thirty centimeters thick that lay on a table before him. "Is this it?"

"Yes Sam, it is. I want to thank you for this. My batteries are nearing an end and even if I had reserves left, I do not think the incoming asteroid would leave me at all capable."

"No problem," Sam replied. "In a way, without knowing it, this is what I came for. Time for me to go. Not much of a window left."

The projection nodded from the waist almost as if it was bowing. "Goodbye Sam. It has been a distinct pleasure to have met you and the others."

"Goodbye, Protector, and thank you for everything."

Sam carried the square in both hands, wishing it had a handle. He placed it carefully on the back of the transport bot and hopped up alongside of it. He checked his time display and realized he was running late.

"Bot forty-seven, take me to the lander site and do so at maximum speed,"

The bot answered, "Maximum speed is not recommended. There is debris along the way from previous mining operations."

"Never mind the debris, use maximum speed. Plow through anything small enough and evade larger items."

"Initiating maximum speed as instructed."

It was four minutes later when the transport bot lurched to avoid a sizable rock. This sent the square flying off of the back platform and bouncing end over end across the lunar surface. Without hesitating, Sam jumped off of the platform and bounced, rolling across the lunar surface as well. As he finally stopped rolling, he saw the transport bot over one hundred meters away and moving away at maximum speed.

Chapter Eighty-Eight

Inside Lunar Lander 2
Nearing Asteroid

Major Zhang's head snapped forward and he shook it, trying to clear his mind. He raised his hand to rub his eyes and felt the faceplate through his gloves. Then he remembered. He was in the lander and had taken off from the Moon. The thought woke him fully as adrenaline suddenly pumped through his veins.

He took stock of his situation. His faceplate display announced he was entering visible range of the asteroid. He looked out of the window, squinting. There! He saw a faint, blurry blob almost dead ahead. Setting his faceplate to offer a magnified view, he held his breath.

The reason it looked blurry was because there was not one asteroid. There were five large rocks spinning around each other with thousands of smaller rocks circling them. The large rocks ranged in size from a football field to an airport. The spectral analysis on his faceplate told him some of the small rocks had come from the Moon.

His best guess was that the Moon rocks managed to crack the asteroid, breaking it into the large parts and thousands of small rocks. This was going to present a challenge since the calculation for his maneuver was based on five large parts.

He made some guesstimates based on the sizes and masses of the different parts. He knew what the over-all mass was. Feeding the data into the on-board AI, he waited until it delivered a new plan. He told the AI it had to come up with a best-case scenario in the next five minutes.

While waiting for the AI to figure things out, he began imagining what the solution might be. Would he need to push the pieces of rocks together? Or would he be able to affect the entire mass in some other way? Was the gravity between the objects enough that if he moved the largest, the others would just follow? This felt like the type of computer game his roommate back at school enjoyed playing so many years ago. He, however, never found that type of game interesting. He wished now he had.

The AI's voice came over his comm unit. "Projected plan is in place. Best case scenario is seventy-two percent effective."

"Do you mean twenty-eight percent of the asteroid mass will not hit the Moon?

"Approximately."

"Show me."

Zhang watched as the display animated the suggested solution. One of the five rocks broke away and went off at a different angle with a few of the smaller pieces following it. Another separated from the bunch, but followed the trajectory for the most part. He watched as the animation showed the rocks slamming into the Moon surface one after another in a line running through the Fermi Base. Finally, the lagging rock missed the Moon entirely and whipped past it curving into the Earth's gravity well. The animation showed the rock breaking as it touched the ionosphere and began heating up. The angle kept it in the ionosphere for quite a while. The majority of the pieces bounced off of the mesosphere and hurtled back into space. A few large pieces came pounding through the stratosphere before becoming white hot on entering the troposphere.

At four kilometers above the Pacific Ocean, the rock, which was the size of a large skyscraper, exploded.

"How accurate are these projections?" Zhang asked.

"Given available data, the projection has a likelihood of seventy-two percent."

"Right, you said that. And what happens on the planet when that rock explodes?"

"Tidal waves with a high amount of water vaporization. Possible earthquakes. Data is incomplete for a more exact projection."

Zhang sighed. It was not the best-case scenario they hoped for, but it didn't sound like an extinction level event. In any case, it was the best option he had. The best option the planet had.

"Okay, let's get started on this plan. Let me see the exact procedural steps we'll be going through. How do we get the big rock to follow us?"

He focused as the AI began to itemize the plan's steps.

Chapter Eighty-Nine

Wenchang Base
Hainan Province

"Ahem, General Sun?" Sun spun his chair around and saw the same nervous captain who had come to see him previously. The captain stood at attention.

"Stand at ease, Captain. Now tell me, what's the news?"

The captain didn't relax despite being ordered to do so. "Major Kwok asks me to let you know the Moon Base has stopped firing rocks. And now they have fired off a lander in the direction of the asteroid. We have attempted to contact the lander but there's no response. It may be unmanned and used as a drone."

"I see." Sun wondered what the lander could possibly be doing. Had the mining system broken or did they have no more rocks? He looked at the captain, whose forehead beaded with sweat despite the climate control in the room.

"Captain, was there anything else?"

"No, General. That was all he sent me to say."

"Then you're dismissed."

Sun turned to his screen and activated the comm with the intention of contacting Major Tsu, when he saw Tsu's face appear with an incoming call indicator.

"Tsu? What do you know?" Sun got right to the point.

Tsu looked a little frazzled. "The Moon has stopped firing rocks and we have put a halt to the EMP plan."

"Is that wise? What if they start up again?"

"They will not. Major Stern came up with the idea of contacting them off the Mars comm satellite. When we connected, we found they thought of that before us. Major Zhang sent a repeating message about their plan along with a complete data set of how they're going to do this. At first shot, it seems feasible."

Sun leaned forward. "Give me the basic overview, I'll worry about details later."

Tsu smiled. "They've fired a lander and they're hoping to use it to bring the asteroid into the Moon. Unfortunately, the Fermi Base may be lost in the process, but they're indicating a high probability of success. My team is crunching the numbers for themselves."

"Good," Sun said, considering the consequences. "Let me know what you know as soon as you know it. In the meantime, load the nuclear ordinance, but keep it on hold until you hear from me."

"General? If we fire the nukes . . ."

"Let me do the thinking, Major. There are elements you aren't privy to right now." Sun stared at him to reassure him he had all the elements in hand.

"Very well, General. I'll contact you as soon as I have more data."

Sun stood up and walked over to the window looking out upon the bay. A fleet of fishing boats was heading into the harbor. Most of them had been out visiting deep-sea farms and were not really fishing the way their fathers and grandfathers had. Their ancestor's methods had proven to be unsustainable. They had almost been disastrous when it came to managing fish stocks. The new deep-sea farms scaled over wide territories and spread the fish out. Over enough area, they prevented a lot of the problems the older farms had. Sometimes, old patterns had to be broken, even if it meant the new ones were hard to implement. Especially if survival was at stake.

He returned to his chair and keyed the connection to Benson. It only took a moment for Benson's face to appear. "Yes?"

"I have important news. We've received a message from the team on the other side of the Moon."

"Really? Were you able to get them to stop firing?"

"We're not actually in touch with them. They sent us a recorded message using our Mars satellite. They've stopped firing the rocks of their own accord. It seems they have a plan to drive the asteroid into the other side of the Moon."

There was a pause before Benson answered. "Do you think they can do this?"

"I'm as yet uncertain. My team is working out the dynamics. If it's the case, we'll disarm the space elevator and bring our warheads back to

Earth. I'll ask you also disarm your missile if this turns out to be a viable plan."

Sun could not help noticing how Benson's eyes looked left and right before responding. Sun was sure Benson was going to tell him what he wanted to hear. Whether that was the truth was another matter.

"Yes, of course. There's no need to have such a missile ready if we don't need it." Benson's voice rose. "By God! Let's hope those boys on the Moon know what they're doing! When will we know if this is going to work?"

"I have a team working out the details and will let you know as soon as I know. In the meantime, we'll share the data the lunar team has sent so your team can work it out for themselves."

Benson nodded, "That's generous of you, General Sun. Thank you."

"Mr. President, my predecessor began an unwarranted and insane war. It will take us all a long time to recover from that. I'm ready to do all I can to assure the peace and set the recovery on the fastest pace possible."

The president showed off the famous smile that got him so many votes. "Thank you, General Sun. I appreciate your candid and peaceful approach. Maybe there is hope for us after all. I look forward to the data and any updates you may have."

The connection severed, leaving Sun wondering what Benson would do next.

In Benson's office, an aide said, "Should I send word about standing down with the missile?"

"Not just yet," Benson responded. "While Sun is sharing everything he's learning with us, it'll be a long time before I trust anyone in the Chinese government. Make sure we have people looking at the data he sent right away. Try to authenticate it with what we're seeing happen between the asteroid and the Moon."

Chapter Ninety

Chang'e 3 Base
Lunar Lander 4

Amanda pulled the strap as tight as she dared to. Then she added some insulation material as padding around Pierre. He looked pale as he smiled at her. She checked his vitals in her display and set his suit to hydrate him a little more. The suit was running short of supplies. They would need to get him to some proper care pretty quickly if he was to make it.

She suddenly realized she'd made a mistake. She was keeping him awake as a way to comfort herself, but there was no need for him to be awake. At least not through the trip off of the Moon and back to Earth. In fact, the added stress of being aware and concerned would deplete his suit's resources even more. She checked what the suit had available for putting him to sleep. She found a mild sedative that wouldn't lower his blood pressure and set the suit to give him a dose.

"You're putting me to sleep?" Pierre's voice was slurring, but still sounded charming with his French accent.

"Just making sure you're comfortable., Pierre. How did you know?" Amanda asked.

"I've been monitoring my vitals, too. Amanda, if I do not wake up from this . . ."

"Don't be silly," she interrupted. "You'll be just fine. We're heading back to Earth and they'll have everything they need to get you back on your feet in no time."

"Well, in that case," his voice was starting to sound quieter. "I'd like to take you to dinner when I'm able to."

She smiled. "That would be wonderful, Pierre. I 'd love that."

Pierre's eyes closed and he muttered, "A French gentleman knows when to take advantage of the situation." He fell asleep with a smile on his face.

Amanda turned to Boris. "How are you doing?"

"I'm doing about as well as I can with this headache. I need to show you how to fly this thing. I have the flight plan in the AI, but you never know what could happen."

"But if the AI has a problem, you'll be there to fly it." Amanda frowned.

"Like I said, you never know what could happen. If the AI is fucked and I'm not capable, you're not going to turn to Pierre to take over."

"But what about Sam? He'll be back any minute."

"Listen, girl!" Boris raised his voice. "I'm telling you if you're the last person alive on board this lander and the AI is fucking it up, you'll need to know what to do! Do you understand?"

Amanda was not one to be cowed, but she'd never heard Boris so angry. "Yes, I'm sorry. Please show me." By habit, Amanda started recording Boris' explanation.

As Boris was explaining the controls, Amanda could not help having her mind wander. Where was Sam? He should have checked in already. She fought the urge to contact him, deciding to wait until Boris was done.

As he finished he said, "So, can you repeat to me what I just told you?"

Amanda blushed. "Er, no. I don't think I can, but I did record everything you said and will replay it as soon as I have a chance."

She was afraid he'd blow up, but instead he said, "Eto nye moya problema. It's not my problem."

"Where do you think Sam is? Shouldn't he be here by now?" Amanda asked.

Boris face went blank in his faceplate and she could tell he was scanning his display.

"Yes," he said. "He should be. Especially because, if my calculations are correct, our launch window closes in less than forty-five minutes."

Sam took ten minutes to fetch the box the Protector made for him. In the low lunar gravity and lack of atmosphere, the box continued bouncing for some distance. It took him a few minutes to see the traces of its passage and follow it to where it lay leaning against a small crater wall.

The fifty-kilo box weighed less than nine kilos in the lunar gravity. Still, its shape made carrying it difficult as he shuffled across the Moon's surface.

Now he was working his way back to the spot where he'd fallen off of the transport bot. It was odd the bot hadn't stopped. It should have when the weight in the back changed, but the high speed at which it was moving may have had to do with that. Sam decided to signal the bot for a pick-up.

A message appeared with an affirmative and an estimated time of arrival just shy of twenty minutes. That made Sam check his suit log and find he'd been lying on the lunar surface for ten minutes before he'd gone to search for the box.

He muttered a curse and then activated his comm unit, "Amanda, Sam here. I've fallen off of a trans bot and am running late."

He waited but didn't hear any answer so he tried again. "Amanda?"

He then tried the Protector, "Protector, are you there?"

Silence prompted him to launch a diagnostic of his audio systems. The result came immediately. His sound system remained undamaged but his microphone was SOL.

"When it rains, it pours shit!" He continued to shuffle-bounce in the direction his faceplate was telling him was the direction of the launch pad.

The Sun was just beginning to rise over the horizon. The lunar surface temperature was about to change from minus one-fifty centigrade to plus one-twenty. That would take four hours. The lunar day was about twenty-seven Earth days. Half of them facing the Sun while the other half saw only blackness and the spectacle that was the Milky Way. Sam knew his suit was designed to deal with both extremes, but it was better at keeping him warm since cooling took more energy from the suit.

He decided to move a little faster until he caught himself stumbling and falling on all fours. He picked himself up, grabbed the box and started again, moving quickly but more carefully now. His time was running out.

Chapter Ninety-One

Lunar Lander 2
Near the Asteroid

Zhang wished he could wipe his brow. He almost jumped as the suit grew a short appendage inside of his faceplate and wiped the sweat from his brow for him. He wasn't sure whether the suit was reacting to moisture or his thinking. He could never get used to wearing something that felt so alive.

The operation was proceeding according to the new AI plan. He'd harpooned three of the major rocks and attached each with carbon Nano-fiber braid. It was the same strong stuff that held up the space elevators. The harpoons were re-purposed from some of the mining equipment used by the lunar bots. They fired a bolt into the rock surface, the end of which expanded in five directions at a ninety-degree angle to the penetrations. Using this method, the lunar bots were able to lift and displace five hundred-ton pieces when needed. Zhang hoped the method would hold when the asteroid train he was building would move from its current direction.

He touched the control pad and pointed to the next rock. It was the largest of the rocks and he added a sixth set of anchors to the braid. He would have preferred to have the largest rock be the first one, but there was no way he could get that alignment to work.

AI pilots made jobs like this a lot easier. He had the pilot come up alongside of the rock, dragging a hundred and seventy meters of the NF braid behind him. He fired the anchors and tested their hold. When he could detect they were not moving, he fused the braid to the end that attached it to the previous rock. Then he took off for the next rock. The entire operation took over an hour along with testing, but he didn't hurry. Having the connections break would have been worse than being late. It would be impossible to predict where the asteroids would arrive if that happened.

Once done, he flew around to the other side of the same rock and looked for a good spot to fire another anchor. Based on the mass of the rock and the placement of the first anchor, he needed a small area that would work. This side of the rock was different with a lot more of the small boulders flying about the asteroid than on the other side. This must have been the side that recently separated from the original stone since he saw a lot of hard edges and shadows. He was starting to wonder if he he'd find a decent spot to anchor it. Then he saw a perfect spot. It was smooth and the instruments told him it was the perfect density for placing an anchor. There was just one problem. It was on the edge of the zone the AI indicated the anchor needed to be in. In fact, if anything, it might be a meter or two outside of the zone.

The major knew he didn't have a lot of time to keep looking, and there was still another rock to attach to the train. He made the decision to go ahead with this spot. He had the AI match velocity with the rock and placed the nose of the ship thirty meters from the target. He fired the harpoon and watched as it moved toward the rock, streaming the long braid behind it. The end struck the surface and immediately drilled itself in before the side anchors fired. He tested by moving it slowly back, satisfied when he felt the braid pull taught.

The last rock was much smaller and only about three hundred meters away. The AI told him this one was receding away from the bunch faster than the others. It must have had a different impact from the Moon rocks. He also saw it had more rocks around it, all roughly the size of his ship. He was sure some of them must be Moon rocks.

Instructing the AI to redirect the output of the impulse engines, he watched as he gained on the wayward final asteroid.

As he got close, he could see that there were dozens of boulders flying around it in a variety of orbits. He watched them zip past, then saw two of them smack into each other breaking apart into smaller boulders. Some of the smaller ones went right into the big rock and others went flying away. Most kept orbiting the big rock the way the two which hit had been doing.

One of them looked as if it was getting bigger when he realized it was heading straight for him.

He woke the piloting AI, stabbed at the image of the rock coming at him and pressed the 'avoidance' button. In less than a second, he felt his

315

ship shift to his upper left. He watched as the growing rock became the size of a school bus and zipped past him at a distance of only five meters.

He took a deep breath, and laughed when he realized he'd been holding his breath in all the time he was roping the asteroids. As a young officer, he raced old cars as a hobby. Often, he found himself less than twenty centimeters from another car, both of them going at speeds that felt absurdly dangerous. Five meters was a huge distance by those standards. He knew the rock's speed relative to his ship would have resulted in opening his ship like a plastic bag of shrimp chips if they collided. And unlike the cars of his youth, outside this ship, there was no air.

"Father Zhang, you almost lost your boy," he said to himself. "That would have been bad timing. He still has to save his family and his nation."

He smiled at the thought of how his father would have been so proud if he were still alive. Although he'd never told him, Zhang knew his father always had high expectations for him.

The AI alerted him they were close enough to the final rock to start finding an anchor target. The boulders circling the rock were distracting. He knew he had to move fast and get away from what would be an eventual collision.

He found a spot in the proper zone and fired the anchors. They held well on the first shot, and he melded the braid to the one trailing from the largest rock. One more anchor and the train would be complete. He overrode the AI pilot for this last bit, worried it might not be able to take all the extra flying boulders into account. He pulled away from the asteroid and started a curved path that would take him to the other side. The path was different from what the AI had been doing. He pulled more acceleration than he'd been getting from the AI's courses. By the time he was opposite the final anchor zone, he was out of breath and feeling a little woozy. He instructed the AI to keep him at the spot for a few minutes before setting the last anchor.

When his head cleared, he approached the rock and placed the last plug, completing the connections.

Now came the delicate process of pulling the entire train—getting all the rocks to align one after the other and follow him to the Moon. This he left to the AI after giving it instructions. The challenge was keeping the braids from snapping and finding a way to keep the rocks from swaying back and forth as they fit into place. Some swaying was going to happen, no matter what. But he had to make sure it didn't put more pressure on the braid than it could handle. Given it was the same braid used for the space elevators, he had a lot of confidence in the tensile strength of the fibers. Still, better to not push the envelope on this one.

The AI indicated the procedure would take about two hours before the train was stable enough to start giving it a new direction.

Zhang let out a deep breath. He pulled up the text he'd been reading a few days earlier. Two hours might be just enough time to finish the book—a collection of Tang Dynasty poems by Li Bai. He decided to reread his favorite, "Waking from Drunkenness on a Spring Day."

Chapter Ninety-Two

Trish wondered if she smelled a rat. Tsu had sequestered himself in his office to contact Sun and hadn't come out, even though more than an hour had passed. Her requests to see him were just met with silence, uneasy eye shifting and shoulder shrugging from his staff.

After her third attempt to get to see him, she stomped back to the room where Helen and Louise were waiting.

"Well, don't you look happy?" Helen said.

"Something's wrong. I'm not sure what, but the way they look at me, something's changed. And Tsu is either locked in his office or MIA. I'm not sure which," Trish snapped.

Helen looked at her with surprise. "You should know by now that this means they're excluding you. More likely they're doing something of which you wouldn't approve."

"Yeah," Trish rolled her eyes. "Don't need to be Sherlock to figure that one out." She sighed. "I'm sorry. I don't mean to snap at you, but I hate when this type of bullshit starts to happen. It never ends well."

Louise was sitting at a comm unit and tapping at the screen. "Then don't just sit there. Do something."

"Like what?"

"Like break into their system and have a look-see," Louise said, smiling.

"What?" Trish moved around so she could see what Louise was looking at. "Holy crap, Louise. What if they catch you doing this?"

"Well, technically, I'm not doing anything. This is Tsu's login. I have to say, he wasn't good at concealing his security credentials. I got in on the seventh try."

Looking over Louise's shoulder, Trish smiled. "Okay, how long before you think they'll notice?"

"Well, if we're quick enough, I'll have the time to wipe out our tracks. So, tell me, what do you want to know?"

Trish bit the tip of her thumb. "What's the status of the nuclear warhead on the elevator?"

Louise tapped the screen a few times, shook her head and then tried something else before responding. "Looks like they're still loaded and primed."

"What?" Helen slammed her fist onto the desktop. "But we know they're not needed. They stopped firing on the Moon and have a solution they're working on."

"Can you tell if anything has changed about the nukes, Louise? Maybe they're just staying charged as an 'in case' precaution?"

Louise manipulated the screen and kept wiping pages. Then she stopped. "The targets have changed. Seems they've been wiped, but I don't see what the new targets are. The system is being primed to accept them. Let me see if I can find what standard plans might be. After all, it takes a while to load brand new targets, but only minutes to restore old ones."

"Can you tell if they'll be using stored targets?" Trish asked.

"Jeez, Trish, and all this time I thought you were sharp as a tack. Of course, they're using stored targets. If not, they'd already be loading custom ones. Nobody wants to waste time waiting."

Trish brushed off Louise's comment. She knew Louise was always trying to make herself look like the smartest one in the room.

"Okay, can you figure out what the stored targets might be?"

"It's really odd," Louise finally said. "Normally one would imagine a few sets of targets. But it looks like all the ones on file are disabled except for this set." She showed Trish a series of columns of numbers scrolling across the screen.

"What are those?" Helen asked.

"Coordinates." Louise responded. "Hold on, let me see if I can figure out what they mean." She held up her small phone comp and began to scan the data. In a few moments, her phone comp played a little tune. Trish recognized the melody as something from the middle of the twentieth century.

"Here we go . . ." Louise's voice stopped. The list on her phone comp displayed most of the major cities in the United States as well as a few other targets across the Rockies and into Canada.

"Fucking asshole!" Trish burst out. "That idiot is planning on bombing North America back into the Stone Age! Just when we're trying to defend the planet. What type of bullshit is this?" She jumped to her feet and went for the door when Helen grabbed her arm.

"Cool down, Trish," Helen spoke evenly. "All you're going to do is get yourself, and probably us, arrested or shot if you barge in there making demands. Especially given the info you're not supposed to be aware of."

Trish stared at her for a moment before acknowledging. "You're right. Say, how did you get to be such a smart spy?"

Helen grinned. "A few years on any university board and you'll be thinking more deviously than any arms salesman."

Trish nodded. "Okay, so what do we do?"

"I have an idea," Louise said. "I could wipe the coordinates in their files and even destroy back-ups. That could set them back a while. But I'm afraid I don't think I can hide who did it that well. After all, Tsu will know it wasn't him."

"Yeah," Trish replied. "But maybe we can set up some sort of dead man's switch that starts erasing the target codes if we don't stop it in time. Something that needs to be reset every few hours?"

Louise thought about it. "I could do that. I could even include a second layer of security in the codes. It would look like they're re-entered and ready to go, but won't load without a hidden password."

Trish laughed and said, "And when did you get on a university board?"

Chapter Ninety-Three

Chang'e 3 Base
Maglev Launcher

S am smiled to see the transport bot slowing down in front of him. "I was afraid you might not find me," he said, knowing the bot could not hear him.

Climbing onto the transporter's back, he tucked the box he was carrying under one arm and grabbed a handrail with the other. He found the bot's messaging panel and directed it to the lander base. The transport bot lurched at its customary pace and Sam resisted the urge to try to get it to speed up.

Only a few minutes later, he saw the lander base and noticed the smaller lander in takeoff position. It sat on the sling rails with light emitting from the cabin. The transport bot stopped in front of the control room. Sam climbed off and went in through the airlock. He was glad to see it was as he'd left it and he plugged his suit into the regeneration tube that followed him around. He walked up to the control panel and fired up the room's comm unit.

"Boris, is that you in the lander?"

"Sam?" Amanda's voice was the first to respond. "We were worried about you."

"No worries," Sam replied. "I took a spill off of the transporter and it seems my comm unit went dead."

"Are you plugged in?" Amanda asked.

"Of course, why?"

"I'll set up a diagnostic scan, Maybe I can fix it. Not good to be without comm."

Boris' voice broke in, "It's good you're here, Sam. I have a problem with the lander."

"What kind of problem?"

"I cannot seem to get any connection to the takeoff piston. No indication of whether it's working or not. Not even that it's there. Very strange."

Sam nodded even though nobody could see him. "Yeah, there was a problem with the latch system when Zhang took off. I had to perform a manual release. Hang on while I check the systems out."

Sam pulled up the checklist and went through each step. Nothing was off until he got to the step that verified the piston hook was in place. There was no response. He tried the switch four times and still got no response.

"Boris, I'm having the same issue. Hang on while I go check the hook assembly itself. I'm going outside."

Amanda's voice came on, "Sam, I don't have an indicator that your comm unit is fixed. Can you wait?"

"Do I need to stay plugged in for the diagnostic to finish?"

"Well, no, not technically, but it might need to load or reload new software to fix it. That won't happen without a functioning connection."

"Okay, well the diagnostics can run while I'm out and then I'll plug back in if a fix is necessary. Don't worry, I'll be right back. A small hop outside won't be bad after the ride I've just been through. And the latch system is just fifty meters away. I'll be back in no time."

He stepped into the airlock and started the process. The sound of receding air was replaced by the silence of the Moon. Or rather the sound of his own breathing, but he had learned to ignore that some time ago.

He shuffled the fifty meters and came up to the latch mechanism. Looking it over, he saw a small part of the casing had broken. He pulled off the cracked part and peered inside. It was a simple system and the problem was easy to see. A cable had come unattached and the end of it snapped. The cable was long enough, so he spliced a bit of the covering. Working fast because the metals were very cold, he wound three centimeters of the cable around the connection. He tugged and decided it would hold steady. Then he squeezed the end of the metal wire into the socket. As he did, he felt the structure pull away. His mouth opened as saw the latch hook pull away and the sling deploy the magnetic mechanism. Losing his balance, he fell on his rear as he watched the lander propel into the lunar sky.

Sam raised himself and shuffle-ran back to the control room. He activated the airlock saying, "Come on, come on, come on!" wishing for it to open faster. When it finally opened, he hopped in and plugged into the system automatically. As the airlock closed and air filled the space, he activated the comm unit in the room, "Boris? What happened? I found a bad connection and reconnected it. I didn't expect you to take off."

The voice that answered was as much a series of groans as words, "Didn't expect it either. System must have been set to launch. Thought it wasn't. G's were bad. Pierre fell. He might be dead. Amanda's unconscious. I'm going to come around and land to pick you up . . ."

Sam realized Boris was not thinking clearly. "Boris, think. How much time will it take for you to land and configure another takeoff?"

There was a long pause before Boris' voice answered, this time clearer. "You're right. Too long. If I come back, none of us gets off in time. Sam, my friend, I'm so sorry."

Sam felt his eyes begin to water. "Listen, tell them all, the people on Earth, tell them all about the Protector and all we've learned here. And Boris?"

"Yes, Sam?"

"Tell my wife Helen that it was all good. Every minute with her was more than I could have ever hoped for." His voice choked.

There was another long pause. "Sam, I'll tell her. But all is not yet lost. There's the old Russian base. If you get on a transport bot now, you might be able to make it before the rocks hit. There may be enough resources there for you to hold out until someone can come back to get you."

Sam knew that was a long shot at best. "Thanks Boris, I'll give that a try. Get yourself, Amanda and I hope Pierre home safe. Signing out now. You need to fire your rockets and get out of here before Crazy Zhang comes in with his rock parade. Goodbye. Boris."

"Goodbye, my friend. Udaci! Good luck"

Sam's faceplate lit up with a message telling him new comm software was being initiated.

"A lot of good that will do me now," he said as he headed to the airlock. Alone on the Moon.

Chapter Ninety-Four

Z hang's head suddenly snapped forward. Something was wrong. He realized he'd fallen asleep and a lurch had woken him. He looked at his screen and saw his heading had changed. Checking with the AI pilot, he found a course change was in progress.

Querying the system, he learned the change was due to a modification in mass. The system said the mass had reduced by thirteen percent. He pulled up the relative masses of all the rocks and it was the tail rock, the one he had first captured, that was missing.

He had the AI run a check and it showed only moments before, a small, fast moving rock struck the last asteroid at its anchor. The connection severed, setting the asteroid segment free.

This sent the train he was guiding off on a different course just as if a terrestrial train lost its caboose in the middle of a tight turn. The AI calculated a course change and was implementing several moves to get the train back on trajectory.

The major double-checked the new trajectory solution. The process would take forty minutes and all his fuel would be spent well before striking the Moon.

As he looked through the solution, he saw the final rock, the caboose, would not strike the Moon. It would still swing around the Moon at a low level and head to the Earth.

He set the AI working on alternate trajectories to see if there was a way to keep all the rocks from hitting Earth. After several minutes looking at options, it showed none avoided Earth impact.

He cursed himself, wondering if the extra time he'd taken at the last rock reduced his options due to fuel consumption. It turned out the AI was implementing the best solution since the last rock would land somewhere in the southern Pacific Ocean, about as far away from massive population densities as it was going to get.

Zhang knew he was still in the Moon's shadow and had no direct connection to Earth. So, he formulated a message and sent it to the Mars comm satellite, hoping someone there was listening.

He sat back and wondered if there was anything else he could do, anything at all.

Chapter Ninety-Five

Space Elevator Facility
Pini Island, Indonesia

"You're not to be in here right now, Major Stern." Tsu's voice was cold and steady. "You must go back to your office at once. Is that clear?"

"Bullshit, Major Tsu!" Trish was unapologetic. "I'm here because something's wrong. You told me you'd be contacting General Sun and then you'd know what the next steps are. That was hours ago and I've heard nothing."

"That's because there's nothing for you to hear. And it's no reason to be rude to an officer of equal rank, Major. Such language is inappropriate. I will let the general know . . ."

"Major Tsu!" Trish raised her voice. "I was sent here by General Sun for precisely the purpose we're discussing! If you're hindering my mission, I'll be forced to relieve you of your command!"

Tsu remained calm. "I suggest you refrain from any such insinuations, Major. You're in my command area and you're a guest. In fact, you're not even a real major since you have only a field commission."

Trish stepped forward and tapped on a screen activating a comm app. She brought up the code she'd been given by Sun in case of an emergency. "We shall see what General Sun has to say."

Major Tsu stepped up and shut off the screen. "Major Stern, General Sun is dealing with important issues. We won't disturb him right now."

"Important issues? Important issues?" Trish raised her voice again. "What's more important than targeting America's population centers with your nuclear warheads? Or is that too trivial for General Sun to know about? Whose side are you on anyway?"

There was silence in the room as Tsu's staff turned to see how he would respond to the accusation.

Tsu made a quick decision. "Captain Fang, please load the targets that are in reserve."

"Yes, Major."

Trish looked him straight in the eyes, "I advise you not to do this. You will regret this, Tsu."

"Is that a threat, Major?"

"No. It's not a threat. It's a piece of advice, but you can take it for whatever you wish."

Displaying a cold smile, Tsu nodded to her. "Then I will take it as a threat. Major Stern. You're under arrest for threatening an officer and . . ."

A lieutenant in the corner suddenly interrupted them. "A new message from the Mars satellite!"

Everyone in the room turned toward him and he set the message to broadcast over a speaker. Major Zhang letting them know there was still a large rock heading toward the Earth made everyone hold their breath. When the message began to repeat, they all jumped into action.

"We need to call General Sun right away!" Trish announced.

"In a moment. Captain Fang, delay that last order and set the original targets back in place. Come with me, Major Stern," he said as he walked into his office.

Once inside he closed the door behind them. "Major, I have not forgotten your contempt for me out there. We'll handle this situation along with General Sun and then we 'll see what becomes of you after that."

"Okay, whatever you say, but first, there's something you need to know."

Chapter Ninety-Six

Wenchang Base
Hainan Province

Sun wasn't sure if it was the temperature in his office that was suddenly higher or if it was the call he had to make. In either case, his brow glistened and the back of his collar was drenched. The news from Tsu at the space elevator crystallized the situation to a place he hoped to avoid. Now, he had to share this new turn of events with Benson. He wiped his brow, remembering the signal he gave that put an end to his mentor Chairman Qi. He hit the connection for a comm session with Benson.

Benson appeared in a few moments. Sun was happy each of them made certain that whenever the other called, the answer came through straight away.

"General Sun. What's the news?"

"We've received a message from the man who's moving the asteroid. I'm transmitting it now. He indicates the majority of the asteroid is going to impact the Moon."

"Just how much of a majority? Or more important, how much is going to miss the Moon and hit Earth?" Benson's eyes were bright red. Sun assumed Benson wasn't sleeping any more than he was.

"The pilot of the ship at the asteroid estimates that thirteen percent of the mass may hit the southern Pacific Ocean."

"That's still a big rock and a big target. Does he mean near Hawaii? Or farther south?"

"We're still attempting to calculate the target. What you and I need to do to minimize the impact. I think that this calls for our mutual use of the nuclear warheads."

Benson furrowed his thick silver eyebrows. "Are you sure? After all, that seems like a lot of firepower for a much smaller rock."

"According to my staff, breaking the rock into smaller pieces will reduce the effect on the impact zone. A group of small pebbles will create some waves in a pool, but many of them will cancel each other out. A lot more will burn up in the atmosphere. Whereas one big rock creates a huge wave emanating from the impact site and causing massive tsunamis that will be far flung. They're advising we hit this rock with everything we've got. I'm dedicated to firing everything I can have ready in time. It would be best if you can add your enormous warhead to that list, Mr. President. It could mean fewer lives lost. Both of our countries would be affected."

"I see. Allow me the luxury of checking with my team as well." Benson smiled in that way that made Sun feel as if he were a mouse about to be eaten by a cat. "What type of window do we have before we must make a final decision?"

"I don't have those details yet. I rushed to get you this information as soon as I had it. I've prepared my nuclear warheads at the space elevator to fire at the rock as soon as it comes around the Moon. The best method would be for your large warhead to hit it first. That would allow my myriad of small warheads to hit the resulting separate rocks. We can deploy our warheads in the same general direction with instructions to pick out unique targets based on size. This would create the right scenario for turning this big rock into as many smaller ones as possible. With a little good fortune, we might even vaporize some of the inbound rocks giving us the best chance of all. It's the best answer we have, President Benson. Destroy the asteroid and then get on with the business of rebuilding the damage Qi left behind with his war. We will sign a treaty to work on that together as full partners. I give you my word on that."

Sun could see in Benson's face he didn't like the idea of having his weapon fired while Sun still had his weapons on the ground. Had the tables been turned, that's what he would be thinking as well. He decided to be as straight forward as possible.

"President Benson, if I was sitting in your shoes, I'd be nervous and hesitant, too. I'd want guarantees my people would be safe from attack and the entire nuclear ordinance in the space elevator was aimed at the asteroid. I don't know how I can give you those guarantees, but perhaps I can give you the next best thing."

Benson raised one eyebrow, "How?"

"Trish Stern is at the space elevator. As you know, I've given her a field commission as a major in the People's Revolutionary Army. I suggest she get a similar American commission as well. I'll give the order for her to be the commanding officer of all military personnel at the elevator. She'll be able to keep you apprised of the ordinance and where it's going. In fact, you can tell her where she should fire the warheads yourself."

Sun stared into Benson's eyes. "Mr. President, I'm giving you control of the majority of my nuclear arsenal. Do you understand?"

Benson slowly nodded. "I understand you think this is the best way to go about it."

"Yes, sir. And I'm putting the responsibility of saving millions of humans in your hands, Mr. President."

"And removing that responsibility from your hands?"

Sun wiped his forehead and smiled, "This is my way of taking responsibility, President Benson. Even if this works as I hope it will, I may be tried as a traitor for what I'm doing. I accept that responsibility for the good of the planet. Let the rest of the chips fall where they may. As Chairman Qi said so often, when the winds of chance blow, some build walls while other build windmills. I'm afraid Chairman Qi chose the walls. However, I choose the windmills.

Chapter Ninety-Seven

B oris jumped as soon as he heard Amanda's scream. "What the fuck happened?" he asked, looking around the cabin to see what was wrong.

She was seated behind him next to where she strapped Pierre in and he couldn't turn his head well enough to see her.

"We launched," he informed her matter-of-factly. "Please check on Pierre, I think he may have had a rough time of it."

Amanda leaned over and saw Pierre was unconscious and hanging off the edge of his seat. The only reason he was not on the floor of the lander was because the straps held him in place. She connected to his suit's life signs and checked his vitals. Pierre was still alive but his blood pressure was low again and his breathing irregular.

"We have to get Pierre to treatment urgently. He's not doing well at all."

"I know. We're heading back to Earth. I'm trying to figure out what the best spot to land might be. Do you have an opinion?"

Amanda said, "I thought Sam said it would be better for us to head to Edwards Landing Field in California. Hey, wait a minute. Where is Sam?"

Boris sighed. "He didn't make it on board. He was working on the latch mechanism on the launcher and managed to set it off. Unfortunately, he was not on the lander when it took off."

"Well, we have to go back to get him!" Amanda lunged for the controls. "You can't just leave him there!"

"We can't go back to get him," Boris said calmly. "The maneuver would use too much time and fuel. We would never be able to refuel in time. Going back would mean we're all lost. Sam understood this."

"You bastard! You've killed Sam!" Her anger turned to tears and she felt the suit wipe them off of her cheeks.

"No, Amanda. I didn't kill Sam. The circumstances have. It was just bad luck. The lander just took off instead of holding as we planned. Zhang has sent a comm. He's coming into the Moon with most of the asteroid. The impact will be on the near side of the Fermi Base. Sam's in a transport on his way to the old Russian outpost. If he hurries, he may be able to get there before Zhang hits the Moon. There's a chance he could survive this. There might be some oxygen left over at the Russian base. He may be able to hold out until we can send help. I know it's a long shot. Sam knows it, too. We'll do everything we can to bring him home."

Amanda let out a long sob. "I never imagined it would be like this. I thought this was going to be a great adventure full of discoveries. That's all bullshit now. We're not amazing people when it comes down to it. We're just fragile little humans pretending we can do great things." She sobbed again.

Undoing his belts, Boris shifted in his seat to look at her. "Amanda, there never has been comfort in discovery. Humans take risks. And because we take risks, we discover, we learn and we share what we've learned. Sam understood this—probably more than most. The discovery we made here—finding the Protector—was the greatest event in his life and maybe in all our lives. And with any luck, there will be at least three of us who live to tell about it. Imagine—finally being able to unravel the mystery of the disappearance of the dinosaurs and understand the true theory of evolution. And to bring home proof that extraterrestrials do exist and have existed for millions of years. That's the stuff people like Sam dreamed of."

"You may be right," Amanda said quietly. "I guess both you and Sam see the world that way, but for me, well, I don't know. I guess individuals matter more than discovery."

"Listen," Boris said. "In a few moments I should have a line of sight with Edwards Base. I'll let them know we're on our way and ask them to start working on the rescue plan for Sam. We're not yet, how do you say, out of the woods? Zhang's message says he lost a rock that will be skirting the Moon along with a bunch of smaller rocks. We need to make sure we steer clear of that."

"Oh!" Amanda said. "We're still in danger?"

"Every moment in space, one is in danger, Amanda," Boris said, stoically.

Chapter Ninety-Eight

Chang'e 3 Base
Maglev Launcher

S am lashed himself to a bar on the back of the transport bot. He knew he had to if he was going to tell it to operate at maximum speed. As he worked out the lashings, he also asked his suit comm to figure out how long it would take to get to the abandoned Russian base. It took several queries. The suit comm didn't understand what he was referring to at first. When he finally got the answer, the estimate was he would get to the base thirty-seven minutes after the impact estimate. This was not the solution he was looking for.

"Sam?" The dulcet voice used by the Protector came into his comm unit. "You must get off of the Moon shortly."

"No shit, Sherlock! But it doesn't seem like that's about to happen any time soon."

After a pause of almost a minute, "You're heading the wrong way. You can still get off of the Moon before impact, but you must turn around."

"Huh? Head back to the impact site? The landers are all gone. There's no way for me to get off of the Moon. All I can do is take shelter at the Russian base and wait."

The Protector's voice, once again, took some time before answering. "I'm very low on energy. You need to listen carefully. You can still get off of the Moon by riding a transport bot off the rail gun. The trip will not be comfortable because the acceleration is more than you're normally able to withstand."

Sam stopped his transport bot. "You think I can leave the Moon just like a rock? I hate to break this to you, but I'm not all that solid."

"I am aware of your frailty, but this is your only viable option at this point. Your suit will help you. I have studied it."

Sam smiled, "Easy for you to say. You won't be the one going through it. And after I'm heading out of the Moon's gravitational pull, how do I avoid falling back in? And as far as I know, these transport bots are surface vehicles only. No way to control it in space and no way to land it either."

This time it took two whole minutes before he got a response and the voice was jerky. "I took the liberty . . . of setting the codes for a launch that would put you in Earth orbit . . . The case you are carrying has a beacon built into it . . . The beacon radiates on a variety of commonly used Earth channels . . . Someone will find you . . . Hopefully in time . . ."

He realized the Protector was right. It might be his best chance. Taking a deep breath and letting it go, he directed the transport bot to return to the rail gun facility.

The bot only took five minutes to get to the airlock. Sam used the time to take a last look at the Moon's surface. He smiled, thinking he never imagined he'd ever have the chance to set foot on the Moon. And he'd communicated with an alien-built intelligence older than all hominids. If this was to end, it may just have been worth it. It was a dream come true for him. He only hoped his three friends would live to tell about it.

Once through the airlock, he automatically plugged in to recharge his suit. It would be his last chance to do so and he might need the resources to last for a long time. He loaded the code the Protector sent him into the rail gun ballistic system. The Protector had chosen one of the heavy-duty bots as it provided more shielding than the regular transport bots. The bot had followed instructions and covered itself in the sticky reflective dust. He had to add the mass of the transport bot as well as his own mass and that of the box he was taking along. The total was far less than the rail gun normally handled.

"Okay Protector, I think I may be ready to go. Will you be able to fire the gun once I let you know I'm in place in the launch bucket?"

Sam waited for a response, remembering each response took more time. After three minutes he tried again. Five minutes later there was still no response. He wondered if Protector had finally run out of energy.

He muttered under his breath as this meant he had to change the rail gun launch to an automated one. After fifteen minutes of tinkering, he decided he wasn't going to be able to start the launch remotely. His only other option was to set up a timed launch and make sure he was ready and aboard when it went off. He set the launch for thirty minutes. That was the longest he dared delay since he knew that Zhang's payload would send a lot of debris flying off down with the Moon's low gravity and he wanted to be well away when it happened.

He doubled-checked the code and verified his suit was loaded with as many resources as it could hold. The suit indicated that, under normal activity, he had seven days of oxygen. Sam felt that it was a very small amount for the voyage he was about to undertake, but it was all the suit would hold.

Just as he turned to activate the airlock, he heard voice of the Protector once again, "Sam, apologies. Change in code. Will spin the bot to protect you from some of the solar radiation. Travel well, my friend."

Sam didn't know if it was his imagination but the voice sounded a little sad.

He loaded the new code and set off for the transport bot, which he instructed to board the rail gun bucket. The bot fit with room to spare and Sam ordered it to adjust to a central position in the bucket. Then he climbed on the back and strapped the case he'd gotten from the Protector to himself. He wrapped himself in several layers of lunar foil and applied the current to it that made it shrink and hold the case tightly to his belly.

Then he strapped a large inflatable mattress onto the back of the transport bot, strapped himself over it and tightened the straps. He inflated the mattress and felt his body fit rigidly against it. He adjusted his suit for 'imminent impact', which would stiffen it preventing bone breakage and protecting his neck when the time came.

He looked at the chronograph display on his faceplate and saw he had four minutes left until the rail gun would fire. He set a visible timer to count down. Sam found himself breathing rapidly. He considered having the suit administer a sedative to save oxygen, but decided he could do that after takeoff. If he survived the ordeal.

The timer was down to thirty seconds and Sam looked up at the black sky splashed and speckled with the bright colors of the Milky Way.

"We really do live in a pretty neighborhood," he said to himself. "Such a shame most people will never get to see it like this."

He was wondering if he could spot Zhang's lander coming into the Moon when the rail gun fired and accelerated the transport bot with him inside it. It had gone just fifty meters when Sam lost consciousness.

Chapter Ninety-Nine

Lunar Lander 2
Moon bound

Major Zhang kept fiddling with the AI projections. He finally came up with what he was looking for. There was no way he was going to be able to get the caboose rock to hit the Moon. It snapped off of the train too soon. But that created an opportunity for him. Using the AI's projections, he found there was a moment when he could detach himself from the train. If his fuel held out, he might be able to avoid hitting the Moon with his lander.

The calculations had him cutting things close. He'd be no more than two hundred meters off of the Moon's surface during the descent. But the effect should be enough to sling him back at the Earth, or into something close to an Earth orbit. If he was lucky.

Zhang didn't believe in luck. "A wise man makes his own luck," his father always told him when he was just a boy. There were several occasions in his life when he felt his father's saying had been true. He was determined to prove it again this time.

He double-checked the calculations. They looked good. The final plan would put him in an orbit close to the Earth. Someone from one of the space elevators could match up with him and bring him back to the planet. He was going to live! He could feel it.

Instructing the AI to follow the new flight plan, he sat back and held on. The automated pilot made the adjustments and described the new course in a visual representation. It showed a solid line for where he'd traveled and a dotted line for where he'd go. He did another check of the numbers and took a deep breath. He was making his own luck.

The lander would detach from the lead rock seven minutes before the first rock impacted just short of the Fermi Base. The other rocks would slam the base and spots beyond it. Zhang felt it was a shame to have so much work done by his country destroyed, but he felt a tremendous sense of relief knowing the planet was not facing the same disaster.

And all because of him.

That was when he realized that not only was he being a hero, he would experience recognition for it. His life was going to change dramatically. There would be a medal, maybe more than one, gala celebrations to attend, speeches to make. Maybe even a parade. He'd get paid for some of the speeches. And there'd be a book. Perhaps even a movie. He was going to be a wealthy man!

Zhang's heart raced as he saw the Moon coming at him, faster than it should. A check of AI projections told him all was as it should be.

When he was just a kilometer off of the surface, he felt the engines in the back of the lander fire. He went from weightlessness to sudden pressure pushing him back in his seat and pinning him there. Still the Moon came on, looking large and ominous.

At half a kilometer he began to see he was starting to aim at the Moon's horizon rather than straight into the surface.

At three hundred meters he could see the lander's nose rise above the horizon.

At two hundred meters he was skimming over the surface, seeing craters race by at a speed far greater than he'd ever seen before.

The lander began to rise. Two hundred and fifty meters, three hundred, four hundred. Zhang pumped his fist into the air as he saw the display show he'd past five hundred meters.

Behind him, the first rock slammed into the Moon raising a cloud of debris that lifted off of the surface at enormous speed.

Zhang had his fist in the air when a piece of the Moon twice the size of his lander crashed into the vehicle, crushing it like aluminum can.

It happened so fast, Major Zhang never felt a thing

Chapter One Hundred

Lunar Lander 4
Earth bound

"Impact!" Boris' voice was shaking. "Lunar impact! He actually did it! He drove the asteroid onto the Moon! That crazy Taikonaut drove the asteroid onto the Moon!"

Amanda looked at him, tearing herself away from Pierre's vitals projected across her faceplate. Her suit recognized her change of attention and faded the stats away. "Where?"

"Looks like about twenty kilometers lunar west of the Fermi Base. Oh! There goes another impact. Looks like this one is almost right on the base itself!"

Amanda requested that her suit show her the Moon. The lander had directional cameras and the suit took control of one of them. She could see spouts of rock and dust rising off of the surface. They looked like huge splashes of water might look but much taller and almost as if they were in slow motion.

"Why does it look so slow?"

"Low lunar gravity makes the splashes rise up a lot higher, so it looks slower compared to the surface. There! Another one. That one was about," he paused while calculating, "one hundred and twenty kilometers beyond the base. The pilot AI is registering two more big ones. There are a lot of smaller ones. Hundreds of them. That side of the Moon will never look the same. I can't imagine the Protector could have survived this in any way."

"What about Sam?" Amanda fretted.

"He was heading on a different path than the rocks are came in. About a seventy-five-degree angle. If he were running at full transport bot speed, he'd be well outside of the impact zone. I'm not sure about the splash when the Moon's gravity brings all that matter back down. It is going to be raining rocks and dust for days, maybe weeks. But lots of it will hit escape velocity."

"Oh, Sam," Amanda whispered. "Is there any way he can make it?"

"Until it's over, there's always hope. Sam's a smart man and can think on his feet. If the old Russian base offers him enough shelter and oxygen, I'd be willing to bet we'll see Sam again."

Amanda nodded, "I wish I had your confidence, Boris."

"There goes the fourth one!" Boris exclaimed. "And it looks like that last one will miss the Moon."

"Oh! Will it hit the Earth?" Amanda put her hand to her faceplate. A habit she never lost.

"It might. Zhang did the best job he could. He is, uh, was a real hero, you know. He never flinched from the task. What a man! They'll build statues in his honor in China."

"That won't help his children," Amanda said.

"Well, let's go home and help our children," Boris replied.

"I only have a nephew. No children of my own yet."

Boris smiled, "I do. And someday you will as well, and you'll have amazing stories to tell them."

"Have you figured out where and how we can land?" she asked.

"I'm working on it," he replied. "I think our best bet is still to take us down at the Edwards Base in California. It's an old base but because it was set up for those old shuttle landings, it has one of the longer runways. It might still have some of the emergency equipment we'll need if the landing is rough."

"Wait. Why would we have a rough landing?"

"Have you ever landed one of these in full Earth gravity?" Boris said.

"No."

"Well neither have I. The AI should be able to handle it, but you never know. If the landing is not a textbook example or conditions on the ground, like weather, are not perfect, we may have a few bumps coming in. Especially if there are rocks coming in with us."

"Oh," Amanda said quietly. She turned back to check on Pierre who was still stable but unconscious.

"Edwards is receiving us and has acknowledged we may land. I have the AI taking us in. We're going to limit the Earth orbits coming in because the sky is full of rocks, but we still need to do at least one breaking orbit. The AI is coming up with bad scenarios if we try a direct entry with no orbits.

The animation looks like we'd bounce off of the atmosphere if we tried that."

"You know, Boris, I usually like to know all the details, but this time I think I'll feel better if you just tell me we're landing," Amanda said.

"Okay, I was just making sure what I'm planning doesn't sound like nonsense."

For the first time in what felt like ages, Amanda actually grinned from ear to ear.

Chapter One Hundred One

Space Elevator Facility
Pini Island, Indonesia

"We have confirmed lunar impacts. Four of them." Captain Fang announced. "It looks as though it hit in four separate locations."

"Is there any sign of a rock that missed the Moon? Anything inbound?" Trish asked.

"We're scanning." Fang replied. "Hold on, affirmative. We have a large object that's just shown over the lunar horizon. And about forty other smaller objects surrounding it. It looks as if some of the matter from the lunar impact is turning into a tail for this object. Calculating trajectory . . ."

Tsu turned to Trish. "I hope you're satisfied now that all the responsibility is yours."

"Get over it, Tsu. I didn't come here looking for power. I came here looking for a way to save lives, so just get over yourself. I need you to focus on solutions instead of bitching about the past."

Behind her, Captain Fang tried to hide his smile. This American born major had obviously not read the People's Revolutionary Army manual on protocol. He liked her style.

Tsu responded. "Yes, Major. Just what are your orders?"

Trish mulled over her response. "We keep tracking the objects. Let's see if the Moon's gravitational pull brings them down. Captain Fang, is there any news from the team on the Moon?"

"Checking now. We have a message from Major Zhang. He's attempting a different maneuver. He says he lost the last rock on his train. That may be the rock we're seeing. It's a large rock according to his estimates. He says it will not hit the Moon. It's going to hit the Earth."

Trish responded, "Can you get a message to him?"

"I am afraid his signal was coming from the other side of the Moon.

He was using the Martian comm satellite and his signal has halted. I think his craft is lost."

The staff in the command center all stood. Trish watched as each of them bowed their heads in honor of Major Zhang.

"He was a hero," she said without emotion. "Now let's be heroes, too, and save this situation. We can honor him when we have time. What's our best estimate for when and where it will hit the Earth?"

After a few minutes, Captain Fang replied. "Current telemetry indicates it will impact a little more than seven hundred kilometers south of Hawaii. It will create a tsunami ring that will hit South America, the Polynesian Islands, Northern Australia, parts of Indonesia, South East Asia and the Hawaiian Islands."

"Do you have an estimate on the wave size?"

"That depends where it hits exactly. The Hawaiian Islands and the Galapagos may be completely overrun. Farther from the impact zone may have a smaller wave. It will be a major disaster wherever it hits."

"Right," Trish responded and looked at her comm tablet. "General Harshaw! This is my official go order. Find that rock and blow that baby up as soon as possible."

Harshaw squinted back at her. "What about the Chinese ordinance?"

"Leave that to me, but get your missile up there now. We need a direct hit as soon as possible. Otherwise we may have to take a star off our flag."

She keyed in President Benson and General Sun, letting them know she authorized the American missile launch. Her plan was to use the Chinese ordinance against any remaining large rock fragments.

Tsu followed her every step of the way. "For someone who says they're not interested in power, you certainly seem comfortable with wielding it."

Trish looked at him dumbfounded. "Tsu, even if we can break this rock in to a bunch of small ones, some of them are going to reach Earth in the South Pacific. There's going to be a tidal wave. Thousands, maybe tens of thousands will die and many others suffer. How could anyone be comfortable with that? I'm only trying to do my best. Power has nothing to do with it. Clearly, we view our roles differently."

Chapter One Hundred Two

Aboard Lunar Transport Bot
Earthbound

A high-pitched beeping tone woke Sam up. He was disoriented upon waking and tried to move around even though he was lashed tight to the back of a transport bot. A transport bot, he remembered, that was flying through space.

Sam knew the best way to fight fear or panic was to take stock of the situation. First, he checked to see if his suit was intact. The takeoff had been rougher than he'd expected and he needed to be sure he wasn't losing air or heat. The suit told him everything was functioning perfectly.

He checked with the plan the Protector gave him. As far as he could tell, he was on target to get to some sort of Earth orbit. He turned his head and looked at the Moon and could see it had been devastated by the asteroid strikes.

As he was looking, a rock twice the size of the transport bot came flying by him just fifteen meters away. It was traveling much faster than he was and in a different direction.

He took a deep breath realizing how close it was to hitting him. There might be others that could still smash into him. He decided to ignore them and focus on achieving an Earth orbit. There was nothing he could do about it and worrying was not going to help. If a rock was going to take him out, well then, so be it.

What did worry him was that he was facing the Sun. While his suit offered some protection, he knew six days in constant solar radiation was not a good idea by any stretch of the imagination. He needed to find some way to shield himself at least part of the time.

The obvious shield would be the body of the transport bot. He thought about it and instructed the bot to turn left for ten meters. While the bot could not turn in space, it did run the wheels on the right side of its length while keeping the left side still. This resulted in the bot beginning to slowly rotate on its axis. It went through three rotations before he sent the signal for it to turn right for three meters.

It took almost an hour before he found himself looking away from the Sun and the bot was no longer turning. He allowed himself a smile as he realized he'd found a good working solution. He smiled because he knew solving problems was the best way to keep his mind occupied. Of course, he hoped he wouldn't face too many more problems.

He took another deep breath as he realized he'd been holding his breath during the last maneuver.

His breath! That was another problem that needed solving. He checked his reserves. He cursed as he saw the reading. He needed six days' worth of oxygen just to get into Earth orbit and the display said he only had five days and fourteen hours left at his current rate of breathing.

Sam could only find one solution to this problem and he didn't like it. The only thing he could do was to slow the rate of consumption. The solution was to have his suit keep him asleep and cool his body down as low as he could get it to keep his metabolism at its lowest level.

He knew that a lot of work had been done in the field of human hibernation, but he didn't think his suit was set up for that. In any case, he knew he could set his suit to wake him if things got dangerous. He quickly found the right combination and dosages to keep himself sedated. He instructed his suit to lower his body temperature and track his life signs. If the temperature started getting too low, he'd have his suit wake him so he could respond. There was always the danger of liquid crystallization but the suit didn't have the chemicals needed to prevent that anyway. He'd use what he had and hope for the best.

After going through his plan twice, he saw he could stretch his oxygen supply to almost eight days. He set himself for a wake-up call in five days and had the suit start to cool and sedate him all at once. Just as he was falling asleep, he noticed a flash of light through his closed eyelids. He waited to see if something struck his transport bot. Nothing did, but he was already fast asleep and no longer worrying. All he could do was sleep and ride it out.

Chapter One Hundred Three

"Yóbany v rot!" Boris exclaimed. "What was that? Amanda, are you and Pierre all right?" he asked, turning his head away from the window.

"What was what?" Amanda asked lifting her head and clearing her faceplate of Pierre's vitals.

"A huge flash between us and the Moon. Closer to the Moon, I think. I didn't look at it until after the flash, just the ghost of it lingers. There." He pointed up through the window of the lander. Amanda detached herself and floated over to the window to see. "Where? Oh, I see. A dim red spot. What do you think it was?"

"Probably a nuclear strike on the asteroid that missed the Moon. Whoever did that may not know we're up here. Govno! We weren't close enough for an EMP effect but some of our sensors are having a hard time with this."

"Nuclear strike! Omygod!" Amanda said. "Lucky you waited before looking at it."

"All Russian kids are taught to not look at something suddenly bright. Were you not taught the same in school?"

"I went to school in California. I was mostly worried about skin cancer from wearing a bikini at the beach and when we would all fall into the ocean."

"Right now, we have bigger problems. The AI pilot is not responding."

Amanda stared at Boris. "I thought the trajectory was already plugged in and we were all set for an automatic ride."

Boris shook his head. "For the most part that's true, but there are always adjustments made at the end. No journey is without some tweaking."

345

"So, what are you saying? Are we screwed?"

"You might say so, but perhaps not. I'm going to have to pilot this thing manually at the end, unless you have some experience at this type of thing?"

"No. None at all. How long before we're in landing mode?" Amanda asked

Boris checked the last trajectory image the AI supplied. "About another day as far as I can tell."

Amanda reconnected to Pierre's suit to check on his vitals, "We need to get Pierre to some more effective care as soon as possible. At least it gives you a day to learn how to fly this thing yourself."

Boris shook his head again. "Nothing on board is going to help me fly this thing. It's all fairly fried in terms of intelligence. I'm going to have to dead stick it in like the old shuttle astronauts."

Amanda's eyes went wide. "Didn't some of those explode?"

Boris nodded. "Yes, two of them did. One during takeoff and one during landing, but I think it had nothing to do with the crew, Just faulty equipment. Most of them did just fine. The only difference between me and them is that they had practice."

"Oh now, that's reassuring."

"Right now, I'm hoping there are no more nuclear bombs being set off near us. We can't take another hit like that."

"Can we get some help from the people at Edwards? Maybe they can figure a way to bring us in."

Boris shook his head. "I'm not getting any response to my messages. Let me try another wavelength."

Amanda checked on Pierre. He was doing better. Blood pressure had risen and pulse was now steady. She let out a sigh of relief and watched the faceplate clean off the fog.

Boris cursed. "That damn EMP has shut off my radio capacity. I can hear Edwards but they can't hear me."

Chapter One Hundred Four

Space Elevator Facility
Pini Island, Indonesia

Trish stared at her split screen. On one side was the face of General Sun, the other showed President Benson's practiced look of concern. She couldn't help but realize one was a professional soldier and the other a professional actor.

She addressed both. "At this point, we have nine pieces at or over the size of a bus and a lot of smaller rocks. One of the items is metallic and advancing faster than the rest of the rocks. We're trying to get a better idea about that one. In any case, I'm setting up a missile trajectory for each rock and we'll be firing in approximately thirty minutes. If we're lucky, this will not only reduce the size of each of the rocks but will also spread the total rock formation. That way less of them will hit the Earth and the ones that do will not create as profound an impact overall."

Sun nodded. "That sounds like our best possible plan."

They both stared at Benson who was staring off to the side, a clear indicator he had another person communicating with him as well.

Benson looked back at the two of them. "I've just gotten a message from Edwards Air Force Base. It seems some of the staff made it off of the Moon in a small lunar lander. The base was hoping to guide them in, but they lost contact with them after the nuke went off."

Sun frowned. "Mr. President, when were you going to tell us about this crew?"

Benson shot back an angry glance. "General, I only learned of this right now! I'm not hiding anything from you."

Trish was surprised to see them so at odds when the Earth was in such danger. "Gentlemen, let's focus. I'm thinking the metallic object might be that lander."

Sun added, "They may have lost electronics, or at least radio from the missile EMP. More missiles will not do them much good."

"You're right!" Trish said. "That's the most likely reason they're not talking back to Edwards. Mr. President, please ask the Edwards team to send us the most probable trajectory for the lander. If it matches up with the metal rock, we'll take them off the target list. Maybe we can send up some kind of ship to match up with them."

Benson broke into the conversation. "Er, how do we even know if they're alive? That was a pretty big blast and if they were close enough, well . . ."

"It's true, we don't know, but we should assume they're alive," Trish said. "If they were able to get off the Moon, they probably had the brains to figure out a way to keep safe. At least we have to give them every chance. We can't just shoot them out of the sky without knowing."

Sun and Benson looked unconvinced.

Trish continued, "Well, the two of you said this was my call. So, unless you're rescinding that order, I'm the one who gets to choose. Okay?"

The two leaders looked at each other and then nodded.

"Good, then I'm going to remove them from the target list for right now and find some way to communicate with them. If they're alive, I intend to bring them home."

Chapter One Hundred Five

Lunar Lander 4
Earth bound

"**A**re you ready for more bad news?" Boris announced, his voice filled with anger and frustration. "Just when we think everything is all right, something else happens."

"What? Don't tell me, we're leaking air?" Amanda responded.

"No, nothing like that, but the nuclear explosion has created fissures in our shield. I was already not so sure our shield would do a great job in landing on the Earth. But I had hoped we'd be able to withstand the heat coming into the atmosphere. Looks like that option is gone now. We would wind up just like that shuttlecraft that fried coming in for a landing."

Amanda rolled her eyes and her voice pitched up. "So, does that mean we're stuck up here?"

"Maybe not." Boris said. "There are still the two space elevators. If they're still functioning after that rock tossing war, we may be able to get near one and slow ourselves down enough. We're not short on fuel. But without the AI to help us pilot, I've got no way of guaranteeing we can do this."

Amanda took a deep breath, "Well, some chance is better than no chance."

Then she heard a different voice say, "Can you identify yourself?"

"What did you just say?" asked Amanda.

"Huh? I said we might still be able to find some way to get to the space elevators, but I'm not sure how we would dock there."

"I just heard someone ask me to identify myself."

"What? On your suit comm unit?"

"Yeah, let me see if I can figure out what wavelength it came in on." Amanda accessed her comm unit history and got the data. She shared it with Boris who tried to connect.

"I'm not getting anything on that frequency," Boris said. "Try to contact them yourself."

"Okay," Amanda said before switching to the frequency she'd found. "This is Lunar Lander 4 from the Fermi Base. We're currently enroute to Earth. But we can't land as planned since we've had our shielding damaged by what seems to be a nuclear explosion."

After a few seconds, she heard, "We copy, Lander 4. This is Space Elevator Pini, Indonesia. What is your current position?"

Amanda asked Boris and then relayed the data. She was rewarded with another response.

"Lander 4, we're tracking you. There are some large asteroids right behind you. The nuclear blast you mentioned broke a large piece into smaller parts. Now that we have you tracked, we can see if we may be able to send a local bus from the space station to try and bring you in. The buses have a fairly limited range so we'll be watching for when you're at closest approach. Can you tell us what your fuel situation is and how much control you have over your ship?"

Amanda explained the conversation to Boris who gave her the answers they needed—manual control of the ship, a fuel tank that was half-full.

She shared the information with the connection in the comm unit and heard a reply. "We think we can catch you when you come by. We'll send a set of instructions, based on our observations. That will help get you near the space elevator here in Indonesia and then we'll send a crew to bring you in. In the meantime, we need you to move to a new trajectory. We'll be firing some smaller nuclear missiles at the remaining large rocks. We don't want you to be subjected to any more EMP's."

Amanda shared the response with Boris who said, "Oh great. We need to fly through more explosions? Okay tell me the new trajectory and I'll get us on it right away."

Chapter One Hundred Six

Space Elevator Facility
Pini Island, Indonesia

Trish walked into the room where Helen and Louise were holed up. The look on Trish's face made Helen inhale and hold her breath. She nodded when she saw Helen's face.

"The majority of the asteroid hit the Moon. As far as we can tell, the Fermi Base was the first place hit. Part of the crew was able to get off of the Moon and is heading this way in a lunar lander. Helen, I'm so sorry, but Sam is not in that lander. Our best guess right now is he may have been involved in the impact. We're continuing to watch for any other signals. From what the crew onboard the lander told us, they advised Sam to seek shelter in an old Russian base. We don't know if he made it. To be honest, the odds were not great. We're working on trying to establish contact with it, but it's been abandoned so long, it's likely all its batteries are drained. But we're trying. If he's there, when all of this is over, we can send someone for him. The crew aboard the lander felt certain the Russian base still had oxygen and supplies that would last a while. Our first missile hit the outstanding asteroid head-on and the EMP that came with it had some impact on the lander with three aboard."

Helen, who had been standing, fell into a chair. Louise rushed to her side and held her in her arms. Trish wanted to do the same, but knew if she began to get emotional, she'd have trouble keeping herself stoic later. She still needed to take care of the rest of the rocks as well as the people in the lander.

"I'm sorry Helen, but I need to go. There are more nukes that need to hit some of the remaining rocks. Sam was a hero. I'll never forget that. We still need to be heroes here and save a lot more people. Once that's done, I'll come back and we can talk. If he's up there, if there's any way to bring him home, we will find it."

Helen just waived her hand at Trish as if pushing her away, unable to speak, her eyes glistening with tears.

"Remember that Sam went to the Moon because we found an ancient alien artifact there. He was the first xenobiologist to ever see an alien artifact," Trish said. "He was there because he wanted to be there."

She turned and left the room, the automatic door closing behind her.

Louise continued to hug Helen as her shock slowly melted into tears and uncontrollable shaking.

"I never met your Sam," Louise whispered, "but he must have been an amazing man when I see the way you've fought for him."

Helen pushed Louise away. "Fought for him and lost him. Yes, he was the best of men. A wonderful man. I loved him and he loved me and now, now I've lost him." She sobbed again. "I never imagined I could lose him. Never! What am I going to do without his smile and his laugh?"

Louise just sat in silence and let Helen weep.

Chapter One Hundred Seven

Space Elevator Facility
Pini Island, Indonesia

C aptain Fang set up the room display to show where the various objects they were tracking were located. They could see the future trajectories of the incoming rocks with the trajectory of the lunar lander curving away. It also showed the eight missiles rapidly closing in on the eight major rocks.

As the missiles drew near, Trish held her breath. The silence in the room made her realize everyone else was holding their breath as well.

Then the display showed the first missile hit its rock, followed quickly by the second and then the third. A few moments later the other five rock's missiles had each scored a direct hit.

A cheer broke out in the room and Trish pitched her voice above the noise. "Good shots, but let's make sure we finish this. Can we get an idea of what the impact has achieved? I need outcome scenarios."

"You!" she said pointing at a lieutenant. "Get in contact with the lander to see what shape they're in."

Tsu stepped up in front of Trish and saluted. "Even if we don't know the result, I must congratulate you on the direct hits."

Trish smiled back at him. She'd seen enough assholes turn into ass kissers through her career to be able to recognize one. "Thank you, Major, but it was you and your staff that did the work. Still, let's stay focused and make sure we're certain the result is what we needed."

The display was shifting and there were now hundreds of rocks with projected trajectories. One by one they displayed their mass and destination as a dotted line.

"No individual rock masses over five hundred kilograms," reported Fang, which prompted another cheer. "We're projecting better than ninety-eight percent of the masses will burn on atmospheric entry. It's going to look

353

like Lunar New Year in the sky tonight."

The lieutenant in touch with Amanda reported he could confirm he was able to continue to communicate with the Lunar Lander. There had not been any major damage from the explosions other than having more of its shielding suffer some additional loss.

This was greeted with more cheers.

The display suddenly showed a blinking blue object appear at the edge of the screen. The mass display showed it was almost half as large as the lander and larger than any of the rocks coming in.

One of the staff members pointed at it. "What is that?"

"Checking," Fang announced. "It's coming in pretty slowly."

Everyone in the room focused on the object as if that would help Captain Fang figure out what it was.

Finally, he spoke. "It's registering as a lunar transport bot, a complete one at that."

"That's ridiculous," said Tsu. "There's no way one of those could be blown off the Moon without being destroyed."

Trish said, "Doesn't each of those have a specific beacon to identify it? Can you see if you can search for its beacon and identify it?"

Fang played with his screen and then his eyes went wide, "Listen to this!"

A throaty masculine voice came over the sound system. "SOS, this is an emergency beacon. This is a lunar transport bot that launched from the Moon before the asteroid impact. Sam Czerny is aboard and requires immediate assistance." The message repeated itself, indicating it was a recording.

Trish was lucky that there was a chair behind her as she fell back. "Holy shit! Fang, get a full trajectory on that thing. We need to see how we can go get that guy."

She got up to leave and Tsu said, "Where are you going"

"Hope," she replied as she walked out. "I'm going to give someone hope."

Chapter One Hundred Eight

Lunar Lander 4
Earthbound

"**N**o way!" Amanda shouted. "Boris, you aren't going to believe this! It just isn't possible! There is no way! I wouldn't believe this if I didn't hear it for myself!"

"What? What is it?" Boris was impatient. He hated to have to wait to get news.

"Sam!" Amanda was grinning. "He got off of the Moon! That crazy man is somehow on a lunar transport bot slowly floating behind us."

"What? That Sam! Ha ha!" Boris slapped his knee. "It looks as though he made it. Can we talk to him?"

"Hold on. Let me find out."

Amanda asked the question. "No, he's not communicating. It's just a recorded beacon saying it's him on a transport bot. The beacon uses the bot voice, but for some reason, it sounds to me like the Protector."

Boris was sporting a wide grin. "When will the pretty boy get to the space elevator?"

Amanda waved at him to let him know she was asking the team at the elevator. Finally, she said, "Oh no! It looks like he's not aimed at the elevator. Right now, they think his ride will bounce off of the atmosphere and then keep going into space. It seems he got hit by a small rock or maybe the explosions had something to do with it, but the trajectory can't be the one he initiated from the Moon."

"Sukin Sin!" Boris cursed. "Will they be able to catch him?"

Amanda waited and then shook her head, "Doesn't look like it. He's too far off." She felt tears pour down her cheeks and her suit wiped them up.

"Can they give you a fix on where he is and where he's going?"

He waited until Amanda replied with the info on Sam's trajectory.

"Okay, fuck this!" Boris said. "I am making Russian executive decision. We're going to save that bastard."

Amanda checked on Pierre's vitals. He was stable. "Fine, but how do we do that?"

Boris grinned. "It will work because whenever you have a Russian Cosmonaut, you have a hero. Time for me to be hero. Tie Pierre up and hang on. We're going to change course."

She barely had time to get Pierre in a stable position before she felt the G's push her back in her seat.

"What is it the American cowboys say?" asked Boris. "Yippee Cow How Okay!"

A while later, Amanda realized Boris was calling her name for the third time. She'd been unconscious since he made the change in course.

"Yes, Boris?" She tried to clear away the cobwebs. Rapid acceleration was not kind to her.

"Oh good. I was afraid you were not surviving. I can see the transport bot."

"Huh? How long have we been accelerating?"

"Four hours and another three hours decelerating. We are almost matched up with the transport bot. It is about fifty meters away."

"Have you been in touch with Sam?"

"I've been trying but have no response. My unit is not working like it should. That's why I have been trying to wake you. Maybe you can talk to him."

"Okay, let me see if I can reach him," Amanda agreed.

After ten minutes of no response, she was frantic. Then she decided to see if she could connect to his health status. She was shocked to find he was in a coma and had a blood temperature of only thirty-one degrees centigrade. She checked his historical charts and found Sam sedated himself and set the suit to lower his temperature. Amanda took control of his health system and started the process of slowly warming his body and bringing him back to consciousness. She informed Boris of what she was doing and explained it would take twenty minutes before he could begin to speak.

Sam opened his eyes and saw a sky filled with stars. It took him a moment to figure out where he was. He could tell the transport bot was spinning slowly, which was not the case when he sedated himself. He was patiently waiting to see the Earth show up in the spin to see how close it might be when a voice came over his comm unit. "Sam? Are you awake?"

"Hello?" He didn't recognize the voice at first. "Amanda? Is that you? How? Where are you?"

"Hi, Sam. Nice to hear your voice. Boris has taken the lander into a matched course with you and we're about fifty meters away. And he did it without an AI. Pretty amazing piloting, I think."

Sam could hear Boris' voice distantly. "Russian Cosmonaut hero piloting!"

Amanda continued, "Sam, we need to get you in the lander. Your transport bot is off course and would not even take you close to the Earth. You'll bounce off the atmosphere and spin out into space."

It took a moment for this news to sink into Sam's mind. "Okay, so how do I get in the lander?"

Amanda replied, "Boris thinks we can get a carbon fiber cord attached to the bot. Then all you need to do is attach yourself to it and break the connection so we can reel you in."

Sam thought about it, "Seems not too unreasonable, but how will you send the cord?"

Amanda took the time to ask Boris.

"Really?" Sam heard her say.

"Okay," she said. 'Boris says he can fire an anchor into the bot. It might go through the bot. He's not sure his aim will be perfect since he's never done this before."

"Oh great. What if the anchor hits me?"

After a moment, "Boris says to try to make yourself as small as you can."

"Oh, great, perfect solution," Sam answered.

"Hang on, here comes the anchor."

Sam was surprised when he heard a *thunk*. Then he remembered he was pressed up against the transport bot and the vibration only needed the air in his helmet to carry the sound.

He looked all around and saw the anchor sticking into the body of the bot in between his ankles.

"Okay I see it. Tell Boris that the shot was really close. Too close for comfort. But we'll talk about that later."

"Sam, there should be a carabineer at the end of the tether. Find a way to attach it to yourself and when you're ready we will reel you in."

"Okay, looking for it." Sam said.

He saw the device glinting at the end of the anchor. He took his time figuring out how to detach himself from the bot and attach himself to the tether. He got his suit to melt away the tape holding his upper body to the bot. Then he bent over and reached to grab the carabineer. He got a hold of it on the third try—promising himself that once he got home, he'd do sit-ups every day.

Attaching the carabineer to the clasp on his suit's belt, he checked to make sure the box the Protector gave him was still firmly taped to him. Once reassured, he had the suit melt away the lower part of the tape that held him to the transport bot and he was suddenly floating free. A small sense of panic gripped him and he took a deep breath, telling himself this was no different than when he was flying his underwater drones back at the university.

"Okay," he reported to Amanda, "I am on the wire and ready to go."

There was a pause before he heard back. "We have a problem. The wire won't reel back. Can you see if the anchor can be pulled out of the bot?"

Sam turned back to look at the bot. He was floating some two meters away. The carbon fiber cord was extremely strong and flexible as well as lightweight, but it had one downside. It was much thinner than any fishing line and almost impossible to see.

He could not reach the anchor, so he grabbed the space around the carabineer, hoping he was winding some of the cord in his hand and gave it a tug. He was pulled back to the bot so quickly he almost failed to grab the anchor.

Placing his feet flat against the bot, he pulled on the anchor as hard as he could, but it wouldn't budge.

"No good," he said. "I just don't have enough leverage to pull it out."

There was a long pause and then Amanda's voice came back sounding urgent. "Boris says we can try something else. He says you should jump to the lander. He'll make the cord taut and you should be guided right at us that way."

Sam responded, "Can I trade places with Boris? It looks a long way down to where you are."

Amanda replied. "He says it isn't down, it's out. You will float

358

forward, don't think of it as dropping."

"Yeah," Sam said. "Everything's relative. Right. Okay, here I go."

Sam grabbed the anchor to brace himself, and pushed off with his legs, letting it go. Trying to keep from feeling as if he was falling, it felt as if he'd jumped up and was just never coming down. As he got closer to the lander, the illusion failed and suddenly he felt as if he was falling face down at the ship. Instinct made him wave his arms for balance and then hold them out in front of himself.

Amanda voice was more urgent than ever. "As soon as you touch the ship, find a place to attach the carabineer while it's still hooked to your belt. Then hold on to something. Do so immediately."

"Okay. I don't have much time either. My faceplate says I have less than thirty minutes of O2."

"Sam, just do this very quickly. Boris says when he made the cord taught, not only did it guide you, but it also pulled the bot at the ship. It's following you."

Sam tried to turn around but stopped himself, thinking it might change his trajectory. He saw the lander only a few meters away. He knew he had to get out of the way of the bot or it would ram into the lander. Even at slow speeds it could crush him against the side.

Sam hit the lander's side, found a handle and grabbed on to it. Then he saw a slot that would hold the carabineer. He felt clumsy as he moved his body, holding the handle with one hand and twisting the carabineer with the other so it was attached to his belt and the slot. Once finished, he was lying lengthwise along the top of the lander, like a racing motorcyclist at full speed.

"I'm attached," he told Amanda.

He heard her reply, "Releasing cord. Hang on Sam, we won't be going fast, but you will feel acceleration."

"Okay." Sam could feel his lungs pumping. The exercise had made him breathe faster and his O2 supply was dwindling. His body was responding by trying to get more breaths in.

He felt the lander surge forward, glad he was also facing that way. There was a sudden screech and a bump.

"What was that?" he asked.

"The bot scraped our tail. No real damage. Might need a paint job though." Amanda's voice had lost its tension.

Sam said, "Somebody needs to come out and get me. I'm almost out of O2."

"Are you still firmly attached?"

"Yes."

"Okay I'm going to sedate you to slow your metabolism. Boris says one hero Cosmonaut is coming for you."

Sam closed his eyes and fell asleep.

Chapter One Hundred Nine

US Naval Medical Center
San Diego, California

Sam heard voices and tried to lift his head. Something was holding it down. So, he tried to lift his hand and it felt as if he was tied down by bungee cords.

He opened his eyes. The light was bright, but he saw the blurry silhouettes of several people. Then he recognized one of the voices.

"Helen?" he said. His voice came out dry and raspy.

A voice said, "He's awake."

Three faces came into view for Sam. He saw two of them belonged to Helen and Trish Stern. The third was an unknown face, but given the clothes the person wore, he assumed it was a nurse or doctor.

"Helen," he said.

"Shhh," she whispered. "Save your strength. You've been in a hyperbaric oxygen chamber for two days." Her eyes glistened. "We almost lost you, Sam. You've got to take it easy."

"Welcome back, Sam," Trish said. "We need to let you rest, but can you at least tell us what that box you had strapped to you is?"

He saw Helen scowl at the question.

"My box," his voice croaked and his throat felt itchy. "Where is it? Who took it?"

Trish replied, "The Chinese military is holding it for you, Sam. The United States and Chinese governments agreed you're the one to open it."

"They agreed because they can't open it," Helen said. "Whenever they try, they get a message saying only you can access the contents."

Trish got to the point, "What's in the box, Sam?"

Helen interjected. "I've been acting as your legal representative, Sam. You don't need to answer if you don't want to."

Sam smiled, "It's software. Software like we've never seen before.

And I'm going to share it with everyone as soon as I'm able."

Chapter One Hundred Ten

University of California
San Diego

Six weeks later, Sam was standing on a stage in the university amphitheater. The place was packed with scientists, journalists, politicians and military personnel. Nervously, Sam nodded to several of his colleagues. Most of them beamed huge smiles back at him.

He stepped to the podium and saw there were over a dozen cameras recording the event.

"Welcome," he said. "To the opening of the first ever School for Extraterrestrial Studies."

When the applause died down he continued. "The school will have several departments including biology, history, communications, technology and defense."

The crowd mumbled, some visibly angry at the department choices. Sam smiled at the typical academic responses he saw among the audience. One woman raised her hand and Sam nodded to her.

"Can you tell us about the staff? Who will be teaching the classes and running the research?"

It was time to show them why he'd really called the meeting.

"Yes, allow me to introduce to you the one person who will be teaching each and every class as well as guiding all the research studies."

The audience looked to see who would come out from behind the curtain. Instead, a twelve-foot tall bipedal reptilian materialized next to Sam. Two people screamed and a few got up and moved towards the exits.

The Alien creature opened its mouth and in a smooth, deep masculine voice said, "Hello, I am Protector Three Hundred and Four."

Acknowledgements

A long, long time ago, some mysterious chemical combination began to use other chemicals in its proximity to replicate itself and pass along information pertaining to its structure to other instances of this chemical combination. I would like to acknowledge that without that initial occurrence, this book would never have been possible.

There are also a lot of more immediate entities who have been at least as significant in the creation of this story. Far too many to name here but I will mention a few who really stood out.

I am grateful for the constant and consistent support of the Fairfield County Writers Group and especially the terrific nuggets of story-telling wisdom shared by group member Dave D'Alessio. The enthusiasm and support I received from beta readers Diane Johnson and Laura Allgeier was priceless and timely as were the kind words of Robert J. Sawyer.

I have special thanks for my phenomenal editor, Charie D. La Marr. Her insights, questions, and advice helped make this story much so more than what it was when I began.

Biography

ROMAN GODZICH is a polyglot who has lived and worked in several countries. He has worked in ecommerce for more than thirty years and has designed e-commerce solutions, search engines, advertising platforms and online booking engines. He currently manages content and user experience for an online travel company.

He grew up in Manhattan and attended the Bronx High School of Science and New York University. He currently resides in Connecticut.

When not working or writing, Roman enjoys deep sea fishing, reading, and gourmet cooking.

No Higher Ground is his first novel.

For more information:

www.romangodzich.com

COMING SOON

The Artificial Soul
The Second Book in the Sam Czerny Series

Sam Czerny and Protector 304 have been working diligently on a history of alien races. It is a daunting task, as much of the Protector's memory was lost on the moon.

During a break from their work, Sam, Helen, Pierre and Amanda go to China to witness the raising of a statue dedicated to Major Zhang whom the Chinese recognize as the savior of humanity.

But a group whose goal is to get humans to stop using Artificial intelligence, and in particular Alien technology, attacks the people attending the ceremony. Sam is frantic when he can't find Helen after the attack. He looks for help from the new elected Chairman Sun along with Trish Stern, who runs the International Committee on Alien Technology.

The Chinese decide to use their own new AI to help them in the endeavor. As a team, they set out to discover who the mysterious anti AI group is and how they can save Helen Czerny, only to discover that P304 has created some plans of his own

CPSIA information can be obtained
at www.ICGtesting.com
Printed in the USA
LVHW081807220719
624870LV00017B/1628/P